Penelope's Hope

Penelope's Hope

REGENCY SILHOUETTES BOOK ONE

Sarah Baughman

a GraftedHeart book

ISBN: 0692527117
ISBN 13: 9780692527115

Dedication

For my parents,
who encouraged my love of books and writing,
and who taught me about God's heart and His love.

Acknowledgments

I SO GREATLY appreciate the hard work of the team that made my cover possible. Thank you to Shaw Photography by Alex Shaw who produced the lovely photograph. And thank you to Melissa Sue Photo & Design for the amazing graphic design skills.

Thank you to all of those who read my early drafts and gave me feedback. Your input was invaluable! Thanks also to my sounding board, Heidi. I'm so glad to share in this journey with you!

Finally, thank you to my wonderful husband Karl, and my sweet children Chazz, Magdalena, August, and George. I could not have finished this without your patience and support. I love you all!

For in this hope we were saved.
Now hope that is seen is not hope.
For who hopes for what he sees?
But if we hope for what we do not see,
we wait for it with patience.
Romans 8:24-25

Prologue

Claymore Abbey, Leicester
1801

THE LOW VOICES in the room drifted to the young girl's ears. She was only fifteen, yet fully aware of the implications of what had transpired. The solicitor, who had already read the will, conferred in hushed tones with the bailiff and butler beside the large desk.

It had been *his* desk, but no longer.

The uncharacteristically bright light from windows behind the men cast their forms into shadow. The girl could not see their faces from her perch on the wingback chair beside the fireplace, giving her an unsettled feeling in her chest and her stomach. Huddled closely on the other side of the room were the housekeeper and the girl's great-aunt, the only family present at this time.

The wingback chair dwarfed the girl's small frame. Her sweet face, set into the proper expression of placid grief – the late baron had been ill for quite some time, so his demise was not altogether unexpected – hid the inner turmoil which nearly prevented her ability to nod her head politely when Aunt quietly asked her whether she was well. Perhaps she was not hiding the turmoil as well as she had thought.

Beside her chair was another, identical in appearance with one exception: it was conspicuously empty. The new Baron, a young man who should have been the chair's occupant, was at Cambridge, unable to return due to exams. Or that was the reason cited in the hastily-scribbled express received by his sister the previous day.

So it was in loneliness that the girl kept the funeral vigil in the black-draped room with only her aunt for comfort. She rode in the carriage first to the church for the funeral sermon, and then to the burial site for the internment. She did not remember very much of that day, with the exception of the ostrich feathers on the black Belgians' heads, dark ink stains against the dull sky. Those were etched into her memory – the way they danced in the wind, belying the somber occasion. Walking back to the carriage after the body had been buried, she could not look away from the feathers as they joyously dipped and rippled. They reflected the feelings of her heart, feelings she must hide. For the first time, hope was fostered – a hope that she would cling to until the time that she might reach out and grasp her full freedom.

Part I

One

London
Early January 1806

MR. ASHBRIDGE WYNDHAM purposely slowed his steps to accommodate the small, dainty stride of his sister Rose. Violet, born between them, had a tall, willowy frame and easily kept stride with him. Rose never hurried her stride to keep pace with her siblings. She ever acted the lady. *If only her perception of what constitutes a lady was more in line with Violet's,* he thought. The elder of the two sisters, while born only two years before the other, seemed to possess the sense of a woman beyond her years.

"We must be sure to be seen," chirped Rose, her breath fogging in the cold air. He believed with certainty that she was imitating something her mother had said.

"Who would see you?" he queried. "You are not out; no one knows who the devil you are."

"Ash!" murmured Violet. "Rose is of a tender age and should by no means hear such speech."

"Oh Vi," said Rose, blinking her wide eyes, "must you be so picksome? At sixteen, I am nearly of an age to be out in Society. Our brother has said nothing I've not already heard."

Ash glanced at Violet in time to see a blush bloom on her cheeks. She remained irritatingly silent, doing not a thing to deter the younger sister from speaking to her in such a manner.

"You've no reason to be so high in the instep, Rose," he was compelled to retort on Violet's behalf. "You *claim* a lady's sensibilities in refraining from exerting yourself in your pace, and yet show no sensibility in speaking to your own sister."

"She is unfailingly proper!" cried Rose.

"It is my hope that I behave in a manner pleasing to the Lord, though I perhaps am too quiet and ought to speak more openly with others." Violet's quietly-spoken words barely reached Ash's ears, though Rose seemed to hear them quite well.

"You mean to say that you ought to speak more openly with the gentlemen."

"I-I did *not*—"

"A gentleman wishes for some enjoyment in speaking with a lady, Vi," Rose teased her sister. "Gentlemen cannot be secured by strictly proper behavior."

"Indeed?" asked Ash. "And what can you possibly know of securing a gentleman?"

"More than you know of securing a wife!" she bit back.

Ash felt a rush of sound within his ears as his heart raced, pumping his blood fast; he had not expected such a centered attack from the girl. Just as he was about to open his mouth with a scathing dressing-down, Violet spoke up.

"Rose, did your friend Miss Cottsworth have her miniature made, as she had planned?"

Ash half-listened to his silly youngest sister prattle on about the latest gossip surrounding the so-called "Invisible Painter" who had never been seen, and yet his work was inexplicably sought-after.

Perhaps not so terribly inexplicable. All of Society is intrigued by those who live outside of what is expected, but so few dare to do it themselves. Instead they claim to adore and dote on the eccentrics—so long as those eccentrics maintain a healthy distance.

He was not truly interested in what Rose had to say, but he was glad that the situation was diffused. He raised his left hand to briefly squeeze Violet's where it rested on his right forearm, and she smiled shyly at him. He returned her smile, grateful for her consideration.

"*And* it is said," continued Rose, "that there is a two-month delay for a sitting. Lawks! Can you imagine scheduling a sitting *two months* before it is to take place? I would so love to have my portrait painted by him. Amelia Cottsworth showed me hers. She has an uncommonly large nose, and while the painter did a true likeness, he also painted her face at the ideal angle as to disguise its prominence. One can only imagine how well *I* shall appear when portrayed by one so talented!"

They had arrived at the cobbler's shop where Mrs. Wyndham instructed them to meet her, and Ash opened the door and ushered his sisters inside. They passed through the door, over which hung a sign inscribed with the name *Phillips*. Warmth, along with the scent of leather, immediately assaulted him, and the cobbler approached to greet them until Mrs. Wyndham waved him away. Her pale golden hair, grown silvery in recent years, framed her still-handsome face. She had been waiting for them inside the shop, having taken their family carriage to the establishment after adjuring the younger people that a walk would do them good and of greater import – afford them the opportunity to be seen. While many of the members of Society were still arriving in London, those present were already preparing for the upcoming Social Season.

"I do hope at the least three members of the peerage saw you, as you all certainly dawdled long enough for the entirety to have made your acquaintance," she said to Ash, referring to those titled individuals at the top of the *Beau Monde* – those who were at the height of Society and known for their discriminating taste in those whom they deemed worthy of their notice. They set the tone for what was considered fashionable, as was indicated by their favoring the French term for the word *tone*; if a person was considered good *ton*, then he was accepted with open arms into Society.

Mrs. Wyndham's voice, while pleasant in its modulations to an unfamiliar ear, carried an edge recognizable by the brother and sisters. As he was now the master of their family's small estate, Ash knew that the widow would not attempt to cross him. She had been carefully pleasant to him since the passing of the late Mr. Wyndham, but her strict manner toward Violet had by no means abated. Her following words caused him to fear, though, that this shopping trip would be more unpleasant than usual for his sister.

Mrs. Wyndham had shifted her attention to the girl and was saying, "We must purchase items which will show you to advantage, child, or you will never find a suitable match. Shame you are so thin. I daresay Rose–" and here she turned to look fondly at the younger sister "–shall cut a splendid figure when she makes her debut."

Ash found himself gritting his teeth to keep his voice silent. *Why is that woman incapable of using kind words with Violet? The poor girl has never treated her with contempt, or anything other than the respect that a mother deserves, in all her nineteen years.*

Mrs. Wyndham turned back to Violet, with a clearly disappointed glance over the girl's figure. "But we shall do what we are able."

As a means of distracting himself, Ash wandered about the small shop, fingering some of the sample boots set about on small shelves and tables. His own shoes and boots he ordered from a more fashionable establishment, but Mrs. Wyndham had deemed this shop sufficient for Violet. Soon, two pairs of dancing slippers, one pair of half-boots, and three of everyday shoes were ordered. The old cobbler bore any snide remarks from Mrs. Wyndham with a humble fortitude, and was rewarded handsomely for his forbearance with a large order. Ash wished his own reward would be as precious as the cobbler seemed to consider his, if his shining eyes were any indication.

Upon leaving the shop, Mrs. Wyndham directed the three young people into the carriage before entering it first, not even glancing back to see whether they followed. Obedience was expected.

Ash handed up his sisters before climbing into the carriage himself. The seat beside Violet was vacant, thankfully, and he flipped up the tails of his coat beneath his greatcoat before sitting beside her.

"Next is the milliner's," began Mrs. Wyndham.

"Certainly you do not require my presence, ma'am," he interrupted. "I've no useful opinions to offer."

"Indeed I do, Ashbridge!" Mrs. Wyndham insisted. He thought, not for the first time, that she must use his given name as a means of annoying him. "Certainly not for the hats or gloves, but when we order a dress, you *must* give your opinion. You know better than we what a young man would enjoy seeing in a gown, and I *depend* upon your opinion. It is imperative that we find a match for Violet as soon as possible. When Rose makes her come-out, she cannot have an unmarried sister hovering about, or Society shall wonder what is wrong with our family."

A quick glance at Violet revealed a blush stealing up her cheeks at the woman's words, and Ash felt his ire rise in the too-familiar rush of heat and pounding of his heart.

"Indeed they shall not wonder at all, ma'am," he argued, fighting to keep his voice level. He wanted nothing more than to leave and go to the Fencing Academy he and his friends frequented; it was quite close to the milliner's shop, and he had hoped to walk over there after delivering the ladies to their next destination. One look at Violet's face, however, lowered and with eyes blinking at a suspiciously high rate, he decided that she needed his presence more than he needed be rid of Mrs. Wyndham's. With a breath to quiet his nerves, he conceded, "Nevertheless, I can see how my presence with this shopping party might be beneficial. I shall accompany you."

"Excellent!"

Mrs. Wyndham and Rose began discussing which style of bonnet best suited Violet, and to what extreme of fashion she might attain, but Ash pointedly ignored them and turned to the sister beside him. Her eyes no longer blinked as much, but they were noticeably glossy, even in the dim light of the carriage. He knew she had been fighting off tears.

Ash subtly squeezed her hand, offering a slight smile. Her attempt at returning it was almost convincing, and he was satisfied for the time being. *Too dangerous to say more in such close quarters with the others,* he cautioned himself. *Perhaps we may walk to the drapers from the milliner's, and speak then.*

At the milliner's, Ash again wandered about, looking at some of the more extravagant hats, the trim of which he was sure must have surpassed the weight of the actual hat. Feathers, silk flowers, fruits, and fabrics all had their places, some in combination and some alone. He spied a smart little bonnet tucked in amongst the others: blue with white ribbon and a single white flower on the side. A glance at the ladies of his party revealed Mrs. Wyndham and Rose settling an extravagant concoction upon Violet's head. Her eyes were wide in alarm, and her lips pressed together, the tension about her mouth clearly displaying her distress to anyone observant enough to look. Of course the other two ladies were oblivious.

Ash waved over the proprietor's assistant, as the man himself was busy with the ladies. The girl approached immediately, and he saw that her hair was the same color of pale straw as the man's. *His daughter?* He wondered. Her dark blue eyes were clear and her cheeks took on a rosy hue when she drew near. Ash knew that his fair hair, steely blue eyes, and evenly-proportioned features gave him an appearance that was pleasing to the eye, but still it felt odd to him when a female reacted as the milliner's daughter did. His time spent in Society had taught him that for ladies of the upper echelons, it was a man's place in the *ton*, not his character or even necessarily his appearance, that determined his value, and therefore his desirability.

"I should like to purchase this," he began, gesturing to the bonnet.

"Certainly, sir," the girl said, reaching to remove the item from its stand. "Shall I add it to your mother's order?"

"No, thank you, miss. It is a gift."

"I see. For a lady?"

"For my sister," he amended her assumption. "But please wrap it and have it delivered to me; here is my card with the direction."

"Of course." She accepted also the coin he offered, plenty to pay for both the purchase and the delivery boy. "May I be so bold to say she will be pleased with this gift?"

"You may," he smiled. "I fear she does not appreciate the same . . . *extremes* of fashion, shall we say, enjoyed by the other ladies of my family."

"Yes," she said, smiling at him. He returned her gaze until she started, cleared her throat, and said, "I, er–I'll have this delivered before evening."

"Thank you."

Ash made his way back to the ladies, just in time to hear Mrs. Wyndham say to the proprietor, "We shall also need some feathers for her court dress."

"I've an excellent selection, here," said he, bringing out a sampling of feathers.

After some debate, and minimal input from Violet, several plumes were chosen for a fan and a headdress, and the proprietor and his daughter began to wrap up the purchases. Ash carried them to the carriage, and handed Mrs. Wyndham and Rose into it before offering Violet his arm.

"We should enjoy a walk, ma'am, if that is agreeable to you," he said. "Which draper's do you mean to patronize? The one at the corner, near the bookseller's?"

"Indeed," said Mrs. Wyndham. "I shall begin looking for a good silk for your court dress, Violet, for that is of utmost importance. And a velvet for the train. Come as quickly as you may, Ash, but I believe you are correct in suggesting a walk. Violet is looking rather pale after the milliner's, and some fresh air would make her complexion tolerable."

Ash said nothing as he stepped back from the carriage.

"So she means to present you in Court?" he asked Violet as the carriage rolled away.

"Yes."

"Would you like me to accompany you?"

"Would you need a new suit?" she asked. "I know that you do not enjoy shopping, or the formalities associated with Court."

"Likely, yes, but I would gladly suffer through if it would put you at ease."

Violet smiled fondly at him before saying, "I believe this is something I must face alone."

"I see. Quite grown of you, and all that," he intoned, an exaggeratedly pinched expression on his face.

Violet immediately recognized his teasing and giggled. "You are absurd."

"Perhaps, but it did bring a smile to your face."

Violet chuckled, shaking her head. "Have I been so unpleasant this morning?"

"You!" exclaimed Ash. "Indeed not. I was thinking more of Mrs. Wyndham's treatment of you."

Ever one to dismiss other's offenses, Violet frowned slightly and said, "I cannot understand your refusal to refer to our mama by that term. It must always be *Mrs. Wyndham* with you."

"Yes, well." Ash shook his head, unable to explain to his sweet sister just why he refused to acknowledge the woman as his mama.

Violet, almost expectedly sensing his discomfort, and wishing to sooth it, said, "Either way, I think that I am now prepared to face the draper's."

"Excellent. However," he paused dramatically, "are you prepared to face Mrs. Wyndham?"

Violet again giggled. "I believe so."

Ash smiled and patted her hand where it lay upon his arm, and they continued in companionable silence. It was nice to see a glimmer of the girl his sister had once been.

By the time they all returned home after visiting the draper's, fabric for two white dresses, three sets of sleeves for the white dresses, four new day dresses, and several other unmentionables were purchased and promised to be sent directly to the dressmaker's. Several ball gowns had also been ordered, including the one to be worn for Violet's presentation in Court. A pelisse and two spencers Violet had from last winter were deemed sufficient for her outerwear. The party returned to their rented house on Wardour Street, eager for rest after the extensive shopping excursion.

The Honorable Miss Penelope Drayton rinsed her brush, taking care that the tip of the bristles was shaped to her satisfaction before she placed it in a jar with its companions. She had enjoyed painting for as long as she could remember. From her scribbles and splatters treasured by her mother, to the paintings proudly presented to her nurse and then governess, and finally the ones which were deemed of sufficient quality to hang in the family's morning room, she had found escape and happiness at the easel. It was a shared enjoyment of her mother's, and one of the only truly valuable things left of the woman.

Morning sunlight filtered through the windows in her family's Town-house, illuminating the sitting room. The house had been built under the direction of Penelope's ancestor, Mr. Albert Drayton, who became Lord Albert Claymore, the first Baron Claymore. Her brother Cornelius now held the title, and knowing what she did of her brother currently, her father before, and all of their predecessors, it was no surprise at all that their family had never been granted a higher-ranking title over the years. She was curious, rather, that it had not yet been stripped of them.

After her brushes were arranged to her satisfaction, Penelope ensured that her paints were all closed tightly – they would be useless if they dried – and removed her apron. As she was folding the rose-colored fabric, her great-aunt strode gracefully into the room.

I sincerely hope to walk with half her grace when I have reached my sixties, Penelope thought.

"Good morning, Aunt," greeted Penelope with a smile and a curtsy.

"Is it? I slept so soundly that I feared it to be much later than morning."

"Did not your maid inform you of the time?"

"Cannot be relied upon." Miss Esther Breckenridge sank slowly into the chair she usually occupied, which was covered by a sheet. "Why is my chair covered? It was not covered yesterday, was it? I cannot have turned senile overnight."

"You've not, Aunt Essie." Penelope tucked her apron into its place beside her paint-box, and retrieved her fichu from the chair near her aunt's. Shaking out the triangular piece of sheer fabric, she draped it over her shoulders and around her neck, bringing the longest points of the triangle together and tucking them into the front of her gown. "Remember, we are having some updates made to this room. The craftsmen covered the furniture to keep the dust off until they have completed their work."

"Oh yes." Aunt Essie stood from her chair and approached Penelope. "Allow me to assist you," she offered, tucking the shorter point of the triangle into the back of the gown. "Your seams are worn, dear, and the neckline is beginning to fray."

Penelope was immensely glad she was not prone to blushing, as was the case for many other twenty-year-olds of the *ton*; she was sure she otherwise would have. "Yes, Aunt, this is one of my older gowns. You know I do not paint in any dress that is less than two years old." What she did not say was that she had spent much of her monthly allowance on a warm new pelisse for her dear aunt. She did not wish for her to take a chill during the early part of the Season, before the air began to grow warmer with the approach of summer. Parliament was set to open on the twenty-first of January, and the air was still frigid and the winds sharp. The Season would not see warmer temperatures for several weeks, at least.

"You are a good girl, Penny," said Aunt Essie fondly as she settled herself into the chair once again.

"Thank you, Aunt," Penelope grinned, seating herself as well.

Aunt Essie picked up some mending, looked critically for a moment at the damaged dress-hem, and selected a thread and needle. "How long have you been saving for these improvements, dear?"

"Two years," Penelope admitted. "We could not very well entertain visitors with the plaster coming down and the carpets threadbare, could we?"

"Indeed not," agreed her aunt. "Though this room did very well for us during the previous Season."

"Yes, but we did not receive visitors the last Season; we left Town to visit your distant cousin. You know that my hope is to entertain a great deal more this year than last."

"And did your brother contribute to the improvements to *his* home?"

Penelope was perfectly aware that her aunt knew the answer to her own question, and sent the elder woman a wry grin. "You know that he has promised me use of this house, when he did not have any obligation to do so; he comes for the Season, but prefers to remain at Claymore Abbey the rest of the year."

"With his penchant for gaming, lightskirts, and drink, I should think he would prefer Town to the country."

"Aunt! I am shocked that you even know those words!" Penelope was quite pleased at her ability to hide her grin. Her aunt, while a proper lady in every way, was no naïve miss.

"And am I to be shocked that you also give the appearance of familiarity with them?" Aunt Essie quipped. "Let us strike a deal. I shall not mention them again if you do not."

Penelope laughed. "Very well. Regardless of what you should have expected, Cornelius prefers the country because the collectors rarely wish to travel to the Abbey. The roads are in poor repair, and more than one rig has been immobilized on the way."

"Shall we call him clever for this?"

"Neglect of his estate and duties which result in a fortuitous circumstance for him is hardly clever."

"I suppose not," agreed Aunt Essie. "But one must admit that there is a necessary dedication to dereliction in order to achieve such advanced degrees of disrepair."

Penelope again laughed, glad to have a reason for it. Her life had not always presented her opportunity for such cheerful behavior, but she felt that she was finally close to grasping happiness and keeping it.

"How much longer until this room is fit to be seen?" Aunt Essie asked.

"I hope in a few weeks' time; certainly by the start of the Season," Penelope replied. "The master carpenter is nearly finished. Then the carpets may be laid, and the plaster applied. I asked that the wall-treatments remain simple, as simplicity seems to be the rule of the day. And glad I am of it, for pale paints and light draperies are much less costly than scrolling wallpapers and velvet draperies."

"Indeed they are. And then what, Penny? You shall be prepared to entertain your suitors?"

Penelope scoffed. "You are familiar with the plan, Aunt. There will be no suitors. If all proceeds as I wish, we shall be set up quite well by this time next year."

"And you are certain this is your wish, my child?" Aunt Essie's voice became soft and wistful. "Independence comes at a dear cost – that of having someone to call your own."

"You seem to be quite content with your choices, Aunt," returned Penelope.

"I am. I have learned to be content in all circumstances." Aunt Essie smiled in a manner that caused Penelope to wonder if she was keeping a wonderful secret. "But I also know the cost of independence, and how very dear it is."

"So if you could start again, you would choose differently?"

"It is not for me to speculate on what might have been," Aunt Essie replied with a gentle shake of her head. "You, though, you have your life before you. Will you live it closed off and alone, or will you welcome whomever the Lord might send?"

Penelope's aunt seldom chastised or even hinted that she might entertain a difference of opinion; even more seldom did she express herself in so direct a manner. Therefore, it was after a moment's reflection that Penelope answered quietly, almost asking a question with her tone, "I have you, Aunt."

The older woman smiled fondly. "Of course you do, my dear. But remember, I will not be here forever. Before you commit to this path, be sure it is what you truly desire, and what the Lord desires for you."

Penelope had a strong urge to squirm, but forced herself instead to look her aunt in the eye as she replied. "It is what I wish."

Penelope cared little what the Lord wished for her. If the Heavenly Father was anything like her papa had been, she supposed she was better off choosing for herself. There was precious little she could do to command her own life, but Penelope was determined to grasp that precious little and run with it as fast and as far as she possibly could. She knew what she wanted, and she knew that she would allow nothing to stop her.

Ash hurried through his dressing routine, finally donning a different coat with the help of his valet before moving to his study, which was a small room adjacent to his bedchamber. He found a stack of letters, and sorted the ones which required his attention this afternoon, as opposed to the ones which might wait several days.

One in particular caught his attention. The direction on the front of the letter was written in a wavering, unfamiliar hand, and the seal on the back was entirely unknown to him. The seal's crest held a knight's helmet above a flag that was rectangular at the top, but formed a point at the base. Two lines nearer the top than the bottom mimicked the base, converging in a point at the center of the flag.

With an inexplicable sense of trepidation, he broke the red wax seal with his finger, opening the letter to view the contents. Out tumbled several bank notes, their amount lost to him as the letter claimed his full attention.

The body of the letter was written in the same shaky hand, forcing Ash to work a bit harder to discern the meaning of the words than he might have otherwise.

"My dear boy," he began reading. *I've not been called a boy in ages,* he thought before returning his attention to the letter.

Linsdon, Westmorland
15 December 1805
My dear boy,

Of course we are not formally acquainted, but I have been kept apprised of your progress, first by your dear mother, and most lately by your father. Upon his end, however, I have had no news. Are you married, my boy? Have you any children?

I expect that no-one in your family wishes to dwell on the tragic reality of that unfortunate event shortly after your sister's birth, and neither shall I mention it. However, you cannot have remained ignorant of who I am. It is my wish, as I near the end of my own life, to mend the rifts I have caused, and as you surely understand, to become acquainted with my heir. And do not fret, for I've gone through the proper channels and petitioned the correct personages; you have been named my heir and accordingly shall be.

Of course there is no opportunity for a visit until the Season has ended, for if you are married, I sincerely doubt that your wife will wish to leave London before its conclusion. And if you are not, then surely you yourself wish to take advantage of this year's new set of debutantes in choosing a wife for yourself. I shall, however, expect you no later than the week after Parliament shuts its doors.

I am, you will know, much too far into my dotage to participate in the House of Lords as I once did. Perhaps not many more years shall pass before you take my seat there, though you know it shall then be your seat, not mine. But in the meantime, do feel free to make use of our Town-house. Perhaps it is too out-moded for you, but you certainly may order whichever changes you see fit. I cannot presently recall the direction, but I shall have my man send it by express as soon—

Pardon that atrocious ink stain. I write as I sit in my bed, and a ferocious coughing spell overcame me before I could hand off the pen and inkwell to my secretary. Poor man is more of a nursemaid these days than a secretary, but the old coot is faithful, if nothing else. I shall close now, as the coughs have also served to exhaust—

Find enclosed an advance of your annual allowance. Remainder to be sent to your bank, once return dir—

Fondly,

Lord Elton Ashbridge, Marquess of Linsdon

Ash could not move, though his mind raced round and round. *Could it be a hoax? Spence is very fond of this sort of thing.* His eyes flitted to the banknotes, a larger sum than he could believe his friend would throw away on fooling him. Looking back at the letter, his eyes found the ink-stain first, then the places where the words drifted off to a mere scrawl, as though infected by the weakness of their scribe. He followed the words, from the loquacious though somewhat vague beginning, to the rather abrupt ending. Still, he could scarcely comprehend them.

Then his eyes fell upon the gentleman's signature, his name.

Ashbridge.

It cannot be a coincidence, can it? I must be connected to him in some manner. But what?

He dared not allow his thoughts to roam where they wished to go, so he instead hurriedly folded the many bills into his purse, tucked it once again inside his coat, and shuffled several papers and letters to cover the one which left him so very unsettled; it would not do for some members of his family to find this letter before he had determined its full meaning. Ash removed himself from the house for a brisk walk about the neighborhood before luncheon began. He dearly hoped the fresh air would aid in clearing his head.

The painter walked through the door and stepped around the fabric curtain hanging as a divider, before surveying the room in its entirety. It was rectangular, the obvious entrance on one side. The space was ideal in that the door to the room was not far from the door to the street. When considering it for purchase, the painter had immediately been charmed. Though cluttered and rather dusty at first, with a bit of work it had been transformed into two quite useful spaces. A set – with chairs, cushions, a table, and several other props – filled the area near the door. The curtain divided the working area from the set and preserved the painter's anonymity. Windows facing the street afforded good light for working during the day, and candles set about the area offered light for working on the frequent overcast days or in the evenings. Now, having worked in it for several months' time, the room was as charming as ever.

The three o'clock appointment would arrive soon, and the painter needed to fetch a fresh piece of charcoal from the storage room. It was easily accessed from a door hidden behind the curtain, and had been empty upon the painter taking possession of the building. The emptiness provided a good beginning for creating an efficient storage room. Builders installed shelves and drawers for storing supplies – bristles, paper, canvas, pigments, oils, and the like – on the inner wall, as well as a working table near the windows on the outside wall. This room was quite narrow, and it was soon discovered that this was due to the stairs being located between the two rooms; the door between passed below the stairs, a deep alcove separating the two spaces.

The charcoal was easily retrieved. As the painter tidied a few papers and some brushes left out on the work table, footsteps sounding through the inside wall announced the descent of the painter's man of business on the stairway, a man by the name of Mr. Edmund Pelter. He was currently the butler of a peer of the realm, but was facing his elder years and unable to perform his duties for many more years. Currently, he was present at the studio only on Mondays, his day off. He had been in the apartment abovestairs, preparing the space to serve as a gallery for the exhibition of the paintings. It needed to be cleaned and the floors improved, but the floors would require a tradesman. The level above that might be useful for a residence, once Mr. Pelter's time as a butler came to an end. He had already proven invaluable to the painter in caring for the building and preparing the spaces for use. Additionally, Mr. Pelter assisted the painter in welcoming customers and acting as the painter's mouthpiece. Anonymity was essential.

The door at the far end of the storage room, which led to the hall, opened. Mr. Pelter entered the storage room and asked about the posing requirements of the three o'clock appointment. The painter walked with him back to the front room, discussing the pose to display the lady's face to best advantage.

When luncheon was announced, Ash was still in something of a fog. His brisk walk had done little to ease his thoughts, as the contents of the mysterious letter were still tumbling around in his thoughts. He had been mildly concerned about the cost of Violet's Season, and now found that he was to receive quite a more substantial sum per annum than he had ever even dreamt of being in his future – or even that of his children, or their children. He determined quite easily, though, that he would keep the contents of the letter to himself for the time being. He was fixed in the certainty that the moment Mrs. Wyndham learned of this, she would decide that the entirety of the *ton* needed to know of it, and that she would consider the amount of his increased income to be her own. He dared not consider how she would demand they remove to the house mentioned, rather than the nearly-shabby house they rented. Wardour Street was not considered a fashionable place to live by the *Beau Monde*. Perhaps it would not be looked down upon as would a house in Cheapside, but it was quite a bit below the neighborhoods of Grosvenor Square, Hanover Square, and Leicester Square. Not that Ash cared one jot for any of it. He was quite disenchanted with Society, to say the least.

Having refreshed himself after his walk, Ash entered the dining room, ready for the distraction of a light repast. Mrs. Wyndham was already serving herself at the side-board, Rose with her. Violet entered shortly after he did, and he ushered her to precede him in approaching the spread of bread, meats, and cheeses, a pudding left from the night before, and several dried fruits.

Once the four members of the Wyndham household were all seated at the table, Mrs. Wyndham spoke. "I trust that you have put away your purchases, Violet?"

"Yes, ma'am," said Violet quietly.

"And you have plans to use the trims we purchased to update the dresses you have which you can still wear?"

"Yes, ma'am."

"And you are prepared to go in two days' time for fittings?"

At Violet's third meek reply in the affirmative, Ash very nearly spoke and interrupted the unnecessary conversation with a severe tongue-lashing – against Violet's meekness or Mrs. Wyndham's unkind tone, he was undecided. Instead, he merely said, "Violet says you are planning to present her in court, ma'am. Has she been instructed in the etiquette?"

"She shall be," replied Mrs. Wyndham. "I've engaged the services of a very knowledgeable individual to instruct both girls in their court manners. Rose will, of course, have no difficulty remembering what she learns; she has always concerned herself with knowing how to properly behave in Society."

"I only wish I might be presented this year, as well. It seems such a waste for Violet to go," simpered Rose, leaning indolently upon her elbow. She sat up suddenly then, feigning surprise. "Oh forgive me! I did not intend that as it sounded. I simply meant that Violet does not enjoy such displays – do you, dearest? – whereas I do, and if we were both to be presented simultaneously, we might balance one another."

Her sugared tone left a sour taste in Ash's mouth, and it was by sheer force of will that he continued to eat the food on his plate.

"Violet," he said when he had nearly finished, "would you care to walk with me to Soho Square? It is only a few blocks from here."

"Does the park have a locked fence about it?" Violet blushed lightly, and Ash recalled their attempt to enter in a park they encountered while walking two days past. The brother and sister duo had made their way along each of the four sides, looking for an entrance, but all were locked. Finally spotting a woman with two small children leaving the fourth gate they approached, Ash inquired as to how they might enter. The woman had responded in an unequivocally condescending tone that if they were not residents of the square, they most certainly could not enter.

"I cannot say, but Mr. Spencer – with whom I attended Oxford – lives on the Square, and if it is locked, we will be his guests."

"Very well," Violet said. "A walk would be most welcome."

Politeness demanded that Ash include all present in the invitation, "Would either of you care to join us?"

"Mr. Leonard Spence?" asked Mrs. Wyndham. At his affirmative nod, she shook her head decisively. "We've nothing more to gain by furthering our acquaintance with him."

Ash gritted his teeth for a moment. Spence was not the *crème* or best of Society, but he had been a faithful friend to the young Ashbridge attending Oxford and worried sick about how his dear sister would fare without him. Spence had served to lighten Ash's moods and even accompanied him on visits home for the sole purpose of ensuring Violet's contentment. It was most galling to hear his friend disregarded in such a manner. With no small measure of self-control, he was able to maintain a pleasant voice when he spoke.

"Very well. Shall we leave in about half an hour, then, Violet? You may wear that walking dress you made back home."

"Yes." She smiled brightly and hurriedly finished the last bites of food on her plate.

Two

PENELOPE WAS QUITE pleased with the sitting room. It had been finished the day previous, and the sole remaining maid – in an effort at economy, the others had been let go – was shining every piece of wood and polishing each piece of metal, until the room glowed. The walls were now renewed with pale green paint, the carpets replaced, and the draperies refurbished – several pieces of the old ones had been refashioned and combined with new fabric to create the illusion of new draperies. Penelope had felt she must also have most of the pieces of furniture re-upholstered; they had been more worn than she would have liked. The house had been seldom used. Her brother had used the house on occasion, and their father had used it even less. Penelope had, therefore, originally planned to leave the furniture as it was. She soon learned that it appeared that her brother was uncommonly abusive to the furniture. The upholstery and repairs had nearly depleted the last of the funds Penelope had saved for this Season. This had necessitated the release of several of their servants, and now she had next to nothing left for new clothing. It would not do for any person hoping to have a successful Season in London. And for Penelope, a successful Season was all her hope.

As she prepared payment for the craftsman, the butler entered the room, bowing.

"Lord Claymore, just in from the Abbey, miss." Before Mr. Pelter had even finished his sentence, Cornelius strode into the room, waving the old butler away.

"Lawks, Pen! You've done this room up nicely. How many pounds did it set you back?"

"Plenty," she answered, attempting to hide her scowl. Money was not a polite conversational topic. "Are you in Town to stay, then, Cornelius?"

"Indeed I am! You shall now have someone to squire you about, sister. Have you any prospects? I know the Season's not truly begun, but surely you've been keeping an eye on who is here and who is looking to set up his nursery."

"I wish you would not speak so bluntly, brother," Penelope said, closing her accounts book. "You make me blush."

"Eh? You, blushing? Gammon!" Cornelius turned and looked at the door. There was a slight thud from the other side.

"Well, if I was prone to blushing, I would be now." Penelope stood and moved to open the door for Mr. Pelter. He moved in with the tea service in his work-worn but still strong hands. She knew that with the necessity of letting go some of the staff, the faithful servant had taken on more than most butlers would consider complying to. They were known to be very jealous of their higher status, over and above the other staff.

"I've your tea, miss," he offered.

"Indeed?" chortled Cornelius as Mr. Pelter carefully placed the tray upon a table. "I thought you had a gown for her."

"Cornelius!" Penelope scowled at her brother before turning to the servant. "I apologize, Mr. Pelter, for my brother's lack of manners."

"Not at all, miss. Thank you, miss," murmured the servant as he bowed out of the room.

As soon as the door was shut, Penelope wheeled on her brother.

"How could you?"

"How could I what?" He lazily regarded his fingernails.

"Speak to that poor man in such a cavalier manner." Penelope felt her heart accelerate its pace, rushing the blood through her veins.

"Oh!" Cornelius withdrew his snuff-box and flicked the lid, taking a pinch between his forefinger and thumb before answering. "Quite easily."

"You know he has been in service of our family for longer than either of us has been alive. He watched both of us grow from infants to adulthood. Oughtn't he receive more respect than that?"

Her brother raised the pinch to his right nostril and inhaled sharply. *How can that distasteful habit be so very fashionable?*

Cornelius repeated the process with the other nostril before snapping the snuff-box closed and shaking his head. "And here I am, having believed for years that he was fulfilling his duties rather than watching a couple of children grow."

"Oh! You know very well what I mean." She poured tea and took a sip before continuing. "He has been a faithful servant for many years. He deserves more respect than you show him."

"Eh, I daresay he rather expects my behavior by now. In fact, I should go so far as to say that if I were to treat him with kindness, he would be patently discomfited." He drained the rest of his tea. "Haven't we anything stronger?"

Penelope watched in distaste as her brother retrieved a flask from his tailcoat pocket and poured some amber liquid into his teacup.

"Much better," he murmured after taking a sip.

"Really Cornelius," said Penelope. "It is still morning. Will you have coffee, then, if not tea?"

"Eh, what? You know I cannot tolerate the stuff. Even worse than tea, which I tolerate only for the sake of politeness."

"How a British Baron can find himself with a disgust of tea is beyond me," she muttered to herself, rolling her eyes and refreshing her cup. An unexpected grin suddenly threatened to break out across her face. Her brother had always held rather stubbornly to his tastes and opinions. She found his stubbornness endearing at times, though she was loathe to admit it. Most especially at present.

Rather than be swayed by the same charm he had used for so long to keep her as an ally, Penelope pushed to the center of her mind what she knew to be true of him now. An image of the two of them hiding beneath her bed while their drunken father raged belowstairs was pushed aside by the memory of her brother stumbling into the Town-house during her first Season, foxed beyond the ability to speak coherently, but still mumbling about the dashed game which had raised his fortunes substantially before taking all in one fell swoop.

Just then, Mr. Pelter knocked before entering once more, this time carrying a silver tray with a slip of paper upon it. "This just arrived for Lord Claymore," said the butler, bowing before the Baron long enough for the paper to be retrieved.

"Thank you, Mr. Pelter," said Penelope when her brother remained silent. The servant bowed and left.

"What is it, Cornelius?" she asked after a few moments of watching her brother's face shift from disinterest to concern.

"Blasted note from my tailor's." Cornelius crumpled the paper, throwing it into the fire.

"Have you the funds to settle with him?" asked Penelope before sipping her tea.

"Err, no. I am quite cleaned out until the next disbursement of our allowances," he admitted.

Penelope wanted to speak, but held her tongue. Stirring up a quarrel would do nothing to help her plan.

"Might you lend me the blunt?" he asked after a pause.

"You receive more than enough for what you need from your estate."

"But I've nothing left this month!" he cried, almost petulantly.

"Cornelius, you know I am saving carefully so I may remain here in Town when you return to the country after the Season's end. You do not wish for your younger sister, who is very nearly on the shelf and will then expect no offer of marriage at all, to be lurking about while you entertain guests, do you?"

"Indeed not!" he said quickly. "But you are by no means on the shelf yet, Pen."

"My name is Penelope," said she.

"Yes yes," Cornelius said with a dismissive wave of his hand, his signet ring glimmering in the light. "But you've enough for remaking the house; why not pay my bill? It is not so very much."

"I've saved and saved to afford these changes, and now have scarcely anything left." Penelope despised admitting any weakness to her brother, real or perceived. "And regardless of my financial situation, I would never give a ha'pence for your senseless debts, even if I was able."

"You would not?" he asked, the corners of his mouth drooping and his brows furrowing in apparent sadness.

While chewing a bite of biscuit she had taken, Penelope had the fleeting curiosity as to whether his crestfallen expression reached his heart, or if it was merely for show. Either way, she swallowed and answered frankly, "Indeed not, on principle. You frequently exceed your allowance." *And maintain dubious friendships. And frequent brothels. And patronize shady gaming halls.* She spoke none of that aloud, though. "If I continued to pull you out of your pickles, you should never learn to avoid these baser temptations. I would be doing you a disservice to allow you to continue down this shameful path."

"Dash it, Pen, I'm downright hurt."

"No, you are not." At the absurdity of his being hurt, coupled with the overly-emotive face of dejection he wore, Penelope suddenly burst out in laughter.

Cornelius held his crestfallen expression in place briefly. When the grin broke out across his boyishly handsome face, he pushed back the mop of curly black hair from his blue eyes. Penelope, observing her brother looking so similar to the boy she'd grown alongside, nearly wanted to like him. Her laughter died down.

Nearly, but not quite.

When the memory arose in her mind of the two of them exchanging small Christmas gifts with one another – she painted a tin soldier for him and he saved for months to purchase new paints for her – she ruthlessly squashed it with the memory of him begging her two days before a Christmas some years later for some coins to place a wager on "a sure win." She, being still young and wishing to believe the best of him, gave him her last coins. He lost them all. Penelope determined to never again be subject to her brother's careless ways.

His next words cemented her in that.

"I truly am at *Point Non Plus*," he pleaded. "I've nothing else to do, Pen. Surely you've a bit left from the renovations, or what you'd planned to spend for new dresses, that you could scrape together for me."

"Indeed not, Cornelius, as I've said repeatedly, I have very little left at all. And my name is Penelope, if you please," she said with much more civility than she felt. "I see you've finished your drink. I must ask now that you leave me."

"But Pen–" At her stern glower, he corrected himself. "Penelope. I've no options! Mr. Cartwright has been in contact with me–"

"He is your friend from school, yes? Does he not hail from Bristol?" Penelope interrupted, grasping at any subject which might distract him from the current topic of conversation. "How does he get on?"

"Very well, but you see Pen–elope. He is not precisely a *friend*."

"But he visited us at Claymore Abbey. Was he not a schoolmate of yours?"

"Er, no, Penelope, he was not."

Penelope was mildly alarmed to note that her brother blushed as he admitted this. She opened her mouth, a barrage of questions ready to pour forth, but Cornelius hurriedly continued.

"Mr. Cartwright lent money to me, and at a considerable interest, with the understanding that I would repay him in a timely manner. And if I do not, there will be consequences."

My brother has found himself indebted to cent-per-cents? The men were known for the outrageous interest charged for every cent borrowed, and most dangerous when not repaid in a timely manner. The blood rushed from Penelope's face, leaving her skin feeling oddly cold and tight. She attempted to swallow in an effort to find her voice. Upon opening her mouth, however, no sound came forth. Her hands began to tremble and her heart raced within her breast. Finally, after several sips of tea, she was able to speak, albeit scarcely above a whisper. "Cornelius, precisely *how much* did you borrow from this Mr. Cartwright?"

"Not a great deal, initially."

"Initially?"

"You see, Pen, at the first, I merely needed enough to settle my voucher at Boodle's and to pay my tailor."

"The tailor's bill in your hand?"

"Yes. Then I discovered a tip on a horse race, a right beautiful stepper, so I approached Cartwright again. It would have paid well, but the animal sprained an ankle shortly before the race, and I lost it all. Including the ruby set."

The tea and biscuit that Penelope had consumed suddenly turned sour in her stomach and she felt ill. She clenched her hands and her jaw, hoping that by holding them with precise control she might also reign in her emotions with similar control. Through her teeth, Penelope ground out, "Surely that would not require Mama's necklace and bracelet, though."

"It did, Pen."

"Penelope," she bit out frostily. "My name is *Penelope*."

"I needed collateral, a . . . deposit of sorts. I still can get it back, but I need five thousand pounds."

"Five *thousand*!" Penelope stood, unable to remain still with the nervous energy suddenly coursing through her. Her heart thudded painfully.

"Er, yes." He blushed again and pulled a bit at his cravat, as though it was too tight for his neck.

"Five thousand." She paced quickly to the window, glanced out without seeing, and whirled to look again at her brother. "Pounds!"

"Yes! We've established this!"

Penelope struggled to keep her voice even as she asked, "How *ever* could you have required so much money, beyond what you receive in your allowance?"

"Oh Pen, I do not know!" Cornelius' voice was rising with each word, until it matched her own. "I needed a bit more here and there, now and again, and before I knew it, I had accumulated what some might term quite a substantial debt."

"You say that as though it were five *hundred* pounds! The tailor pressing for payment is *nothing* in comparison to this! And Mama's ruby necklace and bracelet!" Her voice reached into the realms of desperation as she cried the last.

"And combs," came the quiet addendum.

She sank once again into her chair.

"And combs?" asked Penelope weakly, feeling a terrible, acute pain in her chest. "Cornelius. How *could* you?"

To his dubious credit, Cornelius did appear chagrined at the least, and embarrassed at the best. Penelope fleetingly wondered if his discomfort was due to actual shame and guilt or was simply a result of her furious outburst.

"You cannot think that I planned for this to happen," he said petulantly, rising suddenly and causing his teacup to clatter into its saucer. In a fit of agitation, he paced around the room. He tugged once again at the knot of his cravat and then raked a hand through his ebony curls. "And now Mr. Cartwright is making threats, Pen. He demands–"

"Do *not* address me as Pen," snapped the young woman, in spite of the desperation she heard creeping into her brother's voice, evoking memories of a time when they were both young.

Their father had decided to send her off to a relative's home, in exchange for a handsome sum. The plan had been for her to be raised by them for the purpose of being a companion for the ailing mistress. Cornelius had promised to speak to their father, and he had been true to his word. Penelope remained in her home. She never asked how her brother had convinced the Baron, and through the years, curiosity occasionally pricked at her mind.

That boy was lost to her, though. With cold determination, she forced her thoughts to the much more recent memory of her brother flippantly giving away nearly the last of their mother's possessions. Coldly, she fixed her eyes on his face.

Cornelius had ceased his pacing and stood staring at her for a moment. He abruptly threw himself into his previous seat. As he slumped in the wingback chair, observing Penelope through narrowed eyes, his leg bounced quickly up and down.

"My given name is Penelope," she began, speaking lowly and carefully, "and you are given *that* intimacy only because of my misfortune of claiming the same parentage as you. You *shall not* purchase with credit anything more during your stay here in London, and you certainly will *never* again gamble or wager anything, even something as trivial as your cufflinks, so long as we reside under the same roof. Not if you expect me to run your house for you. Once we have parted ways, at the end of the Season, you may ruin your life as you please."

"Aw, Pen," Cornelius began, but at her fierce glare, he quickly tacked on, "-elope."

"Do *not* argue with me." Penelope closed her eyes, folding her hands with a pretense of serenity. She remained still until she heard the door open and then click shut as her brother left the room.

She relaxed her posture and lowered her head, but still sat, her mind whirling, her fingers tightened around each other until her knuckles grew white and her hands trembled slightly. *It is of utmost importance now more than ever that my plan succeed. I cannot risk any feelings of fondness for Cornelius. He is so far removed from the brother I once knew that I cannot allow association with him for very much longer.*

Further, she doubted that he would allow her to behave in so commandeering a manner again; as the holder of the title of Baron Claymore, and consequently the head of the family, he was within his rights to do as he pleased with his own funds. Having recently reached his majority, though, the entirety of the estate had only just come into his possession; he was still accustomed to being given orders in regards to his spending as others had held his fortune in trust until nearly a year ago. Soon, though, he would realize that no one could dictate his course of action, and he would do as he pleased. And likely follow his own path to destruction.

When she again spoke, it was a whisper, but filled with all the anxiety bubbling up inside of her. "I refuse to be dragged down with you."

Ash held out his hand for Mrs. Wyndham as she stepped down from their family carriage, watching his breath fog in the cold air as he performed the civil duty. He handed down Rose, as well, before closing the door and arranging with the driver to meet him back at the entrance of Hyde Park in two hours. He had hoped to convince Violet to accompany them to the promenade hour at the popular park, but she claimed that she had several changes to make to her blue gown. He considered for a moment upon hearing her excuse whether he could think of something equally credible by which to make his own excuses, but nothing came to mind. Additionally, he felt he must admit to the necessity of providing escort for the two ladies – if for no other reason than to ensure their proper behavior.

A handful of others were already strolling about the park despite the chilling temperatures. Warm bonnets, muffs, and pelisses adorned the ladies; greatcoats, beaver hats, and gloves kept the gentlemen warm. Parliament was set to open its doors in a week's time, when the much-anticipated Social Season would also begin. Those who did not have a seat in the House of Lords would wait until the weather warmed to travel to London.

The park's plants were as sensible of the chill as were the people: the trees remained barren, with no sign of the colors their blooms would bring once the weather warmed. The grass along the paths was a dull brown, awaiting the spring rains. Ash would have much rather been driving along Rotten Row – the pathway that the gentlemen claimed with their carriages, visiting and competing and jostling for position – and certainly would have kept warmer with blankets and heated bricks on the floorboards. Instead, he would have to content himself with walking sedately along the Serpentine River, as Mrs. Wyndham had insisted. It was her sincere belief that they would have more occasions to visit and with any luck be introduced to members of the *Beau Monde* and therefore be more likely to be accepted as part of the *ton*. Ash did not necessarily agree – they could certainly cover much more ground in a barouche – but he chose not to argue this point.

Truthfully, he was surprised that she had allowed Violet to remain behind and did not wish to do anything to change her mind, including question her plan. He knew his sister was quite nervous about the fast-approaching Season. She was sleeping poorly. He had confronted her the other day after she had yawned repeatedly during breakfast. He noticed when they spoke that she was developing shadows beneath her eyes. He had encouraged her at the time to pursue some activities that she enjoyed, and he expressed sincere hope that time spent alone would give her strength for the time spent for Mrs. Wyndham. Violet, at this, had simply smiled and said, "Time spent for one self is beneficial, indeed, but it is time spent with the Lord that gives one strength." He had not wished to argue, and so he said nothing.

"Ashbridge, are you acquainted with Lady Melton and her children, Mr. Barrett and Miss Barrett?" Mrs. Wyndham's voice cut into his reverie. "Her husband is a *marquis*," she finished in a whisper that he could only surmise she believed was much quieter than it was in actuality.

Ash bowed before looking at the matron, accompanied by a gentleman near his own age and a young lady likely near Violet's. A quick, calculating glance suggested that they all were well-supplied with allowances and pin-money for their attire, if the excellent cut and costly fabric of their clothing were any indication.

"Lady Melton, please allow me to present my son, Mr. Ashbridge Wyndham." Mrs. Wyndham was smiling radiantly as she explained to Ash, "Rose and I made her acquaintance two days past in the drawing room of a mutual friend."

He bowed again when she presented her children to them. The wind suddenly picked up, and the lady's bonnets all began fluttering as the feathers, flowers, and ribbons danced with the gusts, and the skirts of their dresses and pelisses blew about in the wind.

Miss Barrett swiftly fastened the two top buttons on her pelisse, which she had left open. She tucked her hands once more into her muff, and smiled at Rose. "Are you enjoying your time in London, Miss Wyndham?"

"Miss *Rose*, actually," said Mrs. Wyndham. "It is my eldest daughter who is making her come-out this year."

"Forgive me," murmured the girl. "Is she unwell, that she could not accompany you this evening?"

"Oh no," twittered Rose, "she's as likely to venture out in public when it isn't necessary as—"

"As anyone," interrupted Ash. "But she is laboring over a white-work dress she wishes to complete before the first ball of the Season." He knew that mentioning her proficiency in the widely-valued art of embroidering the fine white muslin fabric with patterns of white scrolling flowers, leaves, and the like was something Mrs. Wyndham might do. However, he was reluctant to cast his favored sister into a poor light by saying that she was making over a blue gown from two years past. *I told no terrible falsehood, though; she mentioned this morning that her white muslin dress should be delivered tomorrow, and she is anxious to begin the embroidery on it.*

"Indeed?" said Miss Barrett. "I do wish I had paid better attention when my governess instructed me in needlework, and been more diligent in my practice. What a lovely thing to wear for one's first Season. I shall certainly have nothing so meticulously stitched. I can certainly stitch a simple monogram upon a kerchief, but an entire dress? It would likely take me ten years to accomplish such a feat!"

"Your sister seems quite accomplished with her needle, Mr. Wyndham," said Mr. Barrett with a ready smile. *Too ready*, thought Ash sourly. "Does she sing or play?"

"Violet, play?" chortled Rose. "Indeed she does, and quite well. If only the poor dear could do so among company." She shook her head sadly, presenting a fond younger sister who wished her elder sister could be presented to her best advantage, but Ash saw the devious glint in her eye. He found himself torn between defending his sister and allowing the interest on Mr. Barrett's face to continue to fade, as it had begun to do upon the mention of Violet's shyness.

"Well, we must be off!" said Mrs. Wyndham cheerfully. "Do come and visit us, Lady Melton. Here is my card."

The lady's smile was genuine as she received the card, but it faded as she read the address. "Oh, your house is on Wardour Street?" The disdain in her voice was evident to Ash, but he remained silent.

"How amusing!" cried Mrs. Wyndham. "Of course we would not *purchase* a house there. My son is looking for a permanent house; we have settled for renting this one for the time being."

"I wonder that he did not complete a purchase before the beginning of the Season."

Ash knew when his providence for his family was being called into question, so he answered accordingly, "Rushing into such a monumental purchase is never wise. I have been searching for the better part of a year, and have yet to find anything which meets with my expectation."

Lady Melton regarded him silently for a short time before saying, "A wise decision. We shall call on you after the Season begins in earnest."

"Good day, Lady Melton!" called Mrs. Wyndham as they departed. "Mr. Barrett! Miss Barrett!"

They all then continued along the path which wound its way along the Serpentine. The river in the center of the park was surrounded by foot paths. The paths among the trees and other plants were pleasant, but Ash particularly enjoyed walking along the Serpentine, if walk he must. The river invited waterfowl and the wind created ever-changing ripples in the water; it held his interest better than the rest of the park when on foot.

"What an advantageous acquaintance for us!" cried Mrs. Wyndham after they had walked several paces.

I do hope they cannot hear us, grumbled Ash silently.

"I am certain," continued Mrs. Wyndham obliviously, "that they shall be able to introduce us to much of the *bonne ton* and perhaps even a wallflower such as Violet may find a suitable match!"

The park became a bit more crowded as they walked farther down the path. Ash knew from experience that it was nothing compared to the horde that would be present after the start of the Season. He kept pace with the ladies, spoke when necessary, and soon saw why Mrs. Wyndham had so easily allowed Violet to remain at home.

During each of at least ten conversations, Mrs. Wyndham had Rose stand prominently in their little gathering before mentioning that there was an elder sister. It was obvious to Ash that so many of the young gentlemen they encountered were immediately attracted by Rose's stunning beauty. Her golden curls and bright eyes demanded attention. Her admirers' eyes invariably widened when they discovered that Miss Rose was in fact not even out and that she had a sister who would be newly out this Season.

Ash grudgingly admitted it was a rather clever strategy, though he knew it would not help Violet. She would not know how to receive or react to the attentions which undoubtedly would be coming her way. He hoped that her shyness would not be perceived as haughtiness and thereby prevent a gentleman from bothering to deepen an acquaintance with her. Of course, Ash selfishly hoped that she would never marry and instead keep house for him and allow him to live most of his life without the trouble of a wife; they had in fact planned this for several years. Still, if Violet met someone and grew to love him, Ash hoped the gentleman would appreciate the gem he had and pursue her properly.

Again distracted by his thoughts, Ash found that Mrs. Wyndham and Rose had begun to converse with someone before he was even aware of it.

"Oh indeed. We are *most* happy to be in Town for the Season," Rose was saying with an airy giggle, referring to the city of London in the same manner as many of her countrymen did. London alone was Town, and a town was much smaller and offered much less entertainment and shopping.

Ash looked to see with whom Rose spoke and nearly laughed aloud. Thankfully, though, he was able to clamp his lips together quickly enough to suppress his laughter. The pop-in-jay before them had teased and curled his hair to twice its natural volume. The reddish-gold froth framed his face, which was clearly powdered and with a dark mole painted on the apple of his left cheek. Ash noted that had the mole been placed anywhere lower on his face, it would have become smudged by his terribly high shirt-points. He truly could not understand the trend of young dandies to order their shirts to be made with collars so large and starched that half of their faces were covered by them. The cravat was a complicated, lacey mess, and Ash was certain that had the famous Beau Brummel been present, he would have given this man a severe dressing-down for his ridiculously ostentatious waistcoat of blues and greens and reds. The bright peacock blue coat, decorated with gold cording and buttons, showed beneath a bright red cape. *And is that a diamond cravat-pin or a medallion on a chain? I cannot see.*

"Yeth!" cried the man with a clearly-affected lisp. "Ath am I."

Is this man in earnest? Ash could not help but wonder. *Perhaps he lost a wager?*

"Are your parents staying in Town, Mr. Langley?"

"Oh *no*, Mithith Wyndham. I fear they are *both* much too frail for the *rigorth* of Thothiety. My brother, who will inherit my *father's* title, ith in Town with hith wife." He turned a slimy smile upon Rose. "I mutht admit my great relief in my brother'th married thtate. It ith one leth man with whom I mutht compete for the hand of fair Mith Rothe."

It took several seconds for Ash's brain to catch up with the conversation. And several seconds more to realize that Rose returned his apparent regard. She giggled and batted her eyes at the foppish man. *I had supposed no one less than a Duke would truly fulfill her expectations in a match, and here she is setting her cap for a second son.*

Ash half-listened to the remainder of the conversation, until the crowds at Hyde Park began again to thin, and the natural light of the fading sun gave way to the burning lamps scattered about the park. The colorful gent made an elaborate bow, even daring to take Rose's gloved hand and kiss the knuckles.

"Until we meet again, Miss Rose," he murmured, pronouncing her name correctly.

I knew that lisp was merely for show, thought Ash as they made their way to the waiting carriage. *I should not be surprised if that imbecile waits for Rose until she is out. The question, then, is whether Rose would be content to accept him? I am surprised she is not presently mocking that magnificent leg he swept when taking his leave – I've not seen someone bow so theatrically since being presented in court.*

Oddly enough, Ash did not feel a fraction of the protective rush of indignant heat he experienced with his other sister. Perhaps he felt she needed more protection than did the worldlier, bolder Rose.

Three

PENELOPE HAD SETTLED on the amount she might spend on her clothing for the Season. She sincerely hoped it would prove sufficient, for she was much more accomplished with a paintbrush than with a needle. She knew there were some of her mother's old gowns stored in a trunk up in one of the extra rooms of the house, but they would do her no good at all without someone to make them over. The conical bodice and wide panniers of her mother's heyday were nothing like the natural form currently favored. Penelope nearly considered asking a seamstress to use the dresses, but feared that the gossipmongers would learn of it, and subsequently learn of her poverty. Her plan would never succeed if that were to happen. So it was with the last of her savings tucked securely into her reticule that Penelope ventured forth with her aunt to the dressmaker's shop.

"Bonjour, miss," greeted the plump proprietress when Penelope entered the shop, the bell above the door announcing her presence. Aunt Essie followed her into the warm shop's interior, the bell tinkling again when the door was closed. "Might I asseest you weeth anyzing? A new ballgown, perhaps? Or perhaps you are planning your wedding *trousseau?*"

Penelope smiled, but shook her head and said, "No wedding in my future."

"Ees that how you think? Well, never you are to fear. A fetching thing like you shan't remain unattached for long."

Penelope just smiled while she removed her pelisse, muff, and bonnet. Walking to a table with an assortment of fashion plates scattered about it, she asked, "Are these the latest?"

"But of course!" The woman appeared indignant that her expertise in the latest of fashion was being called into question.

"I meant no offense," smiled Penelope. "I was unsure if you were more guarded with your own designs, and might have kept them in another location."

"Ah! I see you haff heerd of Mees Weatherby down the street sending her girls posing as customers to steal my designs!" The woman bustled over to a cabinet against the back wall.

While Madame Bélanger was otherwise occupied, Penelope turned to her aunt. "Would you care to sit, Aunt Essie? There is a chair here at this table."

"I am not so far into my dotage as to be incapable of such a mundane and simple task as shopping," said her aunt. "However, as no one else seems to have need of it, I believe I shall sit."

Penelope smiled at her aunt before returning her attention to the drawings on the table. There were day dresses, ballgowns, visiting ensembles, spencers and pelisses, underpinnings and countless other items sketched and colored to give customers ideas of gowns they would like to bespeak.

"Here we ahhe," panted Madame Bélanger as she returned to the table, a small paper package in her hands. "My asseestant had placed a box of thread on zee top, so it took longer than I had thought to find them."

Penelope quickly gathered the scattered papers, and stacked them into a neat pile on the corner of the table.

"I've several new designs for court dresses here—"

"I made my come-out two years past," interrupted Penelope, "was presented in Court, and have no intention of repeating the experience."

"Ah yes, all zee young debs say it ees quite the intimidating experience, and only endure it for the promise of the Queen's approval for her entrance into *société*."

"Yes," agreed Penelope, "it was rather intimidating, but with a bit of practice with the hoop and the train, it was not so very difficult."

"You seem a lady born to adorn zee court of zee Queen. Haff you been invited to her drawing room?"

"Heavens, no," laughed Penelope. "I've avoided Society as much as possible since then."

"So a few simple day dresses will be all you need?" asked the proprietress, slightly deflated.

"Perhaps." Penelope accepted the stack of papers from the woman, and began to peruse the sketches of gowns. "May I ask, who does the drawings for your designs?"

"A friend of mine did for years, but her rheumatics all but prevented her thees Season. I must find a new artist for my designs. I can assemble fabric into any dress you might imagine, but to create a creditable representation of it on paper? *Je suis perdu.* I am lost."

"Hmm." Penelope was reflective. "I may have someone who would be interested in assisting you. I've decided to sponsor a promising young painter, and until word spreads of the quality of the paintings, I fear my humble patronage is insufficient. He draws as well as he paints."

"Indeed?" She perked up a bit. "May I have his name?"

"I am afraid not," said Penelope sadly. "Anonymity is very important to this individual. If I may, though, I shall send him with a letter of introduction. He will, of course, bring a sample of his work, and you may then decide whether or not to engage his services. If you can promise to protect his anonymity, that is."

"*Très bien!*"

Penelope smiled again. She had determined that she would have enough for one dress at the least, and would order one at a time, to ensure that she did not overextend her resources. "Now. I believe I need one new ballgown." She knew it would be much easier to pass her old day-dresses as presentable than an old ballgown. After a moment's hesitation, she added, "And gloves."

"To wear with zee dress?"

"Yes. Have you any suggestions on fabric or designs? I am, as you said, quite lost."

"Hmm." She accepted the papers back from Penelope, and began sifting through them thoughtfully. "You've a classic beauty which we ought to display. And I believe a seemple gown will do zhat nicely. Perhaps some minor embellishment only? About zee hem?"

She held out a paper, on which was sketched a feminine form draped in a gown, lovely in its simplicity. The short sleeves fell nicely, and the neckline draped in a manner that preserved modesty while also echoing the Greek and Roman dress of days past, which Penelope knew was wildly popular.

"It is lovely." She feared to ask, and knew that most daughters of peers would not have been required to ask at all – but she could not order the dress in good conscience without first knowing how much it would cost. "If I add a pair of silk gloves, what will be my total?" Penelope reached for her reticule to retrieve the coins.

"You may give payment when zee dress is finished," she said. "Many of my customers pay on credit."

"I would prefer not to do so," said Penelope with what she hoped was a bright smile, but she feared it was as weary and wavering as she felt.

"Very well. Let us go to the back rooms and see what fabric I have on hand." She motioned with a calloused hand for Penelope to follow, before glancing back over her shoulder. "Unless you would prefer to purchase it from the drapers and have it delivered to me?"

"Oh, no, but thank you. I am sure that something you have on hand will do nicely." She turned to her aunt. "Would you care to remain here, or accompany us, Aunt?"

"Oh, I daresay it would not hurt to allow these old bones to rest a bit more."

Penelope grinned at her aunt before turning and following the other woman to the back room of the store.

The room was much more crowded than the one in the front. Fabric on rolls lined the far wall, and shelves held folded stacks of more fabric. A cabinet with small drawers to the left was labeled with numbers, with a tall standing mirror located in the back left corner of the room. Two large tables, scattered with scissors, pins, and scraps of fabric, stood squarely in the center of the room.

Madame Bélanger turned to the right of the room. "Are you nearly finished with zee hem, Marie?"

"*Oui, Mére,*" said the girl.

"Very good. And Angelique, ees zee pelisse assembled?"

At the other girl's nod, Madame Bélanger turned back to Penelope. "Zhey are my daughters. Someday, zee shop weell be theirs."

"How wonderful for them." Penelope envied the girls in that while they would never be able to aspire to the Society into which she herself was born, they were able to make their own way in life, to learn a trade and support themselves in that manner. For a gentlewoman such as herself, though, to work was not a possibility.

"Here we are," said Madame Bélanger as she led Penelope to several rolls of soft, gauzy fabric. "Zhese fabrics weell do nicely. Do you think white or a color? White *is* all zee rage." The woman unrolled several yards of a soft white, draping it over Penelope's shoulder and allowing it to hang over her and cover much of her dress.

Penelope gazed into the mirror. She was surprised by how well her dark blue eyes and mahogany hair were set off in sharp contrast to the white of the fabric. It had been years since she had worn such a frivolous color – white was much more difficult to keep clean and to wash once sullied than a dress with color.

Madame Bélanger stood still, considering the fabric for a moment. Suddenly she started with a cry. "Perhaps with a shawl or overdress of turkey red." She hurried to the shelves containing folded fabric, lifting piles of cloth and searching for something. "I know eet ees here somewhere . . ." she trailed off. "Ah! Just as I thought." And she approached Penelope with a deep burgundy fabric, unfolding it as she walked.

Once the turkey red fabric was draped across her front, hanging back in the shoulders and allowing the white to show beneath and above it, Madame Bélanger nodded her head and clucked her tongue approvingly. "Yees. Zhis weell do nicely."

"What will I owe you for all of this?" Penelope asked hesitantly.

"You are a dear girl, and I am pleeeased to make dress for you." Madame Bélanger smiled and named a price which would certainly drain Penelope's meager funds, but was also certainly something that she could pay right away.

With a deep breath to fortify herself, Penelope said, "Very well. I shall give you the coin today."

Madame Bélanger smiled broadly and gathered the fabric from Penelope. "Allow me to make a few notes while Angelique takes your measurements."

A quarter-hour later, Penelope emerged from the back room, retrieved her reticule from her aunt, and counted out the coins for the dressmaker. She poked her head into the backroom, unintentionally interrupting the three ladies who were gathered at one of the tables and discussing the white and red fabrics on its surface.

"Here is my payment," said Penelope when three pairs of eyes turned toward her.

"*Merci*," said Madame Bélanger, dropping a curtsey as Penelope dropped the coins into her open palm. "I shall send word when zee gown ees feenished."

"Excellent. *Merci*, Madame Bélanger."

Penelope left them in the back room to finish their discussion, and returned to where her pelisse was hanging upon a hook by the door.

"Shall we return to the house, Aunt?" she asked.

Aunt Essie was beginning to answer, but the sound of the bell distracted them both. A tall, slender girl entered, looking shyly about the room. She blushed when she looked up and noticed the two ladies.

"Good morning," said Penelope cheerfully. Now that she had paid the price, she was rather looking forward to her new gown, and her enthusiasm colored her tone.

"G-good morning," murmured the girl quietly, her face flushing anew.

"Are you here by yourself?" asked Penelope, looking toward the door to see whether anyone else was following just behind.

"Oh. Er, my mama sent a groom with me," she said as she removed her gloves. "He is still with the driver at the carriage."

"I see." Penelope smiled again. "I am rather surprised that your mama allowed you to shop for dresses without her guidance. Is this your first Season?"

"It is. Only, we shopped last week. Madame promised my white muslin today."

"Is there a particular reason you are so eager to retrieve it?" Penelope could see that the girl was timid, and supposed that only something of great import would cause her to venture out with only a groom.

"I er- I-I plan to embroider it, and must begin soon if I am to finish it before the Season begins."

"Meess Wyndham!" Madame Bélanger called from the back of the room. "I do apologize! I zink that bell was only Miss Drayton leaving zee store. Are you here for your gown?"

"I am," murmured the girl – Miss Wyndham.

"Allow me to fetch eet."

She rushed back to the work room, and the girl blushed when Penelope looked toward her again.

"Miss Wyndham, was it?"

"Yes, Miss Violet Wyndham." Miss Wyndham curtsied awkwardly.

"Pleased to make your acquaintance. I am Miss Penelope Drayton, and this is my aunt, Miss Esther Breckenridge."

"How do you do?" Miss Wyndham curtsied again. "We've already had a brief discussion, have we not? I suppose asking 'how do you do' is somewhat moot at this point."

Penelope laughed, her heart warming at the refreshing innocence of this girl. "Nonsense! I am pleased say that I am quite well. I've just bespoken an evening gown, and am looking forward to the Season."

"My mama insisted that I have more gowns than I ever have before. I cannot comprehend needing so many," admitted Miss Wyndham quietly.

"Have you spent much time in London, Miss Wyndham?" asked Penelope. When the girl shook her head, Penelope continued. "One can never have too many gowns when residing in Town."

Miss Wyndham smiled in response, but offered no comment. Penelope guessed that her family lived in the country, and had arrived in London for the Season, hoping to find a good match for their daughter. Perhaps they had an aunt or close family friend who had offered to sponsor her. Not wishing the conversation to lag – there was something calming and peaceful about conversing with her – Penelope asked, "Is the dress you are wearing from Madame Bélanger?"

Miss Wyndham blushed again before answering haltingly, "Er, no. It was new two years past. I—ah, I altered it a bit, recently, and purchased some new trim."

"You made this dress?" Penelope asked, amazed. It was a fine dusty blue and of an excellent cut. The bodice fit perfectly, the skirt draped nicely, and the braided dark blue trim at the hem, cuffs, and neckline completed the ensemble. Miss Wyndham's shy affirmation set Penelope's mind whirling.

Miss Wyndham would be a most advantageous friend to have. I doubt that a sufficiently close friendship could be formed in time for that to be of any help to me this Season. Even so, I did enjoy speaking with her these five minutes much more than any conversation I have held with the ladies of the ton. *She has a quiet and calming spirit.*

"Do . . . do you think it to be acceptable for a morning dress?" Miss Wyndham asked, her voice painfully timid.

"Oh! Forgive me, Miss Wyndham. I was lost in thought." Penelope smiled at the girl, and even grasped her hand in sincerity. "It is a lovely gown, and I had no earthly idea that it was not made by a dressmaker."

"Truly?" asked the girl. "My mama says that my dresses look well enough for our small village, but that they cannot withstand the critical eyes of the *bonne ton*."

"These words sound as though they are not your own." Penelope's heart squeezed slightly at the sad smile that formed on Miss Wyndham's face. "It is quite well-suited to you, and it is remarkably well-made. May I ask what changes you made, exactly?"

Miss Wyndham explained that she had wished to adjust the construction of the bodice a bit, and could not use the old one, so she had taken the bodice from the back of the skirt, opening the fabric. It was rather simple to remove a portion of it, and then reassemble the skirt. The extra piece of fabric was used to create the new bodice; it crossed at the front and gathered at the back. A white fichu was tucked into the neckline for modesty and warmth.

"Heere ees zee gown, Mees Wyndham!" came Madame Bélanger's voice from the back room.

Penelope decided it was time to leave. "It was a pleasure making your acquaintance, Miss Wyndham."

"Oh! Yes, it was, Miss Drayton." Miss Wyndham blushed and looked about the shop with nervous, flickering eyes for a moment before suddenly reaching into her reticule and withdrawing a card. Her voice was hushed as she spoke. "I, er- I have a difficult time feeling comfortable right away with new acquaintances, and, Miss Drayton, I felt rather surprisingly at my ease speaking with you." She took a deep breath and held out the card. "Would you care to call? I should like to continue discussing fashion with you, and perhaps even show you another of the dresses I have remade, if that would not be improper."

Warmth bloomed in Penelope's heart, and a spontaneous smile broke out across her face. *How long has it been since I smiled unexpectedly?* Rather than dwell on that and its implications for her happiness, Penelope said, "I should be delighted to call on you. At present, I am rather swamped by preparations for the Season, but have you received an invitation to the Lowry's card-party? I believe it is planned for the first Monday after Parliament opens, in just under a week."

Miss Wyndham nodded. "Yes, I believe my mother mentioned that she planned for us to attend."

"Perhaps we may meet there to decide upon a date for me to call on you. I believe that interesting conversation should greatly improve the party."

"I look forward to seeing you there, then," the girl said with a small smile.

"Wonderful. Now, I had best take my leave, and you should go back to Madame Bélanger before she grows angry."

Miss Wyndham chuckled lightly before curtsying and saying, "Good-day, Miss Drayton."

"Good-day."

Ash realized immediately after Violet's departure for the dressmaker's shop that something was amiss. He ought to have been on his guard when Mrs. Wyndham informed Violet that her gown would not be sent to their home as had been previously arranged. She was sent with a groom as escort to pick up the dress as soon as she had broken her fast. Ash had finished his plate when Violet did and was sitting in the morning room reading the paper. Rose and Mrs. Wyndham remained at the small table, breaking their fast and exchanging bits of gossip – the sought-after *on-dits* passed about by the gossips. Ash, for his part, had no interest in the latest *on-dit* and did his best to ignore the conversation. The day promised to be overcast, and therefore the large widows in the room afforded only a weak light. Ash found it necessary to sit close to the window and angle the paper toward it in order to read.

"What a lovely outing we had at Hyde Park yesterday," Mrs. Wyndham said after a pause. Ash looked up from his paper to see that she was using her fork to push the remains of egg about her plate while looking his way. "Miss Barrett was lovely, was she not?"

Ash raised his brows. They had encountered between ten and fifteen parties at Hyde Park yesterday. He had a vague impression of wispy brown hair, but beyond that could not put a face with the name. "I suppose."

"I should be more than happy to welcome her into our family."

"Madam." Ash filled his voice with stern reprimand and just a touch of scorn. Mrs. Wyndham nodded slightly, and said no more on that subject. He knew that she was aware of the situation. As the current master of the Wyndham estate, he held the purse-strings and could easily restrict the amount he allowed Mrs. Wyndham to spend. Her widow's jointure was surprisingly small — certainly enough to meet her needs, but little else. Extra bonnets, gowns, slippers, and whatnot were obtainable only because Ash elected to be generous with the pin money of the ladies in his family. The estate could certainly afford it at present, and Mrs. Wyndham knew that. *I am exceedingly grateful that she remains unaware of the letter from Lord Ashbridge; she should be positively incorrigible.*

"The furthering of our acquaintanceship with Lady Melton and her children was without doubt our most advantageous connection made yesterday."

It appeared that Mrs. Wyndham was not ready to abandon that topic, after all. Ash was about to change the subject, but Rose did so before he had a chance.

"Mama, I disagree." She widened her eyes, gazing at the older woman through the thick fringe of lashes. "Do you not think that Mr. Langley is an excellent man?"

Ash searched his memory for a face to put with the name.

"He was certainly a colorful character," allowed Mrs. Wyndham. *Who is this?*

"He was so very cultured," effused Rose. "He said he knew all the best venues to see and be seen, and he indicated he was intimately acquainted with several of the opera-dancers."

Oh, indeed? I doubt you would wish your love-interest to be dallying with convenients.

"And he dressed with such extravagance that I cannot help but believe him to have quite a generous allowance."

Extravagance? Ash had a feeling he was beginning to realize who this *Mr. Langley* was and did not care one bit for the image materializing in his mind.

"I am positively smitten!" burst forth from Rose's lips. Ash looked over at her from his paper; her glowing eyes and flushed face caused a sinking sensation in his stomach.

Not that parading pop-in-jay!

Unfortunately, Rose's effusions had their intended influence upon Mrs. Wyndham.

"He did seem knowledgeable of fashion. And his *attentions* were so *flattering*," Mrs. Wyndham giggled.

She is giggling?

"Yes, he did stay and speak with us longer than any of the others we met yesterday, did he not? Was it only my imagination, Mama, or do you think he paid me special attention?" Rose's smile was full of youthful hope, but then it faded a bit. "I fear, though, that someone else will snatch his attention. I am not yet out, and will seldom be in company with him." She positively deflated, much to Ash's alarm. "No, I am sure his affections are not enough engaged to remain steadfast through this Season, let alone the two which will pass before I may come out."

Ash saw immediately that for which she was angling. *Surely she will not be successful in convincing—*

"Oh, you poor dear." Mrs. Wyndham rose from her chair and moved to stand beside Rose, gently rubbing small circles on the girl's back. "I wonder that you are not weeping. You are a very strong girl."

Rose drew a shuddering breath. "I must be, Mama. It would not be fair to Violet were I to come out this year; I am convinced I should destroy her hopes to ever marry were I to outshine her."

Ash did all he could not to roll his eyes heavenward. *Can she be serious? She wants to be out this year? We've not the time to purchase clothes for her, not without greasing the fist of the dressmaker, and cobbler, and milliner to make her items a priority. I could afford it, with the funds coming in now from Lord Ashbridge, but I truly do not wish to fund this foolhardy scheme.*

"My dear, I do not wish for you to suffer," began Mrs. Wyndham, sliding her eyes sideways to meet Ash's.

They are conspiring together!

"And if I made it known from the moment I was out that my feelings are engaged, the gentlemen should not be *too* terribly distracted from Violet," Rose offered.

Ash felt his lungs constrict as he struggled to draw his next breath. *No.*

"And Violet is rather standoffish," continued Rose, "so I shan't be surprised if she is not a favorite of the gentlemen, even if I was not out. So truly, my coming out really would not have a pronounced impact on Violet either way. Or perhaps others would be more likely to take notice of her when she is near me."

Insulting your sister in order to forward your own interests, Rose? While pretending concern for her well-being? I had sincerely hoped you were above that, but I now fear that my hope was ill-placed.

Mrs. Wyndham at this point turned to face Ash. "Son, are you willing to support your other sister in a Season this year? The cost for Violet's Season is already considerably lower than it might have been, as she has graciously agreed to make over some of her old dresses."

"Will Rose do the same?" he asked, though he already knew the answer.

"Oh Ash, you know that I am not as accomplished a seamstress as Vi." Rose stood and walked over to where he sat. "And I have grown a great deal more than she has, have I not?" She turned her shoulders back and forth, twisting at the waist and swishing her skirts. "I am not the child I was even a year ago."

"Rose. You are not old enough to be out."

"Nonsense," said Mrs. Wyndham. "I was out at her age."

"We are not living in the same decade as you did, or even the same century; girls are not marrying as young as they used to."

"No, they are not. But Rose is of a similar age as *some* of the girls out this year, and she has a womanly figure which can easily pass her for older than she is."

Ash was growing significantly uncomfortable with discussing his youngest sister's form – *Likely their angle.* He said hurriedly, "Very well! She shall have her Season."

"Oh Ash!" cried Rose, throwing her arms around his shoulders and crushing his paper. "Thank you!"

"Yes, yes." He was admittedly surprised that Rose thanked him, but decided not to comment on it. Instead, he patted her back awkwardly; he and Violet had long been more affectionate with one another than he and Rose. "Very good."

"Come, Rose. Let us prepare a list for when we visit the dressmaker's." Rose dropped a quick kiss upon his cheek before righting herself and following Mrs. Wyndham from the room. As they left, he could hear the words, "He is not increasing your dowry or pin-money; you need not be so effusive in your thanks. He can certainly afford a bit of generosity with his family."

No, I am simply footing the bill for countless gowns and another voucher at Almack's, while also ensuring Rose does not expose herself to ridicule due to her immature prattle. Why did I capitulate? She would have easily recovered from the lost love of Mr. Leelay. Or was it Lesley? Or Langley?

Ash realized his stomach had turned sour; it was with a sense of foreboding that he looked toward to the fast-approaching Season.

Four

PENELOPE SCOWLED AT the floppy hat. It certainly was not attractive, but if it did its job, she would be very pleased to wear it.

"Aunt Essie, would you mind helping with my hair?"

"Am I now your abigail?" she asked, referring to the ladies' maid a woman of the upper class had to assist with her daily *toilette* and caring for her clothing. In spite of her words, Aunt Essie smiled at Penelope and took the brush from her hands.

Penelope grinned ruefully at her aunt through the looking glass at her dressing-table, shaking her head at the woman's teasing. "No, but we both know that the money saved by dismissing the maids is very much needed. I fear I shall have to let Mary go at the end of the Season."

"True," she conceded, moving to stand behind Penelope. "Now, is it all to be hidden beneath this . . . hat?"

"Yes," Penelope giggled. "I must not allow anyone to see that I am not a young man."

"I feel I must tell you that this seems an ill-advised scheme." Aunt Essie gathered Penelope's curls into her hands, brushing them together as best she could.

"Yes, Aunt, so you have said." Penelope smiled cheekily at her. "Several times."

"It is as true now as it was the first time I said it." She began brushing the hair higher and higher on Penelope's head. "What would happen to your reputation if someone were to recognize you? That the daughter of a peer, of nobility would work for money is too vulgar of an idea for the *Beau Monde* to even consider."

"Which is precisely why my scheme will succeed. You know, as well as I, that not a one of them would deign to look closely enough at a poor street urchin to tell whether he was in actuality the daughter of a peer."

Aunt Essie began twisting Penelope's hair around itself, creating a topknot at the crown of her head. "Perhaps."

"If I did not need to appear as myself any longer, I should have cut it off. Ow!" She could not help but cry out as Aunt Essie jabbed her with a hairpin. *I do hope that was accidental.* "Then it would be much easier to appear as a boy."

"Oh?" She continued sticking hairpins painlessly into Penelope's hair. "Do you plan to wear it short after this Season?"

"Perhaps. Or perhaps earlier. You know it has become most fashionable to wear short hair now."

"Yes. But it is the extreme of fashion, not what the average person does."

"I shall allow you that, but I believe I have the confidence to succeed in wearing such an extreme."

"And *I* shall allow you *that*." Aunt Essie stepped to the side and smiled face-to-face at her niece while she took the floppy hat from her hands. Placing it upon Penelope's head, she said, "You certainly do not look like the daughter of a baron."

Penelope lifted her eyes to the looking glass and could not help but stare. Gazing back at her was a boy of about fourteen. The clothing she had found in one of the chests in the extra rooms used to belong to Cornelius. He had long since out-grown them, but somehow they had not been passed along to any of the servants' children. The suit was certainly out-of-fashion, and worn threadbare at the knees and elbows – perfect for the role she was playing. An essential role, considering the manner in which her brother was slowly undermining all that she had been working to achieve.

Just yesterday, Penelope had ventured to the kitchen to seek out a small morsel and found Mr. Pelter and their cook exchanging a tearful good-bye. Mr. Pelter haltingly explained that he was asked by my lord to gather his belongings and seek another position. Cornelius had apparently claimed that Mr. Pelter had taken something of his, and this was the reason for the man's dismissal, but Penelope did not believe it to be true. The man should be retiring with a generous pension after all of his years of service, not facing a disgraceful termination to his employment. Still, there was little she could do about it, aside from sending the elder man on his way with tears and the promise of an excellent reference should he need it.

It was more urgent now, than ever, that Penelope's plan succeed. It seemed that more than her own welfare was dependent upon her success. Mr. Pelter had no one, and in truth, Aunt Essie really had no one else to care for her, either. Penelope had no desire to see either of them suffer, or for herself to end up in a situation similar to theirs in her old age. Yes, her plan *must* succeed. And this disguise might be an important part of its success.

A half-hour later found Penelope drawing a deep, fortifying breath before she pushed open the door to Madame Bélanger's shop. The front room was occupied by four individuals. In addition to the proprietress, there was a matron and two younger people: a girl with fair ringlets and a man who appeared oddly familiar, but Penelope could not place where she might have seen him. With a mental shake of her head to remind herself of the role she was playing, she lowered her eyes and moved to stand near the wall beside the door, hand resting on her satchel. She would wait to be addressed.

"Now two giulls to be out! How veeery exciting!" Madame Bélanger was saying.

The two females positively beamed, but the gentleman only made a disapproving sound low in his throat.

"And you weell be sending zee fabreecs you desire from zee draper's?"

"Indeed," said the matron.

"Excellent!" cried Madame. "Ees there anything else I may do for you, Madame Wyndham?"

"No, that is all. Come along, Rose. Ashbridge."

The gentleman huffed, and then turned to open the door, but Penelope had hurried to open the door for them. He noticed her just before colliding with her much smaller frame, and Penelope felt the air rush from her lungs as sure as had the impact been physical.

"Pardon me," murmured the man. Penelope ventured a quick glance at his face, and felt her own flame. *I do not blush!*

She nodded, and stepped aside, hand on the door, as the ladies exited. Penelope saw him stare at her paint-stained hand as he followed the ladies through the door. *I ought to have worn gloves.*

"May I help you, young man?" asked Madame Bélanger after the door closed behind Penelope.

Clearing her throat, she lowered her voice slightly and answered, "Yes, ma'am. Miss Drayton sent me." She reached into the satchel and withdrew a folded paper. "Here is her letter."

Penelope watched, doing her best not to fidget, as Madame Bélanger read the letter of introduction she had written the previous evening.

"So you are zee *artiste*, no?"

"Yes, ma'am."

"And you weesh to remain anonymous?"

"I do."

"Vell, I must admeet it to be *très irrégulier*, but I trust Mees Drayton." Madame Bélanger's eyes sparkled with mirth as she peered up at Penelope. "She would not lead me astray."

Penelope nodded, unsure of what to say.

"Very well, zhen." Madame Bélanger offered the letter back to Penelope, taking a bit longer than necessary to release it. She looked intently at Penelope's hands as she did.

Next time, I shall certainly wear gloves.

"May I see zee work you've brought?"

"Yes, of course," Penelope responded and hastened to draw the packet of papers from her satchel. "I've several sketches of gowns I saw while – er, saw in the park the other day. I've colored some, and left others. I've also included several portraits I've done."

"I see." Madame Bélanger took her time perusing the drawings. Her brows rose several times when she revealed a new paper. "These are very good. *Très belle.*"

"Thank you."

"What I cannot understand, *mon cher*, is why a *daughter* of a peer finds herself in need of work."

"Madame, I am a poor *man*, with a need to support my widowed mother."

"Are you? Is that why your hands are so fine, aside from the paint? And your face so smooth?"

"I-I was intended for University until recently." Penelope did her best to keep her voice even and low. "When my father passed, he had considerable debt, and the money my mother had saved went to paying his debt." This was the truth; only, the money had not been for Penelope's education, but a portion of her dowry.

Madame Bélanger considered Penelope for a moment. Her heart raced, and she wished for fewer layers of cloth to be on her body; between the shirt, waistcoat, and jacket – not to mention the cravat – she was perspiring more than ever she had before. "Mees Drayton, I can see it ees you."

Penelope considered continuing to insist upon her altered persona, but only for a moment. If Madame Bélanger could identify her not only as a female, but by name, Penelope could no longer maintain her false identity. She reached up to remove her hat.

"*Non*! Miss Drayton, continue your disguise. Should anyone enter my shop, you would be exposed right away."

"Madame?" Penelope began to feel stirrings of hope that had been absent recently – hope that her secret would be kept and perhaps even that her plan would succeed. "How did you know?"

"I dress thee form of woman for my living, and can eeasily recognize one I have dressed already," said the other woman patiently. "I shall engage your services, *mon chère*. I delight in your spirit. Did I tell you that I came here after my husband was killed in the revolution? We were not peers, but we were wealthy. He was killed with many of the aristocracy. I feared for my life and those of my daughters. I knew of a cousin who lived in London, so I gathered enough for passage, packed clothing, and left our home. I still do not know what became of it. I care not, for we shall never return."

Her heavy accent had faded to a gentle lilt in her pronunciation.

"My cousin was married to an earl here and would only allow us to stay for a short time, and only if we worked. She did not want it to be known that her family was destitute. We cleaned and sewed for her, and I discovered that my hours spent practicing my sewing had not been in vain. I made several dresses for her, and she agreed to tell who had made them – but only if asked. Fortunately, for me, she was asked often. My clientele grew and I was able to move my daughters and myself into this shop. They were seven and five at the time – being three and five when we left our homeland. Now, I sometimes have more orders than I know what to do with. I believe I shall have to hire a new girl soon. God has been good to us."

"You believe it to be God, and not your own determination and labor?" As soon as the words left her mouth, Penelope feared the woman would retract her offer out of anger for the words she spoke. However, Madame Bélanger merely smiled placidly.

"*Oui, mon chère.* I do."

Penelope made a noncommittal sound in the back of her throat, similar to the one Mr. Wyndham had made earlier – Mr. Wyndham! *Could that have been the family of Miss Wyndham?* She wondered.

"Come." The dressmaker's interrupted her thoughts. "Let us design now. I feel *très créatif*!"

Penelope laughed, anticipation for the project bubbling inside of her. "Very well. Shall I begin by sketching an existing gown, or would you prefer to tell me what you see in your mind before I begin drawing?"

"Hmm. Perhaps draw a young lady in a cross-front gown, some frills at the neck."

Penelope's pencil flew for several seconds. "Like so?"

"*Oui*! And matching frills at the hem. And the sleeves. Long sleeves. Yes. *Belle*!."

"What sort of waist?"

"Just under the bosom, of course."

"I meant, what sort of treatment? Simply the seam? Or something more elaborate? A ribbon, perhaps?"

On they went, for at least an hour. By the time Penelope packed up her pencils and papers, they had completed three sketches, with plans for her to make copies with different variations on each. Penelope was surprised with the compensation Madame Bélanger promised. For three weeks' time, she wanted Penelope to come for three days each week. After that, she would be given three new gowns and their work would be finished for the Season. Additionally, Penelope would be given a small sum of money each day she worked with Madame Bélanger.

"I do not quite know what to say," Penelope murmured.

"Did I not understand? Would you rather simply be paid? I had thought you would like to order more dresses, but perhaps I was wrong."

"Oh no!" cried Penelope. "This is perfect! Beyond perfect, truly. Much more than I had anticipated."

Madame Bélanger smiled broadly. "Then we both shall be pleased."

"Indeed." Penelope could not contain her own smile.

"Perhaps thee next time, you weell come dressed as Miss Drayton, no?"

"But how will I keep your customers from recognizing me?"

"Tell me if this plan is not to your liking." Madame Bélanger grinned conspiratorially and said, "If I had many customers see that Miss Drayton is a frequent customer of mine, it would be quite good for my business."

"Ah! I see," interrupted Penelope. "I shall keep my pencils hidden beneath a shawl or reticule, and it will appear that I simply am shopping."

"*Oui.* Situated as we are now, with your back to the door, and me facing it, I may warn you when someone is about to enter."

"You are quite clever, Madame Bélanger." Penelope smiled at the other woman, impressed at the resourcefulness, revealed not only in her tale of how she came to be a rising dress-maker in London, but also in her idea of how to incorporate Penelope into her shop without raising questions.

"One cannot succeed in this city without at least a bit of ingenuity." Her heavy French accent had faded again. She smiled fondly at

Penelope. "And do not fret, *mon chère*. Your secret is safe with me." Mme. Bélanger reached a work-worn hand up to gently pat Penelope's cheek. "You remind me so much of myself, when I was younger."

Penelope smiled.

Madame Bélanger grinned, and spoke once again with the heavy French influence. "I eemprove my Eenglish, but find that my cleeant prefer that I sound very *française*. So, you see Miss Drayton, we both of us haf seecreets." The other woman winked as she walked Penelope to the door. She smiled again and thanked Madame Bélanger before leaving the building, hat pulled low over her eyes to avoid anyone recognizing her, until she arrived at the servants' door of her house.

Ash was terribly bored at the dressmaker's. When he had attended with Violet, he had at least been able to chuckle alongside her as the other ladies of their family chose dresses which were ostentatious and really not embracing the ideals of the simplistic, natural styles which were currently favored. This time, Violet had elected to remain at home to continue working on her white muslin.

As he was preparing to leave, donning his overcoat and gloves, Violet slipped up to him and murmured, "I know you are not thrilled about Rose having her come-out so soon, and truly, neither am I, for her sake: will she ever learn modesty in her mode of life?" She smiled ruefully while straightening one of his lapels. "I am glad, though, to share some of the attention. This way, I may simply fade into the background, and once you are prepared to reside in our country house, I may help with the household responsibilities."

Ash thought of the significant inheritance he was to receive, if Lord Ashbridge's letter was to be believed, and wondered when he should tell Violet. When he should tell anyone. *I cannot abide the idea of females clamoring for my attention for the singular reason that I stand to inherit a great deal from a lonely stranger.*

He determined to continue guarding his secret. It was not any distrust of Violet, but of Mrs. Wyndham and Rose eavesdropping.

Now, standing in the corner of the dressmaker's and doing his utmost to hide his boredom, he wished he might simply offer Mrs. Wyndham an extra thirty-thousand, Rose an increase to her dowry, and the both of them a yearly stipend to simply leave him alone.

Fortune cannot buy peace, he was forced to remind himself. Several times.

Ash also reminded himself to be patient while Rose and Mrs. Wyndham poured over designs. With any luck, this would be the only Season he would be funding. It was a good thing, as gown after gown was added to the order – totaling more than twice as many as Violet had ordered. While the ladies were in the back room for Rose to be fitted and measured, he told himself that at least Violet was not suffering as he.

Finally, the women were ready to leave for the draper's, and Mrs. Wyndham was delivering several last-minute instructions to the dressmaker. His heart soared at the tinkling of the bells by the door of the shop, thinking it would be another customer. *That will hurry along the dressmaker, at the least.* Unfortunately, when he turned to see who had entered, it was simply a young man. Perhaps a boy? He could not discern. The lad was slight and had not yet begun to fill out in the shoulders.

"Now two giuls to be out! How veeery exciting!" Madame Bélanger was saying.

Ash turned his attention back to his party with a slight grunt.

"And you will be sending zee fabrics you desire from zee draper's?"

"Indeed," said Mrs. Wyndham.

"Excellent!" cried the dressmaker, a plump, jolly thing.. "Ees there anything else I may do for you, Madame Wyndham?"

"No, that is all. Come along, Rose. Ashbridge."

Ash huffed at her using his given name in such company and then turned to open the door. The boy, though, had run to do the same, and Ash nearly collided with him. He nearly grasped the boy's arm to steady him, but he regained his footing quickly. The boy exhaled sharply while Ash peered down into his face. *A remarkably smooth, fine face. Almost pretty.*

"Pardon me," he said, lowly. The boy glanced up briefly before blushing and lowering his head to hide his face beneath the brim of his ugly, unfashionable hat.

Almost suddenly, the boy jerked his head in a nod and stepped away to hold the door for the party. Ash waited for Mrs. Wyndham and Rose to exit and then followed them. As he passed the boy, he noticed his hand holding the door. It was slender, smooth, and fine. Not the hand of a street urchin or even message boy, yet stained with smudges of several different colors.

How very odd.

Sensing the boy moving behind him, Ash watched him allow the door to close, sending a slight puff of air out after him, smelling slightly of rosewater.

Five

AFTER LEAVING THE dressmaker's, the Wyndham party went to the fabric drapers, then the milliners' for bonnets and the haberdashery for gloves and other accessories. Ash was more than ready for some time at his club by the time they arrived back home, and he called his valet, changed, and left almost immediately after. He did not even stop to greet Violet.

At Boodle's Club, he immediately went to the salon, to his usual table. Situated with tables spread about and food to be ordered if one so desired, the salon was a comfortable place for a man to visit with his friends. The décor was pleasant but unobtrusive, affording the gentlemen a place apart from the ladies in their lives. The room was already occupied by several other gentlemen, and his friend Spence joined him at his table before much time had passed. Ash was glad for his presence. The man had always served as an effective distraction when worries over his family were weighing him down. Ash ordered bourbon and turned to his friend.

"You look positively down-trodden, Ash," admonished Spence. "Whatever has got you so gloomy?"

"Eh, what?" Ash scowled into his drink. "You know I've been shopping with those two."

"I shouldn't mind overly much gallanting your sisters about."

"You would after about a quarter-hour with Rose." Ash sighed as he swirled the liquid about in his glass, then scowled at his friend. "And you know my feelings on any of you boors paying court to Violet."

"Yes, yes. But you must admit that she would be quite an ideal wife. Never questioning, or reprimanding, and always sewing shirts and embroidering waistcoats and kerchiefs for me."

"Oh, she would reprimand you plenty," scoffed Ash, "but in such a kind and unassuming manner that you would heed her every word without even realizing you were doing it."

"Oh indeed?"

"Yes. Just last month she managed to extract a promise from me to attend services every Sunday for the duration of the Season. I'd given my word before I fully realized what she asked."

"Oh-ho!" laughed Spence. "So she's got a bit of fire in her. That can be its own enjoyment."

"Enough! No more. This is my sister of whom you speak."

"Eh, you must learn to relinquish your imagined hold on her. Or perhaps it is hers on you. Cannot cut the strings of the only female member of your family with any motherly compassion."

Ash glared at his friend for a good minute before draining his glass and calling for another.

"Spence, you go too far."

"Do I?" asked his friend. "You know I am loathe to entertain any brown study of yours, but tell me, Ash: what has you so down? Isn't like you to be so maudlin."

Ash sighed, having feared and longed for this question. "I cannot say with any degree of certainty. Rose coming out now, and fear of Mrs. Wyndham learning of my association with Lord Ashbridge and eventual inheritance from him. He's given me an allowance! If Mrs. Wyndham learns of it, can you imagine how she will make demands? Then there is the matter of Violet. She is content with living a spinster's life, at present. But if she should make the acquaintance of a man who will draw her out and will truly appreciate her . . . can I really live with myself if she gives that up because she is compelled to honor our arrangement? Or if she does not, and marries, can I really live with myself? I cannot bear my presence alone for long, before I tire of myself. Violet brings a light to me that I cannot find elsewhere."

He would have gone on, but Spence interrupted, "Slow yourself, man! None of this has transpired yet! Do not worry over *might* and *may be*, for it may prove to be *might not*, and therefore not be a bother to you. Tell me, though, what you mean about this *Lord Ashbridge*. Some distant relative of yours?"

And so Ash proceeded to, in hushed tones, detail his reception of the letter some few weeks past. Spence listened patiently, asking questions where the bourbon Ash had consumed left his explanation vague. After he had finished, Spence gazed intently down into his drink for a moment, before he swallowed a small sip and looked up to meet Ash's eyes.

"Well, I figured it might happen sooner or later; just hoped that it might be later rather than sooner."

"What is that?"

"You are about to ascend to a height in the *ton* which I could never hope to attain. I always figured you would, whether by marrying a lady from there, or by your clever managing of your estate. I've very modest holdings, surrounded on all sides by very well-established estates; there is no hope for me to increase my wealth on that quarter. And frankly, am rather content with my lot. Sad to lose your friendship, though."

"What are you on about, Spence?" Ash blurted. "Your words make no sense."

"Perhaps not now. But they will."

"Stop. There is nothing which will induce me to abandon our friendship." Ash held his friend's eyes, but the other man shook his head.

"Mrs. Wyndham has no use for me."

"And I've no use for her. What of it?" Ash grasped Spence's arm, compelling him to return his gaze. Both men were silent a moment, until Spence seemed to read Ash's sincerity.

"Very well, Ash," conceded Spence with a nod. "Apologies about my own bit of a maudlin freak, there, man. Let us return to your own dilemma."

"Thank you." Ash sat back and took another sip of his drink.

"I reassert my initial advise: wait and see. P'haps it will not be so bad as you fear."

"Meaning . . ."

"Meaning, Mrs. Wyndham may not find out at all." Spence grinned, hopefulness filling his eyes.

"Oh, she will."

"You cannot know that."

Ash grunted, but said nothing. He did not see how Spence was so optimistic regarding the whole affair.

"And even if she does, it may not be so bad. Your lady might–"

"I've no lady," interrupted Ash testily. "And I'll thank you not to bring up *that* subject ever again."

"Very well," agreed Spence lightly. "Even so, you are infinitely more eligible with this wealthy relation than without, and likely will have your choice of wife."

"I do not know–"

"Of course you do not," laughed Spence, "but you shall. Just wait, and try not to fret."

"I do not fret."

"Of course you do! We all do! We parade ourselves as men of the world, above such silly worries. In truth, though, these worries occupy our whole minds much of the time."

Ash, having tired of the conversation, and wary of where it might lead, changed the subject. "Are we here to socialize or to play at cards?"

Spence regarded him seriously for a moment before a wide grin broke out across his face. "Cards, of course!"

They formed up a table with two other gentlemen. One was a second son, whose brother already claimed the title of Earl, by the family name of Peyton, and the other was a Baron Claymore. Both gentlemen wished to play high, and Ash was prepared to meet their wagers. When his friend Spence went out early, Ash remained in the game. He cast his bids and cards quickly, feeling a temporary need for recklessness. His heart pounded, his brow dampened, and his head swam with drinks repeatedly ordered. He won the game, and the two which followed, before his friend Spence pulled him away from the table. Both the other gentlemen promised to receive Ash's man in the morning to settle with him, and Spence ordered the Wyndham family carriage to carry Ash home before hailing a hackney for himself.

As they waited for their carriages, Spence said, "Right odd of you to be the irresponsible one, Ash."

"That so?"

"Indeed. Left me feeling quite put out."

Ash did not speak, but angled his head to see his friend. His vision swam a bit, but settled quickly enough.

"I've always been the irresponsible one, kicking up larks and whatnot, and purely to assist you in forgetting how much your sister's well-being weighs on you."

"And it did help. It does."

"Yes, I know. You've quite let it go today, though, and I must admit that I worry for you."

"Spence, you know that I've not flown off the handle—"

"Yes, I'll be the first to say that you're allowed the odd distempered fit, but one must acknowledge it to be most unlike you."

"I fear they will destroy everything," Ash said lowly.

"Who?"

"Who else? Mrs. Wyndham and Rose."

"Oh, you did not mean that Miss Wyndham would ruin everything?"

Ash looked up, surprised at his friend until he recognized the teasing expression so familiar to him.

"Just remember, Ash," offered Spence as the carriages rolled up to meet them. "Forgetting yourself for a moment is fine, but you will have to face it all when the bourbon wears off."

He nodded, shook hands with Spence, and clambered into his carriage. The ride, followed by Spence's words, served to sober him slightly.

Ash arrived at the house to find that Mrs. Wyndham and Rose were out, dining with a neighbor. Violet claimed she did not have a close enough acquaintance with the family to feel comfortable in an intimate family dinner. Ash knew what she really meant, but chose not to push it. Instead, he unsteadily joined her at the family dining table.

While sipping the soup, Ash looked up at her and asked, "Would you ever consider marrying Mr. Spence?"

"I beg your pardon, Ash?" she responded.

"Spence. My friend from Oxford." He really could not comprehend what was so difficult for her to understand about the question. "Would you ever marry him? Or consider it, at the least."

"Why do you ask?" Her voice sounded oddly choked. *Hmm. P'haps some soup went down the wrong pipe. Funny word, pipe.*

"Pipe." He chuckled quietly.

"Ash?"

"You could do much worse than Spence. He's a loyal sort of fellow. 'Twould not be a bad alliance."

"Are you trying to marry me off?" Violet placed her spoon in the nearly-full bowl, nodding when a footman silently inquired whether she was finished. Ash waved off his own footman and took a rather slurpy spoonful.

"Certainly not. But if you were looking for a husband, I figured I could lend my assistance."

"But our plan. . ." Violet trailed off, eyes downcast. "I see."

"See what?" he asked, allowing his bowl to be cleared.

"Ash, please be at liberty to always speak to me with openness." Violet raised her head, her face now filled with determination. "If you no longer wish to support your spinster sister as we grow old, do not feel obligated to find a husband for me. I excel at practicing economy."

"I know, Violet, but you ought not to be required to. And if I sent you off, I should give you a handsome settlement. I stand to inherit a great deal, you know."

"Ashbridge, have you been imbibing?"

"Indeed! But I am not so foxed as to be operating under some mis-apprehension of a large inheritance. It is legitimate. Or at the least, I suppose it to be. The letter came with a deposit of sorts, of what is to come. Lord Ashbridge claimed—"

"Lord Ashbridge?"

"But of course, Violet," he laughed. "Would it not be a given that I should be named for the man who intended to bequeath me with his lands and title?"

"And what is this title?"

"He is a marquess."

"A marquess? Indeed?"

"Oh yes. It seems he wishes to meet me after the Season. Odd, is it not?" Ash was lost in thought for a time. Violet was quiet, allowing him time to return to the conversation. She truly was a gem of a sister. "Think you shall be up to running the house of so fine a title?"

"If your offer still stands, I shall do my best."

"If my offer still stands?" Ash could make no sense of her words. "Why would it not?"

"You were asking if I would ever consent to marrying Mr. Spence. I had thought that perhaps—"

"Spence?" Ash stood quickly from the table, sending his chair skidding back across the floor. "You shall do no such thing! Have you been meeting with him? Of course you have not; you are Violet, not Rose, and would never agree to a secret assignation with a man."

"Ash?"

"Yes, Violet?" He looked at her, wondering *Why the devil does she look so uncertain?*

"How much did you drink at your club?"

"Is that all? You seemed as though there was something the matter." He again chuckled. *Funny how the floor is uneven. I shall have to call on the lease manager and ask him to address that.* "I cannot recall. But now, Violet, I believe I shall . . . to be . . . retire."

His legs abruptly gave out on him, and he might have collided with the floor, but for Violet's managing to reach him in time. *She's like an angel. Always ready to catch me when I fall.*

Through the fog in his head, Ash heard Violet sigh, "Come along, Ash. Let's get you to your quarters. I shall call for your man to dress you for bed once you are there. Tomorrow you may explain to me what you mean. And do not fret; I shall not breathe a word to Mama until you give me leave to do so."

The following morning, Ash awoke with a pounding headache and a fuzzy recollection of the previous evening. He called for his valet, strong coffee, and his secretary. The coffee was dispatched first. Once dressed, he sent the secretary to collect his winnings from the previous evening and then ordered a tray be sent to his private study, set up in a small sitting room off the bedchamber he was using.

Ash had sought escape the previous evening from the considerable distress of Rose joining them in the Season. Of course, he had no more against that sister being out than he had against Violet being out. The difficulty with Rose was how exuberant Mrs. Wyndham and the girl herself were about all the particulars and with their words and actions. *If I thought it was miserable outfitting Violet for her Season and seeing her through it, it has been and will be ten times worse with Rose.* Still, he could not hide forever, he could not forget forever.

Ash quickly ate the plate of food which his valet brought and carried his second steaming cup of bitter coffee over to his small writing desk, situated near the window, to begin his tasks. He was quite glad to realize that the light filtering in through the sheers over the windows was pale and soft. Several letters and matters of business required his attention, and battling a sunny day's effect upon his regrettable condition would have been most inconvenient.

Once Ash had penned a letter to Lord Ashbridge – he was quite late in doing so – he also prepared a quick note to the steward of the house which Lord Ashbridge had offered to have opened for his use. The man had called the previous day while Ash was out with Mrs. Wyndham and Rose, and his note was left upon the desk. After writing to the bailiff at the Wyndham estate regarding the complaint of a tenant, Ash searched a bit for the original letter from the Marquess. He was able to quickly locate the letter, though he thought that he had left it open beneath the other papers on his desk, not folded as it was now. *No matter,* he thought,

I really must hurry if I am to avoid Violet. She rises so early. She would never be suited to life in Town – balls and routs and card-parties lasting until the early hours of morn, and rising at noon or later.

Ash called for his greatcoat to be brought to the front hall. Once he put the letters on the silver tray in the hall, he was assisted into his coat. After thanking the maid for his hat and gloves, he hurried out the door with a quick glance over his shoulder to see Violet emerging into the hallway at the top of the stairs.

Once outside, Ash walked briskly along the street. It was not a fashionable hour to be out and about, so he was glad for the lack of people on the street. Maids hurried with empty baskets toward the market or full baskets, overflowing with breads, cheeses, and hothouse fruits on their way toward their employers' houses. On occasion he saw a man carrying an empty coal sack, and as he neared the markets, he could hear the voices of those hawking their wares. When the wind shifted slightly, his coat billowed behind him a bit, and the aroma of baking bread filled his nostrils. He was glad he had taken the time to eat already. Ahead, he could see girls with baskets of goods balanced on their heads, and a maid leading her cow passed him before he turned to avoid the market streets. It would be highly irregular for an obvious member of the gentry to be among the servants and hawkers and he had no desire for human interaction this morning. His head was clearing with the crisp morning air, but it still thudded dully from his overindulgence of the previous evening.

While he was still unhappy with the change of plans for their Season, he had to admit that things were not as bleak as they had seemed the previous evening. *Morning light seems to have that effect.* With Rose making her come-out this year, he would not be required to re-enter Society in a year or two's time to introduce her. If all went according to plan, he could parade his sisters among the *ton* in the coming months and then withdraw from Society until he was required to find a wife to bear him an heir. *Twenty or thirty years from now should be good. Perhaps I can build enough fortune that I can simply persuade someone to marry me for that. Once an heir is born, she may do as she pleases and leave me alone.*

His thoughts shifted to Lord Ashbridge, his possible . . . *namesake? Can it be mere coincidence that we share a name?* Ash shook his head slightly, before returning homeward. He knew he must speak to Violet before Mrs. Wyndham and Rose arose, and while he did not look forward to the interview, he certainly preferred that it occur before Mrs. Wyndham was there to interject her own opinion.

Once he arrived at the house again, Ash quickly handed off his greatcoat, hat, and gloves and made his way to the morning room, where Violet would be breaking her fast. She was not at the small table as he had expected, but was sitting in a settee, sewing.

"Finished eating already?" he asked her as he offered a rather sloppy, half-hearted bow. He and his nearest sister had never stood much on formalities.

"Yes." Violet smiled lightly as she took a small pair of scissors from the chatelaine hanging from its place pinned to her dress and snipped a thread. "Did you enjoy your walk?"

"It helped me to clear my head, so yes, I suppose so." Ash lowered himself into a seat next to her own and cleared his throat. He was not looking forward to the admission he must make. He was embarrassed that she had witnessed such a sign of weakness in him, and that she had been exposed to a more vulgar side of himself. "I apologize for the state in which you saw me last evening, Violet."

"Ash," began Violet, a calm smile curving her lips. She tied a knot in the end of the thread that was left on her needle and began sewing another portion of the fabric in her lap. "I have known for quite some time from your occasional headaches in the mornings that you over-imbibe now and again."

"But how are you to know that?"

"You will recall that our father did so at times. Not often, but I did assist him once or twice, and you and he share the expression the following morning."

Ash frowned and felt his respect for his father drop a bit.

"I know what you are thinking, brother, and please do not." Ash relaxed his frown and raised his eyebrows to silently ask her to continue. She did so, but not before ceasing her sewing for a moment and raising the cloth in front of her and looking at it with an assessing eye. She was apparently able to see what she needed and make any necessary adjustments, for she lowered the cloth and began sewing again before speaking. "You are upset that our father would expose me to that. He did not do so intentionally. I most likely ought to have kept to my chambers when I heard him stumbling about the hall, but I feared he might injure himself, and no one else was there to assist him."

"Still, he ought—"

"Maybe so, but I can certainly sympathize with needing a few moments of escape."

"Surely you would never—"

"No! But that does not mean that I am entirely ignorant of these matters."

"You ought to be," he groused. Violet just shot him a mildly exasperated look. "Very well, I shall not disparage our father's memory by complaining about what he ought to have done. Do not try to dissuade me, however, from my mortification over my own actions."

"I am not mortified by them, so why should you be?" Violet shook her head at him and clipped the thread again. "Your morning headaches occur rarely, so I am led to believe that your overindulgence is equally rare."

"That is true," Ash allowed.

"I think no less of you, Ash, than I did before I learned that you take part in that activity. As I did with our father."

"Still . . ." he protested half-heartedly.

"Might we strike a deal, Ash?" asked Violet, shaking out the fabric in her lap to reveal what appeared to be a man's shirt. "I shall attempt to be more assertive when Mama and Rose offer their opinion on my dress and behavior, and you shall attempt to seek other means of escape when you need it."

"But those are hardly similar behaviors!"

"They are both born of fear," Violet countered. "My fear of incurring Mama's displeasure and your fear of what is to come. And to some extent, also a fear of incurring her displeasure."

Ash had to admit that she was correct. Most of his . . . *headaches* were related to Mrs. Wyndham and Rose, in some manner or another. "Very well."

"Are you prepared for the start of the season?" asked Violet, changing the subject.

"Yes," said Ash, glad that the conversation had moved to more comfortable territory. "Are you? I had thought you were still sewing that muslin?"

"Oh, I finished that two days ago."

"And now you are sewing my birthday gift?"

"No, Ash," laughed Violet. "Your birthday is not for another eight months."

"Have you a secret gentleman friend, then?"

"Indeed not! I am sewing shirts for the poor. There is a poorhouse near the river which accepts donated items of clothing, and I had several yards left from each of the dresses Mama agreed that I might make, so I decided to make shirts with the rest."

Ash was delighted to see this evidence that his sister had retained her compassionate heart through the continual onslaught of disparaging remarks from the other females in the family. He smiled at her.

"You are a good girl, Violet."

Violet blushed, but said, "Thank you, Ash. I am doing my best to be prepared for keeping house for you until you marry."

Ash smiled at her, glad that she seemed to be as happy with the arrangement they had planned as he was. *She certainly will be an idyllic person to preside over the domestic side of the estate.* An uncomfortable twinge in his chest caused Ash to pause. *She certainly would be an idyllic wife for some great man. Am I doing her a disservice by keeping her at my side?*

Deciding that he would simply watch her, and if it seemed that she favored a gentleman they would meet this Season, he would be sure to speak to her.

"You will be more than capable as a housekeeper, whether of my house, or of a husband's."

Violet pressed her lips together and said nothing, but gave him a decidedly skeptical glance before returning to her sewing.

The painter, who had only recently begun to sign paintings with "P. Greene," peered cautiously from the back door of the studio. Since beginning to mix paints, rather than purchase them, it quickly became obvious that mixing out-of-doors was preferable. Seeing no one in the vicinity, and using an old cap and coat as an easy disguise – in addition to the old gloves worn for protection against staining by the pigments – the painter carried out a small table and the box of supplies tucked under one arm. There were no mews behind the building, due to the modest structure of the studio and the buildings surrounding it. With this area of Town being occupied by tradespeople, there was no need for a carriage house or large servant quarters, as none of the residents could afford to keep a horse or support a large detachment of servants.

The painter was no exception. At present, none of the rooms was even hospitable. Someday soon, it was hoped that there would be resources to re-appoint the middle level, making it into a gallery as planned. But first, the painter must establish a reputation in London.

And to do that, there must be paint.

With practiced movements, the two-by-three feet glass plate was set upon the table, and a small amount of pale pink pigment poured out. Using a palette knife, a well was made in the center, which provided a place for a small amount of linseed oil to be carefully poured. Once the oil was poured, the pigment it touched turned a deep red. The painter then spent a considerable time using the palette knife to mix the pigment and oil, the pigment and oil eventually blending to the deep red color.

After it was all rather well-mixed, the knife was put away and the glass muller taken in hand. It appeared slightly similar to a pestle, which the painter occasionally used to further grind lower-quality pigments than these. The muller, however, had a wider base, which lay flat against the glass plate. The painter's gloved hands began to spread the oil-wetted pigment on the glass plate, using small circles until the paint was spread over the entire surface of the glass plate. The palette knife was used to scrape the paint into a pile in the center and again the muller was employed to press the paint flat on the surface. The process was repeated several times, until the paint was of a consistency which the painter might use.

Having used the pallet knife to pack the paint into a glass tube, the painter set about cleaning the tools. After everything was clean, blue pigment was drawn from the box, poured onto the glass plate, and the process started over again. By the time the small table was carried back into the studio, the painter had mixed five different paints, and knew that more would need to be mixed soon. The popularity of the miniatures was thrilling, but the increased demand for them was likewise creating a demand for more paint and surfaces. Just yesterday, a man had ordered a ring with his wife's eye painted, and a widow had ordered an image of her deceased husband to be painted upon a medallion which she planned to hang from a ribbon about her neck. This was excellent for business, but also required more time to keep up with the orders.

Things will be much easier, the painter thought, *once I am able to devote all of my time to my craft.*

Part II

Six

Lowry House, London
Late January 1806

MRS. WYNDHAM GLANCED about the crowded drawing room of Lord and Lady Lowry. Her eyes landed on Mr. Ashbridge Wyndham as he led his sister Violet through a crowd of people. His tall frame put him at least a head taller than most of the gentlemen in the room, his pale hair glinting in the chandelier's light. He was a handsome young man, already five-and-twenty, of an age to take his place in the world. A satisfied smile spread across Mrs. Wyndham's face at finding him thus occupied, for it suited her purposes to perfection.

She turned to her youngest daughter and smiled. In a voice which would easily carry to the ears of the mothers in the surrounding area (but not to the ears of her son who was still across the room), she said, "Rose, dear, is it not fortuitous that your brother was named Lord Ashbridge's heir? His estate comes with quite a large income, even more than your late father's, rest his soul. Whoever Ashbridge weds will certainly not want for anything."

"Indeed," agreed Rose with several nods of her head which set her fair ringlets to bobbing. "Any woman would indeed be eager to become his wife."

The two ladies continued their conversation, expounding upon his pleasing frame, informed mind, and even temper. They were vastly satisfied at the numerous heads turning ever-so-slightly in their direction. By the time their discourse on the positive attributes of Mr. Ashbridge Wyndham had reached its conclusion, seven mothers and their daughters had become aware of the man's newly acquired fortune, as well as his unwed status. By the end of the evening, each of those women had informed three or four of their acquaintances, at the least, of their discovery. By the end of the week, the information had spread throughout the *Beau Monde*, as well as reached the ears of those aspiring to its level of Society.

The man himself, however, was blissfully unaware at the card-party that news of his carefully-guarded secret was beginning to spread. He had successfully escorted Violet to a settee, via the table with drinks to fetch a glass of lemonade for her, without being detained to exchange pleasantries with anyone. He promised to bring her a plate of food from the other room, where a sumptuous spread awaited hungry party-goers. Making his way toward the food, he found himself glancing about the large drawing room.

Lord and Lady Lowry had certainly attracted the *crème* of London society to their card-party. Tables scattered about the elegantly appointed room provided the surfaces for play. Some of the games were for small wagers, others for none at all, and still others offered people the chance to win large sums of money – or to lose them. Ash, however, elected to forsake all of them. He had more than satisfied any desire for the thrill of wagering the other evening at his club. Seeing his mama and youngest sister, Rose, sitting down to a table across the room with several other ladies nearly made him cringe. He had no idea what their wagging tongues might say, but he felt with certainty that less would be said were he to keep himself from their company.

Upon reaching the tables located in an adjacent salon, he pointed out to the servants which foods he would like for each plate, waiting for them to do his bidding. *Rather ridiculous,* he thought, *I could have had my plate filled and half-way consumed by this point.* He received the plates from the giggling house-maid and beat a hasty retreat from the room.

As Ash returned to Violet, he felt a renewed thankfulness for her kind spirit. The lack of gossip on her tongue was one of the reasons he got along so very well with her. Although sometimes painfully shy and apprehensive in the midst of large parties such as this one, she was scarcely able to speak when a gentleman was in her vicinity. Unless, of course, that gentleman was her brother. Conversation with ladies was only slightly less stilted. Gossip was, for Violet, out of the question.

It was rather startling, therefore, when he approached the settee on which he had left his sister to find that another young lady occupied the empty space beside her. She appeared to be close to Violet's age, perhaps one or two years her senior, and the two ladies sat conversing, heads bent closely together. Ash fought to keep the shock from his face as he took in the scene before him. Had he not known better, he would have thought that the two were lifelong friends.

The other young lady was quite a bit shorter than his rather tall, willowy sister; he could see that even in their seated postures. Her ebony ringlets framed a face of cream and rose petals. As he drew nearer, he saw that her eyes were a startling shade of deep indigo blue set in a delicate, heart-shaped face. Feeling a stirring of attraction, Ash quickly quashed it, bringing to mind an image of the woman who had crushed his heart. The pale red hair and spring-green eyes floated in his memory, turning his blood cold.

Finding himself in a rather foul mood from the thoughts swarming in his head, Ash forced them all aside as he approached the ladies.

Before he reached them, however, the unknown lady rose from the settee and walked away.

Standing before Violet, plates of food in hand, Ash managed a smile. There was an essence of rose in the air, and it seemed familiar, but he could not place it. *Likely it is Rose who also wears that scent.* Violet carefully raised her glass of lemonade to her lips, sipping demurely, as she watched him with questioning eyes. He decided not to inquire after Violet's companion.

"How are you enjoying the party, Ash?" she asked as he seated himself in the vacated seat and passed her a plate. "Thank you."

"As well as can be expected, I daresay." Ash's feelings remained agitated, and he knew his voice reflected it. "These gatherings are ridiculous."

"Ridiculous? Indeed? I cannot find what would give you cause to call them so." Violet batted her mossy green eyes at him before craning her head in several directions, searching the room for something. As her hair neared his face when she turned to look away from him, Ash caught the scent of lavender, and it chased away the roses lingering in his nostrils. He ate some fruits from his plate and continued watching Violet. He found himself reminded of a sparrow, as she cocked her head in all directions, her pale brown hair giving off a dull sheen in the candle-light. "Where are the sumptuous bouquets of plumes nestling in the ladies' hair? Or the pop-in-jays parading themselves about in their ostentatious colors and fifteen pounds' worth of fobs and seals?"

Ash bit back a chuckle and said through twitching lips, "Very well, sister dear, not ridiculous. Perhaps 'insidious' would be a more apt descriptive."

"Oh, but *there* is an excellent example of the ridiculous," Violet said lowly.

Ash followed her gaze to see Mr. Langley bowing theatrically to their sister Rose. He laughed.

"Forgive me," said Violet as she shook her head. "That was a mean-spirited comment which I ought not to have said."

"I will not repeat it, then," Ash said to her, smiling.

Before eating more of her food, Violet grinned triumphantly at him, though he knew not why. He had not admitted to liking the party as he supposed was her aim in teasing him. "I shall not venture to change your mind about the term 'insidious', though," said she, "for I find it to be the same. But I am glad, *brother dear*, to have drawn you from your unhappy thoughts."

"Unhappy thoughts?" he asked.

"Oh, indeed. And do not think that pitiful excuse for a smile which you gave me upon your return could fool me into thinking there were no unhappy thoughts."

"And is that all you desired, Violet? To see me smile?"

"Indeed."

"Well, then, you had only to smile at me."

"Flatterer!" Violet laughed.

"'Tis true! You are the only female who can bring me from my decidedly ever-present stupor of gloom."

"Untrue! Though I will allow that I am perhaps the only female *in our family* who can bring you from your gloom. Aside from Cousin Charlotte."

"Cousin Charlotte is not here. And she is not to make her come-out for several years yet, Vi."

"Very well, you are correct in asking for caution." Violet's voice suddenly lost its earlier teasing, and her entire demeanor became subdued. "I beg of you, though, Ash, do not call me that."

"Call you what? Vi? You do not prefer it to Violet?" Ash found himself wondering why she did not. It was what Rose called her constantly.

Oh. Of course.

"No, I do not."

He ought to have known that whatever name Rose conjured would not be a favorite of Violet's. He smiled his apology to her, and said, "Very well, then, little wall-flower. I believe they have started some dancing in the other room. As we have both finished our plates, would you care to stand up with me?"

"Why, yes, sir; I believe I should like nothing better." Violet rose ceremoniously from her seat and accepted Ash's escort.

As they progressed through the house, following the strains of the music played by a small ensemble for the dancers, Ash sensed more people than usual looking at him. Specifically, people of the female variety. He soon decided, though, that he must be mistaken. Every time he returned a lady's gaze who seemed to be looking at him, her gaze would immediately shift, moving on to another subject. It did not occur to him that the forbidding scowl he wore might have influenced a lady's desire to return his gaze.

They arrived at the place where other couples were lining up for the dance and Ash walked with his sister to her place in the line before finding his own opposite her. After the music started, the dancers all bowed to one another before starting the cotillion.

"Are you hoping any of these young bucks ask for a dance, Violet?" asked Ash when the dance brought them into close enough proximity to speak.

"Indeed not," she cried, stumbling a bit as she glanced about. Again they were separated briefly before she was able to continue hurriedly, "Do you think any of them shall? I can scarcely keep my steps as it is; I cannot imagine trying to do so with a man who is not my brother!"

They were again separated as Violet made a turn with the gentleman opposite them. Once she was returned to him, Ash said, "You should get on splendidly, Violet! You must have more faith in yourself. You know that young Haverton from home was quite impressed after dancing with you at the assembly this past autumn."

"Ash." Violet leveled a disbelieving stare on him as they circled round, all eight dancers holding hands. "You do know that he would be equally impressed were we to take Papa's prized sow and dress her up in one of my gowns, yes?"

Ash laughed outright, and as he was unable to argue with her, changed the subject to more benign topics than the possibility of his or her marriage. After the dance ended, Ash stood up with his other sister. She chattered the entire time about all of the young dandies whose acquaintance she had made, and how eager she was for a proper ball.

"You must know, Ash, that while dancing at a card-party is pleasant, and certainly a nice way to meet new people, it is at balls that young men fall in love."

Assailed by memories of a ball, several years past, Ash could not speak for the knot lodged in his throat. It was just as well, for he would never agree aloud with Rose in this matter. He was no longer the naïve, smitten young hopeful, new and eager in the marriage market but woefully unsuited to recommend himself to any young female of notable significance in the *ton*.

With a determined clearing of his throat, Ash returned in a droll tone, "Young men do not fall in love, Rose. Indeed, they may fall into infatuations, but no sensible young man would offer for a lady until he has established himself." The words stung his pride, as suppressed memories fought to his mind's surface, but he felt as Rose's older brother, he must warn her. Or, failing that, to make an honest attempt.

"Faradiddles," huffed Rose. "My Mr. Langley is here tonight, and you shall see. If he is not enamored with me by the end of the evening, then I promise to become as dull and tiresome as Violet."

"And how do you propose to measure affection?"

"Anyone may read it in his eyes," replied Rose.

Ash resisted a rather rude snort at her words, settling with a slight huff. "Rose, if a man offers for you before he has established himself and is able to support you, he is acting on a whim – or worse, on passion – not true concern for your well-being. If he cannot provide for you all that a gentlewoman deserves, he is no gentleman."

"If I recall, *you* offered for that Felicity chit," bit back Rose.

With a tightened jaw, Ash managed to avoid causing a scene. His heart pounded and his face felt hot, but he swallowed the angry words that clogged his throat, and when he spoke, he managed to temper his voice appropriately.

"She was – *is* five years your senior, and yet you attach such a term to her? Rose, you may now be out, and considered of marriageable age by those of the *ton*, and I am sure that you are gathering your own band of admirers–"

"I am," interrupted Rose, "and many more than Violet. She is so dull that not even the third sons are interested in making a match with her."

"Violet may not be as lively as you, but the discretion with which she comports herself is far superior to your habit of speaking without thinking – or, far worse, speaking with design to injure. Do not forget, sister, that I hold the purse-strings and have no compunction in seeking to reign in improper behavior by *whatever* means necessary. Even that of your pin-money."

Rose snapped her mouth closed, as she had been gaping rather openly at him. Ash, for his part, resolved to hold his silence for the remainder of the set. He paid particular attention to his steps, to the placement of his hands and head, to his posture and all that he recalled the dancing master of years past harping upon – *that* gentleman should have been greatly pleased with Ash's performance, had he seen it.

Ash felt otherwise.

He was beginning to feel the responsibility he carried for his youngest sister. He had worked diligently to ensure that Violet was cared for, that she was not injured by their father's disinterested behavior and Mrs. Wyndham's pointed criticism. Rose did not receive the same treatment as did Violet. She took her mother's instruction to heart, lacking though it may be, and did all she could to emulate the woman's behavior. Ash, now seeing Rose's unfeeling attitude even out in Society, realized that he had been remiss in his duties. And his negligence had led to her dredging up memories he had thought long-buried.

Once the final strains of the music ceased, he applauded with the others before bowing stiffly to his partner and for the second time that evening, beating a hasty retreat. He needed time to gather his thoughts and find his equilibrium after this sudden and undesired realization. He did not wish to go to the gardens, as it seemed a likely place for a bold young female to attempt to trap whichever gentleman was foolish enough to go there alone. Walking as though with a purpose, with the hope of no-one seeking to detain him if he appeared occupied, Ash made his way about the rooms which were open for the party. Finally, he found a room filled with gentlemen, drink, and real wagers. Rather than joining any of the games, he accepted a glass full of amber liquid from a servant and found a place near a group of other gentlemen, careful to distance himself sufficiently that they would not speak to him overly much. It seemed they were discussing the passing of the prime minister, and its implications for Parliament. While Ash usually enjoyed discussing political concerns with other gentlemen, he could do no more than nurse his drink and his wounds.

He could scarcely believe the strength of the memories dredged up by the conversation with Rose.

It was at the first ball of his first Season that he first noticed Miss Felicity Giles. She was a unique beauty, her hair reflecting browns and golds and reds in the candlelight. Her complexion was clear and radiant, set off beautifully by her soft white gown, embroidered with emerald green at the hem, neck, and sleeves. He now despised the color.

He learned her name and her favorite flower. She was reputed to have a lovely voice, a rich alto, and her skill at the pianoforte was renowned. With all of her admirers, he was slightly disheartened, but resolved to solicit her for a dance regardless of the many others who would undoubtedly also ask. He was introduced to her and to her parents, and was shown favor.

When their set was about to begin, he offered his hand, nearly shivering at the warmth which passed through their gloves from her palm to his own. Her fingers were long and slender, graceful in a way that he could have admired for the entirety of the evening. They spoke few words during the dance. He inquired as to her Season, her family, her home. She answered his questions, but otherwise said very little. At the end of the set, he ventured a glance at her face. Her eyes, the color of new grass in the spring, were hooded under heavily-fringed lids. Her rose-petal lips were quirked into a slight smile. He saw, at this close range, that her nose was sprinkled with a few freckles, which he found altogether charming. He could see children with pale golden hair and freckles running about the rooms of his home while he and his wife lingered over the breakfast table. He now no longer imagined future children gracing the halls of Wyndmere.

A week later, Ash saw her at Hyde Park, and they walked together with several other young people and chaperones. This time, he learned a great deal more about her, but had little opportunity to share about himself. He cared not. Two days passed, and he gathered the courage to send a posy to her home and visited the next day. He was received cordially, and noted that while she had received a great number of tokens similar to his own, none of the others claimed a place on the table beside her chair as did his. He was now resolved never again to send a posy to a woman.

Three weeks after making her acquaintance, he went again to visit, as he had been doing regularly, and when her mama stepped out of the room briefly to call for tea, he threw himself on the ground at her feet and made his addresses. She accepted his proposal of marriage, but begged him to keep it secret until she could convince her father. He did not approve of a country gentleman for his daughter, whom he believed to be destined for greater things. By the end of the Season, Ash was heartbroken to realize that her views were the same as her father's.

With a shuddering breath, Ash recalled where he was – the Lowry's card-party – and realized that his glass was empty. He blinked, unable to recall taking a drink after his first. Placing the empty glass upon the nearest surface – a small table beside the wall – he withdrew his watch-fob, seeing that he had been in his hiding place for only half of an hour. He glanced at the place where the servant was still filling glasses for the other gentlemen, debating briefly whether he wanted another to further dull his pain. Beyond the servant, though, was the door. He saw his sister Violet through it, blushing deeply as she danced with a dandy of a gent, his hands grasping hers more firmly than necessary whenever the steps brought them together.

With a purposeful tamping-down of the ghosts of his hurt and anger, Ash left the room and went to cut in on the dance. The gentleman began to protest, but when he met Ash's eyes and heard the proclamation that he was the lady's brother, he bowed and retreated. Violet's appreciative smile warmed Ash's tired heart.

"I am in need of an alternative means of escape," was all he said.

Violet nodded knowingly, but thankfully let the conversation rest at that. They both moved through the remainder of the dance lost in their own thoughts. Looking about the room, he saw other couples dancing. Ladies offered coy smiles, sometimes genuinely shy. Gentlemen postured and boasted with their movements and covertly did the same with their comments. It was so familiar and yet so foreign at the same time. He could not help but think it all a masquerade, that no one spoke the truth or was open about who they were. Not until either the vows were exchanged – as with Mrs. Wyndham and his late father – or until one spilled his heart as an offering to the other and was summarily trod upon – as with he.

In an attempt to distract himself from his maudlin thoughts, Ash cast his eyes about the room without seeing the faces of the couples. Suddenly, though, his gaze landed on a slightly familiar head of deep brown, curly hair. The lady's petite frame was encased in a gown of white, wine-colored trim at the waist and hem. Her dancing partner was only inches taller, his hair shorter but just as richly-colored and curly. When they turned in the dance, and he saw her face, he realized that it was the young lady with whom his sister was conversing earlier in the evening. For the space of a breath, her annoyance and anger was betrayed in the clench of her jaw and the narrowing of her eyes. She had been so pleasant and kind-looking with his sister; Ash found his curiosity peaked, but knew he would do little to satisfy it.

Penelope took the opportunity offered by the brief separation from her brother in the dance to recompose herself. She feared that had it not been so fortuitously placed, her temper might have gotten the better of her, and she would have caused a scene. *That* would certainly not have been conducive to her plans. When she faced Cornelius again, she was able to maintain a placid expression as she said, "Surely, brother, you know that if I married tomorrow, it would not benefit you one jot."

"Would it not, Pen?" he asked, a great deal more confidence in his voice and posture now than there had been at their last conversation in the sitting room. "If you married well enough, I would have a wealthy brother. What is several thousand pounds between family?" The dance separated them again momentarily.

"I should advise my husband not to feed your destructive habits," she countered when they were near again, saluting one another with a bow and curtsy at the end of the dance.

As they applauded the musicians, he leaned near her and said, "And he would not heed you, if I have chosen him for you, thereby ensuring his loyalty to me."

Fury simmered in Penelope's breast, causing her face to grow hot and her hands to tremble. Not wishing to acknowledge the fear behind that rage, she clung tightly to the anger as she grasped her brother's arm and hurried him to a hallway near the ballroom. Its only occupants were several chairs and benches lining the walls and the paintings that hung above them.

"I shall never marry," she whispered to herself. Cornelius stepped back from her, forcibly ripping his arm from her grasp and causing her to stumble. She righted herself with a huff and said, more loudly, "You have no control of my funds. Our mama ensured that I should have enough to modestly support myself while living under the protection of my family."

"But where will you live?" he asked, a mocking whine in his voice. Her heart went cold with his words. She could provide for her needs, and those of her aunt and Mr. Pelter, but she could not afford the rent of a house. Cornelius continued with biting superiority, "It is my plan to sell the Town-house at the end of the Season."

"But – but you cannot!" Penelope cried, regardless of her impotence to change anything which her brother decreed regarding the holdings of their family. *Certainly, I hoped to have a new residence eventually, but so soon! It was my plan to live there while carrying out my plan in the next two years at least!* But he was now the head of their family, with complete control of the family's holdings, regardless of how inept he might be at filling that role. With a quick glance about the hall, she saw several other people had entered the space and were now looking their way. Lowering her voice, she continued, "We'd discussed my living there and you living at Claymore Abbey. You cannot go back on your word."

"Nothing was written, nothing was binding. The house is mine to do with as I please."

Fear flowed through her veins, sending her heart racing. *He cannot be serious! His meek attitude, where I could command him to stop gaming, has certainly left.* With tremendous effort, she said evenly, "You cannot be in such dire straits as to necessitate the selling of a house. Why not rent it for several seasons and save the income for whatever it is you need?" Surely she could arrange with the renters to allow her to live in the servant's quarters and pay a meager rent for the privilege.

"Too little, too late," he replied, matching her tone. He almost sounded pleasant, but the dangerous spark in his eye told a different story. "I am allowing this last Season for you to find a husband. After that, I will not be returning to Town for some time. You, sister, may do as your husband pleases."

Penelope fought to keep her breathing even, her face expressionless. She could not be this close to escaping the control of her brother, only to fall prey to another man. She had been counting upon having access to her family's Town-house, as her plan depended upon her ability to reside in Town. Her defeat would be assured were she to attempt to disappear to a small hamlet somewhere in the countryside.

I am too close to freedom to capitulate now, she thought desperately.

Penelope knew she must not allow her brother to succeed. Slowly, her plan began to change shape, just a bit. It had been flexible since the earliest days of its conception. That flexibility was a necessity, given her dependence upon so very many outside influences for its execution. The plan's purpose, however, remained true: freedom for Penelope from dependence upon any man. Upon anyone.

"Might I propose a compromise?" she asked, her mind racing to find words that might buy her some time. When he made no objection,

Penelope continued carefully. "Allow me to . . . seek a husband for myself." As the idea took root, and grew, her words came more quickly, with conviction. "We both know that my dowry, forty thousand pounds, will be mine upon my marriage. I shall give it to you. In its entirety. Allow me to marry for love, and my husband shall allow it; I am certain that he will provide for my needs, my settlement, everything. After this, though, you are to leave me alone."

Penelope held her breath, waiting for his reaction. His eyes narrowed in thought, but beyond that, she might have thought him to have completely forgotten their conversation. At length, Cornelius nodded his head slightly. "Very well, Pen – my stubborn sister. You may have the duration of the Season. Once Parliament closes its doors, if you have not found a suitable husband, who will allow you to honor your promise to me, I shall choose one for you."

He did not remain long enough for Penelope to reply, for which she was grateful. The effort to keep up the seemingly impervious façade of strength left her exhausted, and the moment he disappeared through the door to the ballroom, she sank into the chair behind her. She could not decide whether to laugh or to cry, so she concentrated on inhaling and exhaling.

In. Out. Two. Three. Four . . .

Her vow to never marry would not be broken, but she knew that she would need to appear, to her brother at least, that she was searching for a husband. She also needed a place to reside after her plan had reached its completion, or perhaps once it was in its last stages. Worry did not plague her, though, for Penelope knew that her resolve was strong. Ideas formed in her mind and began to connect, one with another, creating a beautiful web of hope and security. She would prevail. Failure simply was not an option.

Five. Six. Seven . . .

Seven

It was not until an additional week had passed that Ash heard some news of his fame. The following Monday found him sitting in the library of his friend Spence, along with their friend Mr. Eadan MacDougal. The three awaited the dinner announcement.

"You are apparently the newest addition to the *crème* of the *ton*," observed Spence, taking a pinch of snuff. "My sister and her silly friends Miss Umberland and Miss Crestly were beside themselves when I let it slip that you were dining here tonight."

"How is that?" asked Ash. "I am not well-acquainted with your sister and I am sure I have never met her friends."

"Sure'n you must know that your name is not unfamiliar to any young lady in Town," chortled MacDougal. "Even my mama, who has no daughters to marry off, knows of you."

"What are you on about, Mac?" asked Ash. "Have you been sneaking something while we wait for dinner?"

"Eh, no!" cried MacDougal, his Scottish brogue becoming more pronounced in his heightened emotional state. "I might've taken a nip before coomin' 'ere, but 'tisn't near 'nough to make me e'en a trifle disguised. D'you mean to suggest that you know noothin' o' the rue-mers?"

"What rumors?" asked Ash. "Would someone *please* be so kind as to enlighten me?"

"They are not rumors, but facts." Spence crossed one ankle over the opposite knee and fidgeted with one of his fobs before continuing. "It's been spread around Town that you, sir, are the heir to the Ashbridge fortune, and the title of Marquess of Linsdon."

Ash cried out, springing up from his wing-chair. "What the devil do you mean to spread that about?"

"Whoa, now, Ash old boy, I never said 'twas I that spread it about." Spence nervously shifted in his chair, placing both feet on the floor and tapping his fingers upon his leg before finally reaching into his pocket for his snuff-box again.

"You are really coomin' to rely on that too much, there, Spence." After MacDougal spoke, he quickly shrank back into the settee in which he reclined, after Spence sent him a withering glare. Though MacDougal was quite a bit broader and taller than Spence, he was a gentle man and kept his aggression within the confines of his sporting.

Spence considered his hand-painted snuff-box for a moment, seeming to wonder if MacDougal had a point with his words. MacDougal brushed imaginary dust from his trousers. Ash found himself growing impatient with the inability of his friends to spell out plainly for him what exactly was being said. "Tell me," he demanded, his voice low and his words clear and slow, "what exactly those hens and their chicks are saying!"

"Ha! Hens an' chicks," MacDougal laughed to himself.

"I doubt you should be so amused by that moniker for the fairer sex if my younger sister was present," Ash grumbled testily. He knew he was venturing into forbidden territory with that comment, but found he was feeling reckless in his annoyance. MacDougal's face reddened and sat back in his chair, silenced for the time being.

Spence apparently decided that MacDougal's previous warning against tobacco was unwarranted, for he deftly flicked the lid of his snuff-box open with his thumb and used his other hand to pinch a small amount of the tobacco. "Ash, calm yourself, man. There is nothing much going about concerning you, save your recent inheritance, which I already told you." He gracefully raised the pinch to his nose, inhaling, before snapping the lid of the box shut and sliding it into his pocket. "The only bit of gossip those old biddies are chirping is that you are on the look-out for a wife."

"I am not!" Ash could stand still no longer and began to pace before the massive fireplace decorating the wall of his friend's library. "The very *last* thing I want at this point is a wife."

"Do ye always answer inquiries into yer matrimonial intentions with sooch vehemence?" MacDougal chuckled.

"Good grief, Mac!" Ash slid one finger gingerly between his neck and his cravat, tugging carefully. He had no desire to rumple or loosen the intricate knot his valet had managed to create that morning, but it suddenly felt too tight. "I simply wish to enjoy my bachelorhood. No woman to nag or wheedle, no little ones running about. I can scarce keep Mrs. Wyndham and Rose within the realm of decency; a man such as I has no business setting up his nursery already! I shall be leg-shackled when I must, but that time is certainly not now. And if *you* did not start that information to circling, Spence, who *did*?"

"I've not the foggiest." Spence shook his head. "Aside from when you told me, I first heard it at the card-party last week and was rather surprised that you had told anyone else."

"Didn't tell me," groused MacDougal.

"Precisely!" cried Ash. "I told no one! Not a soul should know, apart from Spence when I was too foxed to realize what I said, and my sister later that same evening!"

As soon as the last word issued from his mouth, all three men froze, glancing nervously at one another. Ash was certain he knew what they were thinking, for the same thing was racing through his head. *Has Mrs. Wyndham overheard, or even snooped and come across the letter, and said something to someone? Or to several people?*

"D'you think 'twas Mrs. Wyndham?" MacDougal finally muttered.

Gritting his teeth, Ash replied, "It can be no one else. Violet is far too quiet to disclose the information. And I am certain of her inability to injure me so thoroughly." He shook his head, uncertain whether or not he wished to continue this conversation.

Fortunately, at that moment, Spence's butler knocked and entered the room. "Dinner is served, sir." He bowed himself out of the door.

Ash rose quickly and encouraged his friend to lead the way to the dining hall. He wished, for several hours, to forget this difficult position in which he unexpectedly found himself. After dinner, once he had returned home and sequestered himself in his rooms, *then* he would ponder the situation and determine what was to be done. Until that time, though, he wished to simply enjoy the company of his friends as he had in earlier, simpler years. Knowing now that the entirety of the *ton* knew of his recent wealth, he felt that tomorrow would be the first day of a very different existence for him.

Cornelius paced the sitting room before Penelope.

"Would you please be seated!" she cried. "You are *quite* cutting up my peace."

He stopped, dropping roughly into a chair. His bravado of the other evening was all but gone. His eyes were wild, his mouth tense, and his movements erratic.

Choosing to ignore his nervously bouncing knee, Penelope said, "So there is no possibility for an extension on your loan?"

He shook his head, a sour expression on his face. "I told you as much, Pen."

"Penelope."

"The only hope of an extension is a gift of good faith, so to speak. Mr. Cartwright has requested an amount, in addition to what he won from me, in exchange for extending the time until the end of the Season."

"In addition?" she cried. "And until the end of the Season?" *Will this cause Cornelius to act rashly in our agreement?*

"Yes. I must pay in full at the end of the Season, or meet him on the field."

Penelope considered for a moment, unsure of whether she wanted clarification. *As in a duel?* If this Mr. Cartwright would fight with swords only until first blood, she would have no difficulty allowing her wastrel brother to suffer that. If, however, he wished to duel with pistols or fight to the death, she may willingly sacrifice her entire future for his sake. *And very likely regret it the rest of my life.* Perhaps it would be easier not to know.

Still, she found herself asking, "And what are the particulars of meeting him on the field?"

"He is known for being an excellent marksman, and killed a man in a duel two years past, and another several years before that."

This was certainly not what Penelope wished to hear, but she hoped to strike a balance by offering, "If you will use part of your allowance, I have recently sold several of my personal possessions" —there was no need to tell him it was because she was hiring herself out to draw dress designs— "and will give you some of the necessary amount." She moved to a vase on the mantle, withdrawing a small pouch from within.

I shall have to find a new hiding place now. She counted out the coins and carefully drew the top closed again before dropping it back into the vase.

"Here is half," Penelope said as she dropped the coins into her brother's outstretched hand. He grinned crookedly at her, his boyish face reminding her of when they were children and thick as thieves. *Now he very nearly is a thief.* "Please secure the rest of the amount yourself, Cornelius, as I have sacrificed the purchase of several gowns for you already. And if you come to me for more, I promise that I will not have it."

He nodded, thanked her profusely, and took his leave.

Penelope peered through the window and the moment she saw that he had emerged onto the street and begun walking away, she sighed in relief. With a shake of her head, she moved to the vase, took the pouch, and tucked it into the sash at her waist. She would determine another hiding place later; she was in need of more watercolor paint, having used more than she had planned on the design variants for Madame Bélanger, and would need to take the money to the shop on the morrow to secure her supplies.

In an effort to calm her nerves, Penelope determined to do something related to what she loved. She hurried to her writing desk and withdrew from it a paper pouch. She carefully unfolded the paper, tilting it until several smaller packets slid out onto the surface of the desk. She opened them, one at a time, crumpling the papers inside the large one once she had finished.

Before her lay several piles of loose hog bristle, recently arrived from Russia. She immediately began sorting the bristles. Once upon a time, she had been able to purchase finished brushes from the finest master brushmakers, but now she was very grateful to the stodgy old man who had taught her to paint. Not only had he opened to her an entire world of imagination and escape, but he had taught her all of the work behind what was needed to paint. She now always mixed her own paints, and could stretch her own canvases if needed, though she preferred painting on something more solid. She could also assemble her own brushes.

The bristles had already been stripped down to single strands, any bits of dirt or tufts of thicker of hair removed. They had been cleaned, straightened, boiled, and dried. Penelope was glad that she could still afford to purchase the bristles at this later stage from the manufacturers, and hoped that her luck would hold until her plan was implemented. Unbidden, the voice of Aunt Essie floated through her conscious, asking her if it was luck or the providence of God the Father. Penelope shook her head, suddenly uncomfortable with the direction her thoughts were taking. In her experience, fathers lorded over their families, meeting their own needs before even considering those of their charges. With an effort, Penelope forced herself to consider her work. It was difficult enough to hear Aunt Essie speak as often as she did of a heavenly Father. Having her thoughts go there of their own volition would not be tolerated.

Now she worked to sort the bristles into different lengths, stacking them into piles of different sizes. Each pile was incrementally longer than the last, and once every bristle was placed with others of a similar length, Penelope began stacking, tying, and gluing them to a brush handle she retrieved from the drawer. It was a long, tedious process, but as she worked, the tension drained from her shoulders, the throbbing in her head receded, and a small smile curved her lips. She was doing what she loved.

Once the last bristle was in place, the brush was placed carefully into a jar with the other brushes she had assembled in the last few days. There they would wait until they were dried and ready to be shaped with a sharp knife. Penelope stood and stretched, glad that she had found a constructive manner in which to calm her emotions. Now, though, she must refocus her thoughts.

Sitting once again at her desk, she pulled out a piece of paper and began to draw. This frequently calmed her and aided her in thinking. Nothing had necessarily changed in her plan with this latest setback. She feared, though, what aiding her brother in this instance might later lead him to demand of her. His tone and his words at the card-party had rattled her. Had she not known him all her life, she would have thought he cared as little for her as a decent hunting hound. *Or maybe less; he is quite particular about his dogs.*

The brisk strokes of her pencil matched her troubled thoughts, creating a dark room and shadowy figures. Had she unknowingly invited him to make more demands on her?

She knew, though, that if she stood firm, he would have very little ability to truly harm her. If she could just hold him to their agreement, and not give him any more of her money, all would be well. By the end of the Season, if she proceeded as planned, she would be able to live modestly apart from his influence. As she calmed, her pencil slowed also, becoming gentler in its movements, creating variant shades and softening of lines and affectionate emotion.

She was thinking of drawing with her mother. The two would be together for hours, drawing or painting. Lady Claymore had been graciousness embodied. Even as a young girl, Penelope had seen that her mother was a truly excellent hostess, by whom each guest was welcomed and made to feel the single essential person she wished to see. Even more, she cared for her children and even her servants with a generous heart that Penelope had never seen since. Her deep blue eyes and dark ringlets were remembered every time Penelope gazed into her own reflection, but she feared that her mother was being forgotten nonetheless.

Lord Claymore had forgotten her almost immediately. He never remarried, but neither did he honor her memory by emulating her gentle graciousness. Instead, he secluded himself from all others, even his own children. He eventually succumbed to drink, which led to his demise.

It was odd, but Penelope could not recall a single memory of her father before her mother's death. When she tried to remember him, there was nothing. He must have been present at times in the first ten years of her life. When she attempted to identify a memory, though, it was like grasping at mist in the air.

Slowly, Penelope's attention returned to the present and she noticed that her paper had been filled with lines, curves, and shades. This was not particularly surprising, as she often sketched out entire portraits or landscapes when her mind wandered. The subject of this particular sketch was a surprise, though.

On the paper was an image of a young girl, no more than three or four, wearing a dress from the last century – conical bodice, stomacher, and skirt puffed out over panniers – sitting within the circle of a man's arms. He held her carefully, perched upon his knee, a tender expression on his face as she looked at the book in his hands, and he at her face. She could not see whether she had assigned a title to the book, but she suspected by the shape and size that it was likely a family Bible. While the figures were rather indistinct and their features only sketched lightly, there was a familiar set to the man's shoulders, and the girl's dark, curly locks were startlingly recognizable.

Suddenly, a pang shot through her chest, and Penelope shoved the paper roughly into the back of the drawer before standing hastily, calling for her aunt, and making plans to go visiting. It was time to implement the next stage of her plan.

Dearest Charlotte,

I fear that I have not had opportunity to write to you nearly as fre-quently as I should have liked. Mama and Rose have been so very intent on making the most of the Season, with shopping trips and morning visits and numerous evening engagements. And now Ash said that very soon we shall be moving to another house. Some obscure and previously unknown connection has made his house available to us for the Season. The structure itself is in a very fashionable neighborhood – Grosvenor Park! – and I shall post this letter from its direction, that you may know where to address your reply. There are many more rooms and a garden I am most eager to explore. There is a small staff already on hand, so I suppose it will not be overwhelming for our staff. Ash said that there is a separate music room, a library, and even two drawing rooms. The house we are leaving has one room to serve all of those purposes. It will be quite nice to have the ability to keep to myself should I so choose.

Rose, of course, will not want time to herself. She is as eager for Society as ever. Were Rose but the elder sister, my heart should very much be at ease – and I believe so should hers. I would then be free to continue with lessons on the piano-forte, as well as time to write to you and visit museums and attend concerts. And Rose would be very content attending balls and routs and meeting all the demands of the Season.

One of Rose's greatest joys thus far (and yes, it is still early in the Season, and so there may well be more exciting happenings for her) is that she will very soon have a miniature painted of herself. The so-called "Invisible Painter" has become quite the rage amongst fashionable Society. While no-one knows who he is, you can certainly imagine how the rumors are flying. The honorable Miss Cottsworth, a close friend of Rose, recently sat for a portrait with him. Of course, Rose being as she is and wishing to do anything considered even the slightest bit fashionable, promptly persuaded Mama that she must have a miniature made of herself. Miss Cottsworth described her own sitting for Rose, and I happened to be in the room to hear that morning, as we were paying a visit.

She and her mama were received by the painter's man, who offered refreshment while he set up the studio. As for scenery and items to use in the portraits, there are several chairs from which to choose, as well as a low column, vases of flowers, bowls of fruit, tapestries, and so on. Miss Cottsworth raved over the crumbling old column, which she chose for her portrait. Her dress, she said, was of the Greek style, and so she determined it to be fate that she pose as an ancient Greek goddess. The studio is set up in such a way that the painter is hidden behind draperies. How he can see without being seen is rather questionable, but I suppose it is easier to see through a curtain to which one is nearer than far. The painter then worked while she held the pose for a relatively short time. It was only half an hour. Miss Cottsworth said that after the sitting, she waited only three days for the painting to be completed. I believe that the painter must have an excellent memory, or else make incredibly detailed sketches and notes in order to finish the painting without an additional sitting.

"Heavens, Violet," laughed Ash lightly. "By your words, you would appear rather enamored of this Blind Painter."

Violet had been inspecting her quill's tip while her brother read her letter to their younger cousin. At his words, though, she looked up. "They call him the *Invisible* Painter, and you know very well that I am enamored of no one. There is, however, a certain appeal to a mystery. Besides, the letter is for Charlotte, and you know how she delights in intrigue."

"True." Ash began to read again before quickly looking up again to ask, "Would you like to have your miniature done? It seems that all of the *bonne ton* is scheduling a sitting."

His sister flushed and said, "I am not a member of the *bonne ton*; or, at the least, neither a recent nor an enthusiastic one."

Ash smiled fondly at his sister. He knew that she struggled with acknowledging her worth. Handing the letter back to her, he said, "Perhaps, but you've received many invitations to dance at every event we attend, and several of the young ladies counted to be exceptionally bright diamonds this Season have boasted in claiming you as a particular friend."

Violet's astonishment was visible as she asked, "And by whose reckoning are these assertions made?"

"By my own."

"Ash, I never took you for a liar," she laughed.

"No, others have noticed it, too. Just yesterday, I heard two gentlemen at the club speaking of their favorites. I daresay you've surprised more than one person."

"But Mama has always said–"

"And I have always said that she speaks of what she wishes, not of what is."

Violet sighed slightly, shaking her head. "I cannot sway your opinion, I am sure. But neither can you sway mine."

Ash shook his head back at her. "Perhaps not, but someday, someone will."

Violet grinned at him. "Perhaps."

"So are you enjoying your Season more than you anticipated?" he asked, allowing the subject to drop.

"I am. Having so many people everywhere I go is terribly intimidating, but I must own that there is a level of comfort in knowing I will not see most of them ever again after this Season. If I say something foolish, it is unlikely that anyone will recall the next morning."

"That is true," said Ash.

"Are *you* enjoying the Season?"

Ash hesitated before answering thoughtfully, "I believe so." This was the first time in years that he was in London. With the sights and sounds of the Season pressing at him from all sides, memories of his own first Season were proving to be more of an unwanted specter than he had anticipated. Still, with so much that was familiar, there was an equal amount of the unfamiliar. "It has been odd, Violet. This Season is different in so many respects from the one I spent several years ago. Not only am I now my own man, having reached my majority and having command of our family's holdings, but even the others in Town seem to see me differently."

"How so?" she asked.

"There was very little enjoyment for me for the first month of that Season at least. Spence and Mac were both late in arriving and there I was – fresh out of school, with no Grand Tour under my belt due to the unpleasantness on the Continent."

"Oh yes." Violet grinned, apparently quite over her previous embarrassment. "A man cannot be considered good *ton* without having seen the ancient structures in Rome and the art of the true masters. It is quite fortunate that there were those few months of treaty during which it was safe to travel in Europe again, is it not?" Her voice took on a cheeky tone. "An abbreviated Grand Tour *must* be better than none at all. After all, without it, even your recent inheritance might not serve to heighten your respectability in the eyes of the *ton*."

Ash laughed outright at his sister's words. She had a well-hidden clever streak which rarely made an appearance.

"Would that it was so simple," he chuckled. "I cannot say whether it is respectability that I've gained, or simply desirability. Did you know that during my ride this morning, no less than three mothers stopped me to introduce their daughters?"

"Truly?" said Violet. "I am gratified that they can see your value. I do wish, though, that they recognized it apart from what you are now worth."

Ash was mildly discomfited at her words so he changed the subject, even as the question flitted through his head that he could not be entirely worthy if the only woman he had ever offered for rejected him.

"During that first month of my Season," he reminded her. "Our time in the mornings, before the rest of the house was awake, were what sustained me."

"It sustained me, as well, Ash," she replied. "We broke our fast together every morning, and read verses of Scripture. It was so quiet and peaceful. Just as our chat now is quite nice and cozy."

Ash recalled how he enjoyed reading the Word of God during those times – almost as much as Violet did. His opinions on God, as well as a number of other things, had undergone a great change since that time. She, however, had remained faithful. Even now, her Bible sat beside her former place on the settee, where she had been reading before she arose to write to Charlotte. Rather than address that portion of her words, however, he chose to reply to the former. "Ah yes. You were to be given lessons on the pianoforte by a master, rather than the old rector from our parish. If I recall, you were required to bolster your courage before each lesson."

"Yes. Mama thought that I might learn to perform better for others were I to learn from a greater teacher."

"And Rose was given dancing lessons, as well as pianoforte and drawing."

"Of course. I also attended some of the dancing lessons, but Papa said that I needn't have the drawing lessons."

"And you were glad of that."

"Of course," Violet said with a smile. "You have always been quite self-assured, and cannot therefore have a true understanding of the fear which gripped me at the idea of playing in the presence of so great a master."

Ash knew that what she spoke was true, to a point. He had long been possessed of the knowledge of his imminent inheritance of the family estate. He would be an attractive suitor, at least in their small community, and he had always therefore supposed that he would eventually develop a fancy for one of the girls with whom he was acquainted from childhood. His experience with Miss Giles, then, served to lower his ideas of both romance and himself. He understood his sister's poor sense of worth much more than she supposed.

But he said none of this aloud. Instead, he continued along the same vein of conversation. "Yes, Violet. But you will recall that he proclaimed you to have quite surpassed any of his other pupils who resided in Town and had the benefit of his expertise all the year long."

"Perhaps," said Violet dismissively, "but he was a flattering sort, and I never put much stock in his words. I daresay he was hoping to convince our parents that they should keep me in Town, and he would therefore gain another pupil for the whole year, rather than an abbreviated period of time."

Ash smiled at his sister and her characterization of the instructor. "So while you suffered through the torments of instruction on the pianoforte, I floundered for a place in Society."

"After your friends arrived, was it better?" she asked.

"Yes. It was also about that time that I made the acquaintance of Miss Giles. My view of the Season improved greatly after that. If it had ended well, I should look back with fondness upon that time of my life."

Both were silent, as both knew what had been left unsaid: the Season had not ended well.

Violet pressed her lips together, sympathy written in her eyes. After a moment, she asked softly, "Has she made contact with you?"

Ash tensed, having wondered himself if he might see her, and what her – and her parents' – reaction might be to his new prospects. He lived in simultaneous anticipation and trepidation of the day their paths might again cross.

"No, she has not." Ash sighed heavily. "Word is that they have not yet arrived, that the family was called to the bedside of an ailing relative. I am glad for her absence, though, Violet. I am not sure how I would respond if she did try to speak with me."

"Curious." Violet said no more, but regarded him with interest.

Ash explained further. "I was so thoroughly convinced that I loved her, and when she made no attempt whatsoever to convince her father that I could support her, that she did not mind living life as a country gentleman's wife, my heart was crushed. I fear that if she attempted to renew our . . . friendship . . . that I would be weak and grant her whatever she asked for. Which she certainly does not deserve, being as mercenary as her father."

Violet nodded sympathetically, but retained her silence.

"I fear even more, though, that if I see her again, I will want to hurt her as she hurt me, that I will be unable to keep from attacking her with poisonous words and cutting insults. I fear that I shall lose my humanity to her, just as I lost my heart."

Violet shook her head. "Ash, your heart is not lost to you. She may very well have broken it, but there is no reason that you cannot love again. You are healing. I can see it."

"See it?" Ash asked. He could not comprehend that she believed she had evidence of his healing. "How do you mean?"

"In the manner that you show patience with Mama and Rose, even with me. And how you remain polite to anyone who speaks with you. Other dandies about Town seem so quick to slight ladies of little consequence or those who talk to them for longer than they would prefer."

"Brummel has quite earned that right," Ash shrugged. "I hear Lord Reymes, who recently came into his title, seems to think that he is quite too important for any of the ladies about Town."

Violet continued, "And Ash, you are always looking out for me; just recently, you cut in on Mr. Hanley at the card-party."

Ash answered, "You *did* seem rather distressed, and I could not in good conscience leave my favorite sister to suffer at the hands of an overly-eager dancing partner."

"Ash! Do not say such things!"

"But he was *quite* enthusiastic, do you not agree?"

"You know very well that is not what I mean."

"What *do* you mean, Vi?" asked Rose drily, sauntering into the room. Ash stood and bowed, but had not yet resumed his seat before she continued, "Have you two been awake for long? Why *ever* do you rise so early?"

"It is nearly noon, Rose," chuckled Ash.

"Is it now." Rose sank languidly into a chair, covering a small yawn with her fingertips. "I suppose I *should* be exhausted, after dancing every dance last night."

Ash, who had been in a rather buoyant mood and was prepared to be good-natured and even jovial with his youngest sister, instantly frowned at her words.

"Vi, how many times did *you* dance?" Violet flushed at Rose's question, but was unable to answer before the younger girl continued, "No matter. You are not as tired as I am, because you clearly did not dance as often as I did. You really should attempt to exercise more, Vi. It would benefit your complexion."

"Violet walks most mornings when we are in the country," Ash defended. "But she cannot roam the streets of London as she would the country lanes. The house on Grosvenor Square has a small garden behind it, so I suspect that Violet shall resume her walks once we are settled there."

"Oh, yes, Ash," cried Rose excitedly. "I *did* so wish to have you tell me about it; Violet had no prior engagement when you went to survey the house, but I was unable to accompany you."

Ash wisely chose not to mention that he had made the appointment for the tour of the house at a time that he knew both Rose and Mrs. Wyndham would be unable to join him. Instead, he hurriedly launched into a detailed description. As he finished going over every minute detail of the dining-room, Rose asked for his opinion of the neighbors: had he seen any of them, and were any of them noteworthy?

Before he could answer, though, the butler announced a visitor.

Eight

MORNING VISITS WERE the very foundation of social life in London: gossip was exchanged, news shared, balls and routs discussed, along with opera, theatre, and fashion. It was within the structure of these visits that Penelope tirelessly worked at the next stage of her plan. As it would be most impolitic to monopolize the topic of conversation in another woman's morning room, Penelope made sure to wear a miniature portrait on a ribbon round her neck, with the hope that it would catch the attention of others. It was done in oils on a small oval of ivory. The image was of her mother – and father, though including him was a difficult decision. Wearing a likeness of her mother but not her father might indicate to the more observant eye a disdain for her father's memory. Pretended familial fondness would aid her eligibility in the eyes of the *ton*.

"Miss Drayton, what a charming miniature. Is it of your dear parents?" said Lady Melton, seated across from where Penelope and her aunt sat together on a settee. The room was well-appointed in greens and golds, perhaps a bit of the last century in its lavishness, but still quite tasteful. Penelope and Aunt Essie had already conducted three morning visits and were very nearly unable to accept one more cup of tea. They did, though, sipping slowly and enduring the tepid liquid when they took to long to drink it.

Penelope had carefully chosen the houses. She had wanted to visit as many as she could, without wasting valuable time traveling. A morning visit lasting longer than fifteen minutes was universally considered too long, Penelope knew that she must conduct her visits carefully. Too much polite conversation or immaterial *on-dits*, and the purpose of her visits would not be met.

"Yes, my lady, it is." Penelope lightly touched the tiny painting, a wistful expression purposely on her face. "I wanted a remembrance to keep with me always, and so I requisitioned this to be made."

"May I?" At her nod, Lady Melton moved to sit beside Penelope on the settee, leaning in to look at the images. "I was a particular friend of your mother's. This is done from images soon after their marriage, is it not?"

"I believe so. I cannot give the precise year, but they were not very old."

"They both were so handsome. Your father quite doted on your mother."

Penelope smiled, swallowing the bitter scowl that threatened to erupt.

"I was but ten years of age when she passed, and my memories of her fade with every year."

Lady Melton placed a comforting hand on her arm. "I am sorry, dear. She would be most pleased to see what an excellent young lady you have become."

Penelope could not speak for the tears suddenly clogging her throat. She managed a watery smile just as Miss Barrett entered the room, apologizing for the delay. She had just finished with the instructor teaching her court manners. They discussed the rules of court for a moment, as well as Miss Barrett's court dress, before another visitor was announced and Penelope rose to take her leave.

"Before you go, dear," said Lady Melton, "would you mind giving me the address of the artist who did your miniature? I think I should like to have one done of my husband."

Penelope smiled. She would not have bothered visiting were it not for the hope of such a request. "Of course, my lady. It is something of a lark, for the artist protects his anonymity as a she-bear protecting her young. The studio is on Albermarle Street, the small white building. When you go, you will recognize Mr. Pelter, our former butler. My brother had long planned to seek another to fill the role upon his retirement, so when I heard that the artist was looking for a man of business, I thought that Mr. Pelter might be just the person. He conducts all of the artist's business—receives payment, poses the subject, and communicates for him."

"How odd," she commented.

"Quite. But it is something of a lark. I've not sat for him, but others I've spoken with have said it is rather amusing."

"An eccentric."

"Exactly."

Reigning in her triumphant smile, Penelope bade them good-bye and left with her aunt.

Penelope managed to contain her nerves in the hired hack as she and her aunt were driven to Wardour Street, the last visit she planned to make that morning. She knew that Violet had invited her to call, but she was unaccountably anxious about the visit. The girl had a younger sister, as well as an elder brother who was rumored to recently have come into some wealth; Penelope hoped that neither would be present. She had come to a decision to ask Miss Wyndham for some help with a rather delicate matter and hoped that she would be able to do so without an audience.

The hack pulled to a stop, and the equipage jostled as Penelope heard the driver's feet land upon the cobbles of the road and his steps approach the door. When he opened it, Penelope stepped down before her aunt, and then waited while the driver assisted the other woman to the ground. The neighborhood was tidy but worn, and Penelope could see that it would not be considered as the best of residences. It was still respectable, though.

Penelope linked arms with her aunt before turning to the driver. "Here is the fare, and another two fares will be yours if you remain here until we complete our visit." The man's weathered face lit up as he nodded eagerly, tipping his hat and bowing simultaneously. While the triple fare was a costly extravagance at present, it would soon not be so if her plan succeeded. Penelope turned with her aunt, and together they began walking up the handful of steps to the front door.

After she offered her card to the butler and they were announced, she entered the room to find three sets of eyes regarding her. Fortunately, Miss Wyndham's was among them. That pair of eyes lit quickly with recognition, and the girl rose from her seat even before her brother. He was quick to follow, though, and waited patiently while Miss Wyndham rushed forward to clasp Penelope's hands warmly.

"I am so glad you are here," she said gently, accompanied by a genuinely happy smile. "Come meet my brother and sister." Turning to the other two, she said, "Miss Drayton, may I present my brother, Mr. Wyndham, and my sister, Miss Rose. Ash, Rose, this is my friend, the Honorable Miss Penelope Drayton."

They all exchanged the necessary pleasantries before Miss Wyndham ushered Penelope to a seat.

"Where did you make Miss Drayton's acquaintance, Violet?" asked Mr. Wyndham as he sat. Penelope fought an unexpected blush when he flicked his eyes her way, much too appraising for her taste. She knew her gown was rather out-of-date, but it was still in good repair, the elbows being only a bit faded.

"We met at Madame Bélanger's shop, and again several times about Town."

"Ah, you are the one I saw conversing with Violet at Lord and Lady Lowry's card-party?"

Penelope held her breath for a moment, waiting for the warmth on her cheeks to fade. Having the man's light blue eyes settled so intensely on her was somewhat disconcerting.

What on earth is the matter with me?

She quickly gathered herself and answered. "Yes. I find Miss Wyndham to be a valuable friend. She has a peaceful presence and is always ready to listen. Not all ladies of the *ton* are such caring companions."

Mr. Wyndham shifted his eyes to Violet and said with pride in his voice, "She is a gem of the first water, but precious few seem to recognize that. I commend you, Miss Drayton, on your intelligence and good taste."

"Are you enjoying your Season, Miss Drayton?" asked Miss Rose abruptly, in a slightly piqued voice.

"I am," replied Penelope, a bit startled. "And you?"

Miss Rose beamed. "Ever so much! There is much to do and to see! Not to mention the people. It is quite different company than one keeps in the country, is it not? I must say, I greatly prefer Town to the country. Such variety, and so much to entertain."

Penelope nodded and smiled politely, but said, "Though there is a fair amount to entertain in the country, as well, if one but knows where to look."

"And where do you look, Miss Drayton, for entertainment in the country?" came the unexpected question from Mr. Wyndham.

Penelope glanced at him, curious at his question. Since rumors had spread about his recent wealth and forthcoming title, she had heard that he had taken on airs, believing himself to be above others. Of course, having never met him and having heard only kind things about him from his sister Miss Wyndham, Penelope was inclined to dismiss such rumors. His question not only invited her to speak at length, if she was so inclined, but also to share her opinion and interests.

Her own brother would never have posed such a question.

Realizing that she had allowed several moments to pass without replying, Penelope spoke in a rush, desperately trying to ignore the sudden heat in her cheeks. "Forgive me. I . . . was contemplating in what manner it would be best to answer." At his raised brow, she drew a deep breath in hopes of banishing yet another blush, and turned her eyes to Miss Wyndham. *It is a safer place to keep my eyes.* "It would be expected that I answer something along the lines of enjoying house-parties, country balls, and picnics. I must admit, however, to enjoying the open spaces and the views."

"I find that to be my favorite part of being in the country, as well," Miss Wyndham offered shyly.

Penelope smiled warmly at her friend. "I had supposed that to be the case." Feeling in better control of herself, she turned to include everyone when she added, "I am something of an amateur artist, and greatly enjoy the inspiration I find in nature."

"God's creative work is the basis for our own creativity," murmured Miss Wyndham.

Penelope had no desire to disagree with the girl, and planned to keep silent, but Miss Rose spoke up. "Oh, Vi, do not be such a bore! We've enough sermonizing on Sundays without your poor attempts at it during the week."

Penelope wished to defend Miss Wyndham, but was rather inclined to agree with Miss Rose on this subject. Not that she would ever have said so.

Mr. Wyndham, however, spoke up. "I do not believe that it was Violet's intent to *sermonize*, as you so charmingly term it, Rose. You know that she finds more than common comfort in the Scriptures, and that she wishes it for us as well. Never has an unkind word passed her lips in regards to our comparable lack of piety, so please refrain from speaking to her in so condescending a manner." As he turned from the younger girl, Penelope thought she heard him murmur something about a bit more piety on Miss Rose's part being beneficial, but she was unsure.

Deciding a change of subject to be in order, Penelope said, "Miss Wyndham, I believe I recall that you wore particularly sturdy yet also quite fashionable half-boots when we happened to meet at the dress shop. Might I see them now? I would like to inspect them for instructions to my own shoe-maker."

She nodded, stood, and motioned for Penelope to follow her.

"Aunt, will you wish to wait here?" Penelope knew her aunt's answer; they had already discussed this part of the visit. When Aunt Essie declined, Penelope smiled and gave her shoulder a gentle squeeze before following Miss Wyndham down a hall to some stairs.

"We had planned to let this house for the duration of the Season," Miss Wyndham offered as they climbed. "You see, we haven't our own house in Town, but Ash wanted to give me a Season. Well, my mama did, as well, but as Ash is now the head of our family, he is the one to really do so. And now Rose is out, as well."

"I see." They had reached the top of the stairs and followed a short hallway to a door at the end. Hesitantly, because she had no wish to overstep the bounds of propriety, Penelope asked, "Is she not—on the younger side of those who have made their come-out?"

"Yes, she is." Miss Wyndham offered no further explanation, only opening the door to a small chamber and ushering Penelope through it.

"This is a lovely room," Penelope said, looking about the sparsely furnished area. Despite having only a bed, chest, and washstand, not much else would have fit. Two windows allowed ample light to fill the space, chasing away any complaints one might have about the size of the room. Penelope noticed that the view below included the mews at the back of the house.

"Thank you. It shall not be my room for much longer, as we will be leaving soon." Penelope immediately began to protest, thinking that her friend could not possibly leave Town so soon. Miss Wyndham hastened to assure her. "You must have heard the rumors concerning my brother. We are moving to the Town-house that he stands to inherit. It is located in a more fashionable neighborhood, and there is a garden in the back!"

The girl's face positively beamed with delight upon the mention of the gardens.

"Quite a rarity in a Town-house. Are you particularly fond of gardens?" asked Penelope, before continuing by answering her own question. "But of course you must be, fond as you are of the country."

"I am. I have done my best to be content here, but I must admit that I miss my rambles about our home, and I fear that our gardener at home will be unaccustomed to the extra work my absence provides."

"You assist your gardener at home?" Penelope was rather surprised to hear of a gentlewoman doing enough gardening for it to actually affect the work of the gardener. *Perhaps they are not so gently-bred as I had supposed.*

"Only as much as my mama considers appropriate. I still have my sewing and visits to do, as well as practicing the pianoforte."

Penelope smiled, but said nothing. An unaccountable sense of relief washed through her recognizing that Miss Wyndham was not pretending to be more than she was. She would not have allowed it to interfere with her friendship with Miss Wyndham, but it might have required rather creative measures to keep it from interfering with her plan. Her hopes could never be realized were it spread about that she claimed a close association with someone not considered good *ton*. As it was, Penelope hoped that a friendship with Miss Wyndham might in actuality benefit the plan beyond the expected enjoyment of a friendship.

"And you paint?" asked Miss Wyndham, opening the perfect path to that benefit.

Penelope drew a deep breath. Here began the more difficult part of this conversation. She glanced to see the open door, and moved to close it gently before turning to Miss Wyndham.

"I do, but that is not all." The other girl raised her brows with a patient curiosity, encouraging Penelope to continue. "You see, my father ceased to manage his estate after my mother was taken from us. Things fell into disrepair, funds were all but depleted. There was very little that two grieving children could do, especially as the estate was held in trust until my brother would reach his majority." This was true, with the exception of a slight circumvention of the true nature of Penelope's grief.

Miss Wyndham nodded sympathetically, waiting for her to continue. She reached out tentatively to place a comforting hand upon Penelope's arm.

"Now our finances are in shambles. My brother was never taught economy in his spending, and he plans to sell our town-house at the end of the Season." She chose to omit his mandate that she marry by that time, as it seemed rather immaterial at this point. "His management of our family's estate is abysmal, worse even than our father's, and it is my hope to be separated from him." Miss Wyndham's troubled face turned to shock as she began to protest, but Penelope halted her with a raised hand. "Please . . . I know it must seem rather low of me to wish to sever connections with my brother, but he is not my only family. My aunt is advancing in years, with no one to care for her. I also am responsible for a servant; he has been with our family for years, and my brother recently released him from service. It is my hope that separating from my brother and his poor management will allow me to support the three of us.

"I've saved my allowance and pin-money for years and sold several of my personal possessions in order to purchase a small shop in Town. When I said that I am an amateur painter, I was not entirely honest.

I've been selling my paintings under the name of P. Greene for some time now, and the shop is now my studio. Mr. Pelter – the servant I mentioned – acts as Greene's man of business and is the only person customers have seen. Or, if things proceed according to my plan, will ever see. After the Season, Mr. Pelter, my aunt, and I will all live in the small flat above the shop, and I will continue painting as I have been."

Miss Wyndham's mouth had fallen open at the name of P. *Greene*, and her wide eyes indicated that she understood entirely. Penelope waited as patiently as she could to hear what Miss Wyndham would say.

"You. . . *you* are the Invisible Painter!"

"Is that what they call me? I've not spoken at length with anyone since first planting the seed of his brilliant work into several Society ladies' ears. Well, aside from today. In fact, I was doing more planting – or gardening, shall we say? – just before coming here."

"Indeed?" Violet was smiling broadly, excitement lending color to her face. "Rose is desperate to have a miniature made, but my brother is hesitant."

Penelope laughed, relieved to see that Miss Wyndham did not appear to find her decision to work for her living distasteful. If the wrong person should discover Penelope's plans, all would be ruined. Not only would she no longer be included in the first circles, but no one of Society would visit her shop, or request a portrait. She would be ruined, both financially and socially.

"You do understand, Miss Wyndham, that my success rests entirely upon my anonymity?"

"Of course," the girl responded fervently. "Your secret is safe with me, Miss Drayton."

"Thank you." Penelope released a long sigh, unaware she had even been holding her breath. "With my having divulged my most secret hope to you, we are a bit past the formalities of Miss Drayton and Miss Wyndham, are we not?"

Miss Wyndham's smile was wide as she said, "I quite agree, Penelope."

Penelope felt her own smile grow. It had been ages since she felt she had an ally in the world, aside from her aunt and dear, old Mr. Pelter.

"I suppose you may be wondering why I have told you all of this, Violet."

Violet's surprise was slight, but present nonetheless as she considered Penelope's words. "Yes, I suppose I am. Do you need assistance of some sort?"

"Only if you are willing. I recall you saying that you enjoy refashioning old dresses, and I was most impressed with what you wore that day at Madame Bélanger's. Is the dress you are wearing now also one that you made?"

Violet flushed, looking down at her green and white striped gown. "Yes. I made it from some old draperies at my aunt and uncle's house. Mama does not know – please do not mention anything of it, if you see her. She would be appalled, but I had always admired the fabric, and when we visited last autumn and my aunt mentioned that they were planning to replace them, I arranged for her to send them to me. I did use the leftover fabric for two shirts, a girl's dress, and several baby items for some of our tenants."

"Violet, I am in desperate need of your particular talents. I had saved enough for a modest wardrobe to be requisitioned for this Season, that I may wear as I promote P. Greene amongst the *ton*, but I fear that my brother's bad habits have required that I pay some of his debts with that sum. Would you mind terribly assisting me by making several gowns? I would, of course, help with the easy parts, but I am afraid that my sewing talents are not at all up to snuff, as they say."

"I have never sewn for anyone besides myself," Violet said cautiously. She gestured to her frame, tall and willowy, then to Penelope's own shorter stature.

"But you have made dresses for some of the people living on your family's land," Penelope countered.

Violet nodded, but her voice lacked confidence when she answered. "I have, but do you not agree that a lady of the *ton* would be wearing a rather more elegant style than a working-dress?"

Penelope assured her. "Of course, Violet, but the gowns that you've made and wear are lovely. Would you at least be willing to attempt it? I've some old draperies of my own, which would be a good place to start, if you are willing."

Violet was quiet for a moment, seeming to consider. "I . . . I would be glad to, Penny."

Penelope nearly corrected her in her name, but thought better of it.

While she still was not fond of variations on her name, it was still not the same as what her brother used. *In fact, Aunt Essie calls me Penny on occasion.*

"See if you can convince your family to visit soon. I will contrive an excuse to bring you to another room to show you what fabrics I plan to use."

"I thought you said just the draperies?"

"For now, yes. But when the gown that you fashion from them is a success, and your confidence bolstered, I will have more." Penelope grinned cheekily at the girl before adding with a more subdued tone, "If you are willing, that is."

"If you are pleased with the dress, then of course I will be."

"Excellent." Penelope felt happiness welling in her heart for the first time in a very long time.

Several days later, Ash scowled as the carriage stopped at yet another house that was not his own. He was finished with insipid, inane conversation and the scarcely-veiled questions about his newfound wealth, repeated at each morning visit to which he squired his family. When he saw, though, that Violet hopped eagerly from the carriage after Rose and Mrs. Wyndham had disembarked, he followed curiously.

"I do hope this is our last visit this morning," he intoned for Violet's ears alone.

"It is." Violet smiled at him.

Ash raised his brow at her, surprised at her eager expression. "And whom are we visiting?"

"Miss Drayton. She wished to show me something today, if we had the time, and Mama agreed to the visit."

"I see."

As he slowly ascended the steps to the front door – this town-house was considerably smaller than the one belonging to Lord Ashbridge, and yet larger than the rented one his family would soon vacate – Ash felt his curiosity grow at Violet's new friendship. Both ladies seemed rather reticent in company. The mere fact that, at the card-party, Miss Drayton took her leave of Violet before his return was quite telling; if she was an opportunistic female, she would certainly have remained until she made the acquaintance of such an eligible gentleman.

For of course she would have heard the rumors at the party; everyone else did.

Once they had been admitted, it was clear that the sitting room where Miss Drayton was receiving visitors was already full. Once the Wyndham party was announced, all eyes turned to them. Ash could feel the probing eyes of the ladies there – some Society matron and her two daughters, one of whom Ash recognized from two seasons past.

Couldn't marry her off yet? He knew the thought was uncharitable, but the girl's drawn cheeks, dull eyes, and limp hair gave her a sickly appearance. Her younger sister was more tolerable in appearance, but if the babble flowing from her mouth was any indication, her mind was rather underdeveloped. Unfortunately, their mama was looking at him as man with a starving family might look upon a feast. His distaste for the gleam in the woman's eye aided Ash in assuming a haughty demeanor.

Miss Drayton excused herself from the other three ladies to warmly greet Violet.

"Good morning, dear, how good to see you," she exclaimed, reaching to clasp both of the girl's hands. Ash watched her stretch her head up and forward to place an affectionate kiss on his sister's cheek, and he was almost certain that he saw her whisper something into Violet's ear.

His suspicion was confirmed when Violet nodded, and whispered back, "I understand."

Miss Drayton politely extended her greeting to him, Mrs. Wyndham, and Rose, before presenting Mrs. Yardly and her daughters, Miss Yardly and Miss Theodora. Ash bowed at the introduction, then proceeded to pretend he was unaware of any comments or inquiries which were addressed to him. Miss Yardly sat quietly for much of their short time together, as did her sister, but Mrs. Yardly was full of complimentary comments concerning her daughters. As was expected in a morning visit, the Yardly party took its leave soon after the Wyndhams' arrival, giving way to their visit. Ash was glad to see them go, weary as he was of such blatant attempts at impressing him. After the door was shut behind him, Ash felt his posture begin to relax.

"Have you made many visits this morning, Mrs. Wyndham?" asked Miss Drayton politely after the Yardly party took its leave.

"Ever so many," exclaimed Mrs. Wyndham. "Just before we came to see you, we were at Melton House. Unfortunately, the son was out at his fencing academy, but Lady Melton and her daughter were quite impressed with Rose and her conversation. She had excellent commentary on how the popular dresses for the day showcase the seamstress' skills more than the fabrics used. Poor Violet here could think of nothing to offer the conversation besides that of inquiring after the latest plants which Lady Melton has imported from overseas."

"Is that so?" questioned Miss Drayton. "I have heard that Lady Melton invests a great deal in her conservatory at their county seat."

"Oh?"

"Yes, indeed. In fact, I am surprised she did not mention it. She has several exotic fruit-trees such as lemon and orange in her greenhouse, as well as some ferns and flowers which grow natively in India. Her plants are a great source of pride for her."

"Oh dear," murmured Mrs. Wyndham as Ash found it necessary to clear his throat rather forcefully in order to conceal a great burst of laughter which threatened to escape his throat. "How dreadful," whispered Mrs. Wyndham.

"Forgive me, Mrs. Wyndham, but what is dreadful?" asked Miss Drayton.

Ash was able to master his laughter for long enough to answer rather gravely, "I fear that after Violet enquired as to Lady Melton's latest acquisition of flora, Mrs. Wyndham rather sternly adjured her to keep such trivial questions to herself."

Penelope smiled knowingly as she replied, "Ah, yes. That would likely prevent any mention of her extensive collection."

Mrs. Wyndham wrung her hands together as she said, "I do hope I have not offended her."

"Perhaps, next time you are in company with her, you might simply allow Violet to lead the conversation. I am certain that Lady Melton's good humor will allow her to overlook such a trivial offense, especially in the light of your correction of it."

Mrs. Wyndham nodded gravely, if a bit uncertainly as she glanced at Violet.

She was not given opportunity to say more, unfortunately – or perhaps fortunately, Ash mused – for Miss Drayton said, "Violet, have you had opportunity to visit any of the parks or gardens about Town?"

"Oh yes, Ash has taken me to several in the mornings. They are much pleasanter early in the morning before they become crowded. The lovely vistas are not obstructed by so many people."

"Heavens, Violet!" cried Rose. "You are dull indeed if you prefer to look at a tree more than an elegantly dressed countess."

"I am afraid, Miss Rose," said Miss Drayton with a slight edge to her voice, "that I must disagree with you. You see, I too prefer the picturesque to a populated view. I am rather adept at painting portraits, but the country scenes are what truly bring me joy."

Ash was pleasantly surprised to see Rose's face color up. If she could recognize that she had given too strong of an opinion too early in the acquaintance – before she knew of Miss Drayton's own opinions and preferences – perhaps there was hope for her to learn to be more circumspect in her speech.

"I suppose it was somewhat spread about," Miss Drayton said by way of changing the subject, "that I paid some visits the other day, for it seems all of Society has been here yesterday and today."

"Oh indeed?" asked Violet. "I am sorry to have intruded now, then."

"Oh, not at all; I am quite pleased to receive you." Miss Drayton patted Violet's hand fondly. "Only I fear I am unable to show you that item which we discussed. I cannot leave the sitting room for fear of being absent when another person calls. Even if we were to go up now, I am convinced that someone will arrive the moment my slipper touches the stair. Rather, I ought to invite you to tea someday soon, Violet, and we will have ample time to visit and talk."

"I should enjoy that," said Violet. Ash was somewhat curious at the uncharacteristic openness of his sister's manner, but judging by the familiarity between the two ladies, he could not claim that he was entirely surprised. He was, however, stunned that Mrs. Wyndham said little else for the entirety of the visit.

Ten minutes passed before a knock sounded on the sitting room door, and more visitors were announced. The Wyndham party remained long enough to be introduced, then bid Miss Drayton goodbye, with a promise from her to visit soon.

After the family arrived at their rented house, Ash noticed the driver hand Violet a package as he assisted her from the carriage.

"What's this, Violet? Did you manage to get to a shop whilst I was distracted?"

"Oh, no. Penelope had some old fabric for me," she explained, blushing as she did so. "It is my hope that there will be enough good pieces to make some clothes for the poor."

As they climbed the front steps of the house beside one another, Ash said, "You are a good girl, Violet." He placed a gentle arm about her shoulders, and leaned forward to kiss her forehead. "I am proud to have you for my sister."

Nine

In the following days, Violet was very occupied with her sewing. Each time Ash happened upon her, she had some material or another upon her lap, her hands deftly making stitches and hems and other things one did when sewing. He even caught her at it one morning after having begged off from paying calls with Mrs. Wyndham and Rose, citing a headache as her reason for demurring.

"Violet, I was almost certain that you said your head ached at breakfast this morning," said he. "Do you think that straining your eyes to sew will help it?"

Violet glanced up at his voice. "My head is much improved."

Ash paused, unsure. He had never known Violet to prevaricate from the truth, but he also found her present excuse to be terribly flimsy.

"Is that so?" he finally asked.

"Yes indeed." Violet smiled, but quickly returned her gaze to the work in her lap.

Can she not meet my eyes? He raised a brow at her, hoping to encourage the truth from her. *I could not abide if she began to take up some of the habits — telling untruths when it suits her, gossiping voraciously, and flirting shamelessly — of which Rose is so fond.*

"My head ached very little this morning, but I feared that visits would cause the ache to grow. Jane fetched some weak tea for me, and I slept for a short time. When I awoke, I found the pain to be gone."

Ash nodded. "I see." He glanced down at the fabric she held, her needle still pulling thread in and out. He snickered. "And now you are sewing."

Violet nodded innocently. "Yes. Now I am sewing."

"Have you always sewn this much?"

"At home I sewed frequently, but not nearly as much as I am now. Unfortunately, the plants here do not require much of my time," Violet said, nodding toward the potted plants near the window.

"Neither do those at our estate. In fact, the gardener and his staff are more than capable."

"Yes, but I enjoy tending them," countered Violet.

Knowing her time spent in the gardens was a point of contention between Violet and Mrs. Wyndham, he merely said, "As you enjoy this?"

"Yes." Violet very rarely asserted herself, but Ash saw in her eyes an uncharacteristically strong determination, indicating the strength of her opinion on this matter.

I had best not push this topic too far.

He changed the subject. "And what is it that you are making?"

"A dress for someone less fortunate than we are. One difference about being in Town, Ash, is that there are a great many more in need."

"But not for whom we are responsible."

"Oh but we are," she insisted, quickly setting aside her sewing and rising from the settee.

"How do you mean? They are not tenants on my land. How am I responsible?"

"We, all of us, are responsible for the poor. We ought to be doing what we are able to relieve their burden, for so Christ commands us."

No more was said on the subject, for at that moment Rose and Mrs. Wyndham entered the room, having refreshed themselves after their visits. Ash became quiet, which was not altogether out of character for him when in the presence of the newcomers to the room, but only his equally quiet sister noticed. She sat, sewing, while he stared, unseeing, through the window. Only Mrs. Wyndham and Rose spoke, their chatter filling the room.

Ash knew somewhere deep within – quite deep – that what Violet said was correct. Not only in regard to the duty one has to his fellow-man, but her frequent hints that he would find comfort and guidance in the Holy Scriptures. There was a part of him that cried out that he listen to his sister. However, he had long ignored that portion of himself and even wondered at times if it had left him altogether. A disquieting sense that all was not well – beyond his acknowledged frustration with half of his family and with the Society which he strove simultaneously to both please and avoid – began some time ago to pervade his senses. Violet did very well to say her prayers and meditate on the verses found in that ancient tome, but he would much rather keep his time and his will his own. To acknowledge that he had a responsibility to others required an acknowledgement of Who gave him that responsibility. Ash was uncertain he was prepared to allow Him more of a presence in his life than the Sunday mornings he had promised his sister. Certainly Ash was subject to the government, but that was a general governing and a necessity for society. The notion of his being subject in such a far-reaching manner was beyond his ability to tolerate. If he lost his ability to govern himself, what foolish things might he be made to do? What demands of others might he be required to allow?

No. I am my own master, and so I shall remain.

Penelope perched on a stool behind the curtain separating her from Miss Yardly. The girl's mama had sent a message to the studio on Albemarle Street the same day Penelope had called on her. Now, two days later, Penelope was quickly sketching Miss Yardly's image, making notes about colors and shading as she envisioned the portrait she would later paint. She had long retained an excellent visual memory, and that, coupled with her sketch and notes, would allow her to create an accurate and flattering likeness.

She recalled the manner in which the ladies had reacted to Mr. Wyndham's arrival with his mother and sisters. The Yardly family had called, clearly hoping to meet with Penelope's brother, Lord Claymore, and the manner in which they deflated upon learning of his absence was very nearly humorous. Still, it rankled that they were not truly interested in furthering their acquaintance with Penelope herself, aside from how they might benefit from being near her brother.

I suppose though that I am only interested in maintaining an acquaintance-ship with the Yardly household for the purpose of furthering my painting career. We each are interested only in furthering our interests. Are friends ever truly friends? As Penelope sketched Miss Yardly's face from several different angles – looking for the most flattering one – her thoughts turned to Miss Wyndham. *Violet. It has been years since I have had a friend of such intimacy as to use her given name. Come to think of it, have I ever?* Her papa had not the resources to send her to finishing school, and she seldom was permitted to go play with the local children when she was young. Penelope could not help but wonder if Violet was genuine in her friendship. She certainly seemed to be. There was a quality to the girl which she could not quite define, a peacefulness and a kindness which put Penelope in mind of her dear mother.

As with her father, Penelope purposely refrained from thinking about her mother too often. Unlike the painful memories of her father, though, the memories of her mother haunted with a bittersweet quality that she could scarcely bear. Penelope had lived only ten years when her mother was taken from her, preceded by two years of sickness and uncertainty. It began when her mother discovered what the physician later called "a cancerous tumor." Penelope was not told this, but had heard it whispered among the servants. She was never told what happened, but one day, when she was about eight years of age, she was taken with her brother to see their mother. She had grown so weak, and tired very quickly. She lay in bed, propped up with pillows, but seemed relatively well to the young girl.

Cornelius ran to her, embracing his mother without embarrassment. Penelope approached more slowly, allowing her brother a private word. She could see that he desperately needed a moment with their mother.

When Cornelius stepped back from the bed and left the room, Penelope approached cautiously.

"Mama," she had whispered, "what will happen to you?"

"Do not worry about me, dearest. I am in the Lord's hands, and whatever happens, He will be with me, and with you. Trust in His care, and you will see that He gives you all that you need."

Soon, her governess came to collect her. They were going for a picnic. As they walked along the grounds toward a low hill, Penelope thought she heard the low, guttural scream of a woman. When she asked her governess what it was, though, the woman chuckled uncomfortably and said something about the imagination of youth.

After that day, Penelope was unable to see her mother for two weeks. When she was finally admitted to her chamber, her mama was still in bed, with bandages forming odd lumps through her shift and bedjacket. Her mother was weak and pale, and never spoke; she simply smiled at the girl. The girl remembered her mama's words, though, which bade her to trust in God's care.

Penelope tried. She prayed every morning and evening, begging for God to heal her mama. She visited every day she was permitted. Some days, though, the servants rushed about with worried faces and tense shoulders, and she could not see her mama. On those days, Penelope spent a great deal of time in her mama's salon. On the walls were paintings of various things: a young girl, a country scene, a handsome young man. Penelope knew that her mama had painted them, and seeing something that her hand had created was the only comfort that she could find.

Several weeks passed and the baroness felt much improved. Everyone was more cheerful and went about their routines with renewed vigor. After a time, though, she again felt poorly. The house shrouded itself in a cloak of fearful anticipation. And so the pattern went. Improvements in her health brought light and cheer, but they were seemingly inevitably followed by seasons of darkness and uncertainty. Nearly a year passed before Penelope began to notice that her mother found true enjoyment in seeing the work she did with the painting master. Penelope's mother had instructed her at one time, but in recent years her health prevented her. The master tutored the girl in drawing and painting. For the next year, Penelope worked hard to improve her art, and she saw her mother's enjoyment grow while her health declined. Still, Penelope prayed. She prayed and painted, but at the end of that year, her mother succumbed to the disease.

Penelope was devastated.

The sound of a clearing throat, delicately done, startled Penelope from her thoughts. She had not been aware she was distracted for such a long time. The pencil in her hand felt leaden, and her eyes stung. She shoved the maudlin thoughts back to the dark corners of her mind, and forced her hand to raise the pencil to finish her work.

Once she had finished, Penelope stood from her stool, stretched out several knots in her back – *How unladylike of me; thankfully, I am not a lady at present, but a painter!* – and turned to slip through the door to the back room.

"Mr. Pelter, I am finished for the time being. Please inform Miss Yardly that you will deliver her portrait and collect the balance in three days' time."

"Certainly, Miss Drayton," murmured the old man with a bow.

Penelope felt her heart stutter. "Please, Mr. Pelter," was her urgent whisper. "Do not use my name here. If anything, please just call me P. or Greene."

"Of course." With a nod, the man shuffled through the door to the front of the studio. She heard him greet the girl, utter a few indiscernible words, and then usher her to the door. The sound of his footsteps became hollow as he climbed the stairs to the rooms above the studio, then walked a short way and stopped. He would soon be asleep in his chair, dozing until luncheon. Penelope drew a deep sigh when she was certain of being alone again. She enjoyed painting portraits as well as anything – perhaps even more than painting scenic landscapes.

In a portrait, she was able to display so much more than the image of a person. A portrait was an opportunity to show a person's inner self. Miss Yardly may not have been a beauty, but her patience and kindness were their own beauty. Penelope planned to give her a gentle smile, her head tilted at an angle which would soften her features. A rose-colored dress would bring color to her cheeks, and blue walls behind would brighten her eyes. The likeness would be true, but the manner in which it was done would certainly show Miss Yardly to advantage.

And a good thing it is that I've a talent for doing so, for I should not be able to pay rent on the meager income I've managed to secure. I sincerely hope that as I spread the word of P. Greene's skill as a painter, my clientele will grow and be enough to support me. If not . . .

Not wishing to dwell on such thoughts, Penelope decided that a brisk walk was just the thing she needed.

Once outside, she pulled her thin pelisse more tightly about her small frame. The wind was still just as chilled as it had been at the start of the Season, though the trees under which she passed had put out small buds. Some were white in color, others greener, and still others had reddish tints. She could almost feel the yearning of the plants for spring. *Or perhaps it is only my own yearning. Winter leaves one with so much time to think and reflect and remember. I had rather turn my thoughts to the concerns of today, not those of the past.*

While she harbored very few tender memories of her father, she did have painfully fond memories of her brother. He had not always been the unscrupulous man he was now, but the memory of what he once was pained her deeply. She wished those might be chased away as the spring sun would soon chase away the chill in the air and the last of the snow and ice.

Penelope made several turns until she found herself on the more populated Bond Street. She felt the others walking around her, and even nodded in greeting to several, but by and large, she kept her eyes straight, unfocused, and her mind drifted in the recesses of her memories, both long past and those more recent.

She longed for the return of the kind, caring boy Cornelius had been in their youth, but she could not admit that to herself, most days. Today, however, after having such vivid memories of her mother resurface without warning, and having seen Mr. Wyndham on several occasions demonstrate what a kind and supportive brother ought to be, she longed to have that for herself, to have a source of comfort and strength.

In her own brother.

Not in Mr. Wyndham, or in any man, for that matter. And therein was the difficulty. She could never willingly submit herself to a man – not a brother, and certainly not a lover, a husband. She had seen men fall too often to believe that one would not give in to his baser inclinations. Her father fell to drunkenness, her brother to gaming. Should she have a husband, she was certain that he would eventually fall, as well.

To what will Mr. Wyndham finally succumb?

Penelope was not startled at the errant thought, but rather at the truth driving it. *If I wonder at his shortcomings, am I possibly considering him for* . . . But she could not complete the thought.

Considering whatever he stirred in her heart was unthinkable. It was weakness. It was foolishness!

So lost was she in her thoughts that Penelope did not see the large, imposing figure headed in her direction until it was too late. She would have lost her footing had not strong hands closed about her arms, keeping her upright.

"I beg your pardon," said the masculine voice above her head. She tilted it back, until she could see from under her bonnet brim.

Mr. Wyndham.

"Oh dear," came Penelope's voice, disconcertingly shaken. *I am not affected by any gentleman,* she scolded herself, *least of all this one!* "I do apologize, Mr. Wyndham."

"No, the fault is mine," came his own easy voice in much too close proximity to her ear. He released her, stepped back, and bowed. She curtsied in return, fighting the blush that threatened to overcome her cheeks.

"I fear my mind was elsewhere," she admitted.

"Mine, as well," said he with a wry grin. He continued in a higher-pitched, self-important tone. "I've been sent on an errand of utmost importance, one much too lofty for even the most trusted of servants."

"Oh?" she asked, amused at his tone.

He nodded gravely before responding in a monotone, "Yes, for ribbons."

Penelope fought back a laugh and said, "Oh dear, yes. That *is* terribly important."

Mr. Wyndham gestured in the direction that Penelope had been walking, waiting until she started again before falling into step beside her. "It is not any ribbon for which I search, but a very specific sort. Mrs. Wyndham has written it on this paper." He pulled said paper from a pocket in his waist-coat, shifting his greatcoat capes and even his overcoat out of the way in order to retrieve it.

Penelope glanced at it, seeing a feminine script detailing the ribbon to be acquired. "And are you finding this task too much for you?"

"Oh, not at all," he returned with an impish grin as he led them in turning to the left. They proceeded along Brook Street. "It is being delivered to the house in precisely thirty-five minutes, but I plan to tell my dear sister Rose that it was nearly impossible to find."

"And that is why you did not find it necessary to continue on your previous path after we met just now?"

"Indeed. Do you not think my plan ingenious?"

Penelope did not answer, but allowed her laughter to do so for her. *I cannot recall the last time I laughed so freely!*

The buildings they passed gradually became larger and grander, as they moved away from the shopping district and approached Grosvenor Square. After a moment of walking silently together, she asked, "For what occasion are the ribbons necessary, if there is such urgency to your errand?"

"My sisters are being presented in Court."

"I see." Penelope smiled, recalling how unnerving it was to be presented. "Is Violet nervous?"

"Terribly so, though she is doing her best to remain calm. She would rather not have been given a Season at all, but Mrs. Wyndham insisted."

Penelope suddenly wanted to ask whether he enjoyed being in Town for the season, and even went so far as glancing sideways at his profile as they crossed the street before passing the park in Grosvenor

Square. Mr. Wyndham seemed wary of others, and she doubted he would appreciate the intrusion of such a question. She was similarly wary, and rarely made true friends because of it. However, her friendship with Violet and her observation of Mr. Wyndham's genuine affection for his sister caused her to wonder if perhaps in her defense against the negative, she might also be missing the benefits. Rather than ask about him, Penelope hummed in agreement with Mr. Wyndham's assessment of Violet's opinion of the Season. *Anything more would be in excess of what propriety should allow between such new acquaintances.* Just then, a gust of wind blasted down the street, sending a shiver up her spine and through her whole body.

"You must be freezing, Miss Drayton," exclaimed Mr. Wyndham suddenly. "February is too cold to be walking anywhere in London; what were we thinking? Please do come in, and warm yourself. I'll call for the carriage to return you to your home. And perhaps you may visit with Violet a spell, and calm her fears."

"Oh! This is your house?" She turned and craned her neck to look more closely at the imposing structure. The grey stone exterior extended up for several stories, matching bay windows on either side of the front door. The house was located on the corner of North Audley and Upper Brook Streets, diagonally across from the park. The many windows on the front of the building indicated a bright interior, which Penelope admitted to herself that she would like to see.

"Yes, this is the house which Lord Ashbridge made available for our use."

"I see."

"We were established in it only yesterday," he said as they approached the door.

"Is it part of Grosvenor Square?"

"Yes; while a street separates it from the park, the address is Grosvenor. Now, do come in and warm yourself."

"I thank you, Mr. Wyndham."

They approached the front door.

"If you are able to help Violet with this dilemma half as much as you have helped her confidence since making her acquaintance, I ought to be the one thanking you."

"Sir?"

"Violet's moniker suits her, do you not think?"

"Yes, but—"

"Too well." He paused before the door. Turning to face her, Mr. Wyndham said, "She must learn to stand up for herself. I have tried to help her, but am unable to break the hold Mrs. Wyndham and Rose have on her confidence. If anyone can help her, it must be you."

Penelope shook her head and answered, "I cannot claim such power."

"I have never seen her converse freely with anyone, besides myself and our young cousin Charlotte."

"Surely you exaggerate." Her heart beat heavily at the weight of his words. And perhaps a bit because of his proximity.

His brow furrowed sadly as he answered, "I only wish I did."

"I wonder, then, at her comfort with me."

"As do I." He paused a moment, his hand on the door, seeming to contemplate his next words. "Her hesitance to develop close friendships leaves me with the conclusion that those she does deem worthy of intimate acquaintance must be of excellent quality. Therefore, I shall also hold that opinion of you. If, however, you prove otherwise, I will not hesitate to do all that is in my power to return whatever injury you inflict upon my sister."

"I respect your opinion, and am humbled by Violet's," said Penelope slowly. "I give my word that it is not at all my intention to harm her. I am glad to have her friendship, though. True friends are a rare treasure to find."

Mr. Wyndham gazed speculatively at her for a moment before uttering a quiet, "Yes."

With that, he opened the front door and they were greeted by two footmen, who offered to take their outer things. Penelope hesitantly relinquished her pelisse, embarrassed at its light weight in such weather. Unfortunately, her warmer one was too worn to be used where anyone of consequence might see her.

Mr. Wyndham did not seem to notice, though, and simply thanked the footmen before leading her to a small sitting room where a cheery fire blazed on the coals. "Please, Miss Drayton, wait in here. I will go fetch Violet."

Before she could say anything, he bowed and left, closing the door behind him.

With a deep sigh, Penelope neared the hearth and held her hands, stiff with cold, out to the blaze.

What a terribly odd encounter!

She had hoped to avoid thoughts of Mr. Wyndham, only to be confronted by the man himself. And to see such a version of that man! All her past experiences with him had prepared her for a somewhat quiet, stern man.

You ought to have known better! People rarely meet with your expectation of them. Years ago, you expected Cornelius to remain a faithful friend and brother, and he is anything but. It stands to reason that Mr. Wyndham would also be a surprise.

As the warmth of the fire began to loosen her muscles, Penelope sighed again, this time in contentment.

Mr. Wyndham did seem during the first visit to have an undercurrent of humor. He almost appeared to be laughing at the absurdity of Miss Rose's comments. Until she insulted Violet, that is.

Having such a loyal and kind man at one's side would certainly be pleasant. I will say this for him, he was a pleasant surprise. And that is nothing about which to complain.

Penelope put an end to her thoughts then and there. She could no more afford them than she could afford a new trousseau of velvets and silks and gauzes. She instead turned to look about the room. Its three windows were a many-paned affair, beveled and clear and overlooking the street, through a budding tree's branches. The trim work was a deep ebony, the walls painted a soft green. The chairs and rugs, while of a slightly older style, were in excellent condition and the candles positioned about the room, while unlit presently, would provide ample light after dark.

This would be an excellent room in which to paint. Penelope chuckled to herself; every new room she entered was appraised for its lighting, ventilation, and angles. She wondered if she would ever be able to stop.

The door opened then, and she turned to see Violet enter, followed by Mr. Wyndham. Violet rushed across the room to embrace Penelope.

"Oh, I am glad to see you! But your hands are so cold! Come over to the fire. It is warmer away from the windows. Is it not a funny coincidence that you happened to meet my brother? He was not even to be out at all, for he had promised me to stay near all day because I am so terribly terrified at the prospect of Court! But Rose needed some ribbon, and Mama insisted that Ash go, for she feared that a servant might tarry and not return in time. Rose plans to wear it in her hair along with her plumes. What color was your court dress?"

Penelope had never heard the girl so talkative, and from what her brother had said, she was unusually vocal to begin with in Penelope's company. A quick glance at Mr. Wyndham revealed his own raised brows and amused grin. Penelope chose to ignore the manner in which her stomach tried to flip when she met his gaze and his grin widened.

"My dress was a deep rose color."

"Ah, yes, that would suit you very well, Penny," Violet said. "Do you mind that I call you Penny? I never asked your leave to do so. Forgive me."

Penelope knew then, that if the retiring Violet could open herself to a new friendship, she could certainly allow the use of a pet name. Different though they may be, and from such vastly different families, Violet seemed quite like the girl Penelope would hope to have as a sister. Unfortunately, Penelope knew without a doubt that she would rather lose the only friend she had ever had rather than see a sweet girl like Violet married to Cornelius.

There is another way to become Violet's sister, whispered a voice in Penelope's head, which she chose to ignore. Instead, she hastened to answer, "Of course you may call me Penny."

Violet asked, "I am most pleased to receive you at any time, Penny, but what has brought you here today?"

Penelope felt that she might blush if she allowed her thoughts to wander far enough back to what prompted her need for a walk, so she answered quickly, "I was walking, and ran into your brother—"

"Quite literally," came his quip.

It is not so amusing as he seems to find it, she groused inwardly.

"Err, yes. Well, I was walking, and happened upon him, and we found ourselves here."

"In actuality, Miss Drayton, I knew where I was the entire time." He grinned cheekily at her. "I fear it is you who found yourself here."

"Oh, I find when I walk in the country that I lose track of where I am quite often," offered Violet. "I lose myself in thought, or prayer, or even simply enjoying the verdant scape before me."

"Waxing poetic, Vi?" sounded Miss Rose's voice from near the door. "Good day, Miss Drayton. I fear my family is remiss in informing me of your visit."

"It is not a formal visit as such, my dear Miss Rose," replied Penelope, her honeyed tone concealing the irritation she felt — at the least, she hoped it was concealed. Such impolitic behavior, while seemingly common to Miss Rose, was below Penelope. "I popped in when I realized I was quite near Violet's home, and had hoped she might allow me to see her court dress."

Penelope glanced over at Violet, hoping she would confirm the claim.

"But of course you may," replied Violet, rising from her chair. "Shall we go now?"

"Yes, if you please."

"Rose and I shall remain belowstairs, if you do not mind," said Mr. Wyndham. "I've heard enough of court dresses to last me a lifetime."

"I do hope you will change your mind when your own daughters make their come-out," said Violet lowly with a small chuckle, before leading Penelope out into the hall.

Penelope very nearly asked if she ought to be wishing Mr. Wyndham happy, but then feared it would be perceived as over-interest on her part. Instead, she followed Violet through the house, noticing it was much larger and better-furnished than the one which they had rented on Wardour Street

"And you took up residence here only yesterday?" Penelope asked as they reached the top of the stairs.

"Yes. I cannot wait to show you my room."

"You seemed quite pleased with your previous room," commented Penelope.

"Yes, but *this* one–" Violet stopped here and opened a door. The door was located in a corner of the hallway, where it turned, continuing parallel to the back of the house. When Penelope entered the chilly room, she saw why Violet loved it so very much.

On the far wall were two windows of average size, looking out at the house beside them. A comfortably large bed was situated between the door and the windows, with a washstand on the near side and a small table with several books and a basket on the far side. At the foot of the bed was a trunk, open with several garments laid carefully over the side. A few feet from the trunk was a window-seat, scattered with cushions and a book, in front of an enormous, paned window. Penelope saw that one of those panes was propped open, the frigid breeze stealing through it into the room.

Violet rushed over, closing the window while saying, "I do apologize. I had been in a near panic when Ash came to fetch me, and had just opened the window for a breath of fresh air. When I heard that you were here, I forgot about the window entirely. Here, allow me to stoke the fire, and the chill will be gone in a moment."

"Should you not call the servants for such a task?" Penelope asked without thinking.

"Oh but I am perfectly capable. I do not care to trouble them with such a small thing when I am certain they are all quite busy."

Penelope wanted to ask what was so very important that a single servant could not be spared for a moment to stoke the fire, but decided to keep that question to herself.

"I can see why you like this room," she said instead. "Are these walls blue, or green?" Penelope was thinking about what colors she would mix to achieve that particular shade.

"I cannot tell. Perhaps perfectly in the middle."

"Perhaps."

"Oh! But let me show you," began Violet. She did not continue, and Penelope expected her to go to the bed, where was a laid an exquisite gown of deep green velvet. Instead, though, Violet moved to the window-seat, set aside several of the cushions, and lifted the top of the bench. "It is somewhat hidden, and I thought might be a good place to store your dresses while I work on them."

She pulled out a deep green gown, just a bit lighter than the court dress lying on her bed, and held it up to Penelope's slight frame. "I did not have the chance to take any measurements the other day, but thought that a drawstring closure at the top would allow for some leeway, and I recalled that your head came about to my chin when we are both standing. Would you care to try it on now, or take it with you and let me know of changes needed? Of course, you would need to take care with the pins. I have only pinned the skirt to the bodice, and several other seams are simply pinned, as I wanted to ensure that it would fit correctly before I sewed it."

Penelope could not speak at first, and merely listened to Violet prattle on. She was quite impressed that the girl had nearly put together an entire gown in such a short time. Finding her voice, she said, "If you have the time, I would be pleased to try it on now."

Violet smiled, nodded, and moved to close the door. "Shall I assist you with the buttons?

Penelope nearly changed her mind, knowing how her underthings were rather worn, and poorly patched in several places, but then recalled that Violet already knew of her situation. "Please."

As she unfastened the buttons running down Penelope's back, Violet was saying, "I thought that the old gown of your mother's which you included with the drapery fabric would make a lovely open-robe style of gown for you. Only, I would reverse the under and outer dresses. Your mother's print, I believe, would be more fashionable beneath the rose. There you are. May I help you with the other dress? I know where the pins are."

Penelope nodded, and with Violet's help, slipped into the green gown. The bodice was a bit loose, but Violet quickly fixed that by tightening the drawstring running beneath the bust. She had made the gown with short, slightly puffed sleeves, which were tightened to the correct diameter by drawstrings.

"Here are long sleeves, which you may attach. I was thinking of ordering some lace with which to trim the dress. What do you think? Or would you prefer ribbon?"

Penelope smiled at Violet. "I think that as simplicity is the aim of fashion currently, it is quite sufficient as it is."

"I had a very *simple* lace in mind," countered Violet. "And please, consider it a gift. I should be quite beside myself with nothing to do at present. I cannot walk as I usually do at our home, and the plants are still slumbering with this cold weather. Making these dresses has helped me more than you will know. Besides, as there is ample fabric leftover, I will be able to construct several garments to give to the poorhouse."

Penelope shook her head and answered, "Very well. You may trim the gown as you like. Please allow me to purchase any thread or trim which you need for the others, though."

Violet opened her arms to embrace Penelope. "Thank you. I am so glad – so very blessed to have made your acquaintance. God is good, is He not?"

Penelope could not speak due to the emotion clogging her throat. As she returned Violet's embrace, though, she thought, *I cannot speak for God's goodness, Violet, for I have seen but precious little of it. You, however, I am sure are good. Very good.*

Once Penelope was back in her own gown, Violet showed her the court dress. Penelope wished she might paint Violet in it, for the green color of the gown would make her eyes glow, and its richness would certainly bring color to her cheeks. This was nothing, though, when compared to the light in Violet's face when she beckoned Penelope over to the window. Below them, behind the townhouse, was a small garden.

"I could scarcely believe it," admitted Violet. "I did not know that houses in Town could have such a large garden."

"It is rare," agreed Penelope. "Even our house does not have one. How lovely for you, Violet."

"I have yet to explore and learn what sort of plants are down there. It seems terribly overgrown."

Penelope peered through the window again. "It does. Is that a fountain in the center?"

"I cannot tell. It may simply be a statue." Violet mover her face closer to the window, nearly pressing her nose against the pane. "It is my hope that after we are presented in Court, I shall have time to go and clear some of the weeds and prune some of the overgrowth."

"Will that not harm the plants, with it so cold out?"

"The older ones would likely be able to withstand it, but by the time I have cleared the weeds, the weather should be warmer."

"It is somewhat astounding that a plant can continue to thrive after having lost a part of itself."

"Indeed," replied Violet. "But it is no more astounding than our own ability to thrive after the same."

"You speak of a surgeon's work?"

"No, I speak of God's work. Or part of His work, at least. Does He not use some times of our lives to prune away the parts of us which are not beneficial to our living and thriving?"

Penelope was so disarmed by Violet's words that she answered without guarding her tongue. "I cannot say."

"Because you disbelieve it or because you have never considered it?"

"Perhaps both." Penelope usually attempted to keep her opinions of God to herself, but Violet's continually bringing Him into conversation seemed to have removed her guard.

"Yes," Violet's words came softly and slowly. "It might seem rather fantastic for a painful time to produce something good and fruitful."

"To be sure."

"But recall the words of the Psalmist: weeping endures for the night, but joy comes in the morning."

"Does it?" Penelope could hear the disbelief and despair in her own voice, so it was no surprise to her that Violet seemed to hear it, as well.

The younger girl stepped closer, placing a comforting hand upon Penelope's arm. "I believe it does. But let us wait for your morning, and we shall see."

Ash could scarcely believe his foolishness at allowing Violet and Miss Drayton to go by themselves and leave him in the sitting room with Rose. The girl was thrilled to have an audience in her usually standoffish elder brother and demonstrated this with her continual flow of words detailing her excitement at being presented in Court the following day. She spoke first at length about her gown, and how the ribbon just arrived would complete it in a manner worthy of a princess, perfectly complimenting the color and her complexion. She had checked and affirmed that the ribbon matched her ostrich plumes on her headdress to perfection.

Rose had just launched into a detailed description of the practice she had performed with the required hoop beneath her skirts and train – when the monarch would do away with such a ridiculous requirement, Ash did not know. Rose allowed that Violet had been very clever in taking a length of old fabric to imitate the trains, that they may practice walking backwards with it, as they would be required to do once dismissed from the royal presence, in order to keep their faces toward the monarch. However, Rose had practiced ever so much more than Violet had, and would therefore be much more warmly received by the nobility present.

Ash strove to keep his thoughts to himself, for he did not desire an argument. He attempted to restrain his responses to merely nodding, humming periodically, and staring at the clock on the mantle behind Rose's head. However, when she asserted for the third time that the queen would approve of her infinitely more than she would of Violet, he could no longer hold his tongue.

"Why must you do that?"

Rose, startled at having been interrupted, blinked widely at him several times before asking insipidly, "Do what?"

He stood from the wing-chair he had occupied, and paced before the fireplace. "Compare yourself to Violet. And in such an unkind manner."

"I cannot help that she is lacking where I excel."

"And you lack where she excels."

Rose, having lost her placid expression of self-satisfaction, stood and scowled at him. "And well I know it! You and she always thought yourselves above me, just because I am so young and because Mama loves me best!"

"We never thought anything of the sort!" Ash heard the hard edge in his voice and was afraid that Rose could hear it, too.

"You most certainly do! Every time Mama corrects Violet, you jump to her defense. Every time you need consoling, she is right there. No one cares if I've been reprimanded; in fact, you do most of the reprimanding!"

"You have never sought out our company, except to comment on your superiority and our insufficiency."

"And why should I have? There is little we have in common."

"We agree on something, at least," Ash said drily.

"Oh, you're awfully high in the instep for one spurned by his lady love."

"Stop, Rose."

"No! All my life, I've sought first Papa's approval, which no-one could ever gain, and then yours and Violet's. I am finished! I shall only seek the approval of those who care for me, who want my good."

"Of course you would." Even as the bitter words flew from his mouth, Ash knew how Violet would have responded: *I do want your good.* But if Ash was to say it, the words would be a lie. He wondered when he had become so embittered to his youngest sister.

"Well, then," said Rose as she sat once again and picked up a book left on the side-table nearest her.

"Hm." Ash was at a loss as to how to respond. This revelation was rather startling. He had always supposed Rose to simply be a beautiful but vapid person, whose most pressing worry was whether to wear the blue or the rose gown, and whether she would be able to dance every set at a ball. Now he saw that perhaps there was more at work than what was at the surface.

Ash sat, as well, and waited uncomfortably in the nearly-silent room. The clock over the mantle provided steady *tick tick* which heightened his nerves with every passing minute, and occasionally he could hear the rustle of paper as Rose turned a page in her book. He kept his eyes steadfastly on the painting which hung above the mantle and clock. The eyes of the young man, pale blue and terribly piercing, looked back, offering no suggestion on a manner of relieving the tension in the room.

His thoughts that had first appeared at the card-party resurfaced and left him feeling cold and unsettled. *I have truly failed my youngest sister.*

When Violet and Miss Drayton returned, he was indescribably relieved. He sprang from his chair, moving to greet the ladies.

"And what do you think of our dear Violet's court dress, Miss Drayton? Will it do?"

Miss Drayton blushed lightly, but quickly recovered and said, "It will do nicely, I daresay. It will bring out depth of color in her eyes, for they are green as well, are they not? I am certain she will look quite lovely."

Violet blushed, of course. "Shall I call for some tea, Penny?"

"Thank you, but no. I really must return home. I fear my aunt will begin to worry."

"Allow me to call for the carriage to take you to your house," Ash said.

"Oh, no, that is not necessary. It is not far."

"I insist." He leveled his eyes upon her.

He could see Miss Drayton struggle internally before lowering her eyes and murmuring, "Very well."

Ash walked away to make the arrangements, but before he left, he could hear Violet's low murmur. "Return in a few days' time. Tomorrow we will be out, but any time after will be acceptable. I shall have completed at least the green. . ." But then he was out of earshot, and could contrive no good reason to retrace his steps.

How very curious.

Penelope entered her art studio after glancing quickly about to assure that no-one saw her. The hour was early, and only servants were out and about. Still, she must be cautious.

She hung her pelisse on a peg near the door in the back storage room before reaching for her apron. She had brought the rose-colored one from the house, deciding she did not want any incriminating evidence about her home with people visiting every day. Quickly slipping it on and tying it in the back – she had very little time before she needed to be home for morning visits – she walked to her painting area.

A portrait was left on the easel, and she set it against the wall. She considered her incomplete works just a moment before choosing a nearly-finished painting. She had a few details to complete on the newly-married subjects' clothing, so she drew a palette from the old box in which she kept them, along with her paints and a few other things. She scooped a bit of several colors of paint out onto her palette and started painting.

Some time later, a quick glance at the watch hanging from her chatelaine revealed that she had about a quarter-hour before she needed to leave. *Thirty minutes have already passed?* She quickly set aside the portrait and went to clean up her materials. Fortunately, she had used her paint sparingly and the little bit left was easily washed away. She had ten minutes to work on some of the sketches for Madame Bélanger before she left for the quick walk to her home. Fifteen minutes later saw her hastily drawing her gloves over paint-stained hands as she hurried down the street, her open pelisse catching the wind and billowing out behind her.

I must beg Aunt Essie to use some of her cream again, to remove the paint. It will not do to receive a visitor in such a state.

Penelope knew that it would be a difficult transition from her life as a gently-bred woman to that of a tradesperson, but the most trying aspect at present was balancing the two lives. Every day, she arose early after late evenings of parties, routs, or assemblies and hurried to her studio to paint or draw in what little time she had before she must rush back to the house to dress for morning visits, whether she was paying them or receiving them. Following that, she hurried through a sparse luncheon, unless she had been invited to join someone else. Then it was off to the studio for as much painting as she could manage, until it was time to dress for whatever event was being held in the evening. Most nights, Penelope scarcely made it through said event due to exhaustion. It seemed her entire existence was given to either painting or pleasing Society. She was growing weary.

But it would be well worth the difficulty, she reminded herself daily. After she was established as an artist, she would be able to live above her studio, paint, and not worry about pleasing a Society for which she cared very little. If only she could continue through this Season.

Ten

THE NEXT DAY, the Wyndham ladies were all fluttering about, preparing for Court. Mrs. Wyndham, in light of Ash's new fortune, had ordered a new gown for herself, as well, and all of the female servants were occupied with one person or another. Ash concerned himself primarily with staying away from the excitement, but was invariably drawn into the thick of it. From his quarters, almost an hour before the ladies were to depart, he heard a screeching which rivaled that of an injured cat. He hurried into the hall, to see Rose in her dressing gown, pounding upon Violet's door.

"I need Jane! Elsie has *ruined* my hair *entirely*! Jane, come out right *now* and *fix this*!"

Ash hurried down the hall, and grasped Rose's hand just as she was about to reach for the door-handle. "Rose, *do not*." He kept his voice low but intense. Rose knew he meant what he said.

"Why ever not? Jane must come and *fix* this mess!"

He only just now looked at his youngest sister's hair. It was terribly curly, with enormous height. The sides and front were pulled up to the top, the ends left loose and erupting in curls, and the back of her hair was fashioned into four ringlets, which fell down her back. Elsie emerged just then, her face and eyes red.

"I do 'pologize, miss," said the girl. "I di'na' know whay-ther I could concoct the style you d'sired, miss, an' I *did* do my bayst."

"Sometimes," sneered Rose, "your best is still a failure."

"Elsie, please go see if Mrs. Wyndham needs anything pressed," Ash gently instructed. "The irons are still hot, I take it?"

"Yessir," said the girl with a blush, before curtsying and hurrying away.

"Rose, you insulted that poor girl."

"I did no such thing."

"Did you not see her face? She was shamed and very likely crying." He shook his head at her, disbelieving that his sister failed to notice that the poor servant girl was so distressed. Though after what she revealed yesterday, he supposed he ought not be surprised. "You have hurt her feelings."

"Servants are not meant to have feelings," Rose grumbled, crossing her arms with a huff.

"I am of a mind to tell you that you will wear your hair as it is, for such speech." This changed Rose's attitude quickly, and she straightened and turned to face him with wide eyes and a trembling lower lip. "But," he relented, "as it will reflect poorly upon all of us if you arrive at Court looking as you do, I will not."

Just then, Violet's door opened. "I am sorry, Rose, but Jane had just begun pulling my locks up when you first knocked, and we both did our best to call out to you that Jane would be available in a moment, but I fear you could not hear us."

Rose's face flushed red. "I see."

"Thank you, Violet," said Ash. He smiled at her, glad to see that her hair had easily obeyed the wishes of Jane. "You look well. Jane, can you be spared to assist Rose now?"

"Yessir," said she with a curtsy, and followed Rose to her room.

"Violet, you will be a beautiful addition to the queen's drawing room."

"If a temporary one," added Violet with a wry smile.

"That is the plan, but perhaps you shall marry an Earl and be required to appear at court with more regularity."

"Ash, you know that it is not my plan to marry."

"You often speak of God's plans. What will you do if He should desire something different from what you desire?"

Violet smiled weakly, but answered, "I shall do my best to follow where I believe He leads. If that is to a husband –"

"An earl." Ash could not keep the teasing laughter from his voice.

Violet squared her shoulders and looked him in the eye. "–then so be it."

"How will you speak to him?" Ash laughed outright this time at the idea of his sweet, quiet sister filling the role of a countess, and all the social engagements and requirements of such a status. *A mouse married to a lion,* he mused. Then the idea of his kind-hearted sister married to an important man and all that would entail – *he had better not keep a mistress* – soon sobered him.

Violet blushed, but said nothing as she returned to her room to continue preparing. Ash wandered back to his own chambers, but soon was feeling antsy. Because he had earlier determined not to accompany them on this particular portion of a first Season, and therefore had no court suit made, he could not attend today even if he so desired. After remaining in his rooms for another half-hour, Ash decided that it was time to leave the house. He called for his valet to assist him into clothing more suitable for sporting, bade his sisters good-bye and good-luck, and set off for his fencing club at a brisk pace.

Upon arrival, he found that both Spence and MacDougal were there, in the midst of a match. He observed the two lunge and parry for a time, scoring points here and there, until MacDougal emerged the victor. The two gentlemen moved to the side where Ash awaited them.

"You fought poorly, Spence," admonished Ash once the two men were in earshot.

"Think you so?" said Spence. "I should like to see you do better! Mac here has been instructed in swordplay since he was able to stand."

All three laughed, knowing how important MacDougal's father considered the art of swordsmanship to be. He had been a military man, as was his father before him, who joined soon after the union of Scotland with England. MacDougal's father, however, had been given a substantial piece of land following his particularly heroic actions in the War of Rebellion, which resulted in Great Britain losing the colonies. After he returned home, he was able to retire from the military and set himself up as a gentleman on his land. His holdings were nowhere near as extensive as Wyndham's, even before he stood to possibly inherit more. Even so, it was enough that when he married and his wife bore him children, those children were raised in quite a different manner of living than had been enjoyed by his father and himself. The military training remained strong, though, and all of his sons were taught to handle steel well.

"I shall do better." Ash quickly shed his coat and waist coat. "Come, Mac. Are you ready for another match?"

The two gentlemen moved to the floor, Ash pausing first to choose a weapon. Once the cool metal was in his hand, he walked slowly to where MacDougal stood, looking to see how tired his friend appeared. Aside from a bit of perspiration, he appeared unaffected by the previous match. *Good.* Ash was ready for a good round.

They began easily, their blades meeting quickly and sharply, before again lowering to a casually defensive position. Ash, spoiling as he was for the fight, lunged first, with MacDougal answering with a parry-riposte. Ash immediately answered that with his own offensive movements.

"I see y'are in need of some exertion," commented MacDougal, his Scottish brogue strong. Ash kept his eyes on the movements of the saber in his friend's hand, rather than his face while he spoke.

Lunge. Parry-Riposte.

"Indeed. The three females in my house are attending the Queen's drawing-room today."

Parry. Lunge.

"And ye've sought escape in a fight?"

Parry. Lunge. Parry. Touch!

"That is a point for you, Mac. I see your plan to distract me with conversation has succeeded."

The two separated by a few steps, slowly circling, swords at the ready.

"No such thing, Ash," laughed MacDougal. "Ye've distracted yeer-self by answerin' my friendly inquiry."

Lunge. Parry-riposte.

"Hm. Then I shall make that mistake no more."

Lunge. Parry. Lunge. Disengage. Touch!

"A point for me," grinned Ash.

"And anoother for me," declared MacDougal before attacking with an energy that Ash was not expecting. His friend did not appear winded, but he had already fought a match, and Ash certainly did not believe him to have such energy to spare.

Touch!

"Y'must practice more than when ye're in need of escape, if ye wish to best me," taunted MacDougal. "Yeer form is worse than Spence's, and he attends the Academy with even less frequency than you!"

Ash scowled, then lunged. MacDougal easily deflected the attack.

Back and forth they went, their movements gaining momentum until their swords were simply a flurry of lunges and parries. When it was over, Ash had made a respectable showing, but still was easily beaten by MacDougal. As they left the floor, the later gave the former a resounding clap upon the back, causing Ash to stagger forward a bit. He was in good health, but not nearly as committed to his physical training as his friend.

"Not so quick to scorn me now, eh, Ash?" chuckled Spence as Ash mopped sweat from his face.

"But you've not been distracted from your training as I have been by sisters and a mother. You are a happy bachelor, content in your complaisance."

"Either way, I daresay 'tis a good thing for Ash that we placed no wager on the match, or I'd sure'n have cleaned him out, same as I did you," said MacDougal to Spence.

A while later, the three gentlemen left the Fencing Academy and walked toward their club.

"So your sisters are likely in the Queen's drawing room this very moment?" asked Spence.

"Aye. And I cannot think of it without fear creeping into my heart."

"Why? Afraid young Miss Wyndham will faint dead away?"

"Not at all. She was a fretful little thing, but oddly composed under pressure. I fear for Rose." Ash contemplated relaying the conversation of yesterday to his friends, but thought better of it; MacDougal was particularly fond of Rose and would likely allow his affection cloud any sounds advice which might otherwise be offered. Instead, he simply said, "She is too young to have her come-out, and I fear she will embarrass my family by speaking out of turn, or forgetting to keep facing the queen as she exits the drawing room."

"Sure'n she must have the sense to remember protocol and all that," MacDougal did his best to comfort him. Ash nodded, but mostly for his friend's sake. Considering MacDougal's feelings for his sister, Ash also did his best to refrain from criticizing Rose too harshly when in his presence. He still had not the heart to divulge to him the reason for his sister's hurried come-out: another suitor.

Continuing, he said, "Either way, gentlemen, after today my life will be drastically different. I go from being a man with two younger sisters still in the schoolroom, to a man with two younger sisters out, and more – endorsed by the Queen for marriage."

"Or scorned by the Queen; one for refusal to answer her questions and the other for hoydenism," jested Spence.

Ash leveled a scowl at his friend, but remained silent.

"And do not forget," added MacDougal, "two younger sisters with the possibility of increased dowries, due to your recently elevated position in Society."

"How can I forget?" muttered Ash.

They reached their club, and Ash entered first, eager to forget his woes for a time with a fine meal and a rousing game of cards.

Penelope eagerly rang the bell. *At last!* Her Aunt Essie had accompanied her on this visit, which had slowed Penelope's progress up the steps, and she was eager to hear how the girls' presentation in Court yesterday had passed. She knew how uneasy Violet was about it, and hoped to hear that her fears had been ill-founded.

The butler opened the door and immediately showed the two ladies to the sitting room, where Violet and Mr. Wyndham sat. The later was reading a paper, and when he looked up to see Penelope and her aunt, he immediately set aside his paper and rose to greet them. When their eye contact ceased in the midst of his bow, Penelope realized that her eyes had sought him first, and she had yet to even look in the direction of her friend.

"Violet! Mr. Wyndham. How do you do this morning?"

"Quite well, Penny, thank you!" said Violet. Mr. Wyndham made a sound in agreement, but Penelope studiously ignored him in an attempt to correct her perceived lapse. Having seen her aunt situate herself in a chair near the fire, she hurried to sit beside Violet, finding a bundle of rose-colored fabric in the other girl's hands.

"Is this one of the dresses you are making for the poor?" asked Penelope, seeing Mr. Wyndham sit from the corner of her eye.

Violet shook her head, much to Penelope's surprise. "No, this is a gift I am making for a friend. But if you would care to see what I am making for the poor, that is still in my chambers."

"I should like that very much."

The two ladies rose from the settee, and Penelope immediately heard the rustle of Mr. Wyndham's newspaper.

"Ash, please do not trouble yourself with standing," said Violet. "We are an informal party this morning, are we not?"

Penelope feared her presence might prevent his heeding his sister's words, so she quickly added, "Yes indeed. As a matter of fact, I should be quite distressed if you were to rise, Mr. Wyndham."

At his quirked brow, she found she could not suppress a grin. "You see, sir, if you rise and make the polite gesture of a bow, I shall then be required to return said gesture with a curtsey. And I simply cannot be bothered this morning. I am near to fainting with the anticipation of hearing how fared our dear Violet during her presentation at Court."

"By all means, then, Miss Drayton. I should not wish to inconvenience you or to keep you from your information." Laughter bubbled in his voice as he added, "Or worse, cause a fainting spell."

Penelope glanced toward Violet to find the girl looking at her with a quizzical expression.

"Shall we?"

"Hm?" Violet shook her head slightly, then smiled brightly. "Oh, yes. Let's. Will Miss Breckenridge be joining us?"

"Oh no," said Aunt Essie, "but I do thank you for thinking to include me. No, I have brought my knitting to occupy me if Mr. Wyndham is of a mind to talk, and a book if he is not."

Penelope chuckled at her aunt's ever-present practicality, but still asked, "If you are certain?"

"Quite. These old bones cannot go traipsing about houses. I much prefer to sit by the fire."

"Very well, Aunt. I imagine we shall return shortly."

Despite Mr. Wyndham's acquiescence to the request that he not rise at their departure from the room, Penelope nevertheless heard a shuffling as his voice followed them through the door.

"Miss Breckenridge, are you warm enough? I can certainly remove that screen easily enough if you should prefer more warmth from the fire."

She could not hear her aunt's response, though, for they moved away from the door. On their way to Violet's room, Penelope inquired as to the whereabouts of Mrs. Wyndham and Miss Rose.

"They both enjoy sleeping in and breaking their fast in their chambers, but Ash and I have always been early risers."

"Even in Town?" asked Penelope. "I myself am an early riser, but find that the schedule of late balls and routes often cause me to sleep later here than in the country."

"Oh, yes, I do sleep later here, but still cannot remain abed for very long. I am usually up by half-past seven, at the latest."

"Even after the most trying day you had yesterday?" teased Penelope as they arrived at Violet's chamber.

Violet smiled as she opened the door and gestured for Penelope to enter before her. "Especially so. I needed extra time with the Scriptures."

Penelope was so surprised by Violet's words that she blurted out, "Do you not receive enough of that on Sundays?"

Violet set the bundle of deep rose fabric she had carried from the sitting room upon the bench before her window before turning to Penelope and saying with a gentle smile, "I find that I cannot receive enough, regardless of how much I read."

"You sound like my aunt," chuckled Penelope, slightly uneasy. *I cannot imagine why I feel so . . . odd. Aunt Essie has said similar things all my life.*

"Your aunt seems like a wise woman."

"She is. Only . . ."

Penelope was uncertain that she wanted to say what was on her mind. But Violet looked expectantly at her.

Heaving a great sigh, Penelope said, "I cannot see what draw that Book has for you. I have attempted to read it, I will admit, but find that I am not engaged."

Violet nodded sadly. "I suppose you would not be. Many people are in a similar place."

"Place?"

"Yes. Of wondering, of lacking conviction."

"Conviction of what?"

"Any number of things. For some, I suppose they are unconvinced of the Lord's hand in their lives. For others, they may fear that He cannot possibly be pleased with them. And still others simply cannot be bothered with Him. I've been in each of those places, to varying degrees, before. But He brought me from them."

"I see." But Penelope did not truly see.

Violet had a knowing expression, but did not pursue the topic.

"This gown," she said while gesturing to the bundle upon the bench, "is your over-gown. I am finishing the hem, but it should be ready soon."

Violet held it aloft, giving the garment a few gentle shakes to straighten out the folds of fabric. Penelope saw immediately how the open-robe would complement the flowered fabric of the underdress, covering the back and sides, as well as the sleeves, and fastening with a frog closure in the front, just beneath the bust.

"It is not an open robe like most of the ladies have," commented Penelope.

"You do not like it?" asked Violet, uncertainty coloring her face for the first time.

"Oh, I do! I am glad it is different. Perhaps it will set a trend."

Violet nodded as she moved to lay the gown upon her bed. After removing a basket from the bench, she opened the lid and retrieved several items.

"Here is your green dress. The sleeves are only whip-stitched on, so do take care not to tear the stitches. I hoped that would be easier for you to remove them, should you choose to wear it for an evening occasion."

The dress had been decorated with thin braiding of a blue color to match the printed flowers on the fabric.

"It is lovely," said Penelope.

Violet flushed, and reached for a white gown. "This I was able to make from muslin left over from a gown my sister wanted, but then decided that this particular shade of white made her look too washed-out. I asked if I might have it, to repurpose for myself, and she agreed. But now, I've more gowns than I need. As you are so petite, I suspected that there would be plenty of fabric to cut a new dress. Again, the sleeves may be removed. I thought that perhaps you might wear it on occasion beneath the open robe."

"Thank you, Violet." Penelope could not say more just then, for she was looking closely at the whitework embroidery about the hem and bodice of the gown in an effort to keep tears at bay.

Never before has someone made such an extraordinary effort on my behalf.

Finally, Penelope managed to choke out, "This must have taken you quite some time."

Violet shook her head. "I actually began the embroidery some time ago. It was originally from two years past, but I had grown too much by the time I finished the stitching. With careful cutting of the new pattern, it was a simple thing to incorporate it into the new gown for you."

Penelope merely shook her head with a watery smile.

Finally, Violet pulled out two final garments. One was clearly the flower-printed underdress which Penelope already knew to expect. The other appeared to be a wool item that Penelope could neither recognize nor identify. Violet first held aloft the underdress for her inspection, and Penelope happily gave her approval. When Violet reached for the wool item, though, she hesitated.

"I hope you do not mind, but I made this pelisse for you. It is re-made from one I had last year, but I am now too tall for it."

"Oh, you needn't have done that. I am quite pleased to have these dresses."

"To be sure, Penny, for you are so very kind and would never have asked; but Ash mentioned that the pelisse you wore the other day was quite light, and seemed to keep out absolutely none of the cold."

Penelope felt simultaneously mortified and grateful. She could not countenance that Mr. Wyndham had noticed her shivers; she had worked so hard to hide them! However, Violet's kindness and ingenuity in creating a new garment from her old one was most appreciated. She was even rather touched that Mr. Wyndham was concerned enough to mention it to his sister.

"Very well, Violet. I will accept it all, though there are not sufficient words to express my appreciation for your kindness. I count myself indescribably fortunate to have made your acquaintance."

Violet answered, "You are most welcome, Penny. I am glad to be the instrument God uses to bless you."

The uncomfortable twinge Penelope felt at her friend's words seemed to come from anywhere but a compassionate, caring God.

Several days later, Ash sat comfortably by the fire in the front sitting room, his mind calmly drifting and his nerves calm. From elsewhere in the house, he could hear Rose's shrieks and Mrs. Wyndham's less frantic but equally piercing voice answer – but he would not allow it to intrude upon his peace. Violet's room, of course, issued no sound. He imagined her to be sitting nervously before the looking-glass, face flushed and fingers trembling, while Jane arranged her hair. She would soon be finished preparing for the assembly, and join him in the room.

He intended to ask her why she had been avoiding many of the recent morning visits. Already he had attempted to broach the subject gently with her, but to no avail. Today, he would be direct if need be. Having to question Violet about her behavior was most uncommon and left him unsure of how to proceed. Most times, it was Violet attempting to address his behavior. But Ash had observed a pattern developing that left him with an odd discomfort in his belly. This morning, she had plead a head-ache and yesterday a slight ague evidenced by a fit of sneezing and red nose and glossy eyes. Two days past, she accompanied them on visits, but asked to return home early and was conveyed there while the rest of the family visited a third house that day. If it had been anyone else, Ash would have been certain that she was hiding something.

Surely not Violet, he attempted to reassure himself. Still, when the sitting-room door opened, and Violet hesitantly entered, he knew he would need to address her odd behavior of late.

She wore her whitework muslin – *At least she has been truthful about working on this.* – and the candlelight of the room drew a lovely glow from the dress. Ash knew precious little of ladies' fashion and needlework, but even he could tell that his sister's skills were exceptional. The tiny flowers about her sleeves and neckline, which modestly covered most of her décolletage, and the intricate swirls and flowers and leaves which lined the hem of the gown and ran up the center to her waist were all precise and even. Over the white gown, she wore a long green shawl that dragged on the floor even after being generously draped over both her arms. It brought out brighter shades of green in her eyes. She was a vision and he feared that some dashing man would be able to break through the timidity which shielded her, and take her away from him. Since they were both very young, their father had been reclusive in his study, and Ash had been the one to console his sister when she cried at Rose's teasing, or helped her with a sliver in her finger following time spend in the gardens. Seeing her now as a blossoming young woman, he was overcome with emotion.

"You look very well this evening, Violet." He rose to offer the customary bow, quite quickly and informally, and then clasped her hands. "I can scarcely believe you are so very grown-up."

Violet laughed a bit nervously and answered, "I am eighteen years of age, Ash. How else should I be?"

Just then, a wail from Rose's room echoed through the whole house. Ash and Violet looked at each other, then Ash raised a brow at Violet, a grin quirking his lips.

"She is but sixteen!" Violet protested his silent comment. "She will settle as she matures."

"Very well. While I do not necessarily share your optimism, I am cognizant of her youth." Ash moved to assist Violet to a chair, then seated himself. "Let us sit, and I shall interrogate you concerning your odd behavior of late."

Violet visibly paled, but he saw her swallow and draw a breath before saying in a studiously innocent voice, "My odd behavior? Whatever can you mean?"

"You have claimed various ailments the past several days, excusing yourself from visiting about Town." Violet pressed her lips together, and Ash could see that she was uncomfortable. Instinctually, he allowed a wry tone to color his voice in order to ease her discomfort. "You know I can scarcely endure those visits, even with your presence. When you are absent, they are utterly intolerable."

"Are you suggesting I have purgered myself?" asked Violet, her voice only trembling slightly. He raised a questioning brow to send the question back to her, while she coughed delicately. When she spoke again, her voice was stronger. "I have told no lie. My head did ache yesterday when I woke, likely because I did not eat enough for supper the previous evening. I cannot be blamed if a hearty breakfast and a bit of rest cured me."

"And the day before that? You so rarely succumb to any illness."

Violet hesitantly admitted, "I have not been getting the rest I should."

Ash waited a brief moment for her to explain, but when she offered nothing more, he asked, "Why ever not?"

"I have been eager to finish some dresses . . ."

"Surely not for you," Ash interrupted. "We ordered a sufficient wardrobe for you at the beginning of the Season."

"Of course they are not for me; I have more than enough."

"Have you finished yet? The poorhouse must be lacking severely if there is such urgency to require your work when you ought to be sleeping. Is that perhaps why your head ached? Were you working in poor light?"

Violet furrowed her eyebrows and the corners of her mouth turned down in a slight frown as she answered, "Very likely. But I have finished enough that I may work at my leisure on the rest, and so I shall very soon be rested and ready to accompany the family on any visits Mama requires."

"How is it that having finished two allows you to take your time now? Are there so few ladies connected with the poorhouse that they only need two dresses with urgency?"

"Oh!" Violet's face blushed brightly and her eyes widened. "They are not for the poorhouse."

Ash was confused. "But you said-"

"I said no such thing, you merely assumed." Violet smiled slightly. "I do not enjoy keeping things from you, Ash, but it is not my tale to tell. It must suffice that I was made aware of a young lady who was in need of several gowns, and I was happy to assist."

"Do I know her?" asked Ash.

"Only a very little."

"Do *you* know her?" he asked, dry humor leaking into his voice.

"I do to an extent, but we have not been long acquainted. Beyond that, I am certain that she would not wish for me to reveal her identity."

Ash began thinking of the ladies with whom he knew Violet to be acquainted. His first thought was Miss Drayton, but surely a Baron's sister could afford gowns. Perhaps it was a friend of Rose.

Deciding that he did not necessarily need to know the lady's identity, Ash shook his head and said, "Very well, I will not ask that you disclose her identity. But you *will* be resting sufficiently after this?"

"Oh yes indeed," Violet beamed. "It has been delightful, Ash, refashioning old garments into new ones. I daresay my work has been so careful and thorough that you would not be able to discern it from a gown made by a dressmaker from new fabric."

"Truly?" Ash laughed at his sister's rare show of confidence. "I daresay that says very little, considering my limited knowledge of ladies' fashion."

"You know more than you let on," returned Violet. "Do you recall your comment to Mama last week, at the dressmaker's shop, concerning the purple organza Rose wanted for a gown?"

"Yes, I said that she would appear sickly in that hue, due to her coloring."

"Yes, well, she did, and she said that she did not wish to keep the dress."

"Wasteful chit."

Violet's disapproving frown spoke more than did her words. "Ash, do not speak so of your sister!"

"She is wasteful."

"Even so."

At that moment, the door opened, and Mrs. Wyndham entered. "Violet, why are you sitting? Your gown will wrinkle."

Violet stood immediately, smoothing out her gown and blushing. Ash felt his ire rise and stood as well.

"Will not sitting in the carriage also wrinkle her gown?"

"Perhaps, but not to the degree of a chair for such a length of time." She turned to Violet again. "I believe that Jane favors you unnecessarily. You are always finished dressing long before your sister. Jane must learn to divide her time more evenly between you two girls. I will speak with her about it at first opportunity."

Ash saw Violet clasp her hands, her white gloves straining over her knuckles. "Mama, might I speak to her later, perhaps tomorrow morning? We . . . we wouldn't want her to be distracted while assisting Rose."

"Indeed not." Mrs. Wyndham leveled her gaze on Violet, seeming to weigh things in her mind. "Very well, tomorrow you will tell her that she must devote more time to Rose."

Ash was annoyed that Mrs. Wyndham was raising an issue which stemmed more from Rose being difficult to please than from a servant shirking her duties, but he remained quiet. He was, however, enormously proud of his sister for speaking. If only Mrs. Wyndham had not turned it from an even division of time to more time for Rose. Still, he chose not to say anything.

"Ashbridge, dear, it is quite an exciting thing to have obtained vouchers for Almack's."

"Did you not attend when you were younger, ma'am?" he asked, merely to goad her. He knew the answer, that Mrs. Wyndham came from a family which was not high-up enough in Society to have been able to go anywhere near the exclusive club. They held assemblies only on Wednesdays, and one could only attend by obtaining a voucher from one of the patronesses. They were notoriously picksome concerning who was allowed to attend. He supposed that if they knew the truth of Mrs. Wyndham's family, they would not have allowed her admittance. However, she had done well to cover it, and he had no plans to out her, when it would reflect so poorly upon his sisters and even himself, though the connection between him and Mrs. Wyndham was tenuous at best.

Not much longer, and Rose was prepared to leave. Ash handed each of the ladies into the carriage, and they rode to Almack's. Violet was visibly nervous, twisting the ends of her scarf and her face was pale. She stepped down from the carriage last, and Ash leaned in to whisper to her.

"Cheer up, sister, for you may meet your Earl here."

She giggled lightly and dropped the ends of her shawl. "I shall do no such thing."

By this time, they had entered the exclusive club, and made their way to the assembly rooms abovestairs. After they were announced, the party stepped into the cavernous space. After glancing about the room,

Ash looked over and saw that Violet was rather awe-struck by the sumptuous I, the high ceilings, rich curtains, and highly-polished floors. The *ntil* of London Society was present, all in their finest gowns and suits. Violet paled again for a moment, until she looked to their right. She visibly brightened, and a smile appeared upon her face. Ash followed her gaze and spotted Miss Drayton approaching them. Ash had not the slightest idea with what type of fabric her dress was made, but it was white with red trim, and it was of the first fashion.

What an absurd thought that she might be the one for whom Violet is toiling over those dresses.

Eleven

PENELOPE COULD NOT at all account for the disdainful glances cast her way. Just yesterday, she was greeted by Lady Sefton, one of the esteemed patronesses of the club, while walking on Bond Street. Penelope had been permitted to purchase a voucher for the exclusive club during her first season, and every season since. And yet, this evening she was being avoided by most of the *bonne ton*. Upon arriving at Almack's with Aunt Essie, Penelope was immediately snubbed. *And not only by the patronesses,* she thought, *but by everyone present! It is terribly disconcerting, especially after the last couple of days I have had.*

Twenty-four hours ago, her brother had arrived at the house in a terrible state. She had not seen him for several weeks, so she assumed he had been staying with friends. His clothes were rumpled, his face bruised, and his eyes glassy with too much drink. Penelope had struggled to assist him to his rooms, where he collapsed on the bed. This morning, when she awoke, he was still sound asleep. Fear and disappointment mounting, she had retreated to her studio to paint for the day. It was a place of refuge for her, the rhythmic motion of brush against canvas soothing to her spirit. In the evening, she returned to the house to prepare for the assembly.

She wore her only new evening gown, the one which she purchased from Madame Bélanger. The dressmaker had been true to her promise, and after Penelope drew designs for the duration of three weeks, she was given her choice of fabrics and patterns; the three dresses were yet to be finished, but with the generous assistance of Violet Wyndham, Penelope was turned out quite well.

They cannot be snubbing me for my dress . . . can they?

Truly, Penelope could think of no other reason for the change. She had arrived at the assembly rooms with her Aunt Essie, who still acted as chaperone as she had ever since Penelope's come-out, in a newly-made gown of the first fashion.

I still am meeting every requirement of Polite Society, at least to their eyes.

Even so, the number of whispers which followed her and the slights given her by those turning away rather than speaking with her bore evidence that all was not as it had been.

It was with great relief that Penelope noticed Violet Wyndham's arrival with her party. So great was her relief, in fact, that she hurried toward her friend before having time to consider whether she would still be well-received. As she drew near, though, a disconcerting thought caused her to slow her pace.

Has whatever <u>on-dit</u> circulating about me also reached Violet's ears? Her family? Perhaps she will no longer wish to associate with me.

Penelope nearly halted her steps.

She needn't have worried, though, for when Violet's eyes turned her way, she quickly moved to greet her. "Penny! I am so glad to see you," Violet said in a rush. "There are so very *many* people here with whom I am not acquainted, and I *cannot* bear to face them. Ash is very kind, but not at all understanding of my discomfort. He simply ignores those with whom he does not wish to converse, but I cannot. But neither can I speak to them!"

Penelope was greatly relieved that Violet apparently had not heard or had simply discounted whatever gossip was circulating. So much so, in fact, that she watched Violet's smiling face grow more serious, until her smile dropped altogether and her brows furrowed.

"Are you unwell, Penny?"

"Hm?" Penelope shook her head and smiled back belatedly. "Oh! Forgive me. I was distracted."

"Whatever is the matter?"

Penelope's smile dropped. "Have you heard anything lately concerning me?"

"From where?" Violet leaned closer and lowered her voice to a whisper. "Has someone revealed your secret? I promise, 'twas not I."

"I do not believe so, but it has been so odd. Upon my arrival, everyone has been avoiding me, and a few even opened their fans when I passed by and began whispering furiously whilst glancing my way."

"Heavens!" cried Violet. "Are you certain?"

"I am afraid so. I wondered if you had heard what is the matter."

"I have not. But it is quite certain that my sister or mama would have heard. Shall I go inquire?"

The idea of knowing what was circulating about her brought Penelope both trepidation and relief. As she could not decide which would be better – knowing the worst, or not knowing and wondering – she decided she would rather know.

"Would you, please?"

"Of course." Violet glanced about, Penelope with her, and the two spied several sets of eyes following their movement as they strolled about the ballroom. She looked about some more, then pulled Penelope toward the wall. "Perhaps wait behind this curtain, and I will return when I have ascertained the rumors?"

"Thank you, Violet." Penelope almost said no more, but just as Violet was turning to leave, she said in a rush, "And do not think that I am unaware of the sacrifice you will make. Your sister and mother do not treat you with anywhere near the respect you deserve. I imagine that you had hoped to pass much of the evening out of their presence."

Violet grinned ruefully. "I can abide them, especially in the service of a friend."

"You are a gem, Violet. Truly."

Penelope saw that no eyes were upon her, so she slipped behind the curtain. She found herself in a small alcove, the far side of which was a large window. The space was small, but would certainly accommodate two people upon Violet's return.

Peering through the curtain, Penelope saw that Violet did not have far to go to find her family. Penelope believed she could have heard the conversation had the room not already been filled with music and conversation which drowned out whatever words were being uttered most emphatically by Mrs. Wyndham. Penelope watched from her hiding place until finally Violet broke away from them, but instead of returning, she walked in the opposite direction.

At first glance, Penelope was inclined to feel hurt, until she noticed what Violet was doing. With steady progress, she made her way around the outside of the room, with an occasional glance toward her family, which was even less frequently followed by a glance in Penelope's direction. At one point, Violet was detained by a young man approaching her. He bowed, she curtsied, and he gestured toward someone whom Penelope could not see. She could see, though, that Violet blushed, hurriedly nodded her head, and then moved on her way.

After several more minutes, Violet had made her way about the entire room, and joined Penelope behind the curtain. While she was certainly eager for information regarding the rumors, Penelope could not help but tease her friend.

"Did that young man ask you to dance?"

Violet's face reddened anew, much to Penelope's amusement, and said breathlessly, "No, he did not. He . . . asked if he might introduce me to his friend just before the next set. And if I might consider . . . gracing his friend with a dance."

"And you agreed?"

"I suppose I did. I scarcely know! I was in such a hurry to get back to you." Violet's face grew serious and she paused to catch her breath before continuing. "My mama forbade me from continuing my acquaintance with you, so I could not very well immediately return to you, or she would see. I told her that I was greatly troubled to hear that, and wished to take a turn about the room, to collect myself. I fear, though, that until we find a way to fix this, our friendship must be hidden."

Violet was apologetic as she said this, her face displaying such misery that Penelope could not help the laughter which bubbled up her throat. She could only laugh and watch as Violet's face became more and more troubled.

"Oh, I do hope I have not sent you into hysterics, Penny!" the girl cried.

"No!" gasped out Penelope. "Not in the least!"

"Then why *ever* are you laughing? I see nothing humorous in this situation."

Penelope drew a deep breath to calm her laughter before speaking. "I feared that you would not want to associate with me any longer, and now you say that you will continue to do so, even after your mother has said that you may not. I can hardly believe that you would defy her."

Violet fidgeted with her shawl for a moment before she stood up straighter and looked Penelope straight in the eye." I cannot agree with her reasons. You have done nothing wrong, and I will not scorn our friendship because some terrible rumors are circulating about your brother."

This brought Penelope up short. "My brother?"

"I know you had mentioned that his management left much to be desired, but I cannot believe the rumors being spread about him."

Penelope felt all the levity leave her in a heartbeat, a very heavy heartbeat.

"What are these rumors?"

"Of nonsense!" Violet tried to avoid answering.

"Of drunkenness, over-spending, and keeping company with the wrong sort of people? Of excess gaming and cheating and all sorts of terrible things?"

Violet's stunned silence said enough.

"It is true. He is worse than a cad." Penelope found she could not meet Violet's innocent, shocked eyes any longer. She dropped her head, and began to fidget with the trim on the front of her skirt. "I did not reveal the extent of his transgressions because I had hoped they would never touch me in any manner which mattered. I see I was wrong."

Violet's tentative hand upon Penelope's forearm stilled her hands, and she glanced up to meet her friend's sad eyes.

"Penelope, they are not your sins."

"And yet I am the one to pay for them, am I not?"

Violet shook her head, and smiled ruefully ash she whispered, "But you needn't. Your plan to be free can succeed still. We must simply find a way to add credibility to your name, that your connection with P. Greene is not a deterrent of others frequenting his studio. I suppose that this unpleasantness could prove harmful for P. Greene's business?"

"Yes, at such an early stage in his career it would be most detrimental. And as I am his only outright patroness, the only one promoting him as an artist, I can see no other way to save him."

"I am not well-known enough to help much. Perhaps my brother..."

"Pray do not tell him!"

"Oh, no. But if he could be persuaded to support the artist?"

"Perhaps." But Penelope was unconvinced, and fear made her hesitate before suggesting, "Perhaps we might arrange a meeting tomorrow at Hyde Park. Your mama will not allow you to call at my house, and I am fairly certain I would not be well-received at your house. However, if we should happen to see one another at a park, no one could fault us."

"This is true. I am certain that Ash and I could very easily slip away from Mama and Rose tomorrow."

"Will your brother not dislike my presence, same as your mother?"

Violet shook her head before saying, "He has not spoken to me about it yet, but he did not looked pleased while Mama was speaking to me. He frowned more and more with every word she spoke."

Penelope experienced an unexpected current of happiness at her words, but quickly suppressed it. She did not know why she should feel happy at his approbation. *His good opinion would allow him to assist Violet in meeting with me. That is all.*

Violet was silent for a moment, but her face indicated a strong desire to speak. She pressed her lips together for a moment, brows furrowed, until she finally opened her mouth and spoke. "Penelope, I know that you are wary of informing anyone else of your circumstances, but I truly believe that Ash would be a discreet and trustworthy confidant. He has a disdain for Society that I have only ever seen rivaled in yourself, so I cannot believe that he would think less of you for your plan." Penelope wanted to protest, and began to do so, but Violet held up a hand to hush her and continued. "Now, as for his ability to help. He is quickly becoming a sought-after guest; even if I was inclined to enjoy parties, it would be impossible to attend all to which he has been invited. Mama and Rose are ecstatic with his new popularity. At any rate, his popularity, used in support of P. Greene, might be just the thing to help get you past this difficult time."

Penelope considered her options for a moment. *There is really very little I can do alone to salvage this situation. Unfortunately, this might be a time that*

I must rely on others. And I must admit to feeling that Mr. Wyndham is likely one of the only men of my acquaintance who might prove trustworthy.

Feeling that there was very little else she might say, Penelope murmured, "Very well."

Violet asked gently, "Shall I go and fetch him?"

Penelope hesitated a moment before nodding. "Please."

Violet peeked through the curtains briefly before stepping out of the alcove. In very little time at all, Violet returned, followed closely by the tall figure of Mr. Wyndham.

"Mr. Wyndham," Penelope greeted him. She felt her control of the situation slipping from her fingers, and hoped that by greeting him first, she might regain it.

"Miss Drayton," he returned, bowing as she curtsied. "Allow me to assure you that I am most certainly not in agreement with Mrs. Wyndham and her dictates. I shall have Violet at Hyde Park tomorrow at whatever time suits her."

"Thank you, sir." Penelope did her best to hide the discomfort she felt at someone else knowing her shame. "I greatly appreciate your sympathy, as well as your kindness."

"It is shameful to fault one person for the actions of someone to whom they are simply related." He shook his head, and Penelope saw his eyes flit to the side, where Mrs. Wyndham and Rose had last been. "In fact, because I am my own master, and must not bend to her wishes, I believe I can aid your farther. Would you care to dance?"

Penelope felt her stomach give an odd swoop at the thought of repeatedly holding his hand whenever the steps of the dance brought them together, even with both of their hands covered by gloves. Another thought occurred to her, though, and she felt compelled to say, "A dance would be lovely, especially as it is likely to be the only offer I receive all evening, but will it not harm your own reputation?"

Mr. Wyndham laughed darkly and said, "I fear that in the eyes of these mothers and their daughters, I can do no wrong."

"They have been rather like bees buzzing about the only flower in a meadow, have they not?" commented Violet.

"Worse."

Penelope offered a hesitant smile and said, "As it appears that you have thought of the possible repercussions of a dance with me, and still extend the offer, I cannot very well decline, can I?"

Mr. Wyndham extended his hand. Penelope delicately placed her fingertips in his palm.

"Ash, I see what you are doing," said Violet knowingly.

Surprised, Penelope asked, "Whatever do you mean, Violet?"

"Only that Ash's motives are not entirely altruistic."

Fear, cold and prickly, began growing in her midsection. *I finally venture to trust, and now this. I ought to have known he would have a selfish motive.*

But the deep voice of Mr. Wyndham cut into her thoughts. "My approbation should aid you at least for the evening, Miss Drayton. As for the benefit to me, if I am left alone, even if only for the evening, I will certainly count our dance a success."

Penelope nearly laughed with relief.

Never before had Penelope found her suspicious nature anything less than logical, but now the thought occurred to her that perhaps she needn't fear the worst in everyone. She did not have time to dwell on it, though, for the fair gentleman with whom Violet had been speaking earlier was approaching.

"Oh, Violet," Penelope said, "are you not engaged with someone for this dance? I suppose you had better go meet him."

Violet's eyes widened and her lips parted in surprise. "B-but I cannot!"

"She needn't dance if she does not wish it," said Mr. Wyndham, his face concerned and watchful.

Penelope smiled at Violet assuringly and said, "You will be fine, Violet. Pretend it is Mr. Wyndham here with whom you dance." She gently tugged on Mr. Wyndham's arm. She meant to lead them to another area to talk, and allow Violet a moment with her dance partner. Mr. Wyndham, however, led toward the floor where dancers milled about, waiting for the orchestra to finish their break.

"The dance will not start for several moments yet, will it?" asked Penelope.

"Yes, but we may as well take our places. The longer we are seen together, the better for you, as well as for me."

As they walked, Mr. Wyndham glanced about to find his sister.

"She is there, a bit to your left," Penelope said lowly.

He turned his head in that direction, where Violet stood with two gentlemen. The fair one from earlier was smiling a great deal while the other, who boasted dark hair and a grand stature, had a terribly stern visage. After a moment, the smiling gentleman bowed and walked away, leaving Violet and the other man, whose face slowly formed into a scowl.

"He needn't look so pleased to be in my sister's company." Mr. Wyndham's sarcastic words caught Penelope's attention and she turned to see a frown on his face that rivaled that of Violet's dancing partner.

More dancers soon gathered, while the musicians tuned their instruments and practiced a bar here and there. Penelope was forced, by necessity, to stand a bit closer to Mr. Wyndham. She said quietly, so as to prevent eaves-droppers, "Perhaps he is as uncomfortable in company as is she, and not so skilled at hiding it."

Mr. Wyndham turned to look at her, surprise on his face. "You would speak against me?"

"Why would I not when you are drawing negative attention to your sweet sister? If others heard you complain, they would likely draw the conclusion that your family hoped for a match between Violet and Lord Reymes."

"Who is Reymes?"

"The man standing up with Violet."

"Is that him? I have heard rumors of him, but never seen the man."

"Yes. He has only recently come into his title."

"Poor man, dealing simultaneously with the loss of his father and the barrage of females hoping to snare him."

"You do not think that the income associated with his title and his newfound fame might ease the pain of his loss?" she asked, amused.

"I think that very little can ease the loss of a beloved parent."

"I would not know how that feels."

Mr. Wyndham looked at her askance, and Penelope was mortified that she had spoken aloud. She knew she was bitter about her father and his habits, and bitter that her mother had been taken from her at so young an age. However, she was used to exercising much more skill at hiding that bitterness when in company.

The music started, and Penelope determined to behave as though she had not spoken those words.

"Have you before attended an assembly at Almack's, Mr. Wyndham?"

The dance separated them for a moment, but he answered as their steps led down the row. "No, I've not. You?"

"Yes. While my brother is not highly-ranked, he is still a member of the peerage. While I suppose that does not guarantee one a voucher, it is beneficial."

Mr. Wyndham laughed, and she found the sound pleasing to her ears. After a brief separation in the dance, he answered with a wry grin, "To be sure. In my case, it was not until I was known to stand to inherit a title and a fortune that I was considered good *ton*."

"And allowed to purchase a voucher?"

"Indeed."

They danced the remainder of the time with little conversation between them. Penelope could feel the eyes and hear the whispers about them, but she chose to ignore it. For the time, she had two allies amongst this Society, in Violet and now in Mr. Wyndham. Tomorrow they would attempt to find a solution. Truly, this was more than she had expected upon the start of the Season.

After the dance, she received one or two nods from ladies who had previously snubbed her. Penelope hoped to engage them in conversation, to ascertain whether the snubbing was truly over. First, though, she desperately needed to find Violet and ask how she had enjoyed her dance. Penelope found her on the other side of the room.

"Violet!" she called and walked over to her. "Did you enjoy your dance?"

Glancing about, Violet motioned for her to follow. Once they were partially hidden from Mrs. Wyndham and Rose – whom Penelope had not seen or even thought to avoid – Violet smiled slightly.

"I do hope that you understand that I am not ashamed to be seen with you. But if Mama should see me talking with you, after she told me to not, she would watch more closely, and I would surely never be able to see or speak –"

"Violet, I understand. Please do not trouble yourself." Penelope clasped her friend's hand warmly. "Tell me about your dance."

The girl's face was suddenly aflame, and she looked down, fiddling with her gloves. When she spoke, her voice was subdued. "He danced very well."

"He was Lord Reymes, was he not? He ought to have."

"Yes. His friend, Lord Stallingsworth, introduced us. I met *him* at the park earlier in the Season. Both gentlemen seemed most surprised that I had no idea who Lord Reymes was."

"I must confess that I myself am rather surprised as well."

Violet gave a small shrug of her shoulders.

"Well, never mind that." Penelope smiled. "Did he make intelligent conversation?"

"We scarcely spoke."

"Why ever not?"

"Penelope. You know how much difficulty I have speaking to others."

"And he was no better?"

"I do not know if it was discomfort, or if he simply did not care for my company."

"Or anyone's company?"

Violet paused, pressing her lips together for a moment before speaking. "His eyes were sad. I believe that he grieves deeply for his father. Perhaps he does not feel equal to the task of making conversation, but was forced to dance by his friend?"

"You are too kind, Violet. Not all men are as good as your brother." Penelope could hear the bitterness in her voice, but could not find it in herself to hide it.

"Oh I know that, Penny."

Violet's sad smile as she spoke brought a question to Penelope's lips.

"Who has made this known to you?"

An unasked question echoed in her mind: *If this is true, how are you still able to believe the best about this stranger?*

Violet glanced about before speaking. "I do not wish to malign the deceased, but my own papa was oppressed by great sadness and could rarely find it in himself to behave in a fatherly manner. Oh, he was never unkind or hurtful, but he avoided my presence. I cannot say why, for while he was not an attentive father, he did not ignore Ash or Rose to the extent he did me. I fear that my presence gave him pain."

"How could your presence give anyone pain, Violet?" Penelope asked, indignant for the sake of her friend.

"I cannot say why," repeated Violet patiently, "only that such anguish was present whenever he looked at me, especially as I began to mature. I did my best to spare him."

"How absurd!" Penelope was incensed. That anyone could spurn such a dear girl's presence was unbelievable. "There must have been another reason."

Violet shook her head sadly. "I've tried and tried, and cannot for the life of me imagine another explanation. Perhaps it is the reason my mama does not care much for my presence, either."

Penelope had a great deal to say about *that*, but as it was, a gentleman arrived to collect Violet for the next set. To her surprise, another young man approached soon after, asking Penelope to stand up with him. Indeed, it appeared that Mr. Wyndham was rather insightful; his dancing with her had restored at least a modicum of her respectability in the eyes of some of the *bonne ton* present that evening.

After her third dance, Penelope decided to leave. Her aunt, sitting along the walls of the room with the other ladies who were not her dancing, was amenable to leaving early, and the two rode quietly in the hackney back to the house in Leicester Square.

Penelope's mind swirled with all the events of the evening. She was dismayed that Violet's parents had been so unfeeling toward her, but she supposed it did rather explain the girl's low opinion of herself. Penelope knew that had she been in the same place as Violet, though, she would certainly not be seeking an explanation which left any excuse for her parents' treatment of her. These thoughts, coupled with the disconcerting events of the evening, made for a rather melancholy mood as Penelope arrived home and readied for bed.

Twelve

I⊤ WAS NOT often that Ash allowed himself to indulge in thoughts of Miss Giles. She had, after all, spurned him at her father's displeasure with the match. Following the assembly at Almack's, however, he allowed his mind to travel down those dark and winding paths to the place where he stored his memories of her.

She had been light and joy upon their meeting. Never before had he so strongly desired a deeper acquaintance with another person. He was overwhelmed by the unfamiliar sensibility which accompanied his making her acquaintance. As their affection deepened, a betrothal was mentioned and she had allowed him to kiss her. He had never kissed a girl before, and the meeting of their lips overwhelmed his senses, leaving him thirsting for more of the same. She did not suffer the same affliction, however, and easily broke off all contact with him at the merest word from her father. A hastily-scribbled note delivered by an errand boy told him that she would no longer receive his attentions. It was after her cold rejection of him that Ash hardened his heart to love.

An idea had taken seed during the assembly at Almack's, however, and as he and Violet drove to Hyde Park early the following evening, Ash was all shades of uncertain. It was true that he had determined to avoid allying himself with a woman for as long as possible, but what he had in mind was not necessarily a true alliance. Furthermore, if all occurred as he hoped it might, the arrangement could very well benefit him, as well as Miss Drayton. There was no time to dwell further upon it, though, for they arrived at the park.

Already there were many pedestrians ambling about the footpaths surrounding the Serpentine, and horse-drawn equipages moved along the lanes. Ash drove his curricle into Rotten Row; the horses moved quickly and gracefully along the lane. Back and forth they went, turning at the end to race again toward the other side. Ash could tell his animals were enjoying themselves, with their head-tossing and whinnying. He kept them driving for upwards of a quarter-hour before he turned to another driving lane where they could set a more sedate pace. Ash and Violet both began looking for Miss Drayton.

"I do hope that nothing has detained her," murmured Violet. Ash glanced over to see her brow furrowed and her lips thinned as she cast her eyes about for her friend.

"She will be along presently, I am sure," Ash said, but when another quarter-hour had passed, and they still had not seen her, Ash felt his own brow begin to crease and his heart fill with an unfamiliar discomfort. *What if her brother's unscrupulous ways are not limited to harming his own self?* The sensation in his heart was similar to that which he felt once, a long time ago, when Violet lost herself in the labyrinth behind their home. He spent hours searching for her.

"There she is," said Violet suddenly, and Ash felt the air leave his lungs in a rush, relief flooding him before he could even consider whether he ought to be relieved. It was short-lived, though – if relief indeed it was – for when he turned to look where Violet had indicated, he saw the disconcerting sight of Miss Drayton seated in a carriage with another gentleman. Ash was not bothered by her being preset with a gentleman, but rather by who that gentleman was. The man's dark curls and vibrant eyes marked him as none other than the infamous brother, Lord Claymore. Seeing him seated now beside Miss Drayton, Ash realized that he had been one of those at the card-table at his club all those weeks ago.

Another glance in Violet's direction and Ash saw that the presence of the strange gentleman had thrown his sister into something of a dilemma. If he knew his sister as he thought he did, she was struggling between her desire to remain quiet and unseen in the presence of a man whom she did not know, and the desire to speak up and alert her friend to their presence. Violet's worried eyes and wringing hands certainly indicated that he was likely correct. With a sigh, Ash pulled up on his animal's reins and called out, "Miss Drayton!"

She looked in their direction. Her smile was ready, but her voice hesitant. "Mr. Wyndham, Miss Wyndham. How good to see you!"

"Indeed," intoned Ash drily. He took on a haughty demeanor, as it had proved useful in some circumstances. "I am all astonishment to see the *both* of you this morning. Unfortunately, Miss Drayton, I am unfamiliar with your companion."

"Of course. Brother, may I present Mr. and Miss Wyndham. Violet, Mr. Wyndham: this is my brother, Lord Claymore."

Lord Claymore stood in his equipage and reaching out, bowed deeply over Violet's outstretched hand, causing her face to color up. "A pleasure," Ash heard him murmur against Violet's hand.

"Yes, it is." Ash leveled his eyes at the other man's, his gaze scarcely friendlier than a glare.

"How do you do," sounded Violet's quiet murmur just before Miss Drayton hurriedly grasped her brother's arm, rather forcefully pulling him from Violet. Ash smiled at Miss Drayton and was rather surprised to see her blush lightly.

"Cornelius, Miss Wyndham is my friend. I shall tolerate none of your usual behavior with her." From Miss Drayton's low tone, Ash suspected that she did not intend for him or Violet to hear. The effect of the words was immediately apparent, however, as Lord Claymore's suave grin immediately dropped.

"She likely is a dead bore, at any rate," he grumbled to himself. Ash was disinclined to be offended for his sister's sake, as he suspected it was better for a lady if this gentleman thought her a bore rather than someone he would like to know. As it was, Ash had no time to react to the comment, for Lord Claymore continued speaking almost immediately. "So Wyndham, you are the one who has been foolish enough for fall for my sister."

Ash's surprise was great, not only at the man's forward statement – *Although why I should be I cannot say; he has already said much worse since our introduction.* – but at the similarity of their thoughts. Not that he had in actuality fallen for Miss Drayton, but it certainly must appear so if he should decide to follow through with his idea. *If Miss Drayton is amenable to my idea, that is,* he amended his thoughts.

"I cannot say at this point," Ash said loftily, "as I've not yet had a chance to discuss it with the lady."

Lord Claymore gazed at Ash for a moment, his eyes calculating, before bowing deeply. "Indeed. In that case, I shall leave you to it. Pleasure to make your acquaintance, and all that. Miss Wyndham, would you care to accompany me in a ride about the park? Leave your brother and my sister to settle their understanding, if one is to be reached."

"No!" cried Miss Drayton at the same time as Ash. He demurred to her, however, for further comment. "Brother, Miss Wyndham is such a close friend that I have no objection to her presence. It would be inappropriate, after all, for us to lack a chaperone." Her questioning gaze behind Lord Claymore's back caused Ash to squirm a bit.

At his nod, though, Lord Claymore proceeded to hand Miss Drayton down from the carriage. Ash stood and stretched out his hand to assist her in climbing into the curricle. As she stepped up, he saw the front of her pelisse skirts fall open, revealing the green skirt of her gown—the very same material which Violet had been sewing just the week previous. He said nothing, though, and assisted her in sitting beside Violet, on the end of the bench.

"Very well, Pen." Claymore gathered up the reins of his animals. "I shall see you at home, I suppose. Do remember our discussion the other day."

Miss Drayton nodded stiffly as Ash flicked the reins, commanding the horses to walk on. The animals had not taken ten steps before Miss Drayton drew an audible breath and spoke.

"I do apologize, Violet," she began, "for my brother's abominable behavior. I had hoped that you would never meet with him, but he arrived home at the time I was about to leave, and insisted upon accompanying me. That is why I am late."

Ash felt his sister shift uncomfortably beside him, and glanced at her in time to see a fresh blush fading from her cheeks as she said, "It is of little consequence, Penny. He did not importune me in the least, and if he would have, you were a most excellent deterrent."

Miss Drayton caught his eye with a small grin. "Yes, but do not discount the part your brother played in preventing his advances. I wish that I had a brother who protected me similarly."

Surprised by Miss Drayton's warm words, Ash sucked in a large amount of air and did his best to calm his suddenly racing heart. *What on earth?*

"Forgive me," murmured Miss Drayton. "That was an impolitic thought to voice."

Thinking of his sister Violet without the support which he did his best to provide, Ash said with feeling, "There is nothing to forgive. Each of us ought to have the support of someone. Dare I be so bold as to say that I suspect you have lacked much of that in your life, Miss Drayton?"

"Ash," cautioned Violet, "you speak too familiarly and without the knowledge necessary to make such an assertion."

Ash hesitated, knowing his familiar speech had grown from not only his thoughts regarding his own sister, but also from his thoughts regarding Miss Drayton and the necessary deepening of the relationship there, should she agree to his proposal. And he would make it, Ash realized. If she was amenable, there really was no reason not to do so.

"Of course you are right, Violet." He steered the horses from Hyde Park and down the street. "Now *you* must forgive *me*, Miss Drayton."

"Of course," she returned immediately.

"While we are on the topic of overly-familiar behavior, might I broach a subject of some delicacy?"

The curious tilt of Miss Drayton's head contrasted with the cautious and rather alarmed expression upon Violet's face. When the latter did not answer, the former nodded her head.

"While I do not know – and neither do I care to know – all of the particulars of your brother's indiscretions, Miss Drayton, I am aware that you are suffering personally as a result. I am not one to pander to the demands of Society, having been burned by it too severely to do so, but I am not averse to manipulating it in order to achieve some nobler goal."

The alarm on Violet's face faded as confusion began to take its place. "Speak plainly, brother. Whatever can you mean?"

"I believe, Miss Drayton, that it would be mutually beneficial for you and me to put forth the appearance of our having formed an attachment."

Ash did not know what Miss Drayton's reaction might be, but fear certainly was not one for which he was prepared. Her face fell ashen, her eyes round and her mouth tight and worried.

"Ash," scolded Violet gently, "You cannot be in earnest! Not that I would object to having Miss Drayton as a sister – I should like that very much indeed! But what a thing to ask a lady in company, especially one with whom you are so little acquainted!"

He glanced to Miss Drayton, hoping she might say something. For a brief moment, he felt as foolish as when he received the note from Miss Giles, but he forcibly reminded himself that was the past. He must remain in the present if his idea was to be explained.

"I beg your pardon, Miss Drayton. I meant no offense. Merely that a staged engagement would benefit your standing in the *ton*, and it would certainly aid me in keeping the match-making mamas and their debutant daughters at bay."

"Oh! I had thought—"

"I suppose I was not entirely clear," interrupted Ash. "When I said that we ought to *put forth the appearance* of an attachment, I meant it quite literally. Please understand, Miss Drayton — you are a lovely girl, and would make someone an excellent wife. But I have no plans to marry until it is a necessity."

"Well, I plan never to marry, Mr. Wyndham," said Miss Drayton lowly. Ash noticed that her face had begun to regain some of its color.

"Then we are in good company, Miss Drayton," smiled Ash.

"How can you become engaged and yet never marry?" asked Violet. "Would not everyone expect a wedding to follow an engagement?"

"Perhaps," allowed Ash, "but I am certain we can manage to avoid that."

"My brother would likely seek satisfaction, Mr. Wyndham. Not in the form of a duel, but he might sue you for breach of contract." She smiled suddenly. "But if you plan to remain single for quite some time, your reputation would certainly have sufficient time to recover from my having cried off, would it not?"

Ash could not decide whether to be pleased that the lady was so much relieved at his *not* desiring to marry her that she could assist in planning their subterfuge, or to be offended. Pushing those thoughts aside, however, he cleared his throat and answered, "Yes, that would certainly accomplish our purposes."

"Would you speak to my brother, to have all things official and to avoid suspicion?"

"Do you think it necessary?"

"Likely it is, but I fear that his interest in my marrying is not born of his desire to see me well-settled." Miss Drayton hesitated, her gaze dropping to her fingers fidgeting in her lap. "You see, his debt is so great and so pressing that he was prepared to marry me off to the highest bidder. I was able to delay this, begging him to allow me to marry for love, in exchange for the promise of my dowry being given to him once it is accessible to me."

Violet spoke for the first time in a while. "He would agree to this, knowing you are determined not to marry?"

Miss Drayton's voice was chagrined as she answered, "He does not know my true feelings in this matter."

In light of this newfound knowledge, Ash feared that perhaps this plan, while of immediate benefit to the lady, might in actuality bring her pain after all was done. He spoke cautiously. "He would likely be angry as a result of the deception, though, would he not? Would you be in danger of being cut off?" It would not do for Miss Drayton to lose everything after the effort of assisting her.

"It matters not," said Miss Drayton, "for if all goes according to plan, *he* shall be cut off from *me*, and I will never be required to see him again."

Ash was mildly shocked at the force of her words, but before he could decide to comment upon it, Violet spoke.

"Never, Penny?" Violet's furrowed brow and frowning mouth gave away her distress at such a lack of sensibility toward Miss Drayton's brother. "I cannot imagine—"

"Never," Miss Drayton asserted. "He has long since ceased brotherly behavior toward me." Her words saddened Ash as he thought of Violet ever speaking such of him.

Then again, I should never treat Violet as deplorably as it seems Lord Claymore has treated his sister. Indeed, if even half of those rumors being circulated are true, I cannot very well blame her for those feelings concerning his impending absence from her life. Would that I might so separate myself from Mrs. Wyndham and Rose. Feeling some guilt from such an unkind thought, regardless of whether he sometimes felt it to be true, Ash amended with, *Or a respite at the least.*

"How very sad," whispered Violet, bringing him back to the present conversation.

"Not all people are as kindly-disposed toward others as you are, Violet, even to their siblings," said Miss Drayton, her face taking on a pinched appearance, as though she had tasted something bitter.

"I am aware," murmured Violet lowly.

Miss Drayton winced, as if realizing with whom she was speaking. "I am sorry, Violet, to have forgotten what you shared with me last evening, or that your own sister and mother are not as concerned for your happiness as they ought to be."

"Think nothing of it," replied Violet. "It cannot be the same as your case, for I cannot imagine being separated from them."

"Even when their treatment of you is so deplorable?"

"Indeed. My mama has lost her husband, and I cannot imagine how terrible a loss that would be."

"Not so terrible as to cause her to treat you with such disdain." Ash shook his head.

Miss Drayton seemed to be considering Violet for a moment before she said, "Violet, do you look very much like your father did? I really see very little resemblance of your mother."

Surprise showed on Violet's face at the unexpected remark, but she answered evenly, "I take after him to an extent. Perhaps it is a grandparent whom I resemble. I do not believe I have ever met any of them."

"Is that so? Neither did I," said Penelope. "Your mother is so much fairer than you, and her eyes a pale blue to your green."

Violet had a smile in her voice as she said, "You and Ash would make quite the striking couple, with your dark, classic looks, and his fair hair and tall stature." But then she shook her head, a frown marring her features. "I really cannot agree, though, with this deception. Do you not feel it unconscionable to perpetuate a falsehood?"

Ash spoke carefully but with determination. "Violet, I have no wish to put down your strong convictions as Rose so often does, but please recall that the *ton* has made the first offense. It has decided that now I am to inherit a title and a fortune, I am a desirable catch. It has also decided that Miss Drayton, due to the ill behavior of her brother, is not good *ton*. We are merely playing the same game as they, using their love for gossip to give creditability to Miss Drayton's person, and to fend off the females who would set their caps for me."

"Even at the expense of the truth?"

Ash was about to speak when Miss Drayton did first. "They have no compunction with condemning me along with my brother, Violet. They have already broken trust."

"And you may therefore disregard the truth?"

Miss Drayton glanced at him briefly before addressing Violet's question. "Our engagement will be real. We both simply know that it will be dissolved before its natural conclusion."

Violet shook her head, facing forward once again. "I do not know . . . "

"All will be well, Violet," declared Ash. "You shall see."

Violet said no more, but assumed a neutral countenance. Ash turned to Miss Drayton and asked, "And so are we engaged? Have we an agreement?"

"It would seem so."

Ash knew that the next topic of discussion he wished to address would likely not be received so well as the first – which, he must admit went much better than it might have. Drawing a deep breath for a bit of courage, he leaned forward to peer around Violet to see Miss Drayton's face.

"Ought you to tell me your full story, then, Miss Drayton? I should not like to be surprised by something which as your fiancé, I ought to know."

Miss Drayton was silent for a time. When Ash glanced over, he saw that she wrung her hands nervously, opening her mouth as if to speak, and immediately shutting it. At length, though, she spoke.

"It began quite a while ago. My mama painted a great deal, and I suppose her love of that passed to me. After my father's passing, it became clear that he did not provide well for my future – he left a great deal of debt, and while my dowry was untouched, I had already determined to never submit myself to the sort of bondage which masquerades as marriage."

"Marriage cannot be all bad," interjected Violet. "With a good man who fears God and who will care for his wife–"

"Even so, I cannot bear to submit myself to any man." Miss Drayton scowled and shook her head.

Wanting to return the conversation to her tale, as well as to diffuse the sudden tension in the air, Ash commented, "Your conviction, Miss Drayton, bodes well for the success of our plan." He smiled when her frown lessened a bit. "You mentioned your father's poor provision?"

"Oh, yes." Miss Drayton's shoulders relaxed. "After learning of my father's lack of economy and abysmal management – and even squandering – of my family's resources, and knowing of my brother's profligate manner of life, I decided then that I must find a way to support myself."

"You do not mean that you intend to engage in a trade?"

"Of a sort. Through careful saving of my allowance, and selling several non-essential items, I have been able to purchase a small studio. I have already opened it as the workplace of P. Greene, and set up my man of business to live in the apartment above it."

"You intend to sponsor the Invisible Painter?"

"I am the Invisible Painter."

Ash's mind was whirling in all sort of different directions, and he realized somewhere in the whirlwind of his thoughts that it was a good thing his horses knew their way about Town so well, or the carriage might very well have run off the road. "Bu-but how are you. . . that is, what have you done to . . . what I mean to say . . ."

But then he decided that it would be best to perhaps simply listen until Miss Drayton had finished speaking. He shook his head and gestured for her to continue.

"I have long practiced strict economy with my own allowance, and have been saving since even before my father's death. It was my plan to promote the artist until he became sufficiently popular and respected to garner his own clientele. After I learned of the great debt my brother had accumulated, I cut my expenses even more. It was a happy coincidence that I met Violet, and she is so very talented with a needle and so obliging as to make over several old gowns of my mother's for me."

"As well as some old draperies?" asked Ash as Violet murmured, "It was entirely providential."

Miss Drayton glanced at Violet for a moment with a gentle smile before shifting her eyes again to Ash. "Yes, some draperies as well. I had hoped no one would know."

"I saw Violet sewing the dress you wear now, and she told me that she was sewing it for the poor."

Ash turned his eyes to his sister at this, curious how she would respond to his unasked question: *How could you lie to me about the recipient of this dress and still scold us for planning this harmless deception?*

Violet blushed before saying, "I did make several items for the poor with what was left after her dresses were finished. I did not intend to lie, Ash. Indeed, I never intended for you to see what I was making at all. That is why I kept it in my chambers and worked there."

Ash laughed, Miss Drayton soon following suit. "Do not fret, Violet. I was merely teasing you."

"I do wish you would not."

"Your deception was similar to this one."

"It is not," countered Violet. "Do you not see? Penny, you stand to lose so very much if it is discovered that you have entered into a deception. Should it be spread about, you must know that everyone will wonder what else you have lied about, what else you are hiding. Your reputation will be ruined. *You* will be ruined!"

Ash was given pause at Violet's words. He had no intention of risking Miss Drayton's reputation. The lady, herself, spoke then, allaying his fears.

"Violet, I know that you mean well, but I truly care nothing for my reputation, saving what it can do to further Mr. Greene's career. It is my sincere hope at the end of the Season to disappear from Society entirely. I will live above my studio with old Mr. Pelter and my aunt, and paint. We shall do quite well, the three of us."

Ash found Miss Drayton's strength as fascinating as it was admirable. His sister Violet was quite dear to him, but she did not possess such pluck as Miss Drayton displayed. Violet was timid where her friend was bold. She spoke quietly and hesitantly where her friend spoke quickly and forcefully. Even now, Violet's warning that a false engagement was immensely more dangerous than a remade gown seemed rather weak after Miss Drayton's easy dismissal.

Ash and Miss Drayton continued to discuss the terms of their agreement and to share what information seemed pertinent to their circumstances, Violet sitting silently and solemnly between them. After they had safely delivered Miss Drayton to her home, and Ash turned the horses toward their own home, he realized that Violet had not spoken for the remainder of the drive. Though he attempted to start conversation and to cajole some sort of response from her, Violet replied in brief syllables only.

Upon their arrival at the house, Mrs. Wyndham was in an uproar over a perceived slight given Rose by an acquaintance in the shopping district earlier that day, and Ash was unable to speak further with Violet. He determined to seek her out tomorrow at first opportunity.

Thirteen

PENELOPE HELD BACK a sigh as the young debutante – too young at fifteen, in her opinion – shifted impatiently again. Miss Theodora, the younger sister of Miss Yardly, was sitting for a portrait. She seemed disinclined to sit still for the time Penelope needed to sketch her features and make the necessary notations as to the colors, lighting, and setting to be used in the final portrait.

It did not help matters that Penelope's thoughts were rather consumed by the events of the previous day. Mr. Wyndham's proposal – she still could scarcely believe that he had offered to assist her in such a manner! – certainly was enough to have left her reeling. She could scarcely believe she had agreed to his scheme, especially considering her distaste for masculine company. What was more, Penelope was troubled to have upset her dear friend.

As she jotted down several notes about the shades of pale brown in the young girl's hair, Penelope noticed that it was quite similar in color to Violet's. *I do hope she is not cross with me. With us. She is too dear a friend, too kind a soul, to upset.* Penelope realized that her distress regarding the situation derived more from Violet's disapproval than from any concern over the trustworthiness of Mr. Wyndham's character.

She understood Violet's objections to a point. There certainly existed the possible danger of a scandal should the truth be discovered. However, if there existed a man whom Penelope trusted with a thing of this magnitude, it was Mr. Wyndham. He had proved to be a kind, trustworthy man, deserving of anyone's admiration; though she certainly would never admire him as more than a brotherly figure. The very idea was absurd.

Penelope finished her sketches and rang for Mr. Pelter with the bell which he had installed in her workroom only yesterday. Very few moments later, and she could hear his raspy but gentle voice informing Miss Theodora that the painter was finished for the day. He ushered her to the entryway, and once the sound of the door hitting its frame reached Penelope's ears, she groaned aloud.

"Good heavens! I thought it would never end!"

She stood and placed her hands upon the small of her back, enjoying the stretch in her tired muscles. She peeked out the window, glancing up to the sky and seeing nothing but grey.

"Business's picked up, of a certainty." Penelope started, not having heard Mr. Pelter enter the room behind her. "You now spend more time drawing and painting than you do in your home."

"Very soon, Mr. Pelter, *this* shall be my home, as well as yours and my aunt's."

The old man shook his head before turning and shuffling in the direction of the stairs. "'taint right, a gentle-bred lady work in' as such to support her old servant and aunt."

Penelope heard his grousing, but chose to ignore it as she often did. He was a faithful servant, and fast become a close friend. She trusted him implicitly. With a start, she realized that there were in fact two men with whom she was acquainted whom she felt truly deserving of her trust. She was certain that she had begun to trust him at the assembly at Almack's, and their time spent at Hyde Park certainly cemented her in that.

Glancing down at her drawing table, Penelope saw that Mr. Pelter had left a letter upon it. Whether he intentionally left it there, or he brought it and set it down before forgetting its existence, she could not say. Penelope broke the seal, blue wax with a stamped W slightly off-center, and opened the page.

Ashbridge House
22 Grosvenor Sq., London
01 March 1806

To Mr. Greene.
As you are proving to be one of the most sought-after painters of this Season, and perhaps very many more, I should like to schedule a sitting for each member of my family, save my youngest sister, who I understand to have already scheduled one with you. Additionally, I wish to commission you to paint my portrait, to be hung in the home which I stand to inherit. Are you agreeable to discussing the terms of this commission at the time I come for my miniature? Enclosed you will find my card, for the purpose of directing your reply.
Sincerely,
Mr. Ashbridge Wyndham

Penelope knew that she should not be as thrilled to receive this letter as she in fact was. While an unmarried woman was not permitted to receive written communication from a gentleman unrelated to her, Mr. P. Greene was. *How very clever of him,* she could not help but think. They would be able now to discuss matters of the "engagement" in a secret and entirely unsuspicious manner.

Penelope, feeling rather like a young girl playing a game, hurriedly found some paper to construct a reply. Fortunately, her work area was rather tidy, having just yesterday put everything to order. In a short time, she was uncapping an inkwell and dipping her pen.

> *My Good Sir,*
> *It is with grateful humility that I grant your request. As to a time for sittings, I am at your disposal. You are welcome to stop by my studio at your convenience to discuss further.*
> *Gratefully yours,*
> *P. Greene*

After the ink had dried, she carefully folded and sealed the missive. Stepping out to the street, Penelope glanced about quickly for a boy whose services she could engage to deliver her missive. A young lad of about eight years was leaning upon a streetlamp several paces down from the door. Clutching her arms about her against the cold – *Why did I not retrieve a shawl?* – Penelope hurried to him.

"Young man, I've two coins for you to deliver a message for my friend to a client."

"Aye?" asked the boy, standing up straight. "Need ye proof of delivery?"

"If you please. I shall give you this coin now, and the other upon your return."

"Very good, miss," said the boy, accepting the coin and folded paper with a grin.

"You may find me in that building, with the red door." Penelope gestured toward her studio before offering a quick smile. The boy scurried off, and she stood for a moment, looking after him and smiling for no real reason.

The voices of an approaching trio of early shoppers penetrated her consciousness. Fearful of being recognized on the street in an old gown and apron, paint all over her hands and hair likely falling from its pins, Penelope went scurrying back into the secrecy and warmth of her studio. She tarried in the short hallway which connected the front door to the rest of the building, unsure where she wished to go. *Perhaps I ought to return to the Townhouse; ensure that Cornelius has not sold the thing yet.*

"You went out?" called Mr. Pelter from abovestairs.

"Only briefly, to deliver a message," replied Penelope.

It was odd, how only a year ago, she had never engaged someone to deliver anything for her. Footmen saw to such trivialities. But now, she was beginning a metamorphosis that would require her seeing to every triviality. *I am moving from being a gentlewoman to being simply a woman.* Truly, the transition was not as difficult as she had feared it would be. Painting for so many hours every day was beginning to wear on her, evidenced by her sore back, arms, and hands. She supposed she would grow accustomed to it. Giving up the life of a lady was not turning out to be so bothersome as she had feared. Learning to style her own hair had taken practice, but she was quickly growing quite adept. Once she no longer had societal engagements to attend, she would not need to worry over it so much. Already she had disposed of her ladies' maid, after assisting the girl in finding employment elsewhere.

Penelope had known that it would be difficult to part with many of the servants, for most of them had served with her family for years. She was not certain what it was that made them remain so loyal after her mother passed; her father was not one to inspire such longevity in household staff. When it was necessary to dismiss some of them in recent years, whether it be her or her brother doing it, Penelope did her best to assist them in finding a new position. None seemed angered or annoyed at being let go, and Penelope still wondered why they were so kind to her when her family had not treated them well.

Shuffling footsteps alerted her to the presence of Mr. Pelter making his way down the stairs. "Now, I've come all this way back down, miss, so I hope that you will tell me what troubles you."

Penelope started at his knowledge that she was troubled. *Then again, I have been standing in front of the door for a good five minutes. It is unlike me.* She turned to face the older man.

"You have always been a faithful servant, Mr. Pelter, and I am immeasurably grateful for your loyalty. What is it, though, that has caused you to remain so?"

The old man looked at her quizzically, then turned and gestured for her to follow him into the back room. Once there, he offered his hand while she perched upon a stool there, and he gingerly leaned against the edge of her work table.

"I poke at you, miss, for being the daughter of a peer and feeling that you must see to my care." He shook his head and chuckled softly. "Even so, it can only be to your credit that you would exert yourself in such a manner."

Penelope began to protest, but he held up a hand, a rare gesture for so deferential a servant as he. "Never, miss, have I spoken against you. However, as you seem quite determined to lower your station to that of my own, I must speak now." After a brief pause, he gingerly raised his gnarled old hand, gently placing it upon the side of her face. "You are quite like a granddaughter to me. I've watched you grow from a wee tot, running about and causing all manner of trouble."

Penelope chuckled at this and raised her hand to cover the old man's.

"And now you are grown and seeking a way to care for me and for your aunt."

She felt another uncharacteristic blush at his words and at the admiring light in his eyes.

He continued thoughtfully, "But I wonder if this is what your dear parents would have wished for you."

Penelope recoiled, throwing off the balance of the elderly man as she did. Upon seeing him teeter, however, she hurried to reach out her hand and steady him. Standing there, her hand upon his arm and her heart pounding at his words, she could not help but ask, "Do you not mean parent in the singular? For I can recall only one of those who I would have considered dear to me."

Mr. Pelter's face was pained as he replied, "Your papa was certainly lacking in his later years, but do you not recall the man he was before the baroness left you?"

Penelope recalled a great deal. Her papa drinking himself into a stupor and the anger and sorrow that resulted. Once in a while, she thought she had the ghost of the memory of a different, kinder papa. Those were elusive, though, and she never could grasp any of them for more than a fleeting breath. She slowly shook her head.

Mr. Pelter smiled sadly. "Your father was a doting and affectionate husband and father until the sickness took your mother."

"I cannot believe you," whimpered Penelope. She heard his words, but they may as well have been in a foreign tongue.

"You were a mere girl at the time, dear," continued Mr. Pelter as though oblivious to her distress, "but when the Baroness was taken, it destroyed your father. Before, when she was alive, he was a man of faith and love and kindness."

"No! He was harsh and unfeeling," said Penelope stubbornly, her heart thundering and her lip and hands trembling.

He continued despite her protests, as though driven to speak. "He witnessed his wife, his love, first suffer with the tumor, then the agony of having a physician cut it out of her—"

"No!"

"—and then she lived only a very short time after—"

"Speak no more! No mo–," but her voice dissolved into a sob.

Mr. Pelter continued, his voice quiet but firm. "After losing her, and in such a horrific manner, he could not face his grief. I tried, as much as I could, to coax him to eat and to hear words of comfort from Scripture. He refused, instead drowning himself in strong drink."

Penelope sat upon the lowest step, no longer able to support herself. She was drowning, the fear and frustration and anger all pouring down on her. It was too much to bear, too much to withstand. She was heated and chilled all at once, her stomach churning and her breaths ragged. After a time, the storm subsided, and she was able to speak again.

"Do you mean to suggest that he merely lost himself in grief?" She despised how her voice sounded, roughened as it was by her sobs of a moment ago. "That he truly was a good man?"

"Is any man truly good?" was Mr. Pelter's rather unexpected reply.

Penelope wished to answer quickly and decisively, but seeing Mr. Pelter before her – a faithful servant of her family for nearly a lifetime – she hesitated. "I cannot say."

He smiled sympathetically at this. "Of course you cannot. I, however, am quick to say that there is undoubtedly no good man. And no good woman. In the eyes of God, we are all in need of grace."

Penelope could not stop a slight scowl. "I had not known that you were such a religious man, Mr. Pelter."

"Ah, but you see, religion is one of those things that one cannot always know about another, without a more intimate acquaintance. Oh sure, there are observations one may make regarding a person's behavior, but to truly know what one believes in his heart? It cannot be done."

"Do you mean to say that the late Baron is one such person?"

"I simply wish to point out, my dear Miss Drayton," Mr. Pelter said gently, "that there is often more at work than meets the eye."

The bell rang suddenly and Penelope started. *I forgot entirely about the boy returning for his other coin!*

"Mr Pelter, I am in no state to be seen," she fretted, wiping hastily at her eyes and hoping to dry the last remnants of her tears. She retrieved a coin and pressed it into one of Mr. Pelter's weathered hands. "Please give this to the boy at the door. He delivered a message for me and has come for his promised coin."

At the man's assent, she hurried into her studio, planning to spend some time with Miss Theodora's portrait while the sitting was still fresh in her mind. Or as fresh as it could be, with the tumult of her thoughts and feeling warring within her.

The door opened with a sudden complaint of old wood being forced to move upon its hinges. Ash raised his head quickly, meeting the eye of an elderly man through the narrow gap made between the door's edge and its frame.

"Yes?" was the single-word greeting given by the man.

Ash frowned slightly, but answered politely, "Good day, sir. I am here in hopes of meeting Mr. Greene."

The man shook his head – or so Ash supposed, for the man's whole head was not visible, but his face passed in and out of view through the narrow gap. "I am afraid that is impossible." The man's voice was rough with age. "Mr. Greene asks that I conduct his business."

Ash nodded, deciding upon a more direct approach. "Very well. In that case, I should like to speak with Miss Penelope Drayton."

What was visible of the man's face paled before he spluttered, "With whom? I-I am afraid you must be mistaken, sir, for–"

"I am not," said Ash firmly. "You see, I am Miss Drayton's fiancé. I am aware of–"

"Very well," came the elderly man's hurried response as he quick-ly pushed the door farther open, eliciting a startling screech from the offended portal, and reached out to grasp Ash's forearm. "Hush now. We would want no one else to hear." Ash allowed himself to be pulled through the door.

"She is in the studio," said the man, still not offering his name. "Forgive me, but I am an old man and must return to my quarters for rest."

Ash thought he detected a swiftness to the man's movements which belied the man's claimed fatigue, but chose to ignore the anomaly and proceeded through the door which the man had indicated.

Upon entrance, he first saw a chair situated before a backdrop of rich draperies, with a waist-high pedestal holding a potted plant. Ash supposed that Violet would know its variety, horticulture enthusiast that she was, but he himself had not a clue as to its identity. When he looked more closely about the room, however, he quickly saw that the fabric was out of date and had been faded by the sun in some places. The drapes of the fabric were arranged, however, to mostly hide those spots from the unobservant eye. Ash also saw that the draperies were not simply for decoration, but concealed shelves full of items. Books, papers, quills, several musical instruments – there were even toys, such as a porcelain doll and an old wooden sword, among others.

Ash turned away from the apparent sitting area and saw a wall of drapes hanging, which appeared to divide the room. The faint light from the cold, cloudy day afforded him only slight shadows of what lie behind, so he strode purposefully toward it and peeked around. The sight on the other side gave him pause.

Miss Drayton, perched upon a stool, held a brush in her right hand and was gazing at the canvas before her with such intensity that Ash was unsure whether she was even aware of his presence. Her hand moved gracefully, flitting back and forth between the painting and the palette held in her other hand. She suddenly moved the brush to hold it delicately between her teeth while she used her fingers to blend some colors on the painting.

"Gust a nonent, Ister Elter," she spoke around the brush. "Ig nearly catchured duh correct angle hoor Iss Heah-dowa's head."

"Certainly, Miss Drayton, take all the time you require," chuckled Ash, "but I am not Mr. Elter. I do hope you are not keeping multiple fiancés upon a string for the mere purpose of toying with us."

Ash nearly laughed outright at the shock on Miss Drayton's face. Her head had snapped to face him at his first words, and her brush had almost immediately fallen from her gaping mouth, to land momentarily upon her lap before falling to the floor with a small clatter. Her gaze immediately followed the sound of her brush, so it was not until he was nearer her that she met his gaze. Still the brush lay upon the floor. The redness about her eyes and nose, as well as the prominent red veins visible in the whites of her eyes, were disconcerting to Ash.

"Heavens! Mr. Wyndham, you startled me!"

"Did I now?" he asked sardonically, choosing not to comment on the redness on her face just yet. "I rather thought you were expecting me." At her incredulous face, he added, "You did invite me in your letter, did you not?"

Ash knew he was teasing her, but could not seem to help himself. Seeing her with such sad eyes, he found that he wished fervently to relieve that sadness. He now became aware of a wariness which lurked behind the congenial exterior she had always presented during each of their previous meetings. Even though her vulnerable openness revealed a longstanding sorrow in her soul, he found he much preferred it to the mask of wary cheerfulness she had apparently worn up to this point.

"Y-yes," she said with a nervous fluttering of her hands, "but I certainly did not expect you to arrive unannounced, interrupting my work!"

It is odd to see her so vulnerable and uncomfortable. How might I put her at ease?

"Come now," cajoled Ash, allowing a smile onto his face which he knew Violet was unable to resist; he only hoped it proved as effective with Miss Drayton. "You cannot truly be so very put out with me as all that."

She scowled, but he soon saw that her glare was not genuine. A light appeared in her eyes and she seemed to be hiding a smile, though very badly. "Oh but I am, Mr. Wyndham. I cannot believe you would treat that poor errand boy with such disdain. I promised him another coin upon returning with proof of delivery."

"I paid him, and is not my presence sufficient proof?"

She said nothing for a time, her face blushing becomingly.

She seems to be blushing a great deal more of late than she did when I first made her acquaintance.

Ash stepped closer, bending to retrieve her errant paintbrush from the floor before he moved to stand slightly behind her. He peered over her shoulder at the painting before them. The background was painted, a picturesque country scene, with gently sloping hills and a deep blue sky. In the foreground, Miss Drayton had begun several items – a tree, a bench, a large urn. The beginning of a face was suspended in the center of the painting.

"Who is this?" he asked, deciding to tease her a bit more. "Miss . . . Heah-dowa, I believe you said?"

This elicited a light chuckle from Miss Drayton, in turn producing immense satisfaction in Ash. "Miss *Theodora*, actually, Miss Yardly's sister. The family was so pleased with that portrait, it was decided one was needed for the younger sister, as well. She was in earlier for a sitting, and I wanted to begin painting before I forgot everything I had planned to do with her."

"I see."

"I had already begun the scenery. I spoke with her a few days past, and immediately thought that an outdoor setting would complement her complexion better than an indoor one."

"Ah. How did you see her without her recognizing you?" Ash noticed with satisfaction that she seemed quite distracted from her earlier discomfiture.

"Oh, I met her as myself, not as a painter. This was, of course, before my brother's reputation complicated the plan." Miss Drayton's expression darkened momentarily.

"So you were analyzing her during a morning visit? Did such a visit provide you with adequate time?"

"Oh, indeed. I needed only three minutes, which would have left me with twelve minutes to actually visit, but you and your family arrived then, preventing me from the dubious pleasure of a true visit."

"Dubious, you say?"

Miss Drayton's eyes widened and became alarmed. "Forgive me, I had not intended—"

Ash lightly touched her hand. "No, please forgive *me*. It was not my intent to cause guilt. After all, I feel similarly." He gestured to the painting. "Please, do not let me keep you from your work."

Miss Drayton turned to back to the portrait and lightly dipped her brush in some paint on her pallet before saying, "Do you feel similarly concerning these ladies in particular, or all ladies of the *ton*?"

Ash recalled that yesterday she had shared much of her reasoning for entering the engagement, and even some of what caused it. He supposed that it would only be fair for him to share some of his own history.

"All ladies, though I suppose Violet would be an exception to that rule," he began.

"She is a darling girl; my first true friend in ages. Perhaps in my life," commented Miss Drayton, mixing two colors on her pallet to achieve a new shade. "Is your disapproval of ladies in general something that is innate to you, Mr. Wyndham, or something learned?"

"Learned, to be sure." Ash could not help but laugh a bit, though it was certainly self-deprecating. "I was as eager to love as could be, at the start of my adulthood. I enjoyed my first London Season immensely, due largely to one lady in particular."

"Is that so?" Miss Drayton's face was sympathetic as she glanced at him over her shoulder. "As you are not currently married, I cannot image that it ended well."

"No. It did not." Ash waited until she turned back around before saying more. He found it much easier to speak of these things when she was engaged in her painting. Despite his heart clenching painfully at the memory, Ash forced nonchalance into his voice as he said, "The lady proclaimed tender feelings for me after I declared myself to her. However, when I asked for her hand, she decided that as a simple country gentleman, I was not quite the illustrious catch she had hoped to secure. Or that her father had hoped for her to secure. She told me as much in a short missive, and I've not seen her since."

Miss Drayton's brush had stilled, but she remained facing away from him. For a time, she said nothing, and Ash was rather confused as to the suspense he felt at her silence. *I was young and foolish at the time; I hope that her opinion of me will not suffer from this intelligence.* It had been quite some time since Ash was concerned with the opinion of a woman who was not Violet.

Miss Drayton turned her head slightly, as if to look at him, but stopped when her chin reached her shoulder. He could not help but notice her profile: the long lashes which brushed her cheeks, the gentle slope of her nose, and the two plump lips, round and slightly pouting. Or did he imagine that? Once he realized that his focus was not where it should be, he looked again to her one visible eye, which was still lowered.

"Do you love her still?" she asked quietly.

This was not what Ash had expected. He cleared his throat and swallowed. *Do I still love Miss Giles, even after her treachery and after so much time has passed?* He wanted to answer that he did not – and not simply for the sadness he feared was hidden in Miss Drayton's lowered eyes. No, he wanted his answer to be no for himself and for his own heart's freedom. He knew that he did not wish to renew a friendship with Miss Giles; at the most, he could tolerate a dispassionate acquaintanceship.

However, he also did not wish to lie to Miss Drayton. They were not engaged to be married, not truly, but he felt that she deserved his honesty. Therefore, he answered, just as lowly as she, "I do not know."

Miss Drayton nodded once before turning back to her painting.

Irrationally worried that Miss Drayton might misunderstand him – *I know that she does not love me, nor I her, but misunderstanding is the birthplace of malcontent.* – Ash continued, "That is, I do not *wish* to still be in love with her. But I fear I will not know for certain until our paths cross once again."

"And if you regret an engagement to another woman when you meet again?"

"I shall not. If anything, our engagement will protect me from foolish sentiment."

Ash thought he heard a hint of laughter in her voice as she asked, "Oh indeed?"

With a grin, he conceded, "Or if not, then it shall protect me from *acting* upon foolish sentiment."

She again laughed at this. "And what if you meet with her after our engagement is dissolved?"

Ash gave a short, self-deprecating laugh. "I shall be left defenseless, unless I learn some of your determination in the meantime."

Miss Drayton turned round fully at these words, her eyes wide and her lips parted in surprise.

Heart pounding and stomach clenching, Ash found that he wanted her to know how greatly he admired her for the determination that carried her so far. Yet at the same time, he feared giving her false hope, should he express any sort of admiration for her. *She has no expectations,* he reminded himself. *I cannot raise what is not there.* Through a tight throat, he pretended disinterest in his tone. "I see that your determination quite surpasses my own. The comparison is cause for mild shame on my part, as there is little I have done to achieve my own ends."

Miss Drayton said, "There is little you must do, Mr. Wyndham. You are a man, the heir of an estate, and therefore may do as you please. The one thing you must avoid is being ensnared in some young deb's or her mama's matchmaking trap, until the time comes that you find a woman you can love and trust."

Ash felt the odd fear leave him in a rush – or most of it, at the least. *Have I not told her of my intent never to marry until it is necessary? Or has she forgotten?* He could not recall. "I suppose that is true," he responded.

Miss Drayton turned upon her stool and now faced him. "I, on the other hand, am entirely dependent upon the estate which my brother holds for the means to provide for myself."

"But soon you will not be."

Miss Drayton's face broke out into a smile that caused her face to glow with the joy of a cherished dream nearing its fruition. "That is my hope."

"And you plan to live here, then? Once our engagement has served its purpose?"

"I do."

"Where will Mr. . . . . Elter, was it? Where will he live?"

Miss Drayton chuckled lightly as she said, "His name is Mr. *Pelter.* He shall retain his room, and my Aunt Essie and I shall share the other."

"Is that so?" Ash could not believe that Miss Drayton had ever shared a room with someone, with the exception of traveling, and wondered silently whether she would manage the change well.

She has shown a remarkable ability to adapt in all other areas. I suppose there should be no reason she will not do so in this one, as well.

"Yes. Mr. Pelter has no one and nowhere to go. And my aunt shall remain with me as my companion and friend; I fear my brother would cast her off, and she has no other means of support."

"You are a thoughtful, generous person, Miss Drayton."

She shook her head. "I do no more than is required of me by common decency. As a human being, I am beholden to care for those close to me."

"I believe Violet would say something similar, but she would certainly say that our beholden nature comes from God, that He calls us to care for others."

"Would you say the same, Mr. Wyndham?"

He felt distinctly uncomfortable at this, but answered as honestly as he could. "I cannot say with certainty. I believe that God . . . is sovereign, and that as His subjects, we are required to behave in a particular manner. But . . . I cannot go to the extreme that Violet would, that His sovereignty extends fully into each area of our lives. Even a King has a limit to his own power."

"Indeed. I fear that I would venture in the other direction to claim that His sovereignty is symbolic. How else could one account for the devastating sadness that exists? He must be a weak King indeed to allow those He would call his children to suffer as He does."

Ash was not certain that he would agree with Miss Drayton's claim, but he was unsure how to respond. *How can I defend an idea I do not myself understand?* For the first time, he began to wonder if he ought to seek answers for his questions and doubts. Unable to voice any of this, he merely made a noncommittal, "Hmm."

"Do forgive me, sir, I fear I spoke out of turn."

"No, Miss Drayton," Ash assured her, placing a hand comfortingly upon her arm. "If this" – and he gestured with his other hand to the space between them – "is to be successful, we must be honest with one another. Entirely."

Miss Drayton nodded slowly and said, "That is very good of you."

"Yes, well." Ash paused, feeling oddly foolish and quickly removing his hand from her arm. "We must make our engagement as close to a true one as possible. If someone else was to witness one of us caught unawares by an opinion of the other, it could cast our union into an undesirable light."

Miss Drayton replied in an impish tone, "Yes indeed. Now, what unpopular opinion do you keep with which you may shock me?"

Ash laughed. "Your opinion was not shocking, given your circumstances; rather, I had not expected it to be voiced. Though I am glad you did."

Miss Dayton nodded, but remained silent and turned back to her work.

"As for my own opinions," Ash began, "there are none shocking, so much as unyielding."

"I shall be the judge of whether or not they are shocking, sir," she quipped.

Ash was delighted that none of Miss Dayton's reserve had yet to return. *She is truly at her ease here, doing that which brings her joy.* He could not help but notice the delicate grace of her hands as she directed the brush where to go and how heavily to apply the paint to her canvas – a delicacy which belied the strength hidden within her person.

She truly is a remarkable woman.

The unbidden thought caused Ash no small amount of discomfort. *I cannot think of her as anything more than my sister's friend, with whom I have come to a mutually beneficial – but temporary – arrangement.*

Ash cleared his throat and, after a moment of floundering as he searched his mind for the topic of their conversation, finally said, "Now for my . . . How did you put it? *Shocking opinions?* You know of my aversion to the ladies of Society, as well as the origin of such sentiments."

"Or lack thereof?" Miss Drayton glanced over her shoulder briefly, sending a wry smile his way.

"Indeed," Ash agreed. "I shall tell you now to what end that aversion has carried me."

"Oh?"

"It is my plan not to marry until it has become necessary."

"Necessary?"

"As there are no brothers to whom I may leave our family's holdings, and my father had no brothers, it shall all fall to a distant cousin, who is almost entirely unconnected to our family, save that familial one. He may or may not choose to support my sister when I am gone. A son, however, could be instructed to care for his aunt."

"And if you reach your demise prematurely?"

"I shall endeavor not to."

"Yes, but it could happen."

"Yes. Violet practices careful economy already and I daresay it would recommend her quite well as a companion to some elderly matron."

"You would have your sister reduced to such demeaning circumstances?"

"Such as painting for a living?" Ash teased. "I have spoken with Violet of the possibilities, and she has expressed her contentment with an arrangement such as this. And if you will recall, it is not my plan to meet an early end."

"Ah yes. How could I have forgotten?" she asked with dry humor.

"You really must be sure to pay closer attention to my every word, Miss Drayton." Ash fixed her with an overly-intense gaze, fighting to keep his smile hidden. "I fear my self-importance shall suffer if I do not have an entirely attentive and doting fiancé."

Miss Drayton stared at him, wide-eyed, for the space of a breath, and then burst out laughing.

"Oh! I-I . . . could not believe," Miss Drayton was scarcely able to speak on account of her laughter, "you to be serious, Mr. Wyndham, but for a moment—"

"Please call me Ash."

The words were spoken before he even knew they were upon his tongue. Miss Drayton's laughter abruptly ceased, and she looked at him with a startled expression that Ash was certain must have mirrored his own.

What rational thought could possibly have led to that outburst? Ash recalled an impression of how lovely he found it to see a lady who could allow herself to truly laugh, rather than the silly giggles of his sister Rose or the constant attempts to suppress chuckles which he saw in Violet. *But is that sufficient to ask such a liberty to be taken? Indeed, to take such a liberty with her?*

"I-I, that is – were we *truly* engaged, we would most likely use our given names when not in company." Ash felt his face warm as the surprise faded from Miss Drayton's face, only to be replaced with a blush. *Excellent, I've made the lady who seems never to blush color up twice in the space of a quarter–hour.* He bowed formally. "Forgive me. I seem to have forgotten myself."

"No, Mr. Wyndham." Miss Drayton spoke quietly. "*Ash.* You are correct. Please feel free to call me Penelope. Or even Penny, if you like."

"Very well, *Penny.* But only away from company."

"Of course."

The remainder of the visit was somewhat stilted – not with discomfort on the part of either party, but with the new and slightly awe-inspiring knowledge that, had circumstances been different in both their lives, each would find a permanency of their present circumstances not entirely undesirable. Each was cognizant enough of the fact that past circumstances were in fact not different, and therefore a permanent understanding between them was out of the question.

Part III

Fourteen

PENELOPE ENTERED ST. George's at Hanover Square with her great-aunt and Mr. Pelter. He bowed to them before heading to where the servants and lower classes could sit. Penelope and her aunt made their way down the large center aisle to the family box. Her grandfather had been a particular friend of the man who built the cathedral in the early eighteenth century. Due to their friendship, the Baron had purchased a box for their family at St. George's rather than at a church closer to their family's London house. Aunt Essie withdrew the key from its place on the chatelaine she wore pinned to her gown, unlocking the door to their box. Penelope motioned for the older woman to precede her before joining her on the pew. The nostalgia of the long-forgotten action consumed her, like a dream forgotten until an action or word resurrected the memories.

Aunt Essie leaned toward Penelope, speaking quietly into her ear, "It has been some years since you attended a service with me, has it not?"

"Indeed," replied Penelope in equally hushed tones. "It is all so familiar and yet so strange at the same time."

Aunt Essie nodded as she withdrew a small prayer-book from her reticule. "I understand. Did I tell you that I stopped attending services for a time?"

Penelope was shocked, but did her utmost to hide her reaction. "Indeed? I had believed you to have been a faithful worshiper all your life."

The older woman replied, "I had a period of questioning, about forty years ago, when I reached my mid-twenties. I was uncertain that God truly cared for me, as He had not seen fit to give me a husband. I felt it my prerogative to not care for Him."

"Aunt!" hushed Penelope. "I cannot believe you would say such a thing in this place!"

"Why ever not?" asked Aunt Essie. "The Lord is aware; I have spent much time in prayer with Him, detailing my feelings about that subject. And even if I had not, He knows all."

"But not everyone else knows."

"I am not here for everyone else."

Penelope felt a scorching shame wash over her. *Am I not here for everyone else? Or at the least, that everyone else may learn of the news which Mr. Wyndham – Ash – and I have to share?* She still did not know what to think of their arrangement to address one another with such an intimacy as given names, but found a shadow of guilt plaguing her now. *Guilt? I do believe that God exists, but He has not concerned Himself with me, and neither have I with Him. Why should I feel guilty?*

Aunt Essie interrupted her dark thoughts by asking, "Have you your prayer book or hymn-book?"

"I do not," relied Penelope. "I left it in our country-house."

Aunt Essie was quiet for a moment before stating, "So you planned never to retrieve it."

For her aunt's sake, Penelope wished she could reply differently. But she could not.

"No, Aunt. I did not."

The older woman sighed and whispered something under her breath which sounded suspiciously similar to "stubborn young thing, is she not?"

Penelope sat quietly, watching others as they entered the church. Each dressed in fine clothing, moving into their boxes and sitting. Large families filled boxes, with generations sitting in the same box. Single elder folk sat alone in the large box belonging to their families, their descendants either gone or non-existent. Penelope realized with a start that her poor aunt must have looked much like those later church-goers, an elder woman with no family who loves her enough to accompany her to Sunday services.

"Aunt, I am sorry that you sit alone week after week." Penelope knew that what she was about to say would be decidedly unpleasant for her, but Aunt Essie was the last of her close relations, one of only two people who had known her as a child and still cared for her. "I will begin attending services with you."

The surprise on her aunt's face was evident in the raising of here thin brows and the whites visible around the pale blue of her eyes. "I would for you to attend for you, and for the Lord, but I suppose that your attendance is good, whatever the reason. The Word of God is effective, whatever the reason for hearing it."

Penelope was unsure how to reply to this, so she kept silent as strains of music from the large pipe organ in the back of the sanctuary began to fill the cavernous space. Aunt Essie's head bowed in what Penelope assumed to be prayer.

The sudden warmth of a large masculine hand upon her shoulder startled Penelope into gasping softly. She looked up and saw that Mr. Wyndham stood above her, just outside their box. His hand remained on her shoulder as he gave it a gentle squeeze and smiled down at her. Penelope felt heat suffuse her face and her stomach turned in a manner that was unfamiliar, but not entirely unpleasant. A small smile formed upon Mr. Wyndham's face before he pulled his hand away and continued on his way, escorting Mrs. Wyndham. Penelope barely saw Violet's friendly smile in time to return it before she had passed, following where her brother lead his family. He stopped at another box, closer to the front and on the other side of the sanctuary.

Penelope felt, more than saw, her aunt lean closer to her. Before the older woman could speak, the prelude music ended and the service began. As Penelope chanted the liturgy, listened to the readings and sermon, and sang the hymns, it was not long before she settled into the familiar rhythm of the service.

After Mr. Hodgson, the rector, had blessed and dismissed them, Penelope turned and began to make her way out of the box. Before she could even open the door, however, it was opened for her, and Mr. Wyndham stood there, ushering her out and holding out his arm for her to take.

"Good morning, Miss Drayton. I trust you are well?"

"I am, Mr. Wyndham, I thank you." She smiled at him and asked, "And how do you do?"

"Quite well, thank you."

Just then, Lady Melton approached, a mildly confused expression gracing her face.

"Good day, Mr. Wyndham, Miss Wyndham," Lady Melton said. Penelope turned saw that her friend stood slightly behind Mr. Wyndham; she was chagrined to see that she had not noticed Violet until that moment. "Miss Drayton. Miss Breckenridge."

"Good day," replied both ladies as they curtsied.

"Is it not rather irregular that you are escorting Miss Drayton, rather than your mama, Mr. Wyndham?" Lady Melton's voice was lightly teasing, but Penelope could see that she was hoping for information.

The gentleman fixed a bland gaze upon the matron's face for a moment before disinterestedly glancing about the room. He had a decided air of being above the paltry questioning of the meddling woman. *Goodness,* thought Penelope. *Is this how he has been discouraging the ladies of the ton? I suppose there may have been something to those rumors of his haughtiness. Thankfully, I know this to be a mere pretense.*

Mr. Wyndham nodded over to their left, where Mrs. Wyndham and Miss Rose were conversing with a rather opulently-dressed young fop.

"I believe she is well escorted by my youngest sister's beau. Quite the pinkest of the pink, is he not?" Mr. Wyndham had a disparaging, slightly sarcastic tone to his voice as he mentioned the extreme of fashion which the gentleman exhibited.

Lady Melton was not satisfied, however, with this elusive answer. She said coyly, "Even so, you seemed quite eager to reach Miss Drayton after the blessing was pronounced."

"What man would not be eager to reach the side of his fiancé?" asked Ash, an adoring grin spreading across his face. He turned to look into Penelope's eyes even as Penelope saw in her periphery the triumphant expression which came across Lady Melton's face. Mr. Wyndham's voice dropped as he added significantly, "Especially one as lovely as Miss Drayton."

The surprise on Lady Melton's face was obvious, and sounded in her voice as she stumbled over her words: "W-what gentleman indeed? I rather think, or would assume at any rate, that a gentleman with your prospects may choose his bride where he will."

Penelope felt her spine stiffen and she opened her mouth to answer to the thinly-veiled insult, but was stayed by Mr. Wyndham placing his other hand upon her own, where it rested on his forearm. Penelope glanced at Violet, to see a look of disapproval on the girl's face. She was unsure whether her friend disapproved of Lady Melton's words or their duplicity in pretending to be a couple in love.

"We are in the house of the Lord, Lady Melton," Mr. Wyndham replied, "and I shall not, therefore, answer in the manner which my heart wishes. I will, however, tell you that I shall tolerate no disparaging remarks concerning my bride, and should you choose to speak thusly to or about her, or concerning our union, I'll not hesitate to use everything at my disposal to . . . How shall I put this? Return the favor, shall we say?"

Lady Melton blanched, and Penelope very nearly laughed. To see the esteemed marchioness quite set-down by a man not even in possession of a title was most amusing. *I suppose it merely shows how much clout he already has with Society and their opinions of others.*

"I do apologize, Miss Drayton," Lady Melton said. "No offense was intended, I assure you. I've not always been such a gossip-seeker; I am afraid that as my children continue to grow, my time is not as well-occupied as it once was. Perhaps it is time I invest in an occupation besides my plants and my children."

Penelope nodded, surprised at the lady's humble tone. "I believe that Miss Wyndham here finds great enjoyment in sewing."

"Perhaps I shall see about taking up my needle again," she smiled. "The plants are nearly all dormant during the winter, and I really must find a winter hobby. Now, tell me how you and Mr. Wyndham became acquainted."

"Miss Wyndham and I became friends at the start of the Season," Penelope offered.

"Yes. Miss Drayton was – is – such an excellent friend to my sister that I could not help but notice. After we became better acquainted, I knew that I could not rest until we reached an understanding."

Penelope felt odd hearing his fabricated story of how they had come to be engaged. She knew it was untrue, but it seemed almost real. The gentleman certainly was able to act well. She would have to keep that in mind, should she ever play charades with him.

The party chatted – that is Lady Melton, Mr. Wyndham, and Penelope chatted while Violet and Aunt Essie conversed in hushed tones behind the others – as they all made their way to the back of the sanctuary. Mrs. Wyndham joined them at one point, Miss Rose and the gentleman, a Mr. Langley, tagging along behind her. When they stepped out onto the columned portico, Penelope was pleasantly surprised to find that the sun had emerged during the services and the first faint scents of spring were in the air.

They greeted the rector before walking a few yards to the corner of the cathedral. Penelope found herself quite firmly between Violet and her brother, each having taken one of her arms. Mr. Wyndham was speaking with Mr. Langley. Or rather, he was listening to that gentleman wax eloquent concerning a new horse he had recently acquired – a right beautiful stepper, according to Mr. Langley. Violet, meanwhile, said enthusiastically, "Spring is very nearly in the air! Can you not smell the thawing earth? See on this tree? Buds are appearing. I am beside myself with anticipation."

"Indeed, but that is still quite a ways off, is it not?"

"Perhaps, but it shall be here before we know it. Some things have a way of sneaking up on us in a decidedly pleasant manner." Violet slanted her eyes sideways at Penelope before leaning close to whisper into her ear. "It rather seemed that my brother was quite eager to perform his role, do you not agree?"

"He is quite the actor," allowed Penelope, somewhat startled at the sudden turn in conversation.

"Do you think so?" queried Violet. "He has always been rather awful at charades, or if we attempted a small play at home."

"I-is that so?" Penelope could not account for her sudden breathlessness at all. "He was quite convincing today."

"He was indeed," whispered Violet.

Penelope glanced about, it having suddenly occurred to her that someone might overhear. Mr. Wyndham had positioned himself, however, so as to shield Penelope and Violet from the rest of their party. Lady Melton, Mrs. Wyndham, Miss Rose, and Aunt Essie were conversing intently on the other side of the gentlemen.

In a low and rushed voice, Penelope said, "Violet, if you are thinking that we will marry after all, I wish you to put that thought from your head immediately. He no more desires a mate than do I."

"People change," offered Violet.

"I do not."

"Hmm," was Violet's reply.

"Violet, you cannot be in earnest," Penelope huffed. She was most exasperated at the patiently serene expression on Violet's face. "Even if I developed tender feelings for your brother – which I have not – there is nothing to say that Ash feels similarly."

Violet raised her brows.

"Now what?" cried Penelope.

"You used his given name."

"A mere slip – it means nothing! He suggested that we might be less formal in our address of one another when not in company," explained Penelope.

"When was that?"

"When he visited me at the studio Friday last."

"He did? When not even I, your closest friend, have yet to visit you there! He told me he was merely going for a walk."

"I imagine he may have walked there."

"And how often are you planning to be alone together, that you will have opportunity to use your given names?"

Were it anyone else, Penelope should have been offended at the implication behind Violet's words. She knew, however, that her friend was merely looking toward her best interest. "Not often, truly. We likely will, however, go out driving together, and it is equally likely that he will visit again at the studio, that we may plan certain aspects of the engagement. Mr. Pelter or my aunt will be present; we will be chaperoned. Please, Violet, trust that I understand everything I do."

Violet looked into Penelope's eyes for a moment and nodded. "Very well. I will speak no more of it."

The ladies' conversation moved to the dresses that Violet was finishing, as well as the ones which Madame Bélanger had made for Penelope. She had all but forgotten about the three new gowns until she had gone into the shop for a new set of underpinnings and been presented with not three, but four dresses ready for final fittings. Madame had expressed her extreme pleasure with Penelope's work, and asked her to return each Season for a similar arrangement.

"Is this one of them?" asked Violet.

"Yes." Penelope wore a simple green spencer over a gown of deep blue with silver motif of leaves embroidered throughout the fabric. "She also gave me a lilac ball gown, a yellow day-dress, and an open-robe of pale blue over a white under-dress."

"I am glad you will have more options than the few I was able to assemble for you."

Penelope detected no bitter or sad tone, but still rushed to assure her friend. "Violet, you were the first person in a long while who did something for me simply because you cared and knew that it would help me. I believe I will always treasure those dresses. And I forgot to tell you. Madame Bélanger said that she believed I was giving my patronage to her competitor until I told her that a dear friend of mine made the green dress for me."

"Impossible," laughed Violet. "She would know that the pattern on the fabric was not new."

"Yes, but she could not otherwise account for the modish design and the excellent fit." Penelope laughed when she saw Violet blush. "She wished for me to tell you that if you ever find yourself in need of a living, to come and see her."

Violet was still giggling when Mr. Wyndham turned to them. Mr Langley was walking away from them, Mrs. Wyndham and Miss Rose moving toward their carriage, and Lady Melton had already joined her family, waiting for their carriage. Search though she may, Penelope could not spot her aunt.

"Where is Aunt Essie?"

"She and Mr. Pelter planned to walk back to the studio," said Violet, motioning down the street, where the pair could be seen making their way along the road at a leisurely pace.

Penelope was quite surprised at her aunt and could not help feeling a measure of petulance which put her in mind of younger days. "I cannot believe that she would leave me here without an escort."

Mr. Wyndham replied, "I assured her that I would see to it that you were returned home."

"I see," Penelope sighed. "But what of her spending time alone in company with Mr. Pelter? Both are unmarried . . . "

"And quite on the shelf," grinned Violet. "Are you truly vexed with them for leaving, Penny, or more upset with yourself for having been distracted and not noticed their departure?"

Penelope grimaced slightly and shook her head. "I am not upset. I supposed that services were somewhat disturbing to me, and I am left now with a decided lack of peace."

The concern on Violet's face was immediate and noticeable, but Mr. Wyndham did not allow her to speak, instead offering his arms to the two ladies. "Let us continue this discussion as we walk along. Your aunt and Mr. Pelter are just ahead; we can follow them to the studio, and then hail a hack to deliver us all home."

Penelope took his right arm while Violet took his left, and they fell into step together. After a moment, Violet spoke up.

"What do you mean, Penny, that you were disturbed today?"

Penelope wished she had not said what she did. *The trouble of keeping intimate friends is that one often forgets to guard one's words.* Keeping her voice purposefully light, she said, "Oh nothing so serious as it seemed; I was rather caught up in my confusion over my aunt and spoke with more feeling than I ought to have."

"I thought that perhaps you referred to the message of the rector. Careful now," said Mr. Wyndham quietly as he assisted the ladies in crossing the street.

"His message? Oh, no. I suppose that the idea of being in the church while spinning our tales was disturbing to me, but it must be done."

Mr. Wyndham hummed, but said no more. They started down Conduit Street, the shops closed and the streets relatively quiet. Penelope knew that by the next morning, it would be once again bustling with life.

"I agree that it was uncomfortable to mislead others in the house of the Lord," piped up Violet. "I am afraid I cannot condone this decision you two have made. Giving false information or even leading others to believe something that is not true can in no way be pleasing to God. I do believe, though, that there might be a solution." Here she paused for a moment, drawing a deep breath before continuing. "Why not simply marry?"

"*Simply marry?*" asked Mr. Wyndham while Penelope choked on her breath. "You say that as though it is nothing of consequence, such as purchasing a new hat or a pair of gloves. Simply marry, indeed."

"Listen to me, Ash," pleaded Violet. "I already love Penny as a sister, and you know that she'll not injure you. While neither of you loves the other, you share a mutual respect. You never would have entered into this arrangement otherwise, and I can see it in your faces, in your actions, hear it in your voices when you speak. Ash, you need an heir. Penny, you need a source of support whom you may trust to seek your best interests. Ash has always done so with me. Besides, you both know that people marry as even greater strangers than are the two of you."

"Would *you* care to marry a stranger, Violet?" asked Mr. Wyndham.

Violet answered, "You know that no one will marry me. I am too quiet, and too dull for anyone to desire a union with me."

"Stop listening to that woman!" Ash spat. Penelope was startled at the vehemence in his voice.

"Ash! How can you speak of Mama in such a manner?"

Penelope was astounded when he hesitated for a moment before responding. He usually seemed so quick to answer any defense of the reprehensible behavior of that woman toward Violet that his hesitance seemed out of place. At length, though, he spoke. "You know as well as I do that her treatment of you is unfair. There are plenty of gentlemen who would welcome your peaceful spirit."

Violet pressed onward. "Perhaps, be we were not speaking of my own prospects. Why will you and Penny not marry?"

They had just turned onto Bond Street, and Mr. Wyndham huffed angrily and increased his pace. Penelope nearly had to run to keep pace with him and Violet. A little out of breath, she explained, "Violet, this is rather unexpected, is all. Please do not blame your brother for being upset. We were aware that you disapproved of our plan from the start, but you had seemed to resign yourself to it. We are not asking for your assistance in the subterfuge, but merely for your silence."

Mr. Wyndham slowed his pace again, glancing apologetically at Penelope before turning to hear his sister's answer.

Violet pulled her lips between her teeth for a moment before she opened her mouth to speak. "I was praying about this last evening, because my discomfort with the situation has not diminished. I've had a sense from the beginning that this will end badly, but I could not put it into words. I still struggle. But I fear, greatly fear, that this will end in heartache, for one or both of you."

Penelope could see Violet's earnestness in the small divot between her brows and in the slight down-turn of the corners of her mouth. Her voice rang with sincerity. After a moment's consideration, Penelope replied. "Violet, dearest, I thank you for thinking me worthy of being your sister, and for seeking the best for both your brother and myself. Marriage is out of the question, though. I've spoken to you on more than one occasion of my resolve never to marry, and I am convinced that your brother would not appreciate being caught in a marriage of this sort so early in his life." She glanced up to meet Mr. Wyndham's eyes, looking for him to collaborate her excuses. What she saw there, though, nearly caused her to stumble. His eyes were open. Thoughtful. Not hopeful, nor repulsed, but contemplative and considering. Penelope's stomach dropped to her knees before flying up again so quickly that it jolted her heart into a hurried cadence. *He cannot be considering her words, can he?*

Suddenly, though, Mr. Wyndham shook his head slightly and his eyes were once again neutral. A slight grin quirked his lips before he spoke. "The lady has spoken, Violet. I am an unfit suitor."

"That is not at all what I intended—"

"Surely you can see that I tease you, Penelope," grinned Mr. Wyndham.

"But you would be so well-suited!" said Violet in a last attempt as they arrived at the door to the studio.

"Perhaps, but neither of us seek that." Penelope reached out across Mr. Wyndham toward Violet. The warmth of her hand came through both their gloves. Penelope was startled to discover that her own hand was so chilled; the air was warmer than it had been for months. An unexplainable shiver ran through her spine. "Violet, I truly appreciate your concern. Be assured, though, that neither of our hearts is engaged. And we will be careful and more circumspect in our words. I do consider us to be engaged. I will not allow the attentions of any other gentlemen, and should we be pressed to marry by an outside party or risk complete ostracism, or should your brother change his mind, then I will honor the engagement and marry him." She glanced at Mr. Wyndham for confirmation.

He raised his brows in silent surprise but nodded his consent. "Likewise, Violet. Should Penelope choose to marry, I will do so gladly, but as of now, the original arrangement stands."

Violet once again bit her lips together, then nodded and said, "Very well. And I know I cannot force my will upon either of you. I cannot help but be concerned, though—"

"Do not be, Violet," interrupted Penelope. With a wry humor, she said, "I am a rather rational creature, for being a female, and you needn't fear for my heart."

"May I hail a hack to convey you and your aunt home?" asked Mr. Wyndham.

"No, but thank you," she answered. "I've some finishing touches to add to Miss Theodora's portrait."

"On a Sunday?" protested Violet.

Penelope opened her mouth to defend herself, but decided against it. Violet seemed to be a kind and even-tempered person most of the time, but she had already expressed displeasure with her that day, and Penelope had no desire to provoke her friend.

"You are right. I shall stay just a moment to take inventory of the paints I must order tomorrow and then my aunt and I will walk home together."

"Are you certain?" asked Mr. Wyndham. "I would hate to have you fall into difficulty on the way."

"It is a mere quarter-hour walk, one we have made many times."

Mr. Wyndham reached for Penelope's hand and she suddenly felt warmth spread up her arm until it washed over her. "Very well, then. Lady Kennard is hosting a rout tomorrow evening. Are you free to attend? If it is agreeable to you, I will bring the Ashbridge carriage for you around nine o'clock."

"Yes, that will be fine."

"Are Mama and Rose to attend, Ash?" asked Violet.

"Yes, but it is my plan to have the carriage convey them to the rout, then return for you and me. After we fetch Penelope – Violet will be a sufficient chaperone, will she not? – then we will arrive at the rout and Mrs. Wyndham and Rose will then leave."

"Must I attend?" Violet's voice was not plaintive, but very near it. "You are aware that I do not enjoy such events."

Regretfully, Penelope said, "I am sorry, but my aunt will not be able to act as chaperone. She does quite well walking on flat surfaces, but her nether limbs are not as strong as they once were. Stairs create much difficulty for her, especially with the amount of people present at a rout. I cannot ask her to risk turning an ankle on the stairs because there were too many people for her to see where to securely place her feet."

Violet simultaneously blanched and gained an expression of sympathy; it was all Penelope could do not to laugh outright. The younger girl's voice was shaken yet determined as she said, "Very well, brother. I shall attend."

"Perhaps you will see your Earl again," Penelope could not help but tease.

Mr. Wyndham's face was so thoroughly shocked that Penelope did laugh aloud.

"He is not my Earl," defended Violet. "We danced only once at Almack's, and I've not seen him since."

"But you were the only lady with whom he danced."

"Because his friend coerced him," returned Violet. "He told me as much."

"Did he?" returned Penelope with interest.

"Please do not mention this to Mama; I've quite put it from my head."

"Yes, let us not mention this further," said Mr. Wyndham. "The *on-dit* concerning that particular Earl, at any rate, is that he is quite the recluse. He resides in Town all year and scarcely sees anyone."

"Very well. Forgive me, Violet, for teasing you. I meant no harm."

"Of course," she replied weakly. "Someday, I shall learn the art of self-assurance and no longer be troubled by a small tease. Really, it should not bother me so now."

Penelope shook her head and in a rare moment of strong affection, she reached out to embrace Violet briefly. "You are a lovely friend just as you are. Your quietness of spirit is a calming influence, often when I need it most."

Violet replied, "Thank you, Penny. Sometimes I find it difficult to see that I have value as a friend, when there is so very much that I must improve."

"No, Violet." Penelope shook her head. "Do not change."

After another brief embrace with Violet and a gentle kiss placed on the back of her hand by Mr. Wyndham – his eyes shone with some emotion unknown to her and left her rather warmer than she had been – Penelope entered her studio.

"Aunt! Mr. Pelter! Are you in here?"

"We are in the store-room," came Mr. Pelter's gruff voice.

Penelope moved toward the door and opened it to find the pair seated at her work-table, sharing a plate of biscuits and two cups of tea.

"However did you come by food here?" she asked. "The cook-stove in the back is not yet functional, is it?"

"Mr. Pelter has apparently been working on it in the afternoons while you paint," said Aunt Essie, a happy flush on her face. "He surprised me with it this morning after we returned from services."

Mr. Pelter's own face flushed slightly. "It was nothing difficult. I asked the driver of Mr. Wyndham's coach if he knew of a man who might assist me. I know Miss Essie has been fretting about how we will eat after we all are living here and you cannot simply bring food over from the house."

"How lovely," smiled Penelope. *Is there something happening to which I've been blind? Miss Essie? Truly?* "Is there another cup?"

"Indeed there is," said Aunt Essie, rising and one from the cupboard on the back wall. Penelope did not recall its being there yesterday afternoon.

She leaned delicately against the table and sipped the tea appreciatively. "Only a few more months, I believe."

"Until?" asked Mr. Pelter.

"We will be able to live here."

"Indeed. So soon?"

"Do you dread giving up your solitude, Mr. Pelter?" asked Penelope with a chuckle.

"N-no, indeed, miss."

She had never heard the stoic man stutter in her life. Deciding not to pursue the matter, she said, "I believe I've enough clientele to support us, but I would much prefer to gain several more."

"You are aware," said Aunt Essie, "that the popularity of an painter is largely due to the whims of the *ton*, my dear?"

"Yes of course, Aunt, but I have an advantage in that Greene cannot offend anyone and therefore lose patronage in that manner, because he never speaks to anyone. Unless someone does not care for a painting, but I hope that will not often happen."

"True."

"Further, I have in mind to hold a showcase at some point, after we are better-established. Currently, the next floor of this building is unsuitable, but if all continues on the present course, it will be quite affordable to have the area refinished."

"Is not the artist usually present for a showcase of his work?"

"Often, yes. However, the eccentricity of being an anonymous painter has worked in my favor thus far, and it is my hope that a showcase with the artist absent will be amusing more than distasteful to the *ton*."

"A reasonable hope," commented Aunt Essie. "Well, I have finished my tea. Are you ready to return to the house, Penelope? I have in mind several passages of Scripture that I wish to read."

"Yes, Aunt. Shall I wash up these dishes?"

"No, miss, I will." Mr. Pelter took the cup and saucer from her hands.

"Will you not be joining us for the afternoon, Mr. Pelter?" Aunt Essie must have read the confusion on Penelope's face, for she continued, "I invited him to our home. It must be rather lonely here."

"Oh! Yes, indeed, Mr. Pelter. Please do join us," said Penelope.

He smiled at them. "You ladies go on, and I will be along after I've cleaned up here."

"Are you certain we cannot help?" asked Penelope.

"Until you move in here, you are still the Honorable Miss Drayton to me, miss, and ntil that day, I shall treat you as such."

Penelope shook her head fondly at the stubborn man. "Very well, Mr. Pelter. We look forward to your visit. Shall we say in about an hour?"

"Of course, miss."

Preparing to leave, Penelope expressed her thanks at Mr. Pelter, who did not seem to even hear her. His gaze was fixed steadfastly on Aunt Essie. Penelope wondered what to make of this new development.

Fifteen

ASH WAS QUITE pleased to discover that Mrs. Wyndham and Rose whole-heartedly approved of his plan for the rout which Lady Kennard was holding. He had feared that she would not wish to arrive separately from one of the most sought-after bachelors in London, but it appeared that the family connection was sufficient for her at this event. Ash handed Violet into the carriage just a quarter-hour after it left with Mrs. Wyndham and Rose. He instructed the driver to go to Claymore House on Leicester Square before climbing in and sitting across from his sister.

"Are you terribly nervous, Violet?"

"Only a little. I believe I shall be fine as long as you do not forget about me in Penelope's captivating presence."

Ash felt a mild discomfort begin in his mid-section, but he fought against it. "I beg your pardon?"

"Do not put on such airs with me, Ash." He felt foolish, both for his insecurity which caused such a reaction, and for his sister having caught him in it. After a short moment, she calmed and said, "I've seen your eyes when you look at her, Ash. They are not the same as when you look at other ladies."

"I do not care for most other ladies," he attempted to explain. "You are an exception. Penelope is, as well, for she is your friend and has no designs on me."

"You do not look at her as you look at me, Ash," Violet pressed. "And you've taken to calling her by her given name, even when she is not present. Does that mean you think of her as Penelope and not as Miss Drayton?"

"Does that matter?" he asked. "She is my fiancé."

"Whom you do not intend to marry," Violet intoned drily.

Ash was unused to his sister pressing so adamantly, and his voice grew a bit defensive. "It is perfectly acceptable, given our understanding."

"Understanding that you will not marry?"

"No, that we are engaged. Certainly engaged couples may allow that minor intimacy between them."

"Yes, because they are to be *married*," Violet insisted, "which you are not."

Violet's impassioned face calmed at his bewildered silence, and she smiled softly. "Ash, I shall speak no more of this, if you will but promise me one thing."

Ash feared that he would regret his words, but could not find the strength to fight against his sister's persistence. "Very well, you have my word."

"Look into your heart, Ash, and see if affection might be growing there."

There was no time to discuss the matter further, as the carriage drew to a stop and jostled as the driver hopped from his perch and opened the door. Ash nodded briefly at his sister and stepped down to the street.

The door was opened after he rang the bell, Mr. Pelter ushering him into the front hall.

"Mr. Wyndham," the older servant greeted him with a bow.

Ash returned the greeting, saying, "Mr. Pelter, I had been led to believe that you were no longer in the employ of Miss Drayton's family."

"That is true, sir, but I could not very well allow Miss Breckenridge or Miss Drayton to open the door so late in the evening. I am here to keep the former company while Miss Drayton is out."

"I see." Ash hesitated a moment. "Forgive me if I am too forward, Mr. Pelter, but you are under no obligation to the ladies."

"Perhaps not, but I am under obligation to my Lord." Mr. Pelter's eyes crinkled at the corners. "He would not wish for me to leave them defenseless, with most of the Drayton staff having been dismissed."

Ash could see his point, and knew that he would feel similarly if Violet was to be left in a house completely alone. But Mr. Pelter had been released of his service by Penelope's brother, and in a most ungracious manner. *Is he not bitter?*

Still not comprehending the old man's actions, Ash attempted a different approach. "It will be quite late when you must return to the shop. Are you not concerned for your own safety?"

The older man shook his head, a knowing look in his eyes. "Perhaps, but I can afford to hire a hack. I could not live with myself if Miss Drayton or Miss Essie came into harm."

Ash did not respond, as the ladies emerged through a door to his left at that time. Ash pushed aside his confusion – and perhaps conviction – at the man's reasoning, and turned his attention to bowing in greeting to the newcomers.

Penelope wore a white gown, similar to the one she wore at Almack's, but with a deep blue shawl wrapped about her shoulders and crossed over the bodice of her gown, finally tying at her side. He did not miss the irony that it looked well beside his deep blue coat.

"Good evening, Mr. Wyndham," said Penelope.

"Good evening, Pe—Miss Drayton." *I do think of her as Penelope, as Violet claimed,* he realized. *I will need to pay close attention that I do not accidentally address her too informally in company.* "You look well."

She lowered her head a moment, trying to hide a smile. "Thank you, sir."

"Shall we?"

"Yes. Aunt, would you please assist me with my pelisse?"

Ash smiled at Miss Breckenridge and took the outer garment from her hands. "Allow me." He held the shoulders of the pelisse as Penelope slid her arms through the sleeves, then lifted the coat onto her shoulders, settling it over her small fame.

"I thank you."

Ash stepped around Penelope and offered his arm.

"Good-bye, Aunt Essie, Mr. Pelter."

"Is someone accompanying you?" asked Miss Breckenridge.

Ash supposed that she was asking whether all the proprieties were being met, so he offered, "My sister is in the carriage. Would you care to come out and greet her?"

"Yes, thank you, I would," Miss Breckenridge answered.

Ash offered his other arm to her after Mr. Pelter had assisted her into a warm shawl. The trio made their way slowly down the steps to the street. He handed Penelope into the carriage, then stepped aside for Miss Breckenridge to speak with Violet.

"Good evening, Miss Wyndham," she said.

"Good evening. How do you do?" Violet asked.

"Quite well. And you?"

"I am well. Perhaps a bit nervous for the rout, but Ash has promised me that he and Penny will be with me the entire time."

"I am sure they will be. Penelope is quite devoted to her friends. She has been most dedicated to mine and Mr. Pelter's care."

"She is an excellent friend."

"Indeed." Miss Breckenridge smiled and briefly clasped Violet's hand, then turned back to Ash.

"May I assist you back to the house?" he asked her. At her nod, he leaned into the door of the carriage and said to the ladies, "I shall return shortly."

He offered Miss Breckenridge his arm once again, and as she took it, she said, "I really ought to be with her, as her chaperone, but I do trust you, sir."

"Ma'am?"

"I know that you will do her no wrong. I fear that I am not as at my ease as I once was with such a multitude of people."

"Understandably so. I myself do not enjoy them, and Violet positively fears them."

"She is a sweet girl."

"Thank you. I quite agree," he said.

"Will you have the bans read soon? I've not spoken at length with Penelope about the wedding plans."

"I er— I am not certain," Ash said cautiously. *Does her aunt not know the true nature of our engagement?*

They reached the door at this point, which was promptly opened by Mr. Pelter.

"Good-bye, Miss Breckenridge," Ash said as he bowed. "We shall return before too long."

"Do enjoy yourselves, dear," said the woman.

"Thank you," replied Ash, hazarding one last glance at Mr. Pelter. His eyes were unchanged, full of understanding and compassion, and entirely befuddling to Ash.

"Good evening," smiled the older man.

When Ash climbed back into the carriage, the ladies were uncharacteristically quiet. He had not often found the two of them silent in one another's company, and he wondered what they were speaking of prior to his return. *I sincerely hope that Violet said nothing to Penelope of what she believes my feelings to be.* He felt his face warm and was immensely glad that the carriage interior was so dim; only one lamp lit the space, and its glow was quite low.

Pushing any discomfort aside, he smiled at Penelope and said, "Are we prepared to become the most talked-about couple in London?"

"Do you think it we will be so much a topic of gossip?"

"Certainly. The man standing to inherit and who believes every lady of Town to be quite beneath his touch has found himself smitten with the sister of a peer who has lost the respect of everyone. I can imagine that they will speak of nothing else for the next two days at least."

Both ladies laughed, and Ash was gratified that Violet seemed less tense than she had on the way to the Claymore House. "In fact," he continued, "Violet, if you could manage a fainting episode during the rout, our fame may well last for three days."

The carriage rolled to a stop, and as Ash prepared to step down, it began to move again. But then stopped. And moved once again. After several stop-and-starts, he turned to the small door behind his head, which he opened to speak to the driver.

"Mason, what is the meaning of this?"

"Apologies, Mr. Wyndham," said the driver, "but they's carriages upwards a block back."

"Oh dear, I do hope this rout will not turn into a crush," Violet worried. "Rose's friend, Miss Cottsworth, was telling us of a rout that did just that. She said that her favorite dress was ripped and that five ladies fainted!"

"Mason? Do all of the carriages appear to be going to the same house?" asked Ash. "Can you see that far?"

"I canna' say, sir," began the coachman. "Oh now wait a trice. Some folks got out a' this 'ouse right 'ere, but others passed it."

"Are many disembarking at the house to which we are headed?"

"I canna' see quite that well, sir, but it 'pears that there are three places the carriages are 'eadin' to."

"All on this street?" Ash was incredulous. "Thank you, Mason," he added before closing the small portal once again. The carriage proceeded to slowly make its way toward their destination, making frequent stops on the way.

"What are the odds?" laughed Penelope wryly. "These neighbors are not coordinating their entertainment efforts very effectively."

"Or . . . perhaps they are." Ash had an idea, but was cautious that the ladies would not support it. "What would you say to attending all three? We could stay for a quarter-hour at the rout before proceeding to the other houses. As they are all rather close, we might walk between them."

"Should we not fear footpads or thieves?" asked Violet.

"The street appears to be well-lit." Penelope reached to squeeze Violet's hand reassuringly before facing Ash, the light of understanding and perhaps excitement in her eyes. "I do see the sense of what you are saying, Ash."

"Which is?" Violet asked.

"Attending three events this evening will certainly assist more in the spreading of our news," said Ash, "than attending only one."

"This is Fitzroy Square, is it not?" asked Penelope. "The houses here are rather new, but many are incomplete. Only the southern and eastern sides are finished. Perhaps the residents are hoping to attract others to the area by presenting it as a lively location to dwell during the Season."

"Why are the other sides of the square not finished?" asked Violet.

"While I am not acquainted with the particulars of this building endeavor, I will say that the war is certainly dampening the desire of many to spend what is required to build a new home," commented Ash.

"I was prepared to look into these properties before the letter from Lord Ashbridge arrived, though."

The coach remained stopped this time, jostling slightly as Mason hopped from his perch. The door opened and Ash quickly stepped out, turning the moment his feet were secure on the cobbles of the street in order to assist the ladies.

"They have all the appearance of being quite fashionable," observed Penelope as she stepped down, her hand secure in his.

"Yes," agreed Ash. The houses were all relatively new construction, quite modish and in excellent condition. He turned to offer his hand to Violet as she emerged from the carriage.

As the three climbed the steps to the door of Lady Kennard's house, Ash had a pervasive sense of well-being. He had his kind, caring sister on one arm, and a lovely lady on the other, whose presence he was growing to enjoy more and more every moment spent with her. Further, he found himself only mildly disconcerted by the question running through his mind: *There cannot be anything to Violet's questioning, can there be?*

Their summons at the door was answered quickly, and they were shown to a waiting-room, where foods and punches were set out on a table. Lady Kennard greeted them near the door to the room.

"Mr. Wyndham, Miss Wyndham," she welcomed them eagerly, but her tone dulled as she said, "Miss Drayton." Ash had been unaware how very young Lady Kennard was; the word about Town was that she was the widow of a wealthy gentleman, but a peer by her own right. He had expected her to be close to the age of her late husband, but she could not have been more than ten years Ash's senior. He was, however, aware of the slight given to Penelope by greeting her last. As the highest-ranking person among the three, she ought to have been greeted first.

· "Good evening, my lady," Ash said as he bowed, his mind searching for an acceptable manner of communicating his displeasure with their hostess. "I daresay this is a most excellent gathering."

"Why thank you, Mr. Wyndham," the lady preened.

"Have you seen my mother yet this evening?" he questioned.

"Yes, she was through here a short while ago. Did you not arrive with her? I had supposed that I simply missed you," and here she boldly placed her hand upon his arm, "but I am happily corrected."

Happily corrected, indeed.

"Yes, well, I had hoped to steal a few moments with my fiancée. Violet is an entirely sufficient and yet discreet chaperone."

He successfully hid his laughter in the face of Lady Kennard's surprise, but only just.

"Is that so? I've not heard of your engagement. May I be the first to wish you happy?"

"No, I fear that distinction has already been granted another," Ash returned smoothly.

Penelope nudged him with her shoulder, an intimately familiar gesture that he enjoyed perhaps more than he should. "Behave yourself, Mr. Wyndham," she said coyly before turning to their hostess. "Lady Kennard, we humbly accept your congratulations."

"Yes, of course." Ash smiled at Penelope, certain he looked like a besotted fool, for that was how he felt. And he could not seem to stop himself. "We are most happily situated."

"Indeed," intoned Lady Kennard.

After this, their hostess turned her attention to other guests who had arrived. Ash escorted Penelope and Violet over to the spread of food. After eating, their plates having been collected by a servant, the three wove their way through the crowds of people to another room, which appeared to be a drawing room. Ash saw three notorious gossips in one corner, all speaking together, but none looking at another, their eyes roaming the other guests. *Likely looking for a new* on-dit. He immediately led Penelope and Violet toward them.

"Good evening, Lady Melton," he greeted.

She happily offered her hand to him. After he bowed, she gestured to the other two ladies. "Have you met Lady Benton and Lady Westly? They are good friends of mine. I was just telling them of your engagement, but I suppose that they would prefer to hear it from the source."

"Oh, I am nowhere near the accomplished orator that I know you to be, Lady Melton. I beg that you would give me leave to demur," Ash knew he was playing it a bit dramatic, but he was also unsurprised to see that Lady Melton happily played along.

"You flatter me, sir," she twittered before reaching to squeeze Penelope's hand affectionately. "But very well. Perhaps you should like to hear the account from an unbiased party.

"Ladies, you see before you a most affectionate and caring trio of friends, for that is the manner in which they all began. You see, Miss Drayton made the acquaintance of Miss Wyndham, and the two became fast friends. I imagine that Miss Drayton drew out the rather shy Violet – that is your given name, is it not, my dear? – and Miss Wyndham clearly was a faithful friend through the difficulties which Miss Drayton suffered on account of her brother – forgive me, Miss Drayton."

"Of course," Penelope said, bowing her head graciously, the touch of an amused grin upon her lips. Ash was impressed with her fortitude.

"At some point in the course of the girls' friendship, and Mr. Wyndham has not yet divulged the exact moment this happened, he fell in love with her. Is that not correct, Mr. Wyndham?"

He nodded slightly, an odd feeling swelled in his chest. Speaking around a strange emotion lodged in his throat, Ash murmured, "Quite."

As Penelope blushed, and his heart pounded in his chest, Ash suddenly realized that nothing was the same. He had been hiding the true nature of his feelings, even from himself. With Lady Melton's succinct and accurate description, it was now clear to him.

The tide of change had crept up on him so slowly that he had not recognized its presence until he was nearly swimming in it. Ash blamed Violet, really. It was she who befriended Penelope in the first place. Otherwise, he would have continued on, happily ignorant of the pulling of his heart. Surrounded by such a crowd of people, though, there was little he could do to address his changing feelings.

They continued through the house of Lady Kennard, Ash feeling surrounded by a fog. He spoke with some people, smiled and nodded at others, and merely moved past the majority of them; even as he acted the perfect gentleman in love, Ash felt that the ground had shifted beneath his feet.

After leaving the rout, they walked to the Smithson Ball, only three doors down from Lady Kennard's house. Ash apologized profusely for having forgotten his invitation (he most likely had thrown it onto the grate in his study's fireplace), but as he had expected, they were welcomed effusively.

Ash and Penelope shared a dance. He attempted to draw his sister Violet out to the floor, but she demurred.

"No Ash, I would much rather sit along the wall with the other chaperones. I must have a moment alone to recompose myself after that terrible crush at Lady Kennard's."

"That was not a crush, Violet, by any means," Penelope said, amusement prevalent in her voice, "In fact, I should say that Lady Kennard is likely rather disappointed with her turn-out."

"But there were so many people," cried Violet, astonished.

"We could still move about the house; therefore, it is not a crush," laughed Ash. He assisted Violet in sitting between two capped, grey-haired ladies before leading Penelope to the set.

There was no time for conversation before the musicians began, and once the dance started, Ash found that he was disinclined to speak.

In the aftermath of admitting his feelings, he would much rather would simply observe her.

They circled one another, along with the other dancing couples, hands held aloft and joined at the palms. She was small in stature, and he believed that most ladies similar to her would appear childish or stunted in their movements. Penelope, however, danced with an assured grace, her movements deliberate and fluid. *She not only dances beautifully, but carries this gracefulness into all of her life.* He also found himself enjoying the contrast between the darkness of her hair and the paleness of her complexion. Her blue eyes stood out like jewels on her face.

The dance separated them for a brief moment before they all danced around the circle. Ash did not recall enjoying himself so much when he danced with her at Almack's. The other evening had been tainted by the disparaging remarks concerning her brother and by Violet's subsequent distress. He grinned cheekily at her as he added pressure to the delicate yet strong hand he held in his own. Indeed, the present evening was turning out to be immensely more enjoyable altogether.

They separated in the dance, joining with the couple across from them. The lady, with whom Ash was only a bit familiar, smiled knowingly as she glanced between him and Penelope, as she danced with the lady's partner around the circle opposite of them. *Now the ladies are hounding me to offer their congratulations and not themselves as potential wives.* The irony was not lost on Ash, especially the deeper irony of his recently-admitted feelings for the woman who was supposed to have been his protection from a romantic entanglement. They came back together, and she smiled up at him as their hands met, her face a rosy hue.

CanI tell her that I love her? He wondered as they circled one another closely. *Is it possible that I am mistaken?*

The past few weeks had allowed him to come to a deeper understanding of Penelope. He saw that she had inspired true friendship in his sister, who previously had always preferred isolation. He also saw that Penelope was concerned with the approval of the *ton* only so much as it benefitted her hidden artistic work. Finally, to his greatest surprise, he learned that he enjoyed spending time with her, talking with her and even teasing her a bit.

He pretended to stumble in the dance, just a bit, and gently knocked his shoulder against hers. She snickered lightly, and shook her head at him.

For the remainder of the dance, Ash kept his eyes intently on Penelope's face, smiling unabashedly when she caught him looking, and grinning like a fool when she returned his smiles. After they had applauded their appreciation for the musicians, he offered his arm, and when she took it, he kept his hand over hers as they went to collect Violet.

Walking to the last house hosting an event on the square, Ash arranged their party so as to keep Penelope in the center of them. The three all walked close together and reached the house in very little time. They were admitted without difficulty and after greeting the host and hostess, passed into another room and found themselves at a card-party. *They did indeed coordinate their entertainments well.*

Ash escorted the ladies to a whist-table, where they might be partners, and decided to go to the faro table himself. Several other gentlemen were already there, and Ash placed his wager after quickly scanning the tally board.

"Good evening, Mr. Wyndham," greeted one of the other players.

"Lord Hollinsley," returned Ash. "How do you do, my lord?"

"Eh, fair to middling. I did quite well earlier in the night, but lately, my luck has run dry."

"Is that so?" asked Ash.

"Indeed," said the man. "Claymore here is making quite a cake of me. Do you know I've attempted to leave this table thrice already, and he says something or other each time questioning whether I've the stomach for another round. But now you're here and can take my place."

"Can I now?" Ash took the opportunity to look around Lord Hollinsley's imposing form to see who this Claymore was – the name seemed vaguely familiar. His stomach sank when he recognized the man as Penelope's brother. Ash had kept Penelope's family name in his memory, but not yet connected her brother with his titular name of Claymore. He nodded politely, but maintained a hard gaze at the man. "Lord Claymore."

"Wyndham. I'd no idea of seeing you here. Come, dealer, continue the play!"

The card was drawn, and Claymore won. Ash placed another wager, modest but not paltry.

"Is my sister here?"

The dealer showed them the card; both lost.

Ash placed another coin on the same card, the seven, and as he waited for Claymore's wager, he said, "She is, as well as my own. I should advise you to maintain your distance from both."

"Is that a threat?" laughed Claymore, laying three coins on the five.

"Eight," said the dealer, showing them the card and collecting the coins.

"No, my lord, it is no threat," Ash said, placing another coin on the seven. "It is, however, a promise of her displeasure should you approach her, and my own displeasure should you approach my sister."

"Is that so?" Claymore scowled. Turning to the dealer, he said, "Will you take ownership of my horses as a bid?" He signed a paper the dealer offered him and placed it on the five.

The dealer pulled the next card, and it was the last eight of the deck. Claymore scowled but offered no objection.

Ash placed a large stack of coins upon the seven, knowing he may lose, but he also knew that only fives, sevens, a two, and a queen were left. *Either way, I shall leave the table after this.* He answered Claymore, "It is so."

"Seven," said the dealer. Ash smiled, collecting his money.

Claymore scowled at him, stepping close. "Remember the arrangement. I've no hesitance in granting my blessing upon your engagement with my sister – I truly do not even care if there is no shared affection. However, you will honor the promise she made me regarding my funds. I've had the devil of a time joining any card-tables of late."

With good reason. "But they'd allow you at the faro table?"

"Eh, the game's falling out of popularity, and the wagers cannot be placed with credit; I suspect the dealer felt secure in his bank, even with my playing."

"You would play even when you have not the resources to support you?"

"Most gentlemen do."

Ash kept quiet.

"The lack of blunt is no reason not to wager it." Claymore laughed loudly. "Tell your sister to stitch that onto a handkerchief for me."

"I'll do no such thing. And how would you know of my sister's fondness for sewing?"

"My sister might have mentioned it." A malicious glint entered his eye. "She has told me a great deal about your family, in fact, including the scheming nature of your mother, the vulnerability of your sister Miss Wyndham, and the immaturity of your sister Miss Rose. Were she not already engaged, I would pursue a dalliance with her."

Ash coolly raised his brows. "The nature of Mrs. Wyndham is known quite well to me, I am my sister Violet's protector, and my other sister Miss Rose will give no gentleman the time of day, save her beau Mr. Langley."

Lord Claymore regarded him for a moment. "You are Miss Wyndham's protector?" The other man's glazed eyes and slight swaying on his feet alerted Ash to his state. *He's more than slightly foxed.* "Perhaps I shall pursue her, simply for the pleasure of seeing your face as I do so."

Ash scowled and took one step closer to Lord Claymore, his heart beating quickly and his muscles tensing.

"Listen well, Claymore. You will go nowhere near my sister, or I will meet you next with pistols on the green at dawn."

The baron seemed unimpressed and raised one hand to disinterestedly examine his fingernails. "I can also withdraw my blessing from your engagement."

"I shall marry Penelope, blessing or no," Ash ground out. He stepped close to Lord Claymore, so close that he smelled brandy on his breath. Rage compelled him to drive two of his fingers firmly into Claymore's chest and his words were forceful as he declared, "You shall cease this behavior while it has the ability to harm her. After she is free of you, it is no concern of mine whether you wish to ruin your own life. But for now, you shall not harm hers."

Once the words were out, Ash felt a great rush of emotion drain him. He did not feel deflated, but rather relieved. Ash sneered at the other man before clapping him on the shoulder and nodding his head once. "Yes, I daresay she will no longer be bothered by you. And if she is, I shall take her away to Gretna Green and you will have no arrangement with us at all."

"You wouldn't." Claymore's voice was shaky, and his eyes wide. Ash could not blame Claymore for his surprised countenance, for he himself could scarcely believe that he had threatened to elope with Penelope to the infamous place just over the Scottish border, where minors were allowed to marry.

"Indeed, I would. Any scandal caused by our elopement would quickly be swept away by the tide of your own scandals which will surely come to light in the wake of your having no promise of her dowry." One more clap on the shoulder. "Have we an understanding?"

Claymore narrowed his eyes, but nodded briefly. "We have."

Ash was struck by the difference between the bitter, angry man and the gentle, older man back at the house with Miss Breckenridge. By all accounts, their temperaments should have been reversed. While Ash knew that he had not an inkling as to the cause, he knew which man he would rather resemble.

After this, Ash returned to the ladies. The whist game was just finishing, so they all stood and moved to a room where food was set out, a modest spread compared to that of Lady Kennard's rout; it did have plenty of punch though, and they all took some.

"It is nearly time to meet Mason and the carriage," said Ash after he sipped the last of his punch. "Are we prepared to depart?"

"Of course," said Violet.

Penelope laughed, "I believe Violet had been prepared to leave since first entering Lady Kennard's house."

Ash agreed. "That is true."

"It is nothing so strange, you know," Violet huffed. "I have never before been accosted with so many gentlemen seeking my attention."

"Most ladies would be beside themselves with joy," intoned Ash, though he was secretly glad she felt this way. He had not noticed Violet's popularity and hoped that the lapse in his awareness of his sister was not indicative of a tendency toward Claymore's personality.

"I am not most ladies," returned Violet, "as you are well aware."

"I do believe, Violet, that your sudden popularity began after your dance with Lord Reymes." She placed a comforting hand on Violet's arm.

"Then I wish I had declined to dance that evening," Violet said, uncharacteristically petulant.

"You would not have been permitted to dance at all, then, even if your favorite had sought your hand."

"I've no favorite, so not dancing would have suited me quite well. The truth is, I had no idea what was happening until it was done, and I found I had accepted his request for a dance."

"Dangerous habit to have," Ash commented drolly.

"Come now, Mr. Wyndham, your sister is uncomfortable; do you see her blush?" Penelope squeezed his arm lightly, causing his heart to thunder in his chest. "Let us away; I should suppose your coachman Mr. Mason is waiting."

"Very well."

As Ash handed the ladies into the carriage some quarter-hour later, a tingling sensation raced up his arm when Penelope placed her hand in his for support. He knew with certainty that his life would never be the same.

Sixteen

PENELOPE KNEW THAT her life would never be the same again. And she was immensely pleased to realize it.

The engagement plan was working. The morning following the rout, ball, and card-party on Fitzroy Square, she received more visitors than ever before. Not only those with whom she had previous acquaintances, but also some new. Most impressive were two of the patronesses of Almack's. With each of the visitors, Penelope received congratulations on her engagement and shared a new piece of the Invisible Painter's that she had requisitioned of her family's estate. While Penelope did not feel any particular attachment to the place, after suffering so much loss there, she thought that she may as well have a memento; after all, she did plan to never return. It was also an advantageous display of another opportunity for promoting P. Greene.

Only a week later, she (or P. Greene, rather) had been engaged to paint three estates after the close of the season. She knew it was rather risky to paint anywhere besides her studio, and even that held its own risks. However, the danger notwithstanding, she knew that expanding her repertoire to include scenic estates would benefit her business. It seemed that she was spending more and more of her time painting, and her muscles still ached some days with the strain of sitting on her stool for so many hours. But business was good and grew every day.

It was a Thursday morning in early April, several weeks after the initial announcement of the engagement, and both Penelope and her aunt were preparing for a picnic they had been invited to attend at a nearby estate. Violet and Ash – she found it easier to think of him by that more familiar name with each passing day – would be fetching them in one hour, at nine o'clock. He had offered the use of his carriage, knowing that her brother had lost his horses at the faro table. She had never heard of such outrageous bids being placed at the game, but supposed that anything was possible.

In a couple of months' time, I shall be free of him entirely.

"I can wear a similar disguise to the one I wore the first time I went to draw for Madame Bélanger," she explained to Aunt Essie, after she questioned precisely how Penelope planned to remain hidden while painting someone's estate.

"And should you be discovered despite your clothing?" asked Aunt Essie. "Madame recognized you."

"I shall not begin painting estates until after the Season, and perhaps I may find some way to further alter my appearance. Perhaps cut my hair?"

Her aunt's face was dismayed as she exclaimed, "Goodness, no! It may be all the crack, as you young folks say, but I fear you will regret it."

"Perhaps," murmured Penelope. "But it certainly would be easier to arrange if it was short."

"Give the matter careful consideration," cautioned Aunt Essie, just before leaving the room to dress herself for the picnic. "Would Mr. Wyndham be pleased if you cut your hair?"

Penelope felt her face flush. She did not make a habit of misleading her aunt, but the opportunity had not yet arisen for her to explain the true nature of their arrangement. It was true that she feared that the truth would disappoint her aunt, as it had Violet. Even more, though, Penelope dreaded what speaking the truth would do to her heart. When Ash had first invited her into this arrangement, she had not intended to grow fond of the man. And his attentive behavior was certainly not helpful. He held her hand just a breath longer than necessary when assisting her from his carriage. Whenever they rode together at Hyde Park, giving the horses their heads going down Rotten Row, he lightly held her hand. In greeting her and in taking his leave of her, he lingered when bowing over that hand.

And the manner in which he looked at her when speaking her name often left her breathless.

Penelope.

Penny.

Pen.

She had allowed use even of the one pet name she despised, for the simple reason that coming from his lips it sounded affectionate. One day, when she was feeling particularly open, she even let it slip that she enjoyed his use of that name, but would not tolerate it from anyone else. She discovered that she enjoyed his attentions, and even returned some of her own – smiling up at him as he covered her hand with his own while they walked; complimenting him on the choice of coat or the quality of his horses; daring to delicately place her hand briefly upon his forearm while they chatted. Still, she told herself that it was all for show, that they did not want to appear unfamiliar with one another. Considering their relationship as all for show made the fast-approaching end of the Season, the time that they would part ways, much easier for her.

Even so, Penelope found herself whispering to the empty room, "*Would* Ash care for my hair if I cut it?" Not that she would allow a man, even one as kind and compassionate as Ash, to have the least influence upon her actions. Though she *had* chosen her yellow day-dress for today's outing due to the fact that he had complimented her the last time she wore it.

Penelope froze. *Is it true? Am I allowing him to dictate what I do, what I wear? He cannot have such power over me!*

She hurried to her wardrobe and threw it open, looking through the dresses there. The green one was a favorite, as Violet had made it for her before any of the others.

But he proposed to me while I wore it.

Hanging beside it was the flowered one Violet had made.

No, I cannot wear that, for I did when he first came to my studio.

She frantically searched until her fingers grasped a pale pink gown, one made several years ago that she wore before any of the new dresses for this season were made. With a firm grasp on the fabric, she ripped it from the wardrobe and tossed it onto her bed. Her fingers were fumbling desperately at the buttons along her back when the door opened, and Aunt Essie re-entered the room.

"Penelope! Whatever are you doing?" she cried.

Hands raised awkwardly above her shoulders, two buttons loose but the other five still fastened, Penelope stood there staring stupidly at her aunt. "I-I . . . I believe I have changed my mind as to . . . which dress . . ."

"There is no time, dear," said her aunt, hurrying to move behind her and refasten the buttons which Penelope had worked so hard to unfasten.

Before she knew it, Penelope was being hurried out of the house and into the Wyndham's open carriage. She and her aunt sat on one side, Ash and Violet on the other. The drive out to the estate, belonging to Lord and Lady Melton, lasted three-quarters of an hour and was filled with light conversation. After about five minutes, Aunt Essie drifted off to sleep. The warmth of the sun, coupled with the beauty of the day, served to relax Penelope, as well.

"I can hardly believe that the air has grown as warm as it has," Violet was saying as they turned onto the lane leading to the great house. "It seems just yesterday that the chill was so bad that we still needed hot stones for our feet. Now, we have lightweight spencers with straw bonnets and light gloves."

"I am eager for the opportunity to paint scenic landscapes again."

"Perhaps you shall find inspiration during our picnic?" asked Ash, his voice warm and his typical small smile curving his lips.

"Perhaps. I've recently begun to offer paintings of estates, as well. I did one of Clayton Abbey recently, and have been telling all who visit me how pleased I am with my newest acquisition of P. Greene's work."

"How clever," said Violet. "But Penny, how will you keep your identity a secret?"

"By wearing a disguise," she said.

"A disguise?" questioned Ash.

"Yes. I've done it before. I've an old pair of my brother's trousers and a coat. Oh, and an old hat I found in our barn at the Abbey to hide my hair. I can easily, if I use my paint to make some light whiskers, pass for a young man."

Ash was silent for a moment, a frown on his face, while Violet and Penelope giggled like young girls about what misadventures Penelope might find for herself. She worried that he might not approve, but then reminded herself that it was not for him to approve or disapprove. He did look terribly dashing this morning, though, in his blue superfine coat, starched white cravat, and a green waistcoat just peeking from behind his coat. Buff pantaloons and highly-polished black boots completed the ensemble. Suddenly he leaned across the carriage to reach for her hand, startling her from her perusal of his form. She held her breath as he gently but swiftly removed her glove, turning her bare hand over in his. His gloved fingertips lightly traced the paint-stains on her fingers, sending all uprising of emotions swirling like butterflies in her midsection.

"Was that you?" he asked quietly.

"I beg your pardon?" she asked, her voice equally hushed.

"Just after it was decided that Rose would make her come-out this Season," Ash said, his eyes on the movement of his fingers over her own, "I attended her and Mrs. Wyndham to the dress-shop. I saw a young man as we were leaving, with eyes just as yours are, and similar markings on his fingers." He gave those fingers a gentle squeeze and looked up to meet her gaze. "Was that you?"

"It was." Penelope inwardly scolded herself for the breathless quality of her voice.

He smiled, then released her hand and sat back.

Penelope hurried to draw her glove back over her hand, breathing deeply to calm the tremors going through her.

The carriage rolled to a stop, and Aunt Essie opened her eyes. They all stepped down, following a servant through the house to the back, across the terrace, and down the steps to the gardens. Blankets, tents, and several tables were set up, punch and fruits and nuts already on them. Penelope knew that their party would not be the first to arrive, but she was still somewhat surprised to see that even Mrs. Wyndham, Miss Rose, and Mr. Langley had already arrived. Ash led the three ladies of their party over to some chairs, set up under a tent for the chaperones and less spry of the picnickers. He assisted Aunt Essie in finding a seat while they all paid their respects to their host and hostess, along with the others sitting there. Penelope noticed Mrs. Wyndham say something to Violet, which caused the girl to color up and shake her head. The woman spoke again, and this time, Violet nodded and retreated to stand behind her brother.

Penelope wished to speak to her friend, but found no opportunity until they were situated on some of the blankets and Ash had gone to fetch them some lemonade and fruits.

"Whatever did she say to you, Violet?"

The girl flushed anew and shook her head. "N-nothing of import."

"Your face suggests otherwise," Penelope countered.

Violet sighed and lowered her eyes. "Mama cautioned me that the season is already half-over. She suggested that I might attempt to become lost in the lanes with an eligible gentleman of our party, thereby forcing an engagement."

"What!" Penelope could not help but think that perhaps depravity of mind was not limited to men, as she had been wont to previously believe. "Who could suggest such a thing to her own daughter? Ruination is not the manner in which to secure a marriage."

"I agree," Violet said, "which is why I told her I could not do that — even if I wanted to, I fear, as I do not have the boldness of spirit to attempt such a thing."

"And?"

"She asked if I would attempt to at least *speak* with the gentlemen."

"I see."

Violet giggled unexpectedly. "I've learned a secret, you see," she divulged, leaning closer to Penelope. "Gentlemen enjoy speaking about their horses, their sport, and themselves. I can manage a brief conversation if I simply ask the gentleman whether he has found time to ride much this Season. Then, he may feel free to expound upon the limited time available for the pastime, due to his many engagements this season — balls and fencing lessons and such; or he may tell me of the fine animal he has which requires daily exercise. Either way, one question and I must simply listen after that."

Penelope laughed. "You are quite clever, Violet."

"She is," said Ash, having returned and handed them each a cup of lemonade. "In what particular aspect do you mean, though, Miss Drayton?"

"Her ability to be considered a great conversationalist with minimal effort on her part."

"Ah yes. Would you believe that I assisted her in coming to that knowledge?" he asked.

"Oh indeed?"

"I once asked Ash if he had much opportunity to ride yet," Violet disclosed dryly, "and he launched into a detailed description of his Season and how little time he truly had for his own interests."

They all laughed briefly, but stopped when Miss Rose, Mr. Langley, Mr. Barrett, and Miss Barrett joined them. Soon cold meats, cheeses and breads were brought out, as well as two puddings and a wine. The young people all ate together and conversation flowed freely. Penelope noticed with amusement that when she asked Mr. Barrett whether he had much time it ride in town, she had nothing else to do to keep that portion of conversation flowing.

After they had all eaten their fill, Mr. Barrett stood and assisted his sister.

"We've a nice little ruin in the back of the grounds here, beyond that bit of wilderness there. Would any of you care to accompany us to see it?"

Several of the ladies expressed their pleasure with the scheme, and soon they were all rising from their places and ambling toward the chaperones.

"Mama, please may we go?" Penelope overheard Miss Rose ask plaintively. "I cannot be the only one to remain behind."

She hid a chuckle at the thought, for of course Violet would also be required to stay behind if she was. Still, Miss Rose's exuberant "Oh, thank you, Mama!" amused Penelope. She glanced at Ash to see him discreetly shaking his head.

"Oh hush," she teased, taking his arm. "Be thankful that she is behaving with decency."

"This is true." He smiled at her, placing his warm hand over hers. "I am immensely grateful to have you by my side; were you not here, I would be stewing in the silliness of my sister."

Penelope laughed along with him, but her heart clenched painfully at his words.

"Are we all prepared to leave?" asked Mr. Barrett.

Penelope was surprised to see Violet on his arm. She caught the younger girl's eye and offered an encouraging smile. She mouthed, "Ask him about riding."

Violet returned her smile.

Soon they all were walking toward the back of the property.

"I had hoped to have a word with Violet before we set out," Ash said to Penelope after they had been walking for several minutes. "I fear that Rose will require a close eye."

"For what reason?" asked Penelope.

"She has a habit of making unwise decisions, especially when caught up in the excitement of the moment. The girl lacks the prudence to know when to refrain from something that seems enjoyable at the time but may not be wise in retrospect."

"She has demonstrated a certain immaturity," Penelope ventured. "Perhaps this is something which time and experience might temper?"

"Perhaps, were she not allowed such leniency. And she is out now, so I fear that if she is to learn, it will be from experience rather than a maturing of spirit."

They continued to follow the rest of the party through the edge of a small stand of trees and wild flowers – the wilderness Mr. Barrett had referenced.

"Would this be a nice scene to paint?" Ash asked.

"It would, but not from this vantage. It is too close to display the depth of beauty of this place. Do you see the greens in the grass out there?" Penelope gestured briefly to her right, where sheep grazed peacefully in a pasture.

"Yes."

"If I had painted from here, we would see only the back of the house, or the plain green pastures if looking in the opposite direction. This aspect appears imbalanced to me. It would be much better to include some variety."

They cleared the trees and saw a crumbling stone structure about fifty paces ahead. Some of the other young people were already reaching the decrepit stone house, while others were still near the trees. Penelope felt Ash quicken his pace at the same time she did. They looked toward one another and grinned.

Before long, they reached the ruins. Several people were already milling about, looking where the fireplaces had been, the holes in the walls which had been windows, and some partial walls inside the structure, delineating rooms. Penelope and Ash ambled over to where Mr. Barrett was pointing out something to Violet near the far exterior wall.

"Do not think that I will allow you to hide back here with my sister, Mr. Barrett," said Ash jovially, though Penelope was certain she heard a hard edge to his voice.

Mr. Barrett responded nervously, "Of course not, Wyndham. I simply wished to show her the old garden."

Part of a stone fence surrounded an overgrown patch of land. Looking more closely, Penelope thought she saw some thorny vines growing over the walls, perhaps roses. She glanced toward Violet, who was gently running her fingers over some of the newly-sprouted leaves on one of the plants.

"I should love to see this space in a month's time," said Violet. "It will be bright with color."

"Perhaps you shall," said Mr. Barrett.

"Are you planning to host another event?" Ash asked.

Penelope suspected that Ash knew as well as she did that Mr. Barrett had been speaking of a more personal invitation for Violet and her family.

Violet could very well find herself happy as the wife of Mr. Barrett, thought Penelope.

"Er, not precisely," Mr. Barrett was saying.

"Come, Mr. Wyndham," Penelope said, taking Ash's arm. "I wish to see the view from that hill." She nodded toward the east, indicating a gently rolling hill just a short walk away.

Ash looked at her questioningly, then offered his arm and nodded. "Very well, Miss Drayton. Watch for us to reach it, Violet, for I will wave to you when we do."

Penelope looked quizzically at Violet, confused as to Ash's request, until she turned and saw that as he had spoken to his sister, his gaze was unwaveringly upon Mr. Barrett.

After parting ways with the others, Penelope and Ash began to climb the gentle incline. Once they were out of earshot, Penelope asked, "Whatever were you attempting to accomplish back there?"

"Beg pardon?" asked Ash, his voice decidedly distracted.

"You caused unnecessary discomfort for Mr. Barrett and embarrassment for Violet," she explained.

"I did no such thing!" he blustered.

"Of course you did."

"I only meant that I did not appreciate his taking so much of my sister's time," he answered defensively.

"Is that so?" Penelope returned skeptically.

"Yes."

"And if she wished to spend her time with him?"

"How could she have?"

"Well, let us examine the situation," Penelope began. "He brought her to a place with many varieties of plants in one place, a sort of wilderness garden."

"Any lady would enjoy seeing that."

"Perhaps, but the fact that he took particular time to ensure that she did not miss it showed his attention to her interests."

"You cannot be in earnest."

"Oh but I am."

"He showed her a poorly-kept garden."

"A whimsical place frozen in time."

"Allowed to run wild."

Penelope huffed and threw up her hands, walking ahead of Ash. "You are being purposely obtuse," she tossed back over her shoulder. "He has noticed an interest of hers, and showed her something that he believes she will enjoy. But let us not argue; I wish to show you something." She turned, having reached the top of the hill, and gestured to the space before her. "Come and see."

After he joined her, she motioned to the view before her with satisfaction. Before them was an expanse of green, with the ruins nearest, to their right, the stand of trees to the left, and Melton House in the distance. The sheep continued grazing placidly in the foreground, and the sky above was a muted blue, soft clouds drifting in its expanse. The view filled her with a sense of peace and she felt the stirring of her creative soul, the desire to paint welling inside of her.

"Do you see, Mr. Wyndham, how from this aspect, the view is shown to best advantage?"

His voice having a slight gravelly quality, Ash said, "I do see."

She turned to glance at him but was immediately arrested by the intensity of his gaze.

"Pen," he breathed, "you are a remarkable woman."

Her cheeks flushed hotly.

"I know that we've not been acquainted for a great length of time," he said slowly and with much feeling, "but I feel already so thoroughly at ease in your presence that I cannot seem to recall a time not knowing you."

Her hands grew clammy.

"I shall not ask of you anything you are unprepared to give, but I would beg you to consider a longer arrangement between us, of a more permanent nature."

Penelope could scarcely catch her breath. Until recently, there was no man of her acquaintance for whom she would consider breaking her most important guiding principle. But for Ash, she might consider it. Still, was she able to tell him so, without truly knowing whether she could do as she believed he was asking her?

Swallowing thickly, she prepared her words before she spoke them. After a deep breath to fortify her nerves, Penelope whispered, "Ash, I cannot say whether I would be capable of giving myself so completely into another's power, no matter how caring he might be. But I will consider this, and do my best to tell you before the Season's end whether I can or not."

"I suspected as much," Ash replied. "I am honored that you would even give the matter consideration."

"Ash, I am not insensible to the honor you do me in making this offer," she said quietly. "Or of the risk you take in order to ask."

He offered his arm and said, "This is a lovely view, but it appears that everyone else is heading back to the gardens. Shall we?"

"Of course," she returned. *What a preposterous situation this would have been for me, even three months ago! To be engaged to a man and more, to be considering marrying him!*

They walked down the hill, nearing the ruins. Just a few more moments and they would be caught up with the group. Suddenly, though, Penelope felt Ash grasp her by the shoulders and twirl her to stand on the other side of him. She found herself in a side-doorway of the ruins, perhaps the only such structure still existing.

"Forgive me," murmured Ash, "but I was unsure whether I might have another such opportunity."

Penelope was mildly alarmed, but his gentle touch and the expression on his face, which held no maliciousness, dissolved any fear in her. Even as he gently backed her farther into the shadows of the ruins, she felt no apprehension.

"Pen, I cannot say whether I love you, though with every day that passes, I am more inclined to say that I do. What I do know is that what I feel for you is infinitely deeper and steadier than the infatuation I entertained for Miss Giles."

Through her eyelashes, Penelope could see his expressive eyes as his face lowered toward hers. She felt a puff of air across her face as he exhaled. Her own breath hitched and she glanced up at his face. He smiled at her, shook his head a bit, and suddenly his lips were against her cheek, low and near her mouth. It was a gentle touch, the barest brushing of lips. They were surprisingly soft – she had thought they would be firmer, by looking at his face and feeling the strength of his hands. But she had been wrong. Her stomach flipped pleasantly and her heart pounded and he was gone before she could decide what she ought to do in response. She nearly moved to kiss him until the sound of distant laughter interrupted her.

"We must join the others," murmured Ash.

"Yes," was her shaky response.

As they stepped from the shadowed shelter of the ruins, Penelope could not help but think that she had been right. *My life will never be the same again.*

Seventeen

After escorting Mrs. Wyndham to the dining box he had rented at Vauxhall Gardens, Ash offered his arms to Penelope and to Violet. Together with Rose and Mr. Langley, they all set out. Ash hoped for easy conversation, as he had been struggling against the near-constant memory of the kiss — or near-kiss. When he asked her, he had not intended a mere kiss of her cheek. But he knew he ought not to allow himself that liberty — it was not entirely proper, even if they were engaged. He had, therefore, kissed her face at the last moment. However, he had not accounted for its effect upon his thoughts and ability to concentrate on anything else.

"I darethay Vauxhall is quite the popular gathering plathe," commented Mr. Langley, staring about at all the people — the *bonne ton* and common tradesmen alike — ambling about on the Grand Walk.

Mr. Langley can always be counted on for conversation, Ash thought thankfully. *Perhaps his one redeeming quality.*

"Of course," said Penelope. "It has been for well over a century."

The party conversed as they went up and down the walk, discussing the Gardens, the songs that the small group of musicians played, the dress of the gentlemen and ladies they encountered. Ash eventually was able to suppress the wish to kiss Penelope properly by clamping the arm she held tightly against his side, bringing her closer to him. He enjoyed the feel of her shoulder brushing against his arm as they walked, and the gentle pressure of her hand on his forearm did much to alleviate the slight ache in his chest.

After two times back and forth, the sun began to fade and the lanterns were lit, glowing with their various colors. Ash saw Penelope glancing about with a calculating eye, and he leaned near to ask what she was doing. With a twinkle in her eye, she answered, "I am determining the paints I would use to create the colorful glow among the trees."

Ash glanced sideways at her, unable to stop a grin from stretching his lips. "You cannot stop yourself, can you?"

Penelope's eyes widened in alarm and she said, "Forgive me! It seems all I do anymore is paint or think of painting. In fact, I've recently realized that my only outings are with you. Were it not for our engagement, I daresay I should simply have holed up in my studio and painted all the time. I really do enjoy it, but I feel as if it has seeped into every corner of my life. I do miss the days where I painted for my own enjoyment, and no other's."

Ash thought he understood. He enjoyed fencing, but if he trained every day, he would soon grow weary of it. Leaning close, as to not be overheard, he asked, "Are you wishing for a change in your plans?"

She hesitated before answering, "Not truly. I still enjoy it. But now there is no choice."

"What are you two whispering about?" interrupted Rose.

Ash felt his face heat as he answered, "Nothing of great import. We were simply admiring the colors of the lanterns."

Everyone looked around them, taking in the glowing colors.

"It is almost magical," murmured Violet.

"Oh Vi, you are such a goose," giggled Rose from where she hanged on Mr. Langley's arm. He was dressed in purples and blues today, rather like a peacock, Ash thought. "Of course it is not magical. I suppose it is very pretty, though."

Penelope tilted her head toward Ash and whispered, "I wonder whether she has the capacity to appreciate something on a level deeper than meets the eye."

Ash was quiet, being initially shocked by her boldness, and then surprised at her rather accurate assessment. He saw that Penelope's eyes were widening with alarm, and she stepped slightly away from him and opened her mouth, beginning to apologize.

"No, no, my dear," he hurried to assure her, drawing her closer with the arm she held and leaning close to speak lowly to her. "I have said much worse about your brother, and truthfully, I was surprised most at your insightful observation. Violet and Rose are as different as their names would indicate. Violet, as you are well aware, is shy and quiet but holds a depth of spirit that sometimes befuddles me. And Rose is beautiful and . . . forgive me, but she is showy, and also holds a shallowness of spirit that equally befuddles me. I have recently come to the conclusion that Rose has the capacity to be more, but for reasons that I cannot fathom, continues to pursue this course of frivolity and self-interest."

Penelope said, "Thank you for your understanding. I had not meant to offend, but merely to make an observation."

"I do understand." Ash was lost in the depth of her deep blue eyes. The variant shades of blue were fascinating, especially in the light of the lanterns, and he suddenly had the irrational wish that he was a painter as she, that he might paint those eyes.

Slowly, the quiet broke through his consciousness. Throughout their walk, the group changed shape in an organic manner, when some members quickened their paces or others slowed theirs. Rose's prattle could be heard before, behind, or near them at all times. But now, there was nothing, save the distant, muted murmurs of the other garden-goers. No prattle. No Rose.

"Where is Rose?" asked Violet at the same time Ash did.

"I do not see her," replied Penelope, looking around.

"Could she be hiding?" asked Violet. "You know how she would love to hide from me in our labyrinth."

They were at the place on the Grand Walk near the back of the gardens, where the Dark Paths began. Ash saw a couple enter the paths, and he hoped dearly that Rose was not among those who sought to "lose" themselves in the notorious Paths. The sort of female entering the area with a gentleman was not the sort that those gentlemen would be likely to marry. While he doubted that Mr. Langley had any rakish tendencies, he also knew that a marriage might need be forced, if it was discovered she had gone there with him.

"You . . . You do not think she would go in *there*, do you?" asked Penelope hesitantly. "She cannot have such little sense."

"I would have hoped not," said Ash. "However, as we cannot see them near us, and there really is nowhere else they could have gotten to, I fear it to be so."

"Should we go after her?" asked Violet.

"I will not allow you or Pen to enter those Paths," he returned.

"You will not allow us, you say?" There was an edge to Penelope's voice which he had seldom heard previously.

"I had not meant to forbid, Pen," he hastened to explain, "but to protect. You cannot be ignorant of the nature of assignations taking place in those Paths, can you?"

Penelope's face reddened a bit and she murmured, "Forgive me, no. I did not mean to react with such sensibility and so little sense. Of course you would only be seeking to protect Violet's and my reputations."

Ash nodded. "Very well. Please allow me to see you both back to the booth and then I will go into the paths to search for her myself. If I can locate them soon, we may yet avoid a scandal."

As they made their way back to the dining booths, Ash attempted to keep up the easy banter of before, but it felt stilted and superficial. Even so, it would hopefully prevent anyone who saw them from suspicion that anything was amiss. Just before they reached the pavilion around which the booths were situated, however, Ash spied his friend MacDougal. *An ally in my search should prove beneficial.*

Hesitating only a moment, he called out, "Mac! Will you not join us?"

The dark-haired Scott looked over from the party with which he was conversing – it looked to Ash to be several gentlemen they had known at school. The others returned his bowed greeting with the same of their own before returning to their conversation. Mac, however, took his leave of them before turning and joining Ash and the ladies.

"Miss Drayton, may I present to you Mr. MacDougal. MacDougal, Miss Drayton, my fiancé. Violet, you remember Mac, yes?"

"Good evening, Mr. MacDougal," she said softly, hesitating only a moment to take his arm when he offered it.

They walked on, coming to the booth before long. Ash handed Penelope into one of the chairs while Mac followed suit with Violet.

Mrs. Wyndham greeted Ash's friend with a tight smile. She had never approved of the Scotsman as a friend for him. Her disdain was clear as she asked, "Will you be joining us for the evening?"

"I had not yet extended him the invitation, ma'am, but he is welcome if he so desires." Ash had no patience for her antics at present. "Just after we see to an urgent matter."

"Oh?" said Mrs. Wyndham. MacDougal disguised his surprise fairly well. A raised brow and an amused grin were the only signs that he had no idea as to what was happening.

"Yes, you asked me to go with you to collect on a wager you had made with Spence."

Never mind that he asked me a week ago and has already collected.

"Very well, Ashbridge," said Mrs. Wyndham.

As though she has the authority to grant me a request. I reached my majority years ago and am my own man.

"I shall return shortly." He bowed to the party assembled around the table. "Please, if the ham and chickens should be brought before our return, do not wait for us."

"Wait a moment," said Mrs. Wyndham. "Why did Rose not return with you?"

"She re-" Ash had not counted on this question, but he ought to have known that she would ask.

"She met with some friends," interjected Penelope, "and asked us to go on, so that she might visit with them."

"Violet, why did you not remain behind with her?"

"I-I, that is—"

"Never mind," huffed Mrs. Wyndham. "You have never looked after your sister as you ought. I should not expect it from you now."

"But—but I – "

"We shall return shortly," interrupted Ash, bowing and turning from the ladies.

"Do bring back your sister when you return, Ashbridge," called Mrs. Wyndham after him.

He did not turn, but silently promised to do just that.

"Think she'll ring a peal o'er poor Violet?" asked Mac.

"Likely so," ground out Ash between clenched teeth. "I cannot comprehend how she expects certain behavior from one daughter, and yet opposite behavior from the other."

"How do you mean?"

"She told Violet to all but be compromised by a gentleman, and yet she expects her to keep Rose from just the same."

"Is that where Miss Rose is?" The question was asked with a studied disinterest, but Ash could see from the tightness of Mac's jaw that he was not as indifferent as he pretended.

"I cannot say with any degree of certainty." He paused, not wishing to injure his friend, but knowing he would learn the truth eventually. "However, we last saw them near the entrance of the Dark Paths."

"The Dark . . .thunder an' turf, man. We'd best find them quickly."

"Then I may count on your assistance?"

"Of course."

"And your discretion?"

"What would cryin' rope on her do for me?"

"Absolutely nothing."

"You have the right of it."

Having kept a quick pace, the two reached the Dark Paths quickly. As they entered, Mac tentatively asked, "So she is quite set on this Mr. Laughley?"

"Langley. And yes."

"And there is no hope . . . that the interest will fade?"

Ash glanced over at his friend sympathetically. "I do not believe so."

They passed a couple engaged in an amorous embrace.

"What a disgraceful place," scoffed Ash.

"Take care, Ash, or you'll be soundin' like that oother sister of yours."

"Violet?"

Mac nodded before saying, "You know that Spence would have been sincere in his professed interest in her, were it not for her radical religious ways."

"She is no radical," said Ash firmly. "She merely takes a more firm grasp on it than many others do." He was unsure how to say that he was beginning to see the sense of such a position – or if he truly wished to divulge that information. He was beginning to sense that his life was not quite as he wished it to be, that *he* was not quite who he wished to be. How to make any changes, though, was beyond him.

Mac shook his head. "Doona' misunderstand me. I do not think her a true radical, but you've spoken of her sermonizing too often for me to believe that she would not be a bit of a naggin' wife."

"She would be too timid to speak to you." Ash knew his attempt at humor would fall flat even before he finished speaking. "Truly, though – if you'd wished to become my brother by means of one of my sisters, Violet would be the more logical choice. I doubt that Rose and I will correspond much, let alone visit, after she marries."

"A man canna' help who he loves," Mac said lowly.

A girl, giggling and leading a young man by the hand, ran past them. Ash shook his head.

"I know. However, rather than dwell on who we love or do not love, I suggest we proceed more quickly to find my wayward sister."

"Aye."

The gentlemen eventually found the pair, near the back part of the Paths. Rose protested loudly at being made to return, until Ash reminded her that incurring Mrs. Wyndham's wrath would do nothing to aid her enjoyment of the Season.

"Oh, very well, Ash. What a bore you are!"

"And what a hoyden you are."

"What a thing to call your baby sister! At any rate, I have decided that I shall not speak to you until we return to the others."

"Have I your word on that?"

"Lawks, Ash!"

"Please refrain from such vulgar speech."

"Hear now, ol' chap," cajoled Mr. Langley. "We meant no harm–"

"No," Ash bit out. "I cannot believe it. Langley, you cannot have been ignorant of what a liaison in such a place as this would do to a young lady's reputation."

"Well, yes, but–"

"And why must you pretend such airs? I know the lisp to be a sham."

"Oh, I think it a charming—" chuckled Langley.

"It is a foolish—"

"Ashbridge!" cried Rose. Even from within his heightened state of emotions, Ash could clearly see that his sister was upset with his close questioning of her beau. Even though he knew his claims to be correct, he was not truly operating within the bounds of proper speech.

"I apologize," he said, "but my ill-behavior does not excuse yours. What can you two mean by going into such a place?"

"We are in love," said Rose, smiling and squeezing her beau's arm.

"Do you mean to offer for her?" Ash asked Langley directly.

"I would, but my father is a bit of a stickler for the old rules of Society. Miss Rose has an unmarried older sister, and my papa has forbidden me from dishonoring Miss Wyndham by offering for her younger sister before she is engaged, at the least."

Ash was pleased with the man's motives, even if they stemmed from an outdated custom that few observed anymore. However, if his and Violet's plan succeeded, she would never marry. *And she would never accede to an engagement such as mine.*

"Is your mother aware of these circumstances?" Ash asked Rose.

"But of course," interjected Langley. *This seems to be a nasty habit of his.* "I was compelled to assure the woman that I was in earnest, but bound not to act until the matter with Miss Wyndham had been resolved."

"Mama has since been searching for a suitor for poor Vi." Rose shook her head with an affected sadness. "It is such a shame that her stodgy ways have driven away so many gentlemen."

Ash wished to speak in defense of his sister, but decided that, as they were nearing the end of the Dark Paths, he would be best to stay the course.

"Never you mind that. Did anyone see you two in the Paths?"

"Thertainly not!" lisped Mr. Langley as Rose laughed, "Oh Ash, you worry too much."

"Mr. Langley, you will refrain from that affectation in my presence."

"Yeth, but–"

"At all times." He turned then to Rose. "*You* will no longer be allowed anywhere with your gentleman without a proper chaperone. And you and Mrs. Wyndham will stop these attempts to force Violet into the notice of gentlemen."

"Oh Mr. Barrett! Miss Barrett!" Rose cried suddenly. "Good evening. Are you here for the firework display?"

After the proper greetings had been observed, Ash observed Mr. Barrett shoot a significant look in Miss Barrett's direction before she said, "Miss Rose, is your sister Miss Wyndham not in attendance this evening?"

"Oh, no, she is," said Rose. "She's so dull, though, that she merely wanted to sit."

"That is not entirely true," Ash said in her defense. "We were all walking together, but my friend Mr. MacDougal here requested my assistance with a matter of some delicacy."

"That is true," corroborated Mac. "So we delivered the ladies to the booth to await supper with the matrons, saw to my errand, and collected Miss Rose from her friends."

"I see," said Miss Barrett, sending a knowing smile toward her brother.

"May we accompany you back to your booth?" inquired Mr. Barrett. "I should like very much to pay my respects to . . . your mother."

"Indeed," said Ash.

It was not long until they were all returned, and Ash invited Mr. Barrett and Miss Barrett to join them. They were a lively party, Violet and Miss Breckenridge being the only quiet ones. Even they spoke, though, when brought into the conversation. Ash found Mr. Barrett doing so for Violet more often than not, and Mac easily charmed several gentle laughs from Miss Breckenridge.

The party moved to the pavilion where the fireworks display could be viewed, and were summarily impressed. It was, therefore, a happy but sleepy gathering of gentlefolk who bade polite good-evenings and separated to their respective homes for the night.

Once Rose and Mrs. Wyndham had retired, Ash knocked lightly upon Violet's door. She opened it after a brief moment, her hair covered by her cap and her dressing gown snugly fastened beneath her chin.

"Yes, Ash?" she whispered.

"Come down to the sitting room for a moment with me?"

"In my dressing gown? Certainly not!"

He stifled a laugh. "But you are more covered and shapeless now than in even a daydress."

"Perhaps, but I've not my – *unmentionables*. I might as well be–" but she blushed brightly and cut off her speech. "Servants may still be about."

He said, "Most are in their beds, sound asleep, as they must rise early in the morning. But very well, Violet; I shan't press the matter. I simply wished to ask you whether Mrs. Wyndham troubled you during my absence at Vauxhall this evening."

"Not . . . so very much," was her dissatisfactory answer.

"Did she at all?"

"Only due to my failure to fulfill my duties as Rose's chaperone."

"But you are not her chaperone. If anything, Mrs. Wyndham should be filling that role. You are only freshly out, quite green indeed, and have no standing to offer that protection. She, on the other hand–"

"I fear that our father's passing has left her quite bereft."

"So you would defend her." He was unaccountably disappointed in his sister's lack of backbone. He knew that she had seldom showed any in the past, but he wished that she might begin to do so now. "Her disdain for *you* is clear enough."

"That cannot be so," Violet attempted to begin, but Ash was feeling quite merciless and impatient with the excuses made by all of the females in his house.

"No, Violet. You must learn to stand up to her, to speak for your own interests, even if that means abandoning our plans. I would much rather you find happiness and peace apart from her, even if it means apart from me, as well."

"Whatever do you mean, Ash?"

"Mr. Barrett has made his interest rather marked."

"Oh, not you, too!" Violet frowned deeply. "Mama has been pestering me with his name for several weeks now."

"But you do not return his regard?"

"Indeed not!" Violet frowned as frustration colored her voice. "That is, he is not ill-looking, and he is a kind and gracious conversant when in company with me. But there are no tender feelings for him in my heart."

"Would you recognize them if you had them?"

"I've never so much as caught my breath because of him."

"But you have with another?"

His sister blushed brightly, but said primly, "It is a lady's prerogative to keep such matters to herself."

"I see."

"Do you?" Violet questioned. "Ash, your behavior has been peculiar of late. Tell me, what is the matter?"

"I-I . . ." But he could not form an answer. After several breaths, he admitted, "I do not rightly know."

"Are you worried about something?" she asked.

"Perhaps. I fear that I am not . . . who I wish to be. But I've no idea what to do about it."

A light dawned on Violet's face. Rather than say anything in response, though, or offer what Ash had hoped might be advice, she simply grasped his hand lightly, and said, "I will pray for you."

Eighteen

PENELOPE MADE BRISK, light strokes with her brush, adding light and shadow to the well-tailored coat of the young dandy. It seemed that P. Greene's recent popularity had spread to the males of London's population, and not only the females. Lord Grenswold, having just come into his title last year, and out of his mourning within the past month, had deemed it an appropriate time to have a portrait done. He was a member of the first circles, and reported to be quite a "swell of the first stare" as the gentlemen were fond of saying. Penelope knew this would be a great assistance to her career.

He is quite a bit darker than Ash, she thought as she lightly rinsed her brush, preparing to add depth of color to some of the man's dark Brutus-styled hair. Ash wore his in a more wind-swept style, and it was much lighter. *Lighter even than Violet's.*

Frustrated to see that she had inadvertently made Lord Grenswold fairer in her painting than he was in life, Penelope threw her pallet and brush down and stood swiftly from her stool. Making fists, she drove them into her lower back and stretched, relishing the release of tension in her muscles.

"Why do my thoughts refuse to leave him?" she asked aloud.

But she knew the answer. She was dangerously close to wishing for far more than she ought. Picking up her palette and brush again, Penelope resumed work. The hair color of Lord Grenswold's likeness was adjusted, and she soon found her thoughts drifting to the invisible qualities of her fiancé, especially those which put her in some danger. Ash was a devoted brother, a fair master (she had never heard him speak harshly to any of his grooms or maids or footmen), a faithful friend, and most pressing – a desirable husband.

She had promised to consider a more permanent alliance between them, beyond the temporary though requisite one which they had formed.

But is it truly requisite? Was there no other manner in which to salvage my reputation as a lady, or at the least, as a painter?

It certainly seemed to be the only way at the time. But now, especially in light of her brother's letter, delivered just this morning . . . Penelope truly did not know what to think anymore. Of anything.

She pulled the paper from her apron-pocket and sat once again upon her stool, opening and spreading the paper flat against her lap.

> *Dearest Pen,*
>
> *I know, I am not to use that name. Forgive me, I cannot seem to help myself. It is likely you do not recall, but our mama had a habit of shortening your name as I do. Likely, there is some connection between her use and my own of a pet name for you, but I cannot travel that path just yet. Perhaps some day.*

At this point in the letter, there were several words scratched out repeatedly. Penelope had attempted to make them out, but was unable. The letter continued in a rather abrupt manner.

I've lost the estate.

There, I've said it.

Written it.

I am certain you are now mourning my abysmal wasting of paper, but I feel that I've already lost everything else, so what does it signify if I also lose my last piece of paper?

So, waste I shall.

I've wasted my life, and what is paper to a man's life?

If you'd like the particulars rather than hear whatever rumor is floating about, here it is: I'd a debt of honor, and was unable to pay. As collateral, I had put up my inheritance. The lure of the game, the thrill of the gamble — it is more than I can resist. Foolish, yes. If I was able to face you, I should gladly stand and hear every word you would throw at me. Lord B, however, has said that if he sees me again, he will call me to pistols, and we both know I am no crack shot. So I am holed up somewhere you shall never find me, until tomorrow morning, when I shall board a ship heading for the Americas. I know, I am a fool. They are not likely to welcome an Englishman. But I've made your life quite hellish, so I figure it quite apt penance that I send myself to hell; or, failing that, to the Americas.

Forgive my vulgar language. I started on my last bottle of cognac at the start of this letter, and have taken another drink with each dip of my pen. I should say that I am quite foxed by now.

Do not worry about Mr. Cartwright; he has been given satisfaction, in the form of a portion of the family silver. I know you had no intent to ever use it, so you cannot be terribly upset with me. About that, at least.

And I know who you are, Pen. When I heard about the rising popularity of the Invisible Painter, and learned the name by which he — or she — goes, it was rather easy to decipher. And do not fret, I've told no one.

When a man has truly been brought to Point Non Plus, and is at his lowest, he begins to see all of his faults in sharp contrast to the goodness of others, to the goodness of God.

I've no right, Penelope, but I beg your pardon. Your forgiveness. I do not know whether redemption is possible for me, and I may awaken in the morning with a raging headache, and no memory I ever wrote this letter. I do hope, though, that I will be lucid enough in five minutes, after I've closed this letter, to go and hail a boy to deliver it to you.

Feel free to live in the Town-house. Or, if you'd rather, let it or sell it — whichever suits you. I am sorry that you cannot return to the Abbey, but I suspect you never intended to do so.

I am your presently-repentant brother,
Cornelius

PS Should Wyndham wish to marry you, and not simply pretend at it, I give my blessing, for what it is worth, which is admittedly not a great deal. Still, I do give it.

He knew. And he was sorry. Or, he was sorry two days ago when he wrote that letter. Penelope wished she knew whether he made his departure on time, whether he was seasick, whether he would survive the journey. *And what of his arrival in America? He has no skills, no money! What can he expect to do?*

She refolded the letter and reached to place it in her reticule on a table behind her. Now that Cornelius was truly out of her life, Penelope was unsure what to think. It was all so overwhelming.

Is forgiveness even an option?

Penelope knew what Violet would say. She wondered what Ash would say.

And now my thoughts are back to him.

With a shake of her head, she again retrieved her palette and brush.

"If only Cornelius had been brought to his *point non plus* earlier; I'd never have found this alliance with Ash to be necessary. I'd never have grown to know him so intimately, and to lo—"

But she refused to say it. Even so her heart whispered, *Do you truly mean that? That you wish you had never deepened your acquaintance with him?*

"Of course! That is, it would have been better for me . . ."

Would it really? The voice of her heart sounded suspiciously similar to Violet's.

"Leave me be! I cannot risk a lasting alliance, no matter how my heart yearns for it! And it does not signify in the least; I will not burden him with my disgraced family."

Would it matter to him?

Penelope suspected that she knew the answer to that question, but refused to give it voice. Instead, she resolutely returned to her painting with a ferocity born of desperation. As she worked, and saw that her renewed vigor was producing an uncommonly excellent portrait, her lips curved into a smile and she began to hum. The song was familiar, but she could not place it at present.

Two hours later, when she stopped to again stretch her back and observe her work, she realized with startling suddenness that the song was one they sang at services the previous Sunday. She could not recall all of the words, but there was a line about Christ the Lord being a willing Sacrifice. That did not fit with her perception of a disinterested God who would allow her to suffer.

If He is God, why would He ever suffer Himself?

Penelope was confused and frustrated as she cleaned her brushes. She set the canvas with the image of Lord Grenswold beside her other partially-completed paintings with a bit more force than necessary, but thankfully, it did not break. Deciding not to do any more work that day, as she was to attend an opera with the Wyndham family that evening, she removed her apron and donned her light pelisse for the walk to the house on Leicester Square. *Which I must now determine whether or not to keep.*

When she arrived home, Penelope found her aunt and Mr. Pelter sitting and chatting over a cup of tea.

"Is no one else here?" she asked.

"No, why do you ask?" returned Aunt Essie.

"Well, you . . . you've never been married, Aunt. Is it permissible for you to entertain a male caller by yourself?"

"Penelope! What are you saying?" cried Aunt Essie.

"Now, now, Essie, calm down," cajoled Mr. Pelted. Penelope did not miss the familiar manner in which he patted her hand and used the pet name.

"What are you–?"

"Your aunt has agreed to marry me," said Mr. Pelter simply.

"W-what?"

"We had planned to wait to speak with you later, Penelope," said her aunt. "With you marrying Mr. Wyndham, and most likely not wanting your aunt who is nearing her dotage hanging off your sleeves–"

"You must know I could never think such a thing of you!"

"I've come to admire your aunt a great deal," offered Mr. Pelter. "And we know it is rather uncommon for a gently-bred woman such as Essie to marry a servant–"

"But my circumstances have been reduced a great deal since my birth. I daresay I am doing quite well to marry an acclaimed artist's man of business."

"The engagement was a sham."

There, I said it, just as Cornelius did.

"I beg your pardon?" asked Aunt Essie.

"We fabricated the entire thing to keep him free from the match-makers and to lend credibility to my name, for the sake of my career."

The room was quiet. Mr. Pelter stood still, with the exception of rubbing his face with his hand. Aunt Essie was similarly stymied, her eyes wide and her face pale.

"Please, I know it was foolish," said Penelope. She could hear the tremor in her voice. "I need no reprimand, for I've done so myself already, numerous times."

"Are you sad?" Aunt Essie asked gently, rising from her seat and coming to put a gentle arm around Penelope's shoulders.

She was mortified to find her eyes well with tears. "I . . . I cannot say. I've only just recently realized that I could love him. But after what my brother has done, I could not marry Ash, even if he asks me again and again."

"He has asked you to consider actual marriage, then?"

"Yes." Penelope's voice sounded small, even to her own ears. "But I cannot." She fished the letter from her reticule and handed it to her aunt. As her aunt read, Mr. Pelter perusing the missive over her shoulder, Penelope walked numbly over to the writing-desk by the window and sat. She gazed out the window for a moment before looking blankly at the surface of the desk. Without thinking, she reached for the drawer, to withdraw a paper for drawing. *It might calm my nerves.*

The paper in her hand, however, was not blank as she had expected. It was the one containing the sketch she had made back when the air was chilled and her hopes were simpler. The father and daughter on the paper were still reading together, the affectionate facial expressions still intact. Now, though, she could see that it was, without a doubt, her father and herself.

"When did you receive this letter?" asked Mr. Pelter.

"Two days past," she answered numbly.

"Lord Claymore is somewhere on the Atlantic, then."

"Yes." Penelope's voice trembled.

"I am sorry, dear," began Aunt Essie, but Penelope interrupted her harshly.

"Why ever would you be sorry? He was a dreadful brother."

"You are crying," said Aunt Essie, coming over to Penelope and gently wrapping a thin arm about the girl's shoulders. "He may not have been a loving brother, but he was yours. It is natural that you should miss him."

"I cry for what could have been," grumbled Penelope, wiping roughly at her tears. Mr. Pelter chose that moment to give her hand a gentle squeeze before quietly slipping from the room.

"And for what is, but never will be again," said Aunt Essie.

"What . . . what do you mean?"

"He is sorry, repentant. He asked for your forgiveness. You may grant it, but he will likely never know."

"Why should I forgive him?" she sniffed.

"We forgive much because we have been forgiven much."

"What have you to be forgiven?"

Aunt Essie merely leveled a gaze at her before raising one hand to gently tap at the place over Penelope's heart. "Only you and the Lord know what is in here."

Penelope said nothing, but merely sat as memories of a thousand times she had thought unkind things about her brother, her father, members of Society, shopkeepers, even strangers – and she knew what was in her heart. And this was not all. Suddenly, she saw her shortcomings, her failings, as they were – sin.

She shook her head violently. "I have much to be forgiven, you are right. But . . . but . . ."

"But how can you know you are?"

Penelope's lips trembled as tingles ran from her eyes, over her nose and mouth, until her whole body was wracked by shivers and trembles. "I cannot."

"You can. Do you recall your mama reading to you and your brother every night?"

"I do. That book is lost, is it not? I'd always thought it was a storybook of some sort."

"No, it was much more significant than that."

"Oh?" Penelope could not think of anything significant about those days.

"She read to you stories from her Bible."

"Stories . . ."

"And not simply stories, but the events recorded there to explain mankind's failure to keep God's laws and the forgiveness that is offered through the cross of Christ. The forgiveness of God that renews a person's heart – casts out the darkness."

"I do not feel that there is light in my heart."

"Then confess your sin, and be filled with His light once again."

"Again?"

"As a child, you were taught by both your mother and your father. Confession will restore you."

Penelope heard her aunts words, that her father had taught her, as well, but could not make sense of the information beyond a fleeting, *Perhaps my drawing was, in fact, a memory.* More importantly, though, she needed to know, "How?"

"The psalmist says 'Create in me a new heart, O Lord, and renew a right spirit within me.' Let that be your prayer until you find words of your own to use, if you so choose. I find that the words of Scripture are more than adequate for me, every time."

With one last gentle squeeze to Penelope's shoulder, Aunt Essie turned to leave, giving Penelope some time alone. Something must have caught her eye, however, for she hesitated a moment and reached out to lightly touch the paper still in Penelope's hands.

"This is lovely."

Penelope followed her aunt's hand to look again at the man and the child, and the Bible they shared. *Perhaps that is a good place to start.*

Nineteen

ASH HURRIED THE ladies of his family through their preparations for the ball, worry and a touch of desperation spurring him to do so. Over a week ago, Penelope had attended the opera with him and with his family. She had not seemed herself that evening, being rather quiet and withdrawn. Her smiles were genuine, but not as ready as they had been, and her eyes seemed tired. He attempted several times to ask her what was troubling her, but she deflected each time. He hoped to steal a moment with her this evening at the Barrett Ball.

Finally, they were all prepared to leave, and off they set. He had thought to have the carriage take Mrs. Wyndham and Rose first, but the location of the ball denied the practicality of such a plan. Thankfully, though, Mrs. Wyndham was quite insistent on no one crushing her gown, so he sat on the side of the carriage with Violet and Penelope – Violet in the middle, of course.

Not half an hour later, Ash was lining up beside Mr. Barrett for the dance. Penelope stood across from him, and Violet was to dance with Mr. Barrett.

"I hope your sister is sensible to the distinction I've paid her by asking for her hand for the opening set."

In other words, you hope that she is aware of the feelings you are so poor at hiding. Aloud, though, he merely said, "I am certain she is. However, perhaps it might be wise to ascertain the lady's feelings before you attempt to proceed farther along this course."

Mr. Barrett had no chance to reply, as the dance began.

Ash and Penelope did not speak. The dance certainly allowed for conversation, but it seemed that neither was inclined to voice their thoughts. They circled, turned, and promenaded with the others, communicating with touches and glances. Ash felt his heart surge with the hope of a future with her.

Once the set ended, he offered his arm, and they went in search of refreshment.

"Do you think that Violet is aware of Mr. Barrett's interest?" Penelope asked as she took his arm.

"Yes. We spoke of it briefly after the Gardens."

"Does she return his regard?"

Ash did not wish to speak of this. "No, she does not."

"Oh." Penelope was quiet for a moment, and Ash wondered if there was a deeper meaning to her line of questioning. "Do you think he will be terribly disappointed when he learns of her disinterest?"

Ash paused. *Could it be that she has a more significant meaning to her questions?* He searched frantically within his memory of their conversation thus far for some clue as to any hidden meaning behind her words. "I . . . I think that should depend upon his level of attachment. He has not known her long—"

"Neither have you known me long," she interjected.

"—and he has only spent time in her presence several times. That would indicate only an inclination toward an attachment."

"That is good." Relief was clear in Penelope's voice.

"Yes." *She must be speaking of more now than simply Violet and Mr. Barrett.* "However . . . this does not preclude a strong attachment."

"How do you mean?" Penelope's voice was almost alarmed.

"For some, attachment is immediate and strong."

"Is it?"

Ash nodded, continuing to guide her toward the table where the punches and lemonade were being served. After they both had a cup, he again led her about the room.

"Would you care for some air?" he asked. "I believe that Lady Melton has lovely gardens in the back. Shall we?"

Penelope answered by bringing her free hand up to give his arm a gentle squeeze.

After they had slipped outside, the couple made its way down the steps from the terrace. The night was dark, but lanterns gave a gentle glow to the area. Ash inhaled deeply and, for the first time that spring was able to detect some sweet notes in the air. Several small blossoms could be seen peeking from the plants. He led her to a corner of the garden, partially hidden behind a small tree.

"Have you had opportunity to consider my suggestion?" he asked, turning abruptly to face her, his voice low and husky.

"I . . . I have," she replied, smiling and reaching up to clasp her hands behind his neck.

Ash felt his heart surge with happiness. "And?" he prompted, allowing a teasing tone to creep into his voice.

"I . . . I . . ." But rather than give an answer, she gently prodded him to lower his head, her fingertips ruffling the hair at the base of his head and her breath fanning his face. His lips tingled with anticipation.

But he jerked his head back at the last moment. "Forgive me."

"For what?" Her voice was unmistakably shaken.

"For nearly giving in to my baser urges, without having your answer."

"My answer?"

"Yes. My attachment to you is strong and it would give me great me happiness if you would consent to be my wife."

"I . . . I . . . "

At her hesitance, he felt his heart drop.

"I have waited, Penelope, and I will wait longer if needed, but it seems that you have already decided. Why can you not answer me?"

She shook her head, unable to speak with the echoes of heartbreak in the depths of his eyes. She knew that hearing her words would hurt him as much as speaking them would hurt her.

"Do you not care for me?" he tried again.

"I do," she breathed.

"But we will not marry." His voice was flat with resignation, and she wanted to shout that yes, of course she would marry him; she loved him dearly! But then his voice took on a hard, cynical edge. "I cannot claim to be surprised, Pen."

"Do not call me that." She folded her arms and rubbed the narrow sliver of skin exposed between her short sleeves and long gloves.

"I am sorry," he murmured, voice once again caring and gentle. "Something is troubling you. Is it your brother?"

It felt quite nice when he rested a warm hand upon her shoulder in a comforting gesture. Penelope was mortified, though, when it elicited a strong swelling of emotion in her breast, which she had for so long fought to eliminate from her sensibilities. The air in the garden had grown damp and heavy with summer's approach bearing down fast upon the city. Penelope struggled to draw the air into her lungs, knowing as she tried that her difficulty had little to do with the humidity and much to do with the constricting of her throat with emotion. She sniffled a bit and, much to her dismay, blinked back a few tears.

"Penelope?"

Unable to speak or meet his gaze, she could do nothing but shake her head. *It is too painful. Please do not press me.*

At this, Ash placed his other hand in mirror to the one upon her shoulder, leaned in, and gently pressed his lips to her forehead.

Much like I have witnessed him do with Violet. Why this sudden change in his actions, in how he treats me?

Before she could stop herself, she blurted out, "Is this how we are to part, then?"

A puff of Ash's breath hit her forehead. "Penny, I do not wish to part." Her heart sank, then she heard him whisper, "But is it right to keep up this charade when *you* are unwilling to marry me?"

"I have not yet answered you." She reminded him.

"Do you love me?" he asked her bluntly.

Penelope hesitated at that.

Yes!

She wished to shout it. However, she knew that if she made her own confession, he would not so easily allow her to break the engagement. Several quick breaths did little to steel her nerves or aid her in arranging her thoughts. "I . . . I believe I could. I nearly do." Ash's face, patronizing in the lifted eyebrow and small quirk of a smile, struck a chord of resentment in Penelope. Her father had looked at her in a similar manner when she asked why he must drink such large quantities of wine. Her brother had affected that manner when she questioned his frivolous spending and cavalier attitude. That the only man her heart had ever believed it could trust would look at her in the same manner was insupportable. She pulled away from him and paced a few steps away.

Perhaps this is a simpler method of achieving my ends.

Turning suddenly, she found him to be watching her closely. Before she could stop the words, a confession poured forth.

"The first time that I saw you, I was struck with your handsomeness but believed that you would be similar to any other gentleman I had met – a gentleman in appearance and in outward manners, but seeking his own interest in everything. However, when I first made your acquaintance, you cared a great deal for your sister and her happiness, perhaps even more than for your own. *Never* before had I encountered a man who valued anything above his own self. I was confused, and intrigued."

Ash's face had long ago lost the expression which set off Penelope's rant, slackening into something unreadable and indescribably more disconcerting. Having begun speaking, though, she found that she could not stop her words. "As our acquaintance deepened, I began to see that while you cared deeply for those you love, there was harshness in your words and manner in regards to those whom you believe to have wronged you, whether directly or indirectly through a loved one. I feared momentarily that you would direct that disdain toward me, if you began to believe that I had taken advantage of Violet's friendship to fulfill my own selfish means."

Here she was interrupted. "Penelope, I could never believe that of you. Your fondness for her shines in your eyes whenever you are in her presence. You are more of a sister to her than Rose is." Penelope began to protest, but Ash continued, "Even had your initial befriending of her been selfish, she has so blossomed with your friendship that I care not."

Penelope interjected, "I am glad to be her friend, and my affection for her has always been genuine. May I continue now?"

Ash nodded, a slight smile quirking his lips.

"Thank you. When I learned that Violet's nature was so entirely good and trustworthy, I decided to confide in her and to ask her assistance. At the time, I never imagined that our lives would become so deeply entwined. They are now, though, and it seems to have been a successful endeavor."

Ash interrupted again. "Indeed it has. I have been able to pass through the Season promoting my sisters in the marriage mart and yet remaining untouched myself. And from what the *crème de societe* is saying, the Invisible Painter is wildly popular."

"I have you to thank for that. My brother had so disgraced our name that I would surely have destroyed the Painter had I attempted to promote him without the benefit of a connection to you. But never mind that; it is not what makes me believe that I love you." She winced at her slip. "That I *could* love you. I admire your devotion to your sister, your honorable manner of conduct, the kindness shown to those less fortunate. I know you to be a good man, a true gentleman." She paused to rally her courage, knowing that the confession would cost her, even if it was merely a partial-confession. "I know that I could love you."

"Tell me, Penelope." She looked closely at him, wondering what caused his suddenly serious tone. "You say that you could love me. Is it enough to marry me?"

Penelope felt the air leave her lungs in a rush. Her heart was pounding more quickly than she could believe, and her hands grew damp. *Can I bind him to a life with me, and the ruination my brother has brought upon my family? He would say it matters not, but does it?*

"I-I . . . I do not know. I know that I could trust you with my well-being, as a wife must trust her husband. But I . . ." Her words caught in her throat, and would not be said. She knew that societal mores dictated that as a wife, she would be subject to her husband. She knew that the man would not abuse that power, ever. But it was the only thing to which she might cling in order to prevent him from learning the true reason for her refusal.

"But you cannot trust yourself to let go of the control of your life?"

Yes! I can! Knowing what she must say, tears pricked at Penelope's eyes. Her breaths were labored, heavy. "I cannot."

"Neither would I ask you to," Ash said as he slowly stepped near to her, "or to compromise yourself for a few moments of pleasure."

Ash again kissed her forehead, his hands remaining at his sides this time, and he turned, walking back into the brightly lit ballroom. The tears which had pooled in Penelope's eyes spilled over and trickled down her trembling face. She had not surrendered to her love for Ash, and she felt empty. In that emptiness was the loss of all that could have been.

Twenty

It was with a heavy heart that Ash prepared to depart from London. It was the beginning of May, and Parliament had yet to close, but he had no desire to remain any longer in Town. His goals had been accomplished, but somehow they no longer held the importance they once did. There was a terrible ache in the center of his chest, and he feared it would never heal.

This is worse than after Felicity's rejection, a thousand times over.

Still, in the midst of his pain, Ash was aware of a calm peace in his soul, which remained even during the times that the pain seemed to grow worse than he could bear. He knew that it had not been present before his conversation with Violet following the outing to Vauxhall Gardens. For the first time in a long time – perhaps ever – his faith was growing. He now understood Violet's thirst for Scripture, and he was glad to share that time with her. Especially for the balm it provided for his wounded heart.

If only he had been able to convince Penelope. He had thought that, when they danced, there was a deeper level of affection in her eyes, in the touch of her gloved hand to his. But she had behaved so oddly out in the garden, without the usual reserve she had. After their dance, she seemed almost . . . that she knew it was the end for them.

Had she planned it the entire time?

It seemed that perhaps she had. Or, barring that, she knew at the start of the evening that it was the end.

Why was she so very upset to reiterate what she had been saying from the beginning?

He was mulling over an answer to his question when a knock sounded on the door to the sitting room. He was startled into glancing back at the paper, quite forgotten on the desk before him. He was composing a list for his journey. He planned to leave London in two days, to meet the mysterious Lord Ashbridge.

The knock sounded again. Ash cleared his throat before calling out, "Enter!"

A footman opened the door, bowed, and said, "A Miss Giles to see you, sir."

Ash thought his heart might have stopped beating. When she walked into the room, he could not catch his breath.

"Good day, Ash," she said, her voice as melodious and soothing as ever.

He blinked once, twice, before suddenly scrambling to his feet and making a bow. After she curtsied, he motioned for her to be seated in a wing-chair near the fire. She demurred, choosing instead the settee near the window. He followed numbly, choosing for himself an adjacent chair.

"Miss Giles," he managed, "to what do I owe this . . . pleasure?"

Excellent, Ash. Much better than the "What are you doing here?" that was on your tongue.

"We only just arrived in London. My papa – you do remember him, yes?"

"Yes," replied Ash. *How could I forget?*

"He was a particular friend of the Viscount Melville, whose impeachment trial began last month. Papa was afraid that he might be negatively affected, so he delayed our departure from our country house."

"So your papa is still concerned with the gain or loss caused by his connections?" Ash did his best to keep his face and tone disinterested, but there was a thread of bitterness which he could not prevent. "I wonder that you were permitted to come and see me. And without an escort or chaperone! Tell me, Miss Giles, did you sneak over here?"

"Indeed not," she asserted. "Papa said that he was sorry you and I parted on such poor terms, and he asked me to run over while the servants unpacked our things. To pay my respects."

"Pay your respects? Has someone died?"

Ash knew he was heading down a dangerous slope toward incivility, but he could not seem to halt the deterioration.

"You understand my meaning, Ash," she gently chided him.

"Yes. Yes, I suppose I do." Ash stood and moved to sit beside her on the settee. Not too close that it would be deemed inappropriate should someone enter the room, but close enough that he could speak quietly and be assured that she would hear every word. "You are come here to ascertain whether our break is so permanent that it cannot be repaired. I suspect that the moment your father arrived in town, ahead of the rest of your family, he went to his club and there learned of my newfound fortune. So now I am no longer a mere country gentleman, but a rich country gentleman. He finds himself reconsidering his opinion of our courtship, but of course he can admit nothing as crass as a concern with money. So he pretends that there was nothing untoward about the manner in which he refused me, or the manner in which *you* refused me. You may therefore tell him, Miss Giles, that the break is entirely irreparable."

"Is this because of her?" she asked lowly.

"Who? Miss Drayton?" Ash stood and moved to peer out of the window. "Perhaps. But even if she had not broken my heart much more thoroughly than you ever did, even if I had never met her, I daresay I would never have accepted you again."

"Never?"

"No. You left me because you had not the courage to even ask your father if he might reconsider. Even further, you had the gall to tell me that it was a simple flirtation."

"It was!"

"It was not, and you know that."

"What was I to do? You had a small fortune, which you had only just come into—"

"Which I had a good, solid plan to build upon."

"—and nothing else!"

"Nothing else? My charm, my smile, my spirit were nothing to you?"

"Of course they—"

"I do not know whether I can believe you. Your words twist all around and leave me with nothing recognizable."

"What if I told you that I loved you? That I lied to protect you, to spare you the depth of sorrow I felt."

Ash shook his head. "No. I cannot believe it. If it was a lie, you spoke it most convincingly. *Too* convincingly; you never were an accomplished liar, with the possible exception of your feelings for me. Or perhaps I was too foolish and in love to see the truth."

"No, I do—"

"No, Miss Giles. If you truly loved me, there would have been some amount of struggle on your part in perjuring yourself, especially considering it was in regards to your feelings."

"You mean to say I did not struggle sufficiently in telling you that I did not love you?"

"Precisely. If you truly loved me, despite your words, those words would have been uttered with difficulty and . . . and . . ."

But Ash could not recall what he planned to say next, for in his mind, he could see Penelope's face as she told him she *could* love him, that she was fearful of giving control of her life into his hands. His grief had blinded him at the time, but now he wondered if perhaps she was not being entirely truthful in her denial, if perhaps she might have another reason for denying him.

"I must go."

"I beg your pardon?"

"You have it. Thank you, Miss Giles, for coming to see me today. I may indeed owe my future happiness to your visit. But I must hurry, or I might miss her."

"Whatever can you mean? Miss who? That Miss Drayton?"

But he did not answer, simply rushing from the room, calling for his greatcoat, hat, and gloves as he raced down the stairs toward the front door. A footman met him there, holding the coat while he slid his arms into the sleeves, then took his hat and gloves. Ash stepped out of the front door and into the sunlight, blinking against the brightness. He placed his hat firmly upon his head, and hopped down the steps while pulling on his first glove.

"Mr. Pelter," Ash called as soon as he stepped into the door of Penelope's studio. "Mr. Pelter, are you here?"

"Yes, Mr. Wyndham, we both are."

Ash's heart sped expectantly at the words, but when he burst through the door into the back room, it was only Mr. Pelter and Miss Breckenridge.

"Why are you not with Penny?" he asked Miss Breckenridge.

"She requested to make this journey on her own," she began.

"Journey? Alone!" He shook his head, attempting to reign in his frustration. "I cannot believe you would allow her to—"

"Essie and I," interjected Mr. Pelter, "are just married, you see, Mr. Wyndham, and Miss Penny insisted that she go alone."

"You are married? Forgive me, er– allow me to offer my congratulations."

"I thank you," said Miss Breckenridge. *No, Mrs. Pelter.* "We both do. But tell me, Mr. Wyndham, are you here in hopes of finding Penelope?"

"I was. If you will but tell me where she has gone, I will go to her."

"I believe she may have left something behind when she traveled to keep her appointment, though it is a good five-hour carriage ride."

"That matters not. Shall I bring it to her?"

"I would greatly appreciate it, and I daresay she would, as well."

She turned to open a drawer in the wall and withdrew a satchel. Placing it upon the edge of the table where things were set out for tea, she withdrew two books. "This small one is her prayer book. She left it at the estate, but I brought it for her, knowing she planned never to return. This other book is her family's Bible. Her parents read from it together every day, but when her mama passed, her father was greatly pained by the sight of it, so I packed it away, until I could find an appropriate time to give it to her. I would be most grateful if you might communicate that to her."

"Of course, but are you certain she will receive such a gift?"

"I suppose she would not have told you."

"Told me what?" he asked.

"The Lord has turned her heart," said Mrs. Pelter simply.

"Turned her heart to what?"

"To Himself."

Ash paused, feeling as though the whole world slowed with him. "Do you mean to say that she has learned to find comfort in these pages?" He indicated the books he held.

"Yes, and moreover, in the heart of a Father who will never leave her or forsake her."

"You speak of God."

It was not a question, but still Mr. Pelter answered. "Yes."

Ash felt his heart thud painfully, similarly to when he realized he loved Penelope. He knew that if he asked the question burning within him, his life would again be forever altered. He spoke in a rush.

"How could she change her mind so entirely?"

"Her eyes were open to the truth of the nature of God, that He is love, that He is good, and he desires all to be saved."

Ash was unsure how to answer, or even if he needed to answer.

"We were just about to take some tea. Would you care for some?" asked Mrs. Pelter, moving to the small stove over by the wall.

He did not at first understand her purpose in such a question, but as soon as she turned back with a tray, and indicated a seat for him, Ash understood. After she and her new husband were seated at the small table, he took the third and last chair.

"What do you know of God, Mr. Wyndham?" asked Mr. Pelter as tea was poured.

"Er-I know that He made everything, that He rules."

"Yes. What else?"

Ash drew a deep breath, thankfully accepting the tea offered him. "Jesus is God. There is the Holy Ghost, as well. We sing and pray to . . . Them? Him? . . . on Sundays."

"Him," offered Mr. Pelter, smiling. "He is but one God, but three Persons."

Ash nodded, but did not entirely understand what the man said.

"Tell me," offered Mrs. Pelter. "What does God want from you?"

"Obedience?"

"Partially." She smiled at him. "Are you obedient?"

"Some of the time."

"Do you think that to be sufficient?"

"I would hope so, but I daresay Violet would say differently."

"As would I," chuckled Mr. Pelter.

"I suppose that compared to His Holiness, my own obedience is lacking."

"And when compared with the obedience of Christ," murmured Mrs. Pelter. "You hold your sister in high esteem, yes? Do you think her obedience is complete?"

Ash wanted to answer right away with a definite "Yes" but was suddenly uncertain. "I cannot say."

"It is not, and before you accuse me of maligning your sister, please consider first whether she would say the same."

He thought about their previous conversations, and her humble heart. "You are right, she would not. But if someone as sweet and good and *correct* as Violet is cannot be obedient, who can?"

"No one. That is what a person must realize before he can begin to understand the heart of God." Mrs. Pelter sipped her tea.

"God cannot abide sin. *Disobedience*, you might say. And all people are full of it. Whether it shows or not, God knows the heart, and everyone's heart is infected. But He also loves all of those people. So He sent His Son, Jesus, to take the punishment for that sin. Because He cannot allow sin to go unpunished."

"And had we served that punishment, it would have been more than we could bear?" Ash speculated.

"Eternal separation from Him."

"But you mentioned understanding the heart of God. He is just, unwilling to ignore sin. But that is not all. Violet has said that He is also love."

"So you listened more than you let on," chuckled Mrs. Pelter as she rose. The gentlemen followed suit. "Forgive me, but I promised a friend to call on her today, and I really must go. If you require anything more of us, please just leave word with my husband—" and she turned to smile widely at the man "—and he will inform me. Godspeed, Ash, and here is her location." She handed him a slip of paper, embraced him briefly, and went out the door.

After the door had closed behind her, Ash looked over at Mr. Pelter and they both sat.

"I did listen, Mr. Pelter," offered Ash. "When Violet spoke of God. I simply was not ready to admit my insufficiency, or my powerlessness in some situations. But I do believe, before I go to Penelope, I would like to be right with my Maker."

"That is encouraging," said Mr. Pelter. "Do you know how this is accomplished?"

Ash did not enjoy lacking any answer, but after thinking for several moments, was forced to shake his head. "No, I do not. I believe I recall hearing, whether from Violet or the Rector or somewhere else, that a man must confess his sin before he can be made whole. Is that right?"

"Partially."

"Must I list them all?" Ash asked, growing slightly uncomfortable.

Mr. Pelter chuckled a bit and shook his head. "Unless it would give you comfort to name them all, it is not needed. God knows them all, and unless you do not wish to because you are not sorry for some particular sin, I would say it is not necessary. However, your confession should be sincere. Again, He knows."

"It is. Lately, whenever I hear readings in the Services, or Violet mentions something about God's goodness or our sinfulness, it pricks at my heart."

"Then you are in a good way to begin."

"Now?" asked Ash.

"If you wish, but the prayer is your speaking to God. Not to me, not to anyone else. You may do so in the privacy of your room, if you so desire."

"Perhaps. Or perhaps in the coach as I travel?"

"We are to pray without ceasing," grinned Mr. Pelter. "Allow me, though, to point out some passages of forgiveness for you. To hear the Law condemn you without then hearing the Gospel uplift you is a woeful way to begin." He took the Bible from where it rested on the table before Ash. "Here, the psalmist says that though your sins are as scarlet, they shall be white as snow." He turned the pages again, finding a passage toward the back of the book. "The Gospel writers often show us when Jesus forgave the sins of a person when he healed them. That was why He came, and where His heart is shown in its fullness. To win forgiveness for others by His death on the cross. We must pray and talk to God, but it is in His Word, the Bible, that He speaks to us, that He shows us His heart. And where He begins to change ours."

"Should I start reading in the Gospels, then?" asked Ash, looking down at the pages which Mr. Pelter had placed back in his hands.

"An excellent idea," said the older man.

Ash stayed a short while longer and the men discussed his plans, particularly the part that the Pelters would play in that. He shook hands with Mr. Pelter and went out the door, only to meet with Mrs. Pelter just outside the door.

"You have the books?" she asked.

"Yes," he said, holding them aloft. He was about to continue on his way, but hesitated. "May I ask . . . is her brother troubling her?"

"She did not tell you then?"

"Tell me what?"

"That her brother wrote her a letter, saying that he has sailed for the Americas."

"He did what?"

"It is true. He lost his fortune in a game of chance, asked her forgiveness in a letter, and left on a ship more than a week ago."

Ash was shocked. *No wonder she put me off; I doubt many men would wish to be connected with a noble family fallen from grace.*

Needing to know if there was a chance he might persuade her, that if he still wished to marry, knowing all, that she would, as well, he asked, "Is she determined to stay this course?"

Miss Breckenridge smiled, patting him on the face gently. "I think she might be persuaded, if the right man should ask her."

"Thank you, Miss Breckenridge."

"Please, we are nearly family. Miss Essie is fine for the time being, though I daresay you will very soon call me Aunt."

He grinned back at her, then turned and hurried down the street, books clasped firmly in his hands. He had much to do if he wished to leave the following morning at first light. He looked forward to the drive tomorrow, when he might sit and pore over the large book in his hands.

Penelope set her folding easel and stool on the ground before carefully placing the box of her pencils and paints beside them. Finally, she was able to take the large portfolio, holding her papers and boards, from beneath her arm and set it against a nearby tree. She set up her stool and easel, then rifled through the papers for the one she had been using yesterday. The breeze, ruffling her bonnet ribbons and tugging on her skirts, brought with it the sweet aroma of fully-arrived spring.

When Penelope departed London, she was in such a high state of emotion that she could scarcely remember to bring all of her painting supplies, let alone a disguise. She had instinctually reached for the oldest of her gowns, those she wore before she had met *him*. Those dresses, coupled with her well-worn apron and oldest bonnet helped to disguise the fact that she was not in actuality a country maid. She enjoyed a quiet walk from the coaching inn to the Benton Estate. Lady Benton had sent her husband to engage the painter to create a representation of their home. Penelope had learned the time that the family was expected home and determined to finish the painting before they departed London.

Easily finding the paper which she had begun sketching yesterday, Penelope smoothed it out on a thin board. She set up her stool and placed the board upon her lap. Taking a pencil in one hand, she used the other to remove her straw bonnet. She began to sketch, finding the faint breeze tickling her hair enjoyable. She soon found that her mind was not keeping to its task, though.

It turned regularly to Ash.

No. He must now be Mr. Wyndham to me.

He was no longer Ash, nor could he ever be again. She must work harder to put him from her mind.

Penelope resumed drawing, making notes on the paper concerning the depth of the spaces between the stones on the house, the color of the flowers in the gardens, the shades of green in the surrounding land. The green farthest in the distance was the same shade as the green of Violet's eyes when Penelope relayed the events of the garden, when she called the morning after the ball. The younger girl's eyes had been so very sad, but she said that she understood. As a last gift to her friend, Penelope had said, "I wanted you to know that the Lord has opened my heart to His guiding."

Violet's face had been confused at first, saying, "I do not understand."

"I know you have been praying for my heart to be softened. I want you to know that it has been, that I am learning to seek Him and His will and Word in my life."

"Oh, Penny! I am indescribably glad to hear you say that!"

"I clearly still have a great deal to learn, but He is guiding me."

Violet joyfully embraced her before pulling back to look her friend in the eyes. "But you still do not believe that Ash has a place in your life?"

Penelope had to swallow some tears before answering. "I am afraid that there are some . . . complications in that arena which would prevent a lasting alliance between us."

"Penny, you must know that he loves you, that nothing else will signify–"

"I know, Violet. But I will not ask him to make that sacrifice."

"Is it not his sacrifice to make?"

Penelope shook her head. "I will not allow–"

But Violet interrupted this time. "So you are willing instead to sacrifice both of your future happiness for the sake of saving Ash from something which you will not even confide in me?"

"He may yet find happiness with another."

"And you?"

"It matters not. I have my painting, and my aunt and Mr. Pelter, and now the Lord is a greater comfort than I'd ever imagined."

"But Ash would understand–"

"I beg of you, Violet, do not try to convince me; my mind is made up." Penelope softened her tone before continuing, "For years, I have acted for my good alone, attempting to protect myself from hurt. Now, I see that I have been selfish in not considering anyone else. Allow me to make this sacrifice for your brother. Christ would have us deny ourselves for the benefit of another, would He not?"

For a moment, Penelope had thought Violet might argue. Her face was clearly troubled, and she opened and shut her mouth once. But in the end, she merely said, "Very well. Will you write to me?"

"Of course."

A drop splashed down on the drawing paper, causing some of the lines to run. Penelope looked up to the sky, expecting to see rainclouds, until she realized it was a tear from her own eyes. Her heart ached – for the friendship with Violet which would now be limited by her circumstances, for the love with Ash which would never be realized, for the years lost with her parents, and now with her brother. The pain radiated outward from her chest, leaving a hollow sensation that she feared would grow numb with time.

Suddenly, there was a firm touch upon her shoulder, and she shrieked, jumping up from her stool and stumbling backward as she spun around. She tripped over the wayward stool and landed on her back, gazing wide-eyed up at his large, imposing figure.

Ash. No, Mr. Wyndham. At any rate, it cannot be.

"Did Violet send you?" She knew it was a poor greeting but could think of nothing else to say.

He shook his head, placing a paper-wrapped parcel on the ground before extending a hand to assist her to her feet. Once she was once again upright, he said, "No, I sent myself. May I?"

She nodded when he gestured to the stool, somewhat confused as to his meaning. *Ash is not the sort to sit in the only seat when there is a lady present.* To her surprise, though, he did just that. He then proceeded to pull her down into his lap, to her even greater surprise.

"Ash! Whatever do you think you are doing?" she hissed, glancing about frantically as she tried to stand. "What if someone were to see us?"

He held fast, though, and said with an innocent smile, "But we are engaged to be married."

"Not any longer, or have you forgotten?"

"No, I've not forgotten our conversation, but you seem to have." She shot him a confused and exasperated look as he continued, "Or perhaps your mind is adding things to our conversation which were never said."

"Speak plainly, sir."

"Our engagement was never terminated. You never spoke the words. And I certainly did not."

"What?"

"We are still engaged."

"It was understood."

"I am curious, Penny—"

"You ought to address me as Miss Drayton," she interrupted primly.

"Or as Mrs. Wyndham, after tomorrow morning."

"What?" She attempted to stand until his next words stayed her.

"I've purchased a special license."

"License?" She could not make sense of his words.

"*Marriage* license."

"Whatever for?"

"So that we may marry. Unless, of course, you wish to marry at St. George's with all the aplomb of a Society wedding."

"No, a simple wedding is more than sufficient." Penelope then realized what she had said. "That is, *if* we were marrying, which we are not."

"You would leave me out four pounds?"

"What?"

"The Special License cost me four pounds."

"I am sorry, but—"

"And the coach for your Aunt and Uncle Pelter – yes, I stopped to see them. It was they, not Violet, who disclosed your location."

"Coach?"

"Yes, of course. You would wish for their presence at our wedding, would you not? And I expect that we both would want for Violet to be present, so the Pelters will fetch her before they leave London."

"What of your mother and other sister?"

"They will not be in attendance."

"No?"

"No. And there is nothing she may say about it."

Penelope shook her head, hoping to clear it of the swirling thoughts. She was still having difficulty comprehending what he was about.

"Stop, please, Mr. Wyndham. You cannot seriously expect me to simply marry you here in this small village without so much as a by-your-leave. It really is too much trouble for my aunt to come all the way here—"

"Would you prefer Gretna Green?" he quipped cheekily.

"I will not elope with you!" she cried. "In point of fact, I've not said that I will marry you at all, here or elsewhere." She attempted again to stand, but his grin grew as he continued to hold her fast.

"Perhaps, but you've neither given me an unequivocal rejection." He grinned and pressed his forehead tenderly against hers. "And I doubt that you will."

"Very well, then. I refuse," she stated officiously. Or as officiously as she could seated upon his lap, her face only a breath away from his.

Ash threw his head back and laughed loudly. She had to bite her lip to hide her grin. When he had calmed, he grasped her more firmly about the waist, drawing her close once again, and murmured, "If you were truly afraid of the loss of control, you would not tease so easily."

"How do you reach that conclusion?"

"Teasing stems from familiarity and ease in a relationship. One does not tease a person who might be considered a threat."

"Is that so?"

"It is." He pressed a gentle kiss to her forehead. "So, will you marry me, Pen?"

"I . . ." She wanted to. Oh how she wanted to marry him! *But can I impose my shame on him?* "I cannot."

"Why? And I will not believe you if you claim what you did at the Melton Ball."

She laughed a bit, despite herself, at his seeing through her previous avoidance. Drawing a deep breath, she turned a bit so that she might look into his eyes. She reached up to smooth a strand of hair which the wind had blown into his eyes. "Ash, I do love you, very much. But I cannot ask you to bear my shame. You do not know—"

"What your brother has done?" She stared, wide-eyed at him for a moment. He reached to pull a paper from his pocket. "I apologize for the breach of propriety, but I read this letter after I found it inside something your aunt gave me."

In his hand was the letter from her brother. The one which she had thought she'd left in a drawer of the small table beside her bed.

"You did?" she whispered. *He knows.*

"Yes. And may I say something?"

She nodded mutely.

"It is my supposition that your refusal of my affection is due to what is contained in this letter. Please, correct me if it is not." Still unable to form words, she shook her head. "Then please allow me to assure you that whatever perceived shame you bear, I will gladly share with you."

"But your mama will not like it," she choked out. "She—"

"Has nothing to do with this. I love you, Penelope, and I wish to share in all of your life, not only the attractive parts. My family has its own share of disgraces."

"I suppose all do."

"Do you mean to say that you will?"

"You really do not mind that my brother has lost our family's fortune, and most likely will be stripped of his title?"

"Not if you do not mind the present Mrs. Wyndham. Or the man you will have the misfortune to call *husband.*"

Penelope laughed, and it felt wonderful. So wonderful that she could not stop. She laughed and laughed, Ash soon joining her. Penelope finally managed to nod her head before resting it upon his shoulder, her laughter having left her breathless.

"You've made me glad beyond measure." His words made a slight breeze, which flitted through her hair as his hands reached to frame her face.

She lifted her head, incredibly aware of his nearness as she nodded and whispered, "As you have made me."

He gently prodded her face upward, lowering his head slowly until his lips were pressed firmly to her own. Her hands reached up, of their own volition, to grasp at his shoulders. He snaked his arms about her waist and drew her nearer. When they parted, at the same moment, both wore matching smiles – slightly dazed, and deliriously happy.

"Would you care to walk a bit with me?" he asked. As they stood and began to amble down the lane behind her stool, she threaded her arm through his and laid her head against him for a moment. After a time, he offered, "Your aunt will be bringing your new gowns tomorrow – did you realize that you left them? – and we may marry in the nearest church, assuming the rector is not otherwise occupied."

"So you really did obtain a special license?"

"I did."

"But how? I am not yet one-and-twenty, and my guardian is somewhere on the Atlantic Ocean."

"His letter."

"His letter?"

"Yes. He said in his postscript that he gave his blessing to our union, and that was sufficient."

"Amazing."

"What is?"

"My brother, who has for years been a burden to me, has himself released me from the chains of my own making."

"How do you suppose?"

"I was so caught up in the wrongs done to me that I allowed the hurt to paralyze me. I never stopped to consider that they each faced their own demons."

"That does not excuse the wrongs they committed."

"No." Penelope shook her head, understanding, clarity, and light from God causing her heart to swell. "Some people do not fight their demons, but ally with them. Others cower. Still others will fight them alone. But I know now that the best opportunity for success lies in understanding that the battle is over, and in Christ, we have already won. Fighting the demons alongside God is our only sure hope of success."

They stopped walking, and stood looking at one another.

"And now you've learned this, you've conquered?" asked Ash.

"Not entirely," smiled Penelope. "But I know that I shall. And at present, that is enough."

Ash smiled broadly back at her, shaking his head slowly. He leaned down to press a sweet kiss to the corner of her mouth before saying, "I could not have put it more aptly. Now, I suppose we have nearly two hours before the others arrive, and you have work to do. May I watch you paint?"

They started back toward the stool and easel, and Penelope asked, "Are you certain? There is little to entertain in watching a person paint."

"Oh I beg to differ. It gives me a glimpse into how you see the world. Besides, you must finish your notes and whatever else needs done today, for tomorrow after we are married, we are expected at Linsdon. Oh, not right away, but I did include several stops along the way to draw out our honeymoon tour. Your aunt gave me the names of the other two estates you are committed to painting, and we shall stay in nearby inns, that you may complete your work in the process of traveling north. Lord Ashbridge expects us in about three weeks' time."

"Is that so?"

"Yes."

He stooped to retrieve the package he had left upon the ground, and looking her in the eye, he settled it into her hands. "Your aunt sent this for you."

"What is it?" she asked, feeling the weight of the package. It felt like a book, a large volume. She could feel that the corners were worn and bent a bit, so it was not new.

"Why not open it and see for yourself?"

She slowly untied the knotted string about the middle, then unfolded the brown paper. What she uncovered evoked so many long-forgotten memories that she could scarcely breathe for a moment. *Gentle hands stroking her hair as a soft, feminine voice read words of love and salvation to her. Strong arms surrounding her as the low, gentle voice of her father recited words that she had long ago forgotten.*

"Do you remember it?" asked Ash, raising his hands to gently brush his fingertips over her hands holding the old Bible.

"I do." Her voice was equally hushed. "I remember my mother and my father, both reading to me and to my brother . . . but how could I have forgotten that for so long?"

"Perhaps some memories were too painful to face? Until now?"

She did not speak for a time, her eyes merely tracing the edges and angles of the book. "Perhaps." She looked up at him, smiling through tears. "Thank you for bringing it to me. I shall have to thank Aunt Essie for bringing it from Claymore Abbey. It would have been lost to me forever if she had not."

"She also gave me your prayer book, but I have it stowed with my things." Ash's arms gently and slowly closed around her, and he held her for a moment. "Your aunt is a remarkable woman. Much like her niece."

Penelope glanced up at him and stepped back. "I suppose my time to complete my notes is drawing to a close. I had best get to work."

He grinned at her as she seated herself upon the stool and took up her paper and pencil once again.

"Will we make our home at Linsdon, do you think?" she asked as she began sketching again.

"No. I am given to understand that Lord Ashbridge is still well enough to be in command of his estate. He simply wished to meet his heir."

"I see."

"Am I correct to assume that you would prefer your aunt and uncle to remain close to us?"

"If it is not too much trouble," Penelope returned.

"None at all. They were instrumental in my finding you, as well as in my finding a greater understanding of the Lord. I would be saddened to have them depart from us."

Penelope's heart warmed to hear that he held the dear couple in as high esteem as did she. She wished to ask about his mention of their involvement in his spiritual growth, but he was speaking and she decided to ask him later, when she was able to devote her full attention to him.

"Would you be agreeable to living in London for a time? My mother and sister can easily dwell at Wyndmere, or if you would prefer a country home, they will live in London quite happily."

"London is fine," Penelope answered. "But what of Violet? Was she not to keep house for you?"

"You will have control of the household now, Pen. But if you would not mind her living with us—"

"Of course I would not mind!"

"Then it is settled," he stated, wry humor coloring his voice.

Penelope felt her face warm as she fumbled over her words. "That is, I-I would like it very much. If you do not mind."

"I would endure even my other sister and the present Mrs. Wyndham, if you desired them to dwell with us. But tell me plainly. Are you agreeing to marry me only to gain a sister?" The tease in his voice was evident.

Penelope refused to look at him. "As a matter of fact, I am," she said loftily. "My brother is now gone, and I had hoped to replace him, but *you* insist on marrying me. I supposed the next best thing would be a sister in the woman who is already as close as I imagine I would like one to be."

"You cut me to the quick!" he lamented. "I shall never recover my broken heart!"

Penelope giggled lightly, shaking her head.

"Oh, I nearly forgot." Penelope angled her head toward him to show she was listening, but kept her eyes on her work. "I should like to engage the services of a skilled painter to create a likeness of myself and my new bride. Do you know of any such painters in the vicinity?"

"I do, but I fear that he is soon to retire."

Ash's voice sounded concerned as he asked, "I had not thought anything would give him the enjoyment that painting did."

Penelope sighed heavily as her hands drifted to a halt. "Nothing did, until that painting became obligatory. I still enjoy it, but I have been growing weary for some time. The late evenings spent in Society followed by early mornings, and hours and hours spent in the same posture, painting every day in every spare moment. I cannot continue that while tending to my responsibilities in your house."

"*Our* house."

A smile curled her lips as she said, "Yes. But even so, I cannot maintain any house of substantial size while keeping up with the demands of a painting career."

"If you are sure of your choice."

"I am." She glanced over at him from her paper, startled to see he had sprawled upon the ground, propping himself up on his elbows behind him, and his long body stretched out before him. "I daresay I may even begin to paint only for enjoyment again. I nearly forget what that is like."

He suddenly scrambled up to his knees, his pale hair being mussed in the process. Kneeling beside her, his hands clasped upon her lap, he pleaded, "Might you manage one more requisitioned piece, do you think? At the request of your most devoted and loving husband?"

"Oh, I may," Penelope laughed, reaching down to place a quick kiss upon his lips.

Epilogue

UPON THEIR ARRIVAL at Linsdon, Mr. And Mrs. Wyndham were shown to a room where they could refresh themselves and change from their traveling attire. Mrs. Weaver, the housekeeper, had then given them a tour of the house – large and imposing to such a degree that both Penelope and Ash felt out of their element. After seeing the house, Mrs. Weaver's husband, the steward, met them at the front door with an open carriage, to show them the grounds. Upon their return, they were told that tea would be served in half an hour, and that the marquess would receive them in the drawing room at that time.

Ash first saw that the room had not been updated in ages, but was kept in excellent repair. Rich carpets and upholsteries and draperies in golds and reds and blues were rivaled only by the sumptuous wood finishes, polished to a deep sheen. Seated in a chair by the fire, blanket over is lap, for the weather had not yet warmed much this far north, sat an elderly man. He and his new wife were announced – *I think I shall never weary of hearing her called "Mrs. Wyndham"* – and moved toward the man.

"Forgive me for not rising." His voice was thin and weak. "Today has been – particularly difficult. My health is deteriorating, you see, which is why I have decided that it was past time to contact you."

Ash bowed formally to the man, and Penelope curtsied.

"None of that, son," said the man. "You must have gathered already that I am Lord Ashbridge, but I suppose you are wondering what possible connection you may have to me. Please be seated. Mrs. Weaver will be here in a moment with tea. First, though, it does my old heart good to finally meet you."

Ash clasped the older man's outstretched hand. "We are most happy to be here."

"You've much of your mother in you," he said with a watery voice. Ash exchanged a brief glance with Penelope and he could see that she was thinking the same as he: *The old man's eyesight must be suffering.* "But more about that later. Ah, here is Mrs. Weaver. Mrs. Wyndham, would you care to pour?"

Ash watched his wife smile, gently and genuinely, before moving to do so. As she did, she said, "Please, Lord Ashbridge, call me Penelope, or Penny if you prefer, as that is what my close friends call me."

Ash's heart swelled with joy. He knew that her request was outside the bounds of propriety of address, but if the old man had contrived some way to name him as heir, then he must be alone in the world, with no close relations, no family. *I am gratified to see her compassionate heart opening to others.*

"Thank you, Penny, dear," said the elderly marquess. "And thank you for the lovely portrait of my estate. Mrs. Weaver showed it to me. She said the artist's name is P. Greene?"

"Yes," returned Penelope. "He has since retired. I believe that yours was the last he made."

"Is that so? A rare gift then, indeed," commented Lord Ashbridge. Penelope could not stop her smile, but listened interestedly as the man continued, "Now, I suppose you are both all curiosity. I shall tell you my tale . . ."

Discussion Questions

1. In what sort of things does Penelope put her hope throughout the novel?
2. Have you ever had a time in your life when your hope just seemed to dry up and you weren't sure what your next step should be?
3. The upper class of Regency England believed that work was beneath them; they were expected to live off the income generated by their estates or investments. This is why it would have been so shocking for Penelope to paint for a living. How do you feel about this?
4. Life during Regency England and life in today's world are vastly different. Are there any traditions within Society that you would like to still have us practice today? Any that you are glad that we do not? Are there any that we still do?
5. Why did Penelope struggle so much with the idea of marriage? Even though she had grown to love Ash, and knew that he would treat her with love and kindness, why did she not jump at the chance to marry him?

6. At the beginning of the novel, Ash was basically through with people. What can you see within the way that Society functioned during this time period that might lead him to this decision? What events led Ash to begin opening his heart to others more?

7. What do you think of Ash's friends Mac and Spence? Are they helpful or harmful in building his character? What about your friends—are they beneficial in building your character? In what ways?

8. Mrs. Wyndham and Rose served as a foil to Ash and Violet. What purpose might they serve in the story? Have you ever had people like Mrs. Wyndham and Rose in your life?

9. How did God care for Penelope in a way that she did not expect? Has there ever been a time in your life that things did not turn out as you had hoped?

10. The Pelters offer a great deal of guidance for Penelope and for Ash. What kind of advice or wisdom that they offered to Penelope or to Ash did you especially appreciate?

11. Have you ever had a person that you looked up to, who offered you wisdom or served as a mentor as you?

12. How do the characters understand (or misunderstand) who God is at the beginning of the novel? How does their understanding of God change as the story progresses?

13. Was there anything in the story that surprised you?

14. Romans 8:24-25 speaks of hope. Penelope attempted to create hope in a plan that she could see in minute detail. God, however, had a different plan. He gave her hope and salvation in His grace. What other verses can you find that speak to the concept of hope? How do these Words of God inform your perception of hope and of God's caring for you?

Sarah grew up in Ohio and currently lives in Texas with her husband and their four children. Besides writing, she enjoys volunteering at church, sewing historic clothing, and spending time with her family.

Having written stories almost since picking up her first pencil as a child, Sarah is thrilled to be publishing her first novel. Look for the release of *Violet's Daybreak*, the second installment of the *Regency Silhouettes* series in the winter of 2015-2016. It is her prayer that her writing will uplift and encourage her readers while also giving glory to God.

Sarah enjoys connecting with her readers and would love for you to visit her blog at www.sarahebaughman.blogspot.com.

47251588R00211

Made in the USA
Lexington, KY
02 December 2015